ADVANCE PRAISE FOR *BID THE GODS ARISE*

Bid the Gods Arise possesses the music of epic and the color of myth. It's a big story, spanning planets, but with a specific human heart. Once read, it lingers in the mind like a dream.

—Lars Walker
author of *The Year of the Warrior,*
West Oversea, and *Troll Valley*

A tour-de-force of mythopoetic imagination blended exquisitely with a well-founded verbal artistry, *Bid the Gods Arise* is a novel richly textured and subtle in its storyline, resonant with the multifarious heights and depths of the human condition. With seamless effort and compelling insight, Mullin weaves together some of those eternal themes that we ignore to our peril and that in the end are unavoidable in our earthly journey—good and evil, love and hate, cowardice and heroism, anarchy and cosmic order.

—Mark Sebanc, co-author
of *The Stoneholding* and *Darkling Fields of Arvon*

Master wordsmith Robert Mullin brings you a classic tale of good versus evil, but with unexpected twists that leave you breathless for more. Fantasy and sci-fi fans alike will fall under the spell of *Bid the Gods Arise* as they embark on a journey of temptation, betrayal, sacrifice and love like none other in this first in the epic series, The Wells of the Worlds.

—JC Lamont
author of *Prophecy of the Heir*

Robert Mullin has a gift for storytelling. In *Bid the Gods Arise*, his characters and the world he's created come alive. Readers will be pulled into Maurin's and Aric's journeys and will find themselves turning the page to see what unfolds. This is a ride you won't want to miss.

—Charlene Newcomb
author of "A Certain Point of View"
in *Star Wars: Tales from the Empire*

In the tradition of the fantasy genre's revered masters, Robert Mullin has crafted a fascinating journey and a powerful love story that encompasses a tapestry deserving of many sequels—and, one can only hope, its eventual place on the big screen. This first installment of The Wells of the Worlds is a riveting, epic work of art. Mullin creates compelling characters and explores powerful, universal themes. If *Bid the Gods Arise* is any indication of what's to come, I predict Mullin will have a long, wonderful career ahead of him—and I, for one, look forward to the ride with great anticipation. Consider me a fan.

—Rich Handley
author of *A Matter of Time: The Back to the Future Lexicon*
hassleinbooks.com

In *Bid the Gods Arise*, Robert Mullin has brought us his long-labored creation of a fully realized world, complete with a real world's conflicts, passions, and dynamic characters. This is an epic fantasy and a thrilling adventure and love story, in the best tradition of the masters of the genre. Hopefully there will be many more to come in the Wells of the Worlds saga!

—Wm. Michael Mott
mottimorphic.com

This book is great. From the moment an interdimensional slave ship appears and tears the heroes' lives apart, you never know what will happen next. You're in for an entertaining, heart-warming, gut-wrenching ride. You're going to meet soul-sucking vampires, a gladiator with an overdeveloped sense of justice, and a faun-like girl who will capture your heart without a word. You're going to see someone kick butt with a staff, experience prophetic dreams, fly airships (and crash them), and venture into the heart of a twisted mountain-sized tree. What are you waiting for? Read it!

—Kessie Carroll
author of the Spacetime Legacy series

Bid the Gods Arise is a mash-up of fantasy and sci-fi, with a bit of Ancient Rome thrown in—and the blending of genres is flawless. Even with action at every turn, it was the strong characters and dialog that kept me engrossed the whole time.

—Kat Heckenbach
author of the Toch Island Chronicles

In *Bid the Gods Arise*, Robert Mullin grants us a story we have not quite seen before. He introduces us to an original world and sympathetic characters, both brought to life with intricate craftsmanship. A rewarding and fascinating book.

—John K. Patterson
author of the Arrivers and Queensland Crater series

Bid the Gods Arise is fantasy/sci-fi at its finest. A turn of the page sends the reader into a sudden new world where nothing is as it first seems, where temptation and loyalty clash. This kind of storytelling builds new worlds, one within another, making for Robert Mullin the apt nickname of "the Architect."

—K.G. Powderly Jr.
author of The Windows of Heaven novel series

A great epic fantasy with compelling characters, a full-orbed plot, and an amazing and believable sci-fi world. *Bid the Gods Arise* is a literary journey you will thoroughly enjoy and not soon forget. Highly recommended!

—Kenneth R. McIntosh, M. Div
author of *Water from an Ancient Well*

Blending fantasy, sci-fi, and horror, *Bid the Gods Arise* is smothered in violence, sprinkled with complex theology, and sticks in your mind long after the final page. Whether you are into swords or spaceships, this book will leave you satisfied yet still hungry for more.

—Mark Carver
author of *Apollyon* and *Black Sun*

Bid the Gods Arise is painted with a vibrant palette. Clever wordsmith Robert Mullin illuminates a tale of the heights and depths of the sentient experience. A vibrant maelstrom of emotionally charged adventure, indeed.

—Victor J. Vieira
author of *Umbral Haiku*

The book was phenomenal. There were so many scenes that contained some of the richest, most delicious writing I've ever read. I was never bored, never skipped a single sentence, and am still in awe of the strong character development and plotting. Very nice work!

—Julian Hernández
author of *Unrelenting Darkness, Inescapable Light*

Bid the Gods Arise is Robert Mullin's stunning breakthrough in a fantasy niche that has long needed a jolt of energy. This book starts with powerful action and the dynamic between the two main characters is intense and keeps you guessing. It's a gripping tale and great read!

—Tom Bielawski
author of the *Chronicles of Llars*
and Heck Thomas series

In *Bid the Gods Arise*, high fantasy fans like those of Tolkien and Guy Gavriel Kay are sure to find an instant favourite. Filled with fast-paced action built around realistic cultures and histories, characters that jump off the pages with fully fleshed personalities, flaws, quirks and passions are coupled a multi-leveled plot that draws you in and keeps you hooked until the last page. In the eternal struggle of finding out what lives inside of us all, and what it means for us, and others, finding purpose in our lives and how and why we live them, Robert Mullin strikes a strong cord that flows seamlessly into the fight for a greater cause and against great evil that threatens to change an entire world. This is a must read for anyone who seeks to get lost in another world and more!

—Amy McDonald
advance reader

Dedicated to the memory of Jeffrey William Chapman
March 23, 1980–July 11, 1997

You were here for the beginning, Jeff, and should have been here for the end. The story was yours as much as it was mine, and a significant part of me died with you. May your memory never fade as the years go by, and may you be pleased with this, my humble attempt to complete our project.

I miss you, cousin, friend, and brother.

I love you always.

THE WELLS OF THE WORLDS

PREFACE TO THE SECOND EDITION

In preparation for the release of the long-delayed sequel, I decided to re-visit the original text and fix some long-standing issues. Most of them were merely minor editing relics, typos, and the like that had managed to slip through previous printings, but there are a couple of short scenes that I have always felt were missing and have now been restored for greater character depth and continuity. If you have already purchased a prior edition of this book, fear not; the canon has not been altered, and you need not read this version to understand the sequel. But if you have not, you are getting the "author's preferred edition."

You will also want to check out the evocative and exciting tie-in score by the talented Dennis S. Mowers, available on dsmowersmusic.com, Amazon, Spotify, Bandcamp, Soundcloud, and iTunes. His liner notes for the album are included at the end of this book.

Immortality is not a gift
Immortality is an achievement;
And only those who strive mightily
Shall possess it.

—Edgar Lee Masters
"The Village Atheist"
Spoon River Anthology

They do not know, nor do they understand; the foundations of the earth are shaken. I said, "You are gods, and all of you are sons of the Most High. Nevertheless, you will die like men, and fall like any one of the princes."

—Psalm 82:5-7

He who most resembles the dead is the most reluctant to die.

— Jean de la Fontaine

The body does not give rise to the soul, then, but is rather the rough instrument by which the spirit manifests itself.

—Sir Arthur Conan Doyle
"The Parasite"

You frighten me with dreams and terrify me with visions.
—Job 7:14

PRELUDE
UNQUIET DREAMS

I'm dreaming again, and that's never a good thing.

We're in a cave; of that much I'm certain. All else is nebulous as the winds. Thirty or forty strangers in the distance, murmuring in the dark. Their language is familiar, though I'm sure I've never heard it before. Like me, they're waiting in the cool damp of the caverns.

Waiting to die.

"I'm scared." The soft voice of a child shatters the silence. I ignore it, indifferent to all but my own growing anxiety. The blow is about to fall. How and when, I don't know.

I grind my teeth, trying not to betray my impatience—or my fear. Something hunts us, something just beyond my comprehension. The expression on each man, woman and child is the same.

The look of prey.

In the dim light of the torches, several people stationed in the upper levels stare at me. What is it they expect me to do? I avoid their scrutiny, discouraging conversation.

"Here they come!" A voice near the mouth of the cave turns into a scream, silenced by a snap and a growl.

My breath quickens. Sweat runs in icy rivers down my back. Baying howls fill the echoing chambers, and people scatter like chaff.

Massive lupine forms rush from the darkness with a grace belying their bulk. Claws click and scrape across the stone floor. Gray-blue fur bristles as the creatures leap upon their quarry, slavering muzzles clamping around throats.

A warm flood of fetid air bathes my neck, and I whirl to face a fanged maw. Glowing green eyes bore into my own.

Paralyzed, nowhere to run.

The beast lunges. I feel the creature's strength, a rush of pain, and then...

In the distance, someone calls my name, and the nightmare is over.

For now.

CHAPTER 1
EVE OF DESCENT

"They're hunting me!"

Shrieks of terror split the night air. Maurin jolted upright in bed, heart racing. Across the room, Aric thrashed and groaned, caught up in the throes of yet another dream. Pass or come to pass, those had to end if there was to be any peace. Maurin lurched over and dragged him upright. "Aric, wake up!"

Aric convulsed and gasped, and his spine stiffened. His eyes flew open and rolled wildly, eyelids fluttering as he strained to focus. Maurin gripped his shoulders and shook him again. "Are you all right?"

Upon recognizing Maurin, he slumped and looked away. "I will be, as soon as you let go of me."

Maurin complied, and Aric flopped back onto his bed with a groan. Maurin stood and leaned against the cool stone wall, wiping his cousin's sweat off his palms. Moonlight still streamed through the window, and the muggy air promised a miserable day to come. The night-wisps chirped outside, and insects trilled by the lake. Sounds of calm. As Aric's breathing slowed to a regular rhythm, Maurin's heart eventually settled back into its usual rate.

"What did you see this time?" Maurin asked softly, after waiting in vain for his cousin to speak.

Scowling, Aric flung his legs over the side of the bed, dragged the sweat-soaked sheets from the mattress, and stripped off his damp garments. "Apparently, you have no intention of letting me go back to sleep."

Maurin snorted. "You think sleep is going to come easily for me after an awakening like that?"

Aric stalked over to the opposite wall, pulled down an ornate sacred tapestry, and wrapped it around himself. Sitting on the edge of the bed, he heaved a sigh and ran his fingers through ash-blond curls.

"Isn't that dusty?" Maurin cringed, admittedly more concerned about the sacrilege than his cousin's comfort.

"Ask me if I care."

Maurin bit down on the first retort that came to mind and shuffled back to his bed. After all, he wasn't accountable for what Aric did. "Aren't you going to tell me about your dream?"

"I don't know." Aric waved dismissively. "Nothing worth bothering about."

"It bothered you enough to make you scream." Maurin leaned on his elbow, forcing the frustration out of his voice. "You haven't done that since you were a boy. You've even been talking in your sleep; you've kept me up half the night for weeks with your doom-saying about ships of fire and eyes of death."

"Everyone has nightmares." Aric squeezed his eyes shut. "And waking up to you hovering over me half-naked and bald-skulled is not exactly comforting."

Maurin grimaced and passed his hand over his scalp. The elders had shaved his head yesterday in the purification ritual. Though he was Aric's senior by only six autumns, he felt older tonight. So much would change in the morning. "Do you remember that time you dreamed about running into Lirican's flockherds?"

"Yes." Aric whipped his head around, eyes gleaming. "So what? That was a long time ago."

"The healers kept me from my temple duties for over a week." Maurin smirked in wry memory. "I kept wondering, as I lay in bed, trying not to scratch at all the herbs and poultices they wrapped me in, if we had stayed away from the woods that day, could we have avoided the whole mess? But no, you said, it was only a dream."

"It *was* only a dream. The same thing would've happened whether or not I'd seen it beforehand."

"I think there's a hole somewhere in your logic." Maurin drummed his fingers on the bed in agitation. "At any rate, you're missing the point: your dreams have this uncanny tendency to come true."

Aric's expression tightened, and he shrugged. "I can't avoid it or prevent it, so I just put up with it. If I had a silver piece for every time I heard Elder Regin give a lecture before he actually gave it, I would be across the seas by now, pirating in the Falores or living it up as a sultan in Danubar.

Do you have any idea how annoying it is to live those things over and over again?"

Maurin forced a laugh, but his smile faded. A lizard tried to stay inconspicuous in the shadows of the stone wall above his head. Maurin sucked in a deep breath for the question he had been dreading, the question he had asked probably a half-dozen times already. "Was it about the wedding?"

Aric lay back down and muttered into the wall. "Is that what it would take?"

"What?"

For a moment Aric said nothing. Then he sat up, gauging Maurin's reaction. "Yeah, it was about the wedding."

Maurin's gut lurched. "What? What happens?"

"I don't know for sure. But it's bad." Aric bit his lip. "You can't go through with it, Maurin."

"I don't have a choice!" Panic threatened to overwhelm him. "And what could I do? Where could I go? The world is not so big that my father wouldn't find me. How can I escape what has been charted for me in the heavens?"

"Or in the deluded minds of our priests," Aric scoffed under his breath.

"Aric! Have a care! What if you're heard?"

He gave an ironic smile. "Maurin, no god or man is going to be able to convince me this is a good idea. And I'll say it loud enough for either to hear."

"Then what should I do?"

"You should—we should go." Aric threw off the tapestry and reached for his breeches. "We need to get out of here."

Maurin remained transfixed, too torn to move.

Aric slipped into trousers and a plain dark tunic, then started tossing clothes into his satchel. "Maurin, hurry up! We have to get out of here tonight."

Still, Maurin hesitated.

"Listen to me: Things are different now. Something very bad is going to happen if you get married tomorrow."

For the first time, Maurin saw the genuine apprehension in his cousin's eyes. He leapt to his feet and pulled on his breeches and vest.

Aric started violently at the padding of canine feet on stone behind him, and whirled in terror to face the hallway.

Maurin stared at him, his own panic escalating now. "It's just Cludes. Are you all right?"

Aric nodded and visibly relaxed at the carob-colored dog prancing around his knees. He scooped her up. "Hey, baby. Where have you been? You trying to send me over the edge?"

Maurin tugged one of Aric's hunting caps over his head to protect his tender scalp. It seemed only yesterday the senior scout of Athure had given Cludes to Aric when his own mongrel went to whelp. In the idealism of youth, the boy had named the pup after the legendary conqueror of the western kingdom of Beneal. Only afterwards had he found out that not only was the animal the wrong sex, but she had an indiscriminately affectionate nature. Maurin had half expected Aric to be disappointed that his animal never approached the ferocious reputation of her namesake, but he didn't care. He loved her all the same, sometimes even carrying her around like an infant.

"She usually comes running when you have a nightmare. She must have been out plying the guards for treats again."

Aric smiled and let her lick him all over the face.

"That's disgusting."

"You just wish you had a dog as good as this."

Maurin tightened the laces of his vest and buckled his boots. "I don't wish I had any dog."

"Right. Who needs a pet when you can have a wife?" Aric set Cludes down.

"That's unkind."

"Come on, Maurin, let's go."

"What about the guards?"

"What are they going to do?" Aric grinned. "You're the son of the high priest."

Maurin shot his cousin an exasperated glare and indicated their outfits and gear. "You think that will make any difference if they catch us running away?"

"Just follow me." Aric clicked his tongue, and Cludes padded along-side him as the cousins sneaked down torch-lit pathways. They avoided the main hall, choosing instead a storage alcove, and pushed their way through a dark labyrinth of cloaks, tallow candles, and bizarre accoutrements of the faith. The smell of incense still hung in the priestly robes, seeming to emanate from the very stone of the temple itself.

The chanting prayers of the priests ended upon sundown, leaving the corridors deathly still. Every step scuffed and echoed more loudly than it should, and Maurin wished for the clanging of the metal gong, or the tinkling of the prayer bracelets, just to have something other than Aric and himself making noise. The late hours filled him with a sense of ancient caution, of trampling on things that did not wish to be disturbed. It didn't help that Aric took pains to avoid the darkest corners of the rooms, as if clawed terrors lurked beyond the light, waiting for them to step off the narrow path. Maurin shook off his agitation, but his cousin had him more spooked than he cared to admit.

They passed the corridor that led to the vault of texts, and a pang of regret stabbed at Maurin. Probably no way to bring any of the scrolls with him. Could he so easily discard the sacred manuscripts that had shaped his life? Perhaps most painful, the amateurish history of Sangrine he was in the middle of writing might well remain forever unfinished.

With a few more twists and turns, they were once again bathed in the pallid light of Ulne, its summertime orb high and proud overhead. At the sound of footsteps, Aric ducked behind a parapet, and Maurin dropped down after him. In the moonlight, he saw the silhouette of a guard making his rounds.

He held his breath as the man drew closer. Above them loomed the observation tower, where the sages studied the heavens and predicted the fates. Despite his trepidation, a thrill of forbidden pleasure surged through Maurin. Many a happy hour had been spent up there as a boy, joking with Aric, listening to stories, and eating contraband foods while the other priests assumed he was meditating somewhere. He might never see the place again.

Maurin swallowed the stone in his throat.

The footsteps passed, and Aric glanced over the wall. He bundled Cludes under his arm, tugged at Maurin's sleeve, and whispered, "He's gone. Come on, it's now or never!"

Then he was over the parapet. Before he could talk himself out of it, Maurin vaulted after him and sprinted toward the little-known corridor that led out the rear of the city. It was designed to be used in times of emergency.

This probably counted, in its own way.

Aric turned sideways and pushed his way through the vines overgrowing the recessed slit in the wall. Maurin sputtered at the rain of earth as his head brushed roots and leaves. Then they were outside, and his pounding heart started to calm.

Cludes barked in excitement as Aric set her down, but he clamped his hand over her muzzle and shushed her. Then he straightened up, laughed, and punched Maurin in the arm. "We made it. You're free, Maurin. Can you believe it? You're free!"

Maurin craned his neck up at the walls now hiding the temple from his sight. "I'm free," he whispered. But free to do what? He had no idea where to go next. This all felt so unreal. In a few hours, Kirai would wake to find her groom had run away in the night, shirking his responsibility to her and to his people.

"I wonder what she looked like?" He pitched his voice low. They weren't out of danger yet.

"What difference does that make?" Aric set off along the edge of the wall. Cludes wagged her tail and scampered after him. "Anyway, you look like a ghoul. Think Kirai would even want to marry you, if she saw you like that?"

Maurin shook his head self-consciously and chuckled. "Why is it the one day of his life a man wants to look his absolute best...?"

"You tell me, Maurin. It's your stupid tradition."

He shrugged. Against his better judgment, Maurin followed his cousin into the woods, attention flitting between the ground and the top of the wall. "Someone got the bright idea centuries ago that a member of the priesthood has to enter the marriage covenant pure."

"Apparently, *pure* meant *hairless* in that day and age. So why don't they shave the girl?"

Maurin bit his lip. That hadn't occurred to him. "I don't know. Maybe they do. I've never been to a wedding like this."

"What, your own?"

"Very funny."

"At any rate," Aric said, pushing aside a branch, "there's one person you've made incredibly happy."

Maurin's brow furrowed. "Who?"

"Jathan."

That gave him pause. The Saronine queen's brother had a son, rumored to worship the gods of the Otherworld. Unlikely, but it was no secret that many believed the royal succession should have gone to Jathan. The Saronine people took great care getting Maurin's bride from Sarone to Athure in safety. Ostensibly, this was because of the bandits in the high country, but he and Aric suspected it was due to her cousin.

"Yes." Maurin gestured for him to keep his eyes ahead. "No doubt he will be quite pleased. Watch your step, would you?"

The island of Beydan was a jagged semicircle of lava rock, the product of a cataclysmic eruption sometime in the ancient past. Athure stretched out at the pinnacle of one of the highest mountains in the region. The edges of the city crowned the volcanic summit, and its walls prevented anyone from entering any other way than the main gates. The surrounding terrain was hardly something Maurin wanted to traverse at night. He trailed his hand along the cold stone, watching for sudden drop-offs.

"Maurin"—Aric paused to regard him over his shoulder—"what do you think my dreams mean?"

Maurin considered carefully before answering. Aric did not wax philosophical very often, and getting him to discuss his feelings was not unlike extracting teeth from a Carnian boar-hound.

"You've been given a great gift by Baelon. This ability to see beyond what is visible, to live things not yet lived, is his way of talking to you." Gravel shifted under his foot, and Maurin grabbed a vine trailing the wall for support. "Or perhaps through you. Warning of dangers to come."

"What, you think I'm a prophet or something?" Aric scoffed. "That is the biggest cart of mule dung I have ever heard. If I wanted cryptic priest-prattle, I'd be off meditating with Regin. And if I'm a prophet, why do I have so many dreams that don't seem to mean anything?"

Maurin shrugged, inclining his head toward the unseen front of the city. "Every day, all manner of people use those gates. Only one road leads to Athure; peddlers, tramps, beggars, thieves, merchants, and royalty all use the same path. It could be your dreams are like that."

"At least we can refuse entry to the city," Aric grumbled, and resumed walking. "The gates in my head are wide open."

Maurin dug his fingers under his cap and scratched at his scalp. If he had known he was going to run away, he would have done so before they shaved him. Even now he felt like turning back. But if Aric was having visions... "They're trying to tell you something."

"They're telling me I'm a freak."

"Can you describe them?"

"Something's always after me. I don't know why, and I can never tell what it is, but I still sense it. And it's getting worse. At times, even when I'm awake I swear I'm in the middle of one of my dreams."

A thin cloud passed over the moon. "What about the one you just had? What would have happened had I stayed?"

Aric shook his head, clearly disturbed, and went silent for several minutes. When he spoke again, it was in a subdued voice. "There is one dream that's not like the others."

"Oh?"

"I'm walking through the streets of a big city. It's hot, the air stinks, and the people all around are dressed in strange clothes. There's a lot of shouting and selling going on. A bunch of people are in chains, and I'm one of them. This woman is on the other side of the street. I can't see much of her face. She's no taller than the rest of them, but she stands out above them somehow. She's dressed different, too; she has on this long green gown like something a princess from Carnia would wear."

Maurin wiped at the sweat dripping into his eyes, and silently cursed the priests for not at least leaving his eyebrows. "What did she look like?"

"What part of *I can't see much of her face* didn't you understand? She's wearing a headdress and a veil. There are people between us, but somehow she sees me, and she doesn't look away. That's when I can see her eyes, and she doesn't even blink. It's like she recognizes me, but I know I've never seen her before. Then, somehow, the people are gone. It's night, and it's just the two of us." Aric paused, no doubt due to the alien excitement of new desires. "She tells me she's been waiting for me, and I will sail across the empty seas for her."

"Hmmm." The blanket of stars began to fade toward the horizon as the first fingers of dawn crept up across the mountains. Below, gauzy mist wreathed the dense woods. Giant forest animals lowed in the distance, mournful and hollow.

Aric glanced back at him. "What does that mean, crossing the empty seas?"

"I have no idea." Maurin shrugged. "Perhaps as you get older, you'll learn not only what these visions mean, but how to discern their importance." He gripped his cousin's shoulder. "You're going to hear many voices in your life, Aric, all of them telling you what to do. You'll have to be careful whose you listen to."

"You're one to talk."

"I listened to you, didn't I?" Maurin frowned. "I don't even know what I'm doing out here."

"Whatever you want. I say we go down to the harbor at Natuna and hire on as cabin crew. We could head to the Falores, or go exploring the tropics. Maybe even find our own island—"

With a gasp, Aric dropped from sight.

Maurin's chest seized. With a cry, he rushed forward to the edge of the deep ravine that had swallowed Aric whole. Cludes barked frantically as Maurin fell to his knees and searched the pitch-black depths for any sign of his cousin.

Numb with shock, Maurin couldn't find his voice. His mind raged. Aric, gone? How could he have been so foolish as to do this?

"Er, you just gonna stand there, or are you going to pull me up?" From the side nearest the wall, Aric dangled from his satchel, caught on a jutting projection of rock. The fear in his eyes gave lie to the jocular tone. The cloth strap holding him up had ripped in the fall and looked ready to give.

Wrought with relief and terror, Maurin crawled on his belly as far over the edge as he could reach.

The strap tore.

Aric spasmed with effort and caught Maurin by the wrist. He grasped at his cousin's arm, and the satchel tumbled quietly down the chasm.

"Pull, Maurin!"

"What do you think I'm doing?"

"Come on. I can't hold on much longer." No joking in his voice this time.

"Hang on." Maurin glanced back over his shoulder at the thick, woody vines creeping up the outer wall of Athure. He wedged his foot between the wall and a root, then inched forward. "Baelon, help me! Please don't let him fall!"

The moment the prayer passed his lips, Maurin heard another plea echo from the depths of another time. *Don't let him die*. Aric was a ward of the temple, an orphan before his seventh birthday. They had been brothers almost instantly, but Aric had fallen deathly ill barely a year after he came to live with them. Maurin had dropped at the feet of Baelon, vowing service and obedience to whatever the heavens decreed in exchange for his cousin's life. Though already born into the order, he submitted himself to an irrevocable priesthood. After Aric recovered, Maurin had all but forgotten his boyhood oath.

His cousin's sweaty fingers began to slip.

Maurin had forsaken his vow, and Aric was going to die for it.

"Forgive me," he prayed desperately. "I swear to you, I shall return. Please don't take Aric."

With a surge of strength, he pulled. Something strained in his back, and for an infinite moment, Maurin thought he was going to drop him.

Then Aric's dangling feet found a foothold, and he climbed up, using Maurin's arm and body as a rope. Together, they panted on the edge of the ravine while Cludes did a dance of joy around Aric. After a few minutes, he laughed. "Our first adventure."

Maurin gaped at him in disbelief. He stood up and walked away from the ravine, running a hand over his nonexistent hair. "Aric, I have to go back."

For a moment, his cousin just stared. Then he exploded. "Are you crazy?"

"No."

Aric tossed a clod of dirt over the ravine. "I can't believe you want to go through with it. This is your last chance to run!"

Can you believe that's how much I care for you? Maurin headed back the way they had come. "I'm not running, Aric."

His cousin leapt after him, fuming. "I knew it! I knew you couldn't go through with it! Always have to play by the rules, don't you?"

"Aric..."

"Nothing I say gets through to you. Even if I had dreamed about it, you—"

Maurin whirled, his feet skidding on loose gravel. "What do you mean, even if you had?"

Aric stood silent, clenching his jaw.

"You never dreamed about the wedding?" Hurt and anger threatened to take Maurin's last bit of composure.

"Break into a sweat, get stomach pains, and feel like running into the woods every time I think about it, yes," Aric said crossly. "Dream, no. Not that I can tell, anyway. I wish I could. It would be nice if one of us felt good about the thing."

"Aric, you lied to me!"

"I'm sorry." Aric's voice nearly broke. "I didn't want to stand by and watch. But can't you just trust me? Something seriously doesn't feel right about this."

Maurin studied him for a long moment, and then pulled him into an embrace. "It'll be all right. Nothing is going to change between you and me. Brothers to the end, remember?"

Aric snorted and pulled away. "Is that what you think I'm worried about?"

"Isn't it?"

He shook his head in disgust. "If only that were all. Gods, Maurin, you're more stubborn than I am!"

Maurin chuckled ruefully and trekked ahead. "Is that possible?"

His cousin fell in behind him, but would not be deflected. "What about Jathan?"

"I can handle Jathan; don't worry about him."

"You think so? His father could rally support from their warriors, and you would have the shortest garland season ever."

"You have a point. Still..." Maurin hesitated. "Still, I think most of Kirai's people are in favor of the marriage."

"They know Jathan. How many of these barbarian Saronines do you suppose are willing to live or die by your word, when none of them has even seen you before? You're not even of royal blood."

"No, but His Majesty isn't getting any younger. He hasn't had any offspring, and my father's authority as high priest is second only to his. If the king produces no heir, the rule will go to my father. And the royal chieftain of Sarone is on his deathbed, and has no heirs."

"He has plenty of daughters!"

"But he has sired no sons." Maurin struggled to be patient, but this was an old argument, and he was in no mood to have it again. Not now. Aric was no traditionalist in any sense of the word, and certainly no advocate of arranged marriage. All the same, Maurin knew Aric wouldn't begin to comprehend the vow. "He wishes security. Most of the people understand that. It's not as if we have a choice. And besides, you don't even know the girl."

"Neither do you! Why do you want to sign your life away?"

Not for the first time, Maurin thanked Baelon that Aric had not been initiated to the priesthood. So many things with which he would never have to be burdened. "My life was signed away the moment I was born and consecrated into the holy order. This is no different. It's just the next step in doing what's expected of me."

"So you're doing this because it's expected of you, or because of a crazy devotion to some pompous, centuries-old tradition? I haven't heard you object once!"

"Inane as it may sound to you," he said, "I think it's the right thing to do."

"Doing the 'right thing' will be the death of you someday," Aric grumbled.

Maurin smiled. "Did you dream that?"

Aric raised an eyebrow.

Maurin held up his hand. "No, don't tell me. At least I know I'll die with a clear conscience."

"You should be so lucky."

They didn't speak for the rest of the return trek. When they reached the passageway, Maurin closed his eyes and put his forehead and palms against the stone wall. Aric sat down with his back against it and swore. Cludes rolled over on her back, inviting him to scratch her belly. He obliged, and Maurin slumped down beside him, thoughts awhirl. After several moments of sitting in silence, he gave Aric's shoulder a squeeze. "I know none of this makes sense to you. Most of the time, it doesn't even make sense to me. I do wish I'd at least had a chance to meet Kirai."

Cludes put her head in Aric's lap, and he stroked her ears morosely. "You'll have your chance soon enough."

"I want her to see she's not marrying a monster. Just a chance to let her know that I will treat her well."

"That's not the reason."

"It's not?" Maurin raised one eyebrow, pretending to be shocked. "I thought that's what I wanted."

Aric smirked. "You want to take a gander at her to make sure you're not the one marrying a monster."

"You could be right." Maurin allowed himself a wan smile. "I agree with you that we should have been allowed to at least talk. It's not as if that's going to corrupt her before we're married."

"I don't know," Aric said, "your breath in the mornings is enough to corrupt the most—"

"All right, that does it!" Maurin grabbed at his cousin, and Aric dodged, laughing. Maurin mock-punched and scuffled with him. If they were caught by some of the sterner members of the order, they would be in for a lecture, at the very least. Cludes barked encouragement from a safe distance.

Aric finally submitted, red-faced and grinning. Maurin turned to the rosy glow on the horizon. His cousin didn't try to grapple with him as often as he had when he was younger, and for that, Maurin was grateful. He didn't know how much longer he would be able to emerge the victor.

"What are you doing out here?"

Maurin and Aric both started. Regin, one of the celibates, pushed his way through the vines, wearing his customary worried pout. Aric had once remarked that the elder had the face of a turnip.

And all its inherent charm, Maurin thought.

Jutting his head forward and his nose out in an odd, birdlike fashion, Regin stalked up and grabbed them by the shirt sleeves. "We've been searching all over for you! You're filthy! Come, we must get you bathed!"

"It's hours until the wedding," Maurin reminded him.

"Have you no respect? The dignity and reputation of our entire kingdom will be represented by you this afternoon." Regin turned on Aric in reproach. "You had better do your part, as well, young Aric. And get that animal out of here!"

Cludes whined; she wasn't that smart, but she knew when she was being talked about.

"All right, all right," Maurin said. "Get Aric ready first."

"What?" Aric skewered his cousin with a glare.

Maurin ignored him. "I'll be there presently. Just give me half an hour."

"And just where are you going?" Aric asked.

"To the inner temple." Maurin ducked into the aperture with a wistful smile and called back over his shoulder, "I need to pray."

Maurin muttered a ritual prayer of thanks to the god of knowledge as he ministered to a torch whose alkaline fluids had gone stale. He poured the bitter acid into the clay cylinder, then dipped the metal wick into the mixture and sealed the top with wax from a long taper. An arc of current leapt between the two upright arms of the metal statue encased in the safety of a sandglass shell, infusing the inner sanctuary in a pale blue glow.

He reflected for a moment on an imperfection, a swirl distorting the face of the miniature god inside into a hideous visage. Why was he seeing omens in everything these days?

"Just a few hours more, and a new life will begin for you," a familiar voice boomed from the hallway.

Maurin bowed to greet the red-bearded man approaching him. "I still think there's something sacrilegious about it, Father."

"Sacrilegious?" Perin sounded genuinely surprised. "What?"

"Having the wedding on the Eve of Descent. I don't know; it just seems wrong." Ten thousand years ago, according to the holy scrolls, the gods had visited this world and lived with them for generations, instructing and ruling in peace. Before the great wars, anyway. Maurin didn't give those events much credence most of the time, but Aric's dreams had him edgier than usual, and he wasn't entirely sure it was due to the upcoming nuptials.

"It's a sacred day, Maurin," Perin reiterated. "We prayed, we sacrificed, we consulted the heavens. The elders all agreed that this is the right time for the sanctification of your union."

Maurin had heard it all before. "I suppose it would take a visit from the gods themselves to get Aric to believe that all is well. But it would appear I don't have much choice."

"Maurin, as my firstborn and my lastborn, you inherited a great deal of responsibility that otherwise might not have been yours. You would always have been a priest, but it might not have fallen upon you to marry without your consent. Yet the Law demands the holy bloodline continue."

Maurin knew that for a fact. He had read their own texts enough, even poring over them when he was not supposed to. He had secretly asked one of the elder priests to teach him the nuances of the ancient tongue, so he might better understand that which he was required to recite every day. Some parts he found amazing, others incredible, and still others boring and pretentious. Of course, he dared not say that aloud, lest he be accused of heresy. Better to contemplate the mysteries of the gods in privacy and silence than to face possible execution for insulting them in public.

"But what of Aric's dreams, Father? What am I to make of them?"

Perin shrugged slightly under the heavy metal breastplate, the motion billowing out the white sleeves of his robe. His expression made it clear that the door of his mind had just been closed. "We've walked this ground before, Maurin, and even if I could change the path, it is too late now. The priests have had no visions, and unless your mother's sister's son has been granted something they have not, we must assume that Aric is simply dreaming as most young men do."

Considering the reason Aric had ended up in the temple in the first place, that struck Maurin as being singularly naïve. Or perhaps just a kind of denial. Aric claimed that he had never dreamed of his mother since that one time, but surely that once was enough?

Maurin studied the craggy features of his father's face, the thick, curly beard that was starting to gray, and wondered if he took more after his mother. Certainly he saw little enough of himself in his father, no matter what anyone else said. For the first time in weeks, he felt bitterness creeping in at the edges of his soul.

Perin's face softened into a smile. "This way is best; you'll see."

Maurin found his reverie interrupted by the sound of bare feet slapping on cut stone, and the sudden appearance of a young acolyte wearing a short tunic. His hair was cut close after the manner of priests in training. Maurin looked down his nose at the boy in disapproval, and was about to chide him for running in the temple, but his father spoke first.

"What is it, Yared?"

"They're almost ready." The acolyte panted for breath. "The King requests your presence."

Demanded it, more likely.

"All right, boy; I'll be along shortly."

Yared nodded and hurried around the corner again.

"And don't run!" Maurin shot after him. The footsteps skidded to a stop, then resumed at a more measured pace, accompanied by some wincing mutters.

"I must go." Perin grasped him by the shoulders. "You have borne up very well, son. I am proud of you."

Guilt twinged in Maurin as he gazed up into those dark eyes, eroded around the corners by the streams of time. Would Father be so proud if he knew that just this morning, Maurin was ready to run away from it all, to leave him and the life he swore to live behind, simply because he was afraid? So many men regarded the high priest's duty and resolve. Would they ever view Maurin with the same respect?

Perin grew wistful, and clutched Maurin's arm one last time. "If only your mother were here to see you now."

———————◆———————

The sun was too bright, the birds were too loud, and this whole day just seemed like another bad dream.

When Aric next saw Maurin, his cousin looked even less like himself than before. The deep blue robe draped over him shimmered like a midnight sea as he joined the procession. His eyelids were tinted with a lighter purple delicately shaded into black. Indigo colored his lips, giving him a slightly cruel, sensual appearance that Aric despised. It reminded him of someone, though at the moment he couldn't quite figure who. It was no wonder looking glasses were not allowed before events such as this. The groom would never show his face in public, let alone to his bride. He didn't even want to think about his own appearance; before he closed his eyes for the priests' ministrations, he had caught a glimpse of a series of rose paint sticks held in a chubby hand.

Another stupid tradition.

The bride, he had to admit, was a jewel. The warm sun glinted in the blonde tresses cascading past her hips. Aric stole an appreciative glance at the soft rise and fall of Kirai's pale bosom. For the first time he felt a touch of envy for Maurin, and the pleasures of marriage, snickered at in low voices long after they were supposed to be asleep.

Several years ago, when Maurin began to wax poetic about the beauties of women, Aric was impatient and disgusted, wanting his older cousin to get his mind back on the adventures they'd planned, exploring the woods, and talking of far-off places. But now, though Aric still yearned for an escape from the general tedium of life in Athure, he also found himself distracted by stirrings he couldn't quite explain. Still, he watched the girl with a scrutiny bordering on suspicion.

In distinct contrast to Maurin, Kirai's face was unpainted and unadorned, with not even a veil between her and the groom. Two dark streamers draped over the girl's shoulders and framed her arms against the light green of her simple gown. The loose garland of white flowers around her neck was attractive, but the wreath nestled on her head was a bit much. It was woven of fresh halaia leaves, replete with the occasional sprigs of red berries. Apparently the Saronine women who dressed her that morning thought it important that there be children in the near future.

Rushing destiny. Everybody tried, but it always took its own course.

Why was he still so troubled? After all, as Aric himself had pointed out, he wasn't the one getting married here. And yet, a vague unease continued to gnaw at him, growing with each passing moment. At first, he dismissed it as mere anxiety, but now he wasn't so sure. Not sure at all. No way to talk to Maurin—even discreetly—without interrupting the ceremony. He had caught his attention once, and gotten an *if-you-mess-this-up-I'm-going-to-murder-you* look.

The procession moved past hundreds of Saronine and Athurian spectators lining the main street of the city. Dancers and singers preceded them to the beat of drums and the strumming of stringed instruments. Torches lined the path at a discreet distance, burning an aromatic mixture of knotted herbs Aric had come to hate. Ostensibly they were sacred incense, meant to further enrich the mystic union. Aric knew from listening to the priests that they were mostly designed to keep the bugs away.

Maurin's father strode several paces ahead of the couple, heralding their nuptials with a loud voice and outstretched arms, allowing people to add their blessings as they passed. Aric shuffled along in their wake.

If only he could figure out this upset in the pit of his stomach.

If only there were some way to escape.

The life of a priest was not conducive to excitement, but Maurin wasn't like the others. For all his stodgy adherence to the ethics of the order, there was a yielding quality to him that came in quiet moments, a suggestion that he wasn't quite happy with the way things were. Aric took advantage of that whenever he could; it was his only hope that his cousin would not become like one of those who ritually prostrated themselves at the stone feet of Baelon until the day their withered knees could no longer bear their own weight.

At last, they stood in the magnificent pyramidal shadow of the temple. It had been built on a series of tiers, with no ground level entry in front. If this was to keep anyone from entering the temple casually, it certainly worked. Aric had always joked that those steep stairs were what kept Maurin from getting soft and saggy like the priests who never left the inner sanctum.

Maurin winked reassuringly as he accepted the chalice from Aric, then tilted his head back for a drink. With reverence, he passed it to Kirai. She held the broad-rimmed cup as if it were a bowl, drinking with care.

Overhead, a large white bird circled twice, and flew on.

Having dutifully performed his part in this farce, Aric was determined to remain in silent disapproval for the duration. He attempted to quell the turbulence in his stomach. Desperate for any reason to distract himself from these odd misgivings, he watched a twig bug scouting out the pleats of Kirai's skirts. Perin droned on, binding Maurin's wrist to hers with a pair of silken ribbons.

Aric's head jerked.

He saw nothing.

He heard nothing.

But his heart raced, and he swallowed hard. His fidgeting drew the attention of several of the spectators and earned another reproachful glance from his cousin. Aric peered intently into the distance, the wedding all but forgotten. Meaningless words murmured on beside him, a steady droning in his ear. A droning that became a buzz, then a hum. If the onlookers around him were any indication, Aric was the only one who heard it.

This wasn't his imagination. Something was wrong... very wrong.

Sweat stood out on Aric's brow, and he clenched and unclenched his fists. Every muscle in his body shouted flight, but ruining the wedding would have dire consequences. He had no intention of suffering lectures and disdain—or worse—while Maurin enjoyed his wedding night.

But with every passing moment, the dread grew stronger. Should he speak up? What would he say? That he wasn't feeling well? Maurin would kill him.

Distantly, Maurin recited the concluding parts of his oath, and Kirai responded.

Then the sky tore open with a scream.

CHAPTER 2
BROKEN VOWS

After the first ear-splitting shriek, a blinding flash and concussion knocked everyone in the courtyard to the ground. The stones of the pavement shook and bounced out of their fittings. Incredible vibrations traveled through Maurin's bruised palms and rattled his teeth, and howling wind whipped his clothes against his body. All around, people buried their faces, quaking and wailing penitent prayers. Others screeched and ran.

Whatever it was blotted out the sun, and yet outshone it, as well. Billows of flame poured off its gray surface, filling the air with a blue mist. Spidery fingers of lightning set nearby trees smoldering. Larger than the temple and the palace put together, the thing formed an unlikely canopy over the entire main court of the city. For one mad moment, Maurin had a fleeting recollection of the few ocean craft he had seen in his young life. Yet this thing hung impossibly in the sky.

Aric swore violently. "I knew it!"

"What's happening?" Kirai screamed.

"The gods have returned!" Perin said, enraptured. "I never thought I'd live to see the day!"

"I'm not sure you have," Aric said, and somehow Maurin knew his words were true. The crowd pressed close.

With a screech, a tremendous maw opened in the underbelly of the titanic beast.

Galvanized, Maurin leapt to his feet, still bound to Kirai by the nuptial ribbons. With a few deft flicks of the wrist, she released herself and ran.

"Kirai!" he called after her.

Those not staring up in stupefied wonder at the intruder clawed and shoved at each other, shouting and screaming. Aric pushed his way toward Maurin through the panicked throng. He stumbled only a few yards away, and Maurin leapt to pull him out of the path of the trampling feet.

Aric grasped his shoulder and screamed into his ear, "We've got to go!"

"Just a moment. Where's my father?"

"I don't know. I lost sight of him." Aric scanned the crowd, focused and intent. Then his face fell, and he pointed. "I think I see him."

Maurin followed his finger to a crumpled heap on the ground.

"No! Father!" He ran against the tumultuous mob, buffeted and jostled from every side. When he reached Perin, he knelt, oblivious to the chaos around him, and turned him over. Perin moaned, and his eyes wandered. His clothes were torn and covered with bootprints, his face bruised and bloodied.

"Father?"

Perin stretched a shaky hand up to his son's face. "Maurin. You must be strong." His voice faltered. "I go to the arms of Baelon now. Don't ever forget I love you."

Maurin's mind spun. When was the last time he had heard those words? Was this what it was like to be caught up in one of Aric's nightmares?

The wind picked up, and dust and leaves blew out in a circular pattern away from the hovering demon. In moments, a tunnel of swirling air surrounded it, reaching to the ground.

Perin's eyes closed.

Maurin cradled his father's head, the world turning to a gray haze. He could no longer hear the pandemonium around him. Yards away, Aric mouthed something at him.

What did he want?

His cousin's face twisted with frustration, and he sprinted over and yanked Maurin to his feet.

"Run!" Aric bawled into his ear.

Shaking himself, Maurin cast about frantically for Kirai. He had to find her. This was another test. It must be.

There she was, huddled with her mother, not too far away. He ran over and tugged at her arm. She shook her head at him and pulled out of his grasp. No amount of coaxing could get her to budge.

Aric screamed back into the gale. "Leave her!"

"I can't! You don't understand!"

"Maurin! Get out of there!"

His innards a cauldron of turmoil, Maurin cast off his outer cloak as he ran to Aric.

It never hit the ground. Instead, it spun up toward the mouth of the flying beast.

His jaw dropped as, one by one, people rose after it, lifted off the pavement by an unseen force. They tumbled much more gently than he would have expected given the stormy violence of the air, but their ascent was inexorable. He sprinted as quickly as he could, breeches and sleeves pulled tight by the wind.

"I couldn't get her to move!"

"Don't worry about it, Maurin."

"But she's my responsibility!"

"If she wants to die with her mother, let her!"

Maurin threw him a shocked glare, then turned back to the intruder. "It's blocked the entrance to the city!" What did Baelon expect of him? How was he supposed to fulfill his vows now?

"We'll have to go through the temple. Once we're inside, it won't be able to get to us."

"But the stairs...!" Maurin bit his lip, calculating how long it would take to run around to the rear entrances.

"Come on; we don't have a choice!"

Maurin swore. Exposed and vulnerable, every step taking him further heavenward, and closer to the unexpected interloper. He gasped and panted as his feet slapped on the ground. He was nearly to the top of the first flight when Aric shouted.

"It's coming this way!"

Maurin glanced back and barked his shin trying to take two steps at

a time.

"Quick, Maurin!" Aric sprinted the fifty feet to the doorway leading to one of the side passages.

Maurin winced and limped after him, blood plastering his breeches to his leg. His stomach lurched as he began to rise from the ground.

"Aric!"

His cousin leapt up and grabbed Maurin's wrist, the ribbon still attached and flapping. When their combined weight caused them to start to sink, Aric grabbed the doorjamb and pulled with all his might. Air rushed out from the tunnel, but they managed to set their feet on the ground long enough to start running again. The wind snuffed the flaming torches lining the outer tunnels, but Maurin ran headlong into the darkness. He could break his nose running into a wall if he wasn't careful, but he knew these passageways. All the same, he held his arm out in front of him.

"Left turn here."

"I know," Aric said beside him.

Maurin slowed to a fast walk; the air no longer whistled in his ears. Within moments, a blue glow appeared ahead. At least those torches were still working.

A soft whining came from one of the corridors.

"Cludes!" Aric called.

After a few seconds, the familiar shape of his cousin's dog emerged from the shadows, running toward them. She did not stop, but scuttled past them and cowered in Aric's shadow.

"Cludes? Come here, girl."

She remained where she was, whimpering.

Maurin's mind raced. Father, gone. Kirai, deserted. Aric...

Icy fingers raked his spine.

"Aric." Maurin shook his shoulder.

"What?"

"We're in trouble."

Another light was growing; a white light that swallowed up the pallid blue of the temple's torches. With every passing moment, it gained intensity.

"What is that?" Aric's voice sounded odd and hollow.

"They're inside. I don't know how, but they've gotten in."

Voices sounded in the hall ahead, but Maurin did not recognize the speech. The source of the light rounded the corner, searing streaks across his vision. He shielded his eyes.

Maurin could just make out the silhouettes of several massive forms, roughly the height of men. He couldn't discern any features, or even tell how many of them there were. Several of them carried long devices of some sort, and the one in front bore the light.

Cludes yipped in fear and shot off down the passageway. Aric ran after her.

"That's not the way out!" Maurin yelled.

"I know that!" Cludes's tail disappeared around a corner.

"Who are they?"

"How should I know?" Aric retorted as they ran through several hallways after the fleeing dog.

"She's headed for our rooms," Maurin said. "We need to get out of the city and into the forest."

Aric nodded. "This won't take long."

"Don't let that dog be the death of us!"

Moments later, they burst through the open door of the room, and found Cludes crouching under the bed. Aric reached for her, but she growled at him. He spoke her name in a soothing tone, then grabbed her by the scruff of the neck and hauled her out. "C'mon, girl. Let's go."

"Too late." Maurin pointed to the balcony.

Jaggedly bizarre dark blue armor encased a figure shaped like a tall man, and sturdy shoulder guards augmented an already broad frame. A menacing helmet hid the creature's face, and a jointed metallic headdress led into the rest of the body. The being held out a long two-pronged staff covered with intricate scrollwork.

The dog growled and barked. Aric shushed her.

Maurin backed slowly toward the doorway. A hard blow to the shoulders nearly bowled him over, and he whirled. Another one of the invaders peered at him through an eyeless visor.

Cludes leapt out of Aric's arms and ran past the knees of the great creature.

"Some protection you are!" Aric groused.

The armored giant closest to the doorway raised his weapon, and another flash of light nearly blinded Maurin. A large portion of the wall disintegrated into a smoking pile of blackened rubble, barely missing Cludes as she skittered into the hall.

Aric drew back his fist.

"Don't!" Maurin held out his hands. "They'll kill you!"

Five invaders now blocked the balcony entryway. Aric cursed in disgust as two of them pinned his arms to his sides.

A thick fog rolled in from outside, shrouding the legs of the invaders in a dismal gray mist. Maurin's vision started to blur. He took a few steps toward Aric, hoping he could break the raiders' hold long enough to give him a fighting chance, but with each successive step, his legs got heavier, and the room grew longer. At the end of a dark tunnel, Aric's distorted body hung slack between the two huge forms. His head lolled on his shoulders. Laboring to breathe, Maurin slid to the ground in despair.

The last thing he remembered before he succumbed was a huge, helmeted form leaning over him.

INTERLUDE
VISITATION

Muted conversations swirl around me as I float free into the darkness. They hold no meaning, and dwindle into silence. The world exists no more. I feel no fear or exultation. I simply am. An eternity passes, and I don't care.

A voice speaks into the void. *Aric.*

Who are you? I ask.

I am the one you seek. Come to me. I long to show you the meaning of your dreams.

What do you want?

To love you, Aric. To make you mine.

For no reason I can name, the words fill me with an icy dread.

I can see her now. Her beauty nearly takes my breath away. Alluring blue-green eyes over prominent cheekbones draw me closer. A floating cloud of thick brown hair moves in an unseen current. It falls to bare shoulders, framing features chiseled as if by the hand of a master sculptor. I see no more; her face fills my vision, her eyes fill my soul.

Eyes of destiny.

I am waiting for you, Aric. Her voice reverberates with alien timbre. Electric green clouds behind her swirl and coruscate with a ghostly light. *Follow me.*

Without warning, she is gone.

In a rustle of wings and a breath of wind, I know what it is to fly. I have no awareness of my body; I am conscious only of the sensation of soaring. I pass over forest, swamp, streams, and hills, and on into a mountainous region.

She is beside me. Had she ever left?

Buried in this dark valley is the grave marker of the gods. Within lies a secret that would freeze the heart of many a brave man, if ever the truth of its existence became known.

The sky turns dark ahead. The terrain is ashen, overgrown with gray vines and brambles. I can't detect a hint of green anywhere. This is not the pewter shine of moonlight; this is a land stripped of color and vibrancy. In the midst of this blighted gorge, stretching far above the mountains around it, a spindly hand reaches up to grasp the moon. As I draw nearer, I see it is more like an antler, or a colossal piece of driftwood, or a tree—yes, that's it. It is a tree, but leafless, and of prodigious proportions. It rises out of the mists ahead like a silent, malevolent titan. Dark abysses like watchful eyes gaze with the omnipotent gloom of the ages. Life in the surrounding lands withers under its unrelenting glare.

It has stood these long ages as a testimony to their conceit. Concealed from the eyes of the outside world is the forgotten remnant of a once-mighty race.

I have flown in a kind of hollow roaring silence up to that point, but now I am aware of a new sound, a chorus of voices. A soft howling permeates the windless canyon, a moaning of souls whose hunger can never be sated. Soon a wordless lament fills the air, a painful banshee wail. It's getting dark; a storm is gathering. A black cloud swirls above the stark citadel.

It has wings.

A vast horde of enormous bat-like creatures fills the sky almost to the bleak horizon. The screeching howl emitting from their apish mouths chills my blood. For a brief moment, I know fear. But that fear does not have time to grow. She draws me toward the heart of the looming mountain-tree.

Why are you showing me this?

Because I wish you to know. Observe, and remember.

At once, we are inside. The room has two occupants, indifferent to the malignant aura of their surroundings, and oblivious to our presence. The chamber's only light is the unholy glow emanating from two braziers perfuming the air with incense. Smokeless green flame shimmers and casts uncertain shadows on distant walls, illuminating bizarre patterns on the thin rug. All is still. In the middle of the room the violet-robed forms of a man and a woman face each other with their eyes closed. Each mirrors the other's posture, legs folded underneath them, arms out and to the sides, palms held upward as if in supplication.

They breathe as one.

The intimacy of their proximity is not romance, but a connection infinitely more potent. A solemn feeling of building power nearly stifles me as they await I know not what. Yet there is nothing passive about the silence. In the absence of motion or sound, I sense the shaping of destiny.

His features distorted by the rippling light, the man leans his head back and sighs, as if burdened by a great weight. His dark complexion makes him seem ageless; only his eyes betray his years, which must be innumerable. It is impossible to determine the color of his hair, as he has none. Prior to the movement, I might have thought him a statue, or an exquisite wood carving.

Across from him, the pale skin of his counterpart stands out above the neck of her robe. Dark hair spills in a straight rush over her shoulders and blankets her back. She pauses a moment, then speaks—quietly, so as not to disrupt the aura of his meditation.

"You have had a vision, my lord." There is no question in her voice, which is as haunting as her presence, a solid, fixed point in the ethereal gloom.

The man speaks, but his eyes remain closed. "One is coming who will bring about the downfall of our race, and the end of our world."

"We must stop this from happening." The dark-haired woman's generous mouth forms the snarl of a predator protecting her cubs.

"Nothing can stop this from happening." His voice is heavy with solemn resignation. "Our time is nearly come. We stand upon the cusp of destruction. Doom is written in the very stars above our heads. The sun must set even on the forgotten Glorious. We must accept this."

"Perhaps," she says at last. "Perhaps not."

There will be no change, no destruction. She will see to that. She has poured her heart and soul into the continued existence of her race. When the die is cast, only the strong will survive. Extinction is not an option.

None of this makes any sense, but I can't help but ask, *What is she going to do?*

My guide pierces me with her gaze.

The Dreaded One will come. Disaster will not be averted. The question is, upon whose head shall it fall?

CHAPTER 3
A NEW WORLD

Maurin shivered on the dank floor of a metallic vault. His head hurt, and his vision took a while to clear. Aric slumped near him toward the end of a semicircular room, which terminated at both ends in a dark hallway. Maurin supposed they had been deposited in the gullet of the flying beast. A deep thrumming sound echoed through the walls and corridors, and the vibration of something distant and massive caused a slight tingling sensation wherever he sat.

Set into recesses in the ceiling, fixtures very much like the current-torches in the temple lit the enormous chamber. One wall curved to form an awning overhead, and the opposite wall continued up into the dark. The sheer number of people inside warmed the air. Maurin recognized hundreds of men of the city, but saw no women among them. He smelled the sweat of fear over the perfumed oil the priests had used to tame Aric's unruly locks.

His stomach roiled. Aric was all he had left now.

"I can't believe it." Maurin rocked with his head in his hands. "A dog. You couldn't leave without the dog."

"Shut up, Maurin. You would have done the same thing."

"I suppose; if she were mine, and I cared for her. As a matter of fact, I seem to remember trying to get Kirai to come with me, if a certain

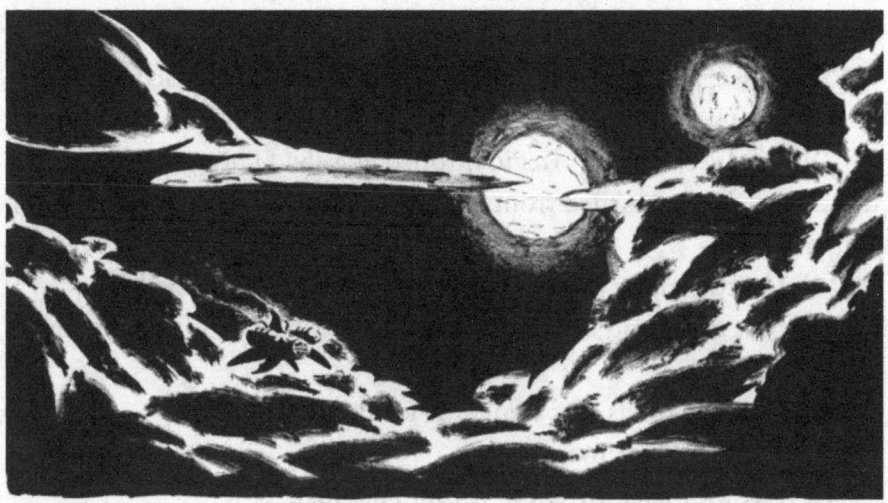

cousin of mine hadn't convinced me to leave her behind." He kicked at the steel floor.

Father. Oh, Father...

"I didn't make you leave her. And you could have made her come with you."

"Oh? And how exactly was I supposed to do that? She was fighting me." Fought, and won. And Aric would be the loser. Baelon would not forget...

"You could have thrown her over your shoulder and brought her if you felt it was so important."

Maurin stewed in silence for a moment. "For some reason, manhandling my new bride didn't occur to me."

"Well, it's kind of a moot point now, anyway. None of this would have happened if you had listened when I said something bad was coming."

"Not to us, anyway." There was too much truth in what Aric said to argue further.

"Silence, young fools!" Regin said from the shadows. "You'll bring the wrath of the gods upon us!"

Aric whirled with a snarl. "It's a little late for that."

"Aric, hush," Maurin said. What did Baelon want? Did the strength to pull Aric from the ravine come from him, or from Maurin himself? Would Baelon understand that Maurin had done all he could to fulfill his vow, or would he still exact a price for failure?

"Elder Regin," Yared the acolyte asked despondently, "do you believe we are in the hands of the gods?"

"What else can it be?" Regin intoned gravely. "This is the Eve of Descent. They have returned from the sky and are taking us to Baelon for judgment."

"I'm a little young to be going to paradise," Aric quipped.

"I don't think you'll have to worry about that, you insolent young pup."

Aric lurched to his feet, clenching his fists.

"Sit down!" Maurin ordered.

Aric acquiesced, muttering, "Stupid old man."

Yared faced the sulky Regin. "If Baelon has come to bring us to the world beyond, what must we do?"

"Be contrite. You must defer to his power at all times, and never contradict his precepts."

"And what if it is not Baelon?" Maurin asked. "What if these messengers are not of the gods at all?"

Regin hissed. "You risk the eternal flames."

"If they aren't the gods, our fear is groundless." Maurin gestured angrily. "And if they are, there's nothing more we can do, anyway. We can only tell them how we have lived our lives. They can but judge us on our deeds. We should have nothing to worry about. On the other hand, one who has not followed the law of the gods might have something to fear indeed."

"And what would a man of Baelon fear?" Aric piped up. "I'm sure you've done nothing deserving the wrath of the gods. Unless all the extra time you spent 'meditating' with the acolytes is going to keep you from the Hills of Splendor."

Even in the dim light, Maurin could see Regin turn pale at the implied accusation.

"How dare you!" the older man gasped.

Had Aric heard something Maurin, as the high priest's son, had not? Another dream vision? Or was he just being his subversive self again?

"He didn't mean anything, Elder Regin." But it was too late. Several of those closest to them heard what Aric said about the priest, and started an uproar. They decided it was Regin's fault they were all in this predicament. Some suggested killing him and offering him as a sacrifice to appease the angry gods. In the end Maurin had to stand between the old priest and a mob of others. His chest ached. If only Father were here. Perin would have known what to say.

It didn't end there, though. Soon the men started accusing one another of various misdeeds, most of which, Maurin guessed, would not have been serious enough to cause the gods to pay attention, but who was to say what the gods deemed worthy of their notice, or what might precipitate their retribution? Baelon always struck Maurin as somewhat indifferent to the affairs of men, but the requisite worship seemed to imply otherwise. The arguments and accusations got heated enough that in one corner of the room the men came to blows, and Maurin had to face them down again until the outrage settled to an angry murmur. The men resumed their places, but resentment and blame radiated from each man toward his neighbor.

When it seemed no more outbursts were forthcoming, Maurin turned to Aric. "I'm going to have a look around. Are you coming with me?"

Aric stood up again—"Do you even have to ask?"— and stepped over the moaning form of one of the men.

"I wouldn't do that," Yared said, his eyes hollow and haunted. "I already tried, while you two were unconscious. They don't let you out."

"What do you mean?"

"Guards are posted at both ends. My uncle went mad and forced his way past them. They pointed one of those wands at him, and fire leaped forth and consumed him before my eyes. They took away his body, and no one has tried to escape since."

Oh, Baelon. Maurin swallowed a lump in his throat and put his arm around the boy. "I'm sorry."

The young man stared straight ahead, not acknowledging him.

"So what do you say to that?" Aric said quietly.

Maurin scowled. "These are not our gods."

"Thank you. I meant beyond that."

"I think they are not gods at all. In fact..." A bitter taste formed in Maurin's mouth, and a fresh wave of nausea hit him. Hunger, the after-effects of whatever had knocked them unconscious, or something else? Every movement felt strange in this place; whenever he stood, his arms seemed light, as if they would just float off if he weren't careful.

"In fact, what?"

"I dare not say." He squeezed his eyes shut.

"Say it, Maurin. You know it's what you're thinking anyway."

"What do you want me to say? That I wonder if there are any gods at all? You know me better than that. But we are being tested, for some reason." Maurin chewed on his lip. He should not have gotten angry at Aric. Maurin was the elder; he was responsible for his bride. He couldn't blame anyone else just because he hadn't taken charge of the situation. He felt out of control enough as it was.

Did you dream this, too, cousin?

How long had it been since he had last eaten? He didn't want anything, but his body told him it must have been quite a while since he and Aric were taken from the temple.

All around, men began to grumble about their empty stomachs as hunger eventually overcame their fear. When the clamor got too loud, some of the armored guards came back, pronged weapons held at the ready, to maintain the quiet. Still, some of the bolder ones stalked up to the massive figures, gesturing and demanding food and drink.

Maurin watched with trepidation as one of the guards loomed over the daring men. The dark-visored helm made it impossible to see its expression. It made a gesture seeming to indicate they should sit and wait. Well, the sit part seemed plain enough. He might have been stretching it a bit for the wait.

"What do you suppose they mean to do with us? They can't intend to starve us to death here."

Aric gave him an odd look. "Why not?"

How was Maurin supposed to reply to that? "Well, it doesn't make any sense. Why would they take people merely to let them starve?"

"Why do people do anything? Or gods, for that matter."

Maurin shrugged. "It just seems wrong somehow."

"Lots of things seem wrong, Maurin."

"But why imprison us all? To my knowledge, they haven't killed anyone. Apart from Yared's uncle, I mean."

"We don't know what has happened to the women."

That gave Maurin pause, and he swore softly. "No, we don't. I hope they're all right."

Aric closed his eyes and concentrated. "I imagine they're as all right as we are. You're right; they don't want us going anywhere, but they don't seem too eager to kill us."

An unsettling realization struck. "Strange."

"What's that?"

Maurin lowered his voice. "Save for Regin and a handful of others, almost none of the older men are here. Did you notice that?"

"Of course I noticed."

"I wonder why."

Aric didn't reply, but Maurin didn't like the look in his eyes. He knew something... or at least suspected. Maurin started to press further, but his cousin merely shook his head. The sound of boots in the corridor tramped into Maurin's reflections, and he leapt to his feet. Aric eyed the dark aperture of the doorway warily.

"They're back," said Yared.

"Oh, really?" Aric growled.

Several of the man-shaped guards emerged, wielding their pronged weapons and taking up residence at each side of the entrance. Some smaller figures followed them in, dressed in a colorless shimmering material. As with the guards, the newcomers' helmets hid their faces. They carried in several small vats of pale, pasty gruel, and set them sloshing on the floor.

The men fought over even this ghastly excuse for nourishment. It wasn't as if they were starving. But Maurin's dismay wasn't enough to keep him from wolfing it down all the same, once the rush had died off. He couldn't tell what it was, and he wasn't sure he wanted to know. It was hard to eat without gagging, and the air in the chamber didn't help. A curved gutter ran along the opposite wall and on through the corridors beyond, and the men had started using it as a latrine. Without water or sand, the smell was getting horrid.

How many days or weeks passed in this place of no sunrise or sunset, Maurin had no way of knowing. He tried to count the days by the number of times he slept or ate, but soon gave it up as a futile exercise. The only indication of time was the stubble growing on the faces of everyone around him, and the slow lengthening of their nails. Everywhere he turned, he saw his father's face, and hated himself for his weakness. Yet what could he have done? What could he do?

More than once, as they lay on the floor avoiding sleep, he speculated with Aric in hushed tones about the possibility of escaping. They could band together to overpower the guards and liberate the rest of the stolen people. Then they could go home, he could find and marry Kirai, and all would be as it had been.

A nice dream. The longer they stayed captive, the more unlikely it seemed. Maurin began to despair of seeing their family—such as it was—and friends again. It was a little alarming how quickly Aric seemed to grow accustomed to the idea.

The meals were always the same, brought at regular intervals. Drinking water must have been precious, though, because they were rationed only a small amount, and Maurin felt constantly parched.

Then several of the men got sick. Within a short time, most of them were retching and heaving, and the air in the chamber grew thick and close. It was bad enough being in the same room with several hundred sick men, but when it took hold of Maurin, he thought he was going to die. The guards had already removed multiple bodies of those who had.

Some time passed in a delirium, and Maurin could vaguely sense someone—was it Aric?—helping him to drink, and fingers forcing paste into his mouth. He slipped in and out of consciousness, his only memories the interminable thrumming of the air and the coughs and moans of the men around him.

He woke up one day aware of his surroundings. He could barely sit up, let alone stand, but he stayed awake, and Aric appeared glad to see him. His cousin would never admit to being worried, but he did complain about having been bored with no one to talk to.

"How long was I ill?" Maurin asked.

"How should I know?" Aric said. "Too long. The water turned bitter for a while, and people started getting better. You woke up just in time, though."

"What do you mean?"

"A few others were as sick as you, and they got dragged out. We never saw them again. One of those armored guys was looking at you a lot this morning. I tried to get him to believe you were just asleep, but I'm not sure it worked."

Maurin shuddered. Who might be counted among the dead? He didn't have the strength to ask. Being a priest meant that one spent relatively little time among the general populace, but he was acquainted with enough people to consider it a personal loss if anyone he knew had succumbed.

"It's just as well you were out. A bunch of men decided there were more of us than of them, and rushed the guards."

"What happened?"

Aric shrugged. "They died."

"I'm sorry. I'm surprised you weren't with them."

"Disappointed?" he asked with a snort.

"Hardly. I just can't see you letting someone else throw a punch if your fists still worked."

"Do you think I'm an idiot? Anyway, someone had to make sure you didn't get thrown out with the refuse."

Maurin managed a smile. "Thanks."

"Don't mention it."

Perhaps an hour had passed since Maurin woke from his stupor when he saw a massive silhouette lurking in the passageway. It seemed to be focused on him.

"Something's going on," Aric whispered. "Our jailers have been running back and forth for hours now, and the guards have doubled. That's the leader."

Maurin nodded and stood. Then he took a few tentative steps in a small circle.

"What are you doing?"

"I can't manage the spring festival dance, but that ought to convince them I'm not dead or dying." Maurin scowled defiantly after the dark figure as he turned around and walked back down the hall.

"I'd sit down if I were you," Aric said, with a faraway stare.

"Oh? Why?

"Because we're here."

"Here? Where? What are you talking about?"

Before Maurin could finish his sentence, the lights overhead dimmed and brightened several times in a row, and the whole room bucked. Maurin landed in a heap on the floor. All around him, men were jolted off their feet or knocked over onto their sides. Only Aric sat unperturbed.

A chill washed over Maurin that had nothing to do with the air. Aric showed no indication he knew he was being stared at. The vibration grew stronger in the floor beneath Maurin's body, and a high-pitched whine and a roar as of distant winds joined the deep throbbing. The guards remained motionless for some time, and the men started to murmur. A metallic sound like a gigantic latch being drawn somewhere echoed through the corridors.

"Get up, Maurin," Aric whispered, standing. "This isn't over yet."

Maurin dizzily complied. Several men followed their lead, while others remained cowering on the floor, fearful of another shock. The guards motioned, signaling them to stand. Within moments, a score of the armored fiends pushed their way in from the right-hand entrance and prodded the prisoners toward the other walkway. This time, the guards at the opposite end stood to one side and herded the quaking and protesting men through the doorway.

Maurin and Aric glanced at each other, not daring to speak. The crowd pushed and jostled them past several more armed guards jabbing them along the way.

They followed the curved hallway to a point where it joined another. The passage into that corridor was blocked, and the only way past was through a tunnel sloping off to the left. One gesture from the guards, and the men in front headed into the opening as quickly as they could while still maintaining their footing on the cold metal.

After everyone was through, a great metallic screech and moan, followed by a reverberating clang, sealed the last of them in.

Light flooded the chamber, and Maurin had to shut his eyes against the glare. With some effort, he forced himself to squint and get a sense of his surroundings. A stone bench ran the length of the chamber on each side, and at one end of the room a round bronze door reached almost to the ceiling. It was through this they had just come. At the other extremity, heavy wooden doors hung open, framing a stairway leading up and outside. Several armored guards blocked the way, and several of the smaller beings waddled down the stairs to inspect the men.

For the first time, one spoke. Maurin couldn't understand the words, but the tone of voice, combined with the gestures, made its meaning clear enough: he was to strip. He protested, but the armored guards lowered their weapons and pointed them casually in his direction. As Maurin complied, the smaller beings nattered out another staccato command, encompassing the room with their arms, and gesturing to the most reluctant of the prisoners with unmistakable intent. Slowly at first, but gaining speed as resignation set in, the men in the chamber doffed their clothing.

Under other circumstances, Maurin supposed, he would have been humiliated, but as it was, he just felt perplexed and vulnerable under the silent vigil of the guards. Only when several even smaller man-forms came into the chamber long enough to collect the piles of stinking clothing did he start to get truly concerned. He managed to wad the ribbon of his marital bonding in his fist as he set aside his clothes.

Without warning, a fine mist emerged from the ceiling. Maurin jumped. A hot milky-white fluid sprayed over the entire chamber at high force, stinging the eyes and nose. The men gasped in surprise and indignation as they tried in vain to flee the onslaught of the shower. When Maurin had blinked enough of the liquid away from his eyes to check on Aric, he gave a violent start.

"Your hair…"

"What about my—agh!" Large clumps of his curly hair rolled down his body and onto the floor, leaving a slick scalp behind. All around, every man had the same unfortunate reaction to whatever was soaking them all. The guards warned off anyone getting too close to the exit with a prod of their flame-wands.

The unexpected shower was over as abruptly as it began. The spray cut off, replaced by a few errant drips. Aric snarled in disgust, and Maurin couldn't help laughing. Apart from the sudden complete hairlessness of every man in the chamber, the fluid did not seem to have harmed them in any way.

"And it was just growing back, too." Maurin rubbed his head.

"I suppose you're happy now." Aric scowled. "We match. This better not be permanent."

Maurin was about to reply when he was hit with another blast of liquid. Like the former, it came out of the ceiling in a high-pressure mist, but unlike the last time, this did not sting. Plain water, though unpleasantly cold. It lasted longer than before, and did not stop until the last patches of matted hair were swept away.

"If this is their idea of cleanliness," Aric said, "I'm starting to reconsider their being gods. It certainly fits. Maybe we're all going to get married."

The light dimmed, and some of the guards left the room. Maurin expected Regin to rebuke Aric for his sacrilege. The scrawny man huddled against the wall farthest away from their jailers. Maurin could think of nothing comforting to say.

"I'm glad the women aren't here with us," Maurin said. "I wish I had something—anything—to put on."

Aric smiled. "You're only naked if someone else is clothed."

"Not sure I agree, but I get your point." Maurin waited on the alert, clutching the crumpled and soggy wedding ribbon in his left hand.

A tall man in the doorway peered into the chamber, seemingly counting the prisoners. Turning to the armored form next to him, he spoke, writing on a tablet with some sort of stylus.

Maurin gritted his teeth in frustration.

"Can you hear what they're saying?" Aric murmured.

"Yes, of course I can," Maurin snapped. "They're not speaking Aran. What's going on here?"

"I'm thinking the more important question is, where is 'here'?"

Maurin gave Aric a curt nod and strained to hear the guard's reply. It reached up under its chin, loosened a connecting strap, and with one motion, pulled the helmet from its head. Piggish eyes twinkled, and an unshaven face with a sneering grin laughed into the room.

The laugh bit into Maurin's very soul.

"I told you." His voice went from a whisper to a roar. "It's a MAN!" Maurin launched himself across the chamber, ready to tear this imposter's head off. "They aren't gods! They're just men!"

Surprised, but hardly taken off guard, one pulled a short baton from his belt and cracked it down on Maurin's head. He struggled to rise again, and was rewarded with another smack across the shoulder. This close, Maurin could smell the sweat on the man, and see the sandy red of his hair. Whoever he was, he didn't seem particularly upset, or even gleeful, but rather practiced and efficient, as he gave Maurin another couple of licks for good measure. Once he made certain Maurin wasn't going to get up again, he said something else to the pale man beside him and closed the great wooden doors.

Through his dizziness and pain, Maurin heard the unmistakable sound of a heavy bar being dropped into place. Then the overhead lights went dark. A pale blue glow streamed in through tiny windows, illuminating the room. It seemed healthier, somehow, than the diseased incandescence in which they had been bathed for the past several weeks, or however long it was.

"You okay?"

Maurin sat up, but his head spun, and he sank back down. "I'll live."

When he felt steady on his feet again, he walked over to the barred window on one side of the room. It was high, but not excessively so. Maurin asked a couple of the men on the bench to move aside for a moment so he could see out. A mere slot in the stone, the window afforded Maurin only a view of the tops of trees, even when he stood on his toes. The forest cut the bottom edge of the golden moon ragged. There was no sign of any other building outside. Probably a sheer drop from here.

"That's a harvest moon." Maurin rubbed his head. "How long were we in there, anyway?"

"I don't know. Judging by that, I'd say a good seven months, but that doesn't seem possible."

"No, it doesn't," Maurin agreed. The craters looked off, and the size was wrong. He meandered over to the opposite side of the chamber and climbed up on the bench. He thrust his head up over the stone ledge of the window.

From outside, a low-pitched rhythmic throbbing—faint at first, but growing steadily nearer—rose above the worried murmurs of the men in the chamber.

"Hey, come see this."

Aric stepped onto the bench and peered out the window.

A small dark silhouette floated limned against the moonlit clouds. It came from the south, growing steadily nearer as the sound got louder. The whirring grew in intensity. A large bird? No. Some sort of ship, sailing through the air.

His jaw dropped as it passed within a few leagues of them and faded into the darkness. "What was that?"

Aric sported an excited smile. "How should I know?"

"It was a rhetorical question." Maurin turned back to the window, heart pounding. "This is too much."

"Whatever it was, I want a closer look." Aric gave him a playful jab. "You're starting to go senile on me. That's a summer moon."

"Huh?" Maurin followed his gaze, then blanched.

"What's the matter?"

Maurin choked out a hoarse whisper. "Wrong... window." He jumped down off the ledge and ran back over to the other side of the room. The men scrambled out of his way as he leapt up to stare out the other aperture. "No, no, no, no, *no*...!"

There was the moon, golden and full. His insides turned to ice water, and all the strength went out of his legs.

Two moons?

He reeled back against the wall. "Where are we?"

CHAPTER 4
WAYFARER

"Name?"

"Valasand Del Siriné."

"Papers?"

"I have none."

The port sentry spread his hands, too bored to be exasperated. "No identification, no certificate of residence? What is your business here?"

"That is my own affair." Valasand pushed a wind-whipped strand of hair out of her eyes. She did not like to lie, and he did not need to know the truth.

"Is that so?" The young man crossed his arms over his chest. "Well, my business is to make sure the vermin stay outside the city, and don't come slinking in through the main gates. What makes you think I'm going to let a wood-rat like you into Caileen?"

"I have come a long way."

He snorted in derision. "I'm sure you have. Go peddle your wares somewhere else. Only authorized traffic goes into the city."

So much for not telling the truth. "I believe"—Valasand reached into the front of her robe and withdrew the Temple medallion she wore around her neck—"that a Warden of the Gates is authorized."

The port sentry went pale in recognition and stammered, "I'm so

sorry, ma'am. I didn't know. Is there anything I can do for you?"

Judging by his expression, he hoped there was not.

"Yes." Valasand tucked the pendant back into her robe. "I need to see the port records, specifically on-world arrivals and tariffs. Anything pertaining to traffic and merchandise for the last five years."

"M-may I ask what your purpose is in wanting this information?"

"My purpose"—she stared into his eyes—"is that I need to know. I am conducting an official investigation for the Temple. I expect your complete cooperation in this matter. You will help me find the records I need, and when I leave, you will forget I was here. Is that clear?"

The man nodded vigorously, sweat shining on his brow.

"Good. Now fetch those logs and stay close at hand. I may need further assistance."

With a slight limp, she followed the clerk inside the small building to a private room lit by a series of tall, narrow windows. He led her to the appropriate records, then hurried back to his post, trying valiantly not to glance back over his shoulder to see what she was doing. Valasand braced her staff against the wall and sat on the hard bench. Leaning over the table, she scanned through the port's books, piecing together the puzzle that had brought her across oceans of space and time. Her eyes and nose itched from the dust, and the text started to blur, but at last she arrived at the entry she wanted. She cross-referenced and double-checked; a strong correlation existed between traffic orders, "cargo" received, and the source of all the transactions. One name kept cropping up, again and again:

Daman Argoneis.

Taking in the last of the man's vital statistics, she whistled softly at his estimated worth. Returning to the port sentry, she said, "Thank you for your cooperation. Now, you can direct me to the local Office of Estates."

After the young man gave her instructions, he warned, "You'll want to be careful. Women of wealth don't generally travel alone here."

Valasand gave him a wry glance. "Do I look like a woman of wealth?"

"No, Ma'am. No offense."

"None taken." She hoped her next task would go a bit more

smoothly. Valasand walked over to the edge of the port, tying her hair into a simple queue with a plain leather thong. She set her staff against the thick stone balustrade and leaned over. The cool mountain air nipped at her face as she took in the panoramic view of the city below, nestled in the protective shadow of several large peaks. A majestic waterfall flowed off to the side, between the city and the port. No doubt it masked much of the sound of air traffic—which was relatively sparse, but perhaps more active than one would have anticipated, given the backworld setting.

A slope at the base of the port led to a lake, into which the waterfall churned ceaselessly. The runoff wound down the mountainside, and several causeways stretched in graceful arcs across the lake toward the gates of the city.

Do not be deceived by appearances, Little Flame. This land is rife with an evil even you cannot fathom.

Valasand took a deep breath, regretful that she could not simply stay and appreciate the scenery. She headed toward the path that led to the main bridge and the city gates.

"Have a pleasant day, Ma'am," the port sentry called after her. "Enjoy your stay in Caileen."

"Somehow," Valasand muttered under her breath, "I very much have my doubts."

The bridge was constructed in such a way that pedestrians had a wide berth on the outer sides of the stone barriers. As the animal-drawn traffic rattled by in the middle, so the more casual walker could traverse the massive expanse without hurry and observe the beauty of the lake. The perpetual splash and foam of the falls misted the stone and kept it damp, but the bridge was specially roughened to accommodate foot traffic.

Towering above the main entrance like ivory sentinels, the gates of the city gazed sternly upon the roving populace. It was a dirty place, dirty in a way that was difficult to put a finger on. She had been in many worse cities, of course, but there was an unshakable gloom to the air of this one. Gloom, and something else, something recent. Fear, perhaps. The sense of wrongness in this place was suffocating, debilitating. She imagined her shoulders bowing under the weight of it.

A large white bird flew overhead toward the heart of the city, and Valasand smiled. Though she had been leaning heavily into her staff, she found her strength renewed, and stepped forward with resolve.

"And just who are you, Daman Argoneis?"

CHAPTER 5
EMISSARY

"Fill my cup, lad."

Aric glared, but at a quiet nod from his owner—he could never quite get himself to think of Krige as his master—he poured Lord Argoneis's flask almost to the brim. The man took a long drink, then cheered his approval with the roaring crowd as the fighter in the arena delivered the final blow.

The victor straightened up to hold her dripping arms to the sky in triumph, knives gleaming in clenched fists. The gladiatrix was a muscular woman with legs like steel pillars and a body crisscrossed with scars. One had to look closely to see them, though, because tattoos decorated her from the top of her shaven head right down into her leather sandals. She bared her teeth in a leer of victory, rasping her blades over her head.

"*Dan-ia! Dan-ia! Dania!*"

People stomped their feet and clapped their hands in rhythmic accompaniment to the chant. The bloodthirsty cries of the crowd seemed to fill her with a darkling power, and Aric could practically taste her euphoria as she drank it all in, riding on the noise, floating above the din, out of the pit.

In the two years since he had last seen Maurin, Aric attended so many of these matches he had grown bored by them. Except for the preliator named Dania, who had a reputation for being undefeated in the arena. She was never boring. He had seen her battle against bigger and better-armed opponents, and often more than one at a time. Rarely did her foes leave the stadium in one piece, let alone alive. Once she was placed in the ring with three wild cats from the nearby forest of Verdine. Each one of them must have been at least double her weight, and Aric expected her to die that time. Yet she had dispatched the great creatures with effortless grace.

People called her Blood Goddess.

Aric stood in attendance to his owner, Lord Aster Krige, and Krige sat next to Lord Daman Argoneis and Baron Seides in the best stall in the stadium. Argoneis liked to entertain various noblemen from time to time, and Lord Krige and Baron Seides seemed to be his favorites. Aric would have thought them friends, but wasn't sure the word really meant anything to Lord Argoneis. If it did, he certainly wouldn't define it the way most people would.

At any rate, in this comfortably furnished booth set aside from the general admission, Aric got a better vantage point than many of the paying customers. The viewing area surrounded the circular arena, protected by a lip of iron-spiked stone jutting out around the rim—a small but necessary barrier between the audience and the participants in the sand below.

Dania strode haughtily out of the stadium, greeted by guards flanking the passageway. Lord Argoneis followed her exit with an appreciative nod, stroking a bit of blond stubble on his chin. "She fights beautifully. But what's she like when she's not in the arena?"

"Oh, much the same." Rominan Seides, a whip-thin man not quite old enough to be Argoneis's father, smiled under a close-cropped mustache. His eyes shone with smug amusement as the body of the defeated fighter was dragged away.

Aric hadn't quite decided which one of them he hated more. He had a pretty good idea now.

"I have to keep her guarded night and day; else she would quite likely murder me in my sleep." Seides chuckled. "She threatens to do so, in fact, quite regularly."

Argoneis laughed once through his nose, and smirked. "That could be changed. Breaking the spirit is half the fun."

On second thought, I hate you most of all. Aric's jaw clenched, and his knuckles went white on the wineskin. Krige tipped his head back for a deeper drink.

"Try breaking this one's spirit, Daman," said Seides. "I guarantee it can't be done."

Aric wasn't so sure. From all the rumors, if anyone could do it, Argoneis could.

The same notion must have occurred to Seides; his thin smile carried more than a hint of warning. "And even if you were able, you'd ruin a perfectly good fighter. So don't get any ideas."

Lord Argoneis gave a bored shrug. "If she's so dangerous, why do you keep her around?"

"Where is the thrill, my boy, without the danger?"

"I prefer submission, myself."

The warmth with which Argoneis said it sent chills down Aric's back. Most likely it would have affected a lesser man than Seides; certainly Aric's owner wore a queasy expression after any extended period of time spent with Lord Argoneis. But Seides just smiled that thin smile of his. "Not everything learns to submit, Daman."

"They do to me." Daman Argoneis gazed dreamily into space and raised his arm, gesturing like a visionary at nothing in particular. "There is nothing quite as gratifying as having someone kneeling before you, begging, knowing you hold his life in your hands. It is as if they pray to me. Maybe they do."

Krige coughed. Aric refilled the bottle for him, his only real task whenever he was dragged to such events. He had a fan in his hand, and was supposed to use it to keep the flies off his owner, but rarely remembered to do so. So long as Krige had something to wash away the sour taste of Argoneis's company, he never seemed to mind much.

"Perhaps so, but why wait for it to come to you?" Seides leaned forward in his seat. "I much prefer the hunt. To stare death in the face, to take it into my own hands and hold it at bay by a mere fraction of an inch. To brush it, touch it, caress it, and know only the barest of restraints keeps you from mortal danger—now that's excitement!"

"Ah, well." Argoneis laughed and tossed back his fine blond hair. "To each man his own poison, I guess." He slapped his older friend on the back in comradely good humor, then switched his attention back to Krige. "Speaking of learning to submit, are you still having trouble training this one? Because Rominan here tells me there are still slots open for the games."

"He's getting better," Krige said, though none too quickly for Aric's taste. Aric hated the look in Lord Argoneis's eyes whenever they turned in his direction, and he longed for the day when he could put them out.

"Oh?"

"He still forgets the proper courtesies most of the time, but he handles my chariot better than any of my former slaves, and he claims he never saw one before being brought here."

Always talking about him as if he weren't there. Aric swore that would be their undoing one day.

Seides shifted his stance and ran a hand through short steel-gray hair. "More's the pity. I think you're wasting a good fighter," he said with a nod toward Aric. "Just look at that physique."

"And what about your slave-girl, that lovely Maolori?" Argoneis pressed. "Are you still resolute about not selling her?"

"My lords," Krige said, "you would soon have me walking everywhere I went and cooking in my own kitchen, were I to sell you every one of my slaves in which you have shown an interest."

Daman Argoneis laughed heartily, but the smile Aric's owner wore was only superficial. The particular slave Argoneis asked after was Krige's pride and joy, not to mention favorite bed-toy. Krige had once sworn in a drunken stupor that there was no way in the seven hells Daman would ever get his filthy paws on her. It was the sort of thing Aric filed away for occasions such as this, but he said nothing.

Argoneis took on a conspiratorial tone. "For the past month you've done nothing but fill my ears with how grand this circus spectacle you're planning will be. How are you doing on the quota?"

Seides settled forward on the bench. "We've more than enough to make the grade."

"Still more slaves are being brought from off-world," Argoneis offered. "We're expecting another shipment any day now."

Krige cleared his throat and shifted a bit in his seat. "You should know, Daman, it's come to my attention that the countess from Sal Dalinde is raising all hells among the other nobles about that sort of thing.

Thinks you're 'destroying our way of life'."

Argoneis laughed and clapped Krige on the shoulder. "She is the least of my worries. Her kind is easily disposed of."

Krige squirmed under Argoneis's touch. Aric almost felt sorry for him.

Almost.

"You need to be careful, old friend," Seides cautioned. "There's a limit to what even you can get away with."

Argoneis's eyes flashed, but a tight smile replaced the sudden dangerous expression. "Not on this planet." His knuckles turned white on Krige's shoulder. "This may be a forgotten corner of the civilized worlds as far as the Temple is concerned, but it's my forgotten corner, and I'll run it the way I please. I'm not going to let some petty slattern daughter of a nobleman dictate to me."

"Traditions die, but grandeur lives on," Seides said, attempting to refocus the conversation. "My circus will be talked about for years."

"If you will excuse me, my lords." Krige spoke before the conversation had a chance to degenerate into a lavish anticipatory fantasy. "Langfort calls."

"Oh, that's right," Argoneis said. "I'd almost forgotten."

"Langfort?" Seides asked. "That's a long trip for this late in the day."

Krige spread his hands in a helpless gesture. "There seems to be a misunderstanding with the Reamar, and Lord Argoneis has asked me to help sort things out."

"The Reamar, the Reamar." Argoneis rolled his eyes. "You know, they've never forgiven me for forgetting to let them inspect that shipment a couple of years back. It doesn't happen often, but they just hate it when I forget."

Krige nodded. "Well, if you hadn't, I might not have my pilot here."

Argoneis's gaze swept Aric. "Yes. They always insist on first pick, and he does seem their sort."

Aric paused. He knew of the Reamar, though few spoke of them in the open. Many thought them some sort of necromantic sorcerers, and a small but growing underground cult worshipped them as gods. The Reamar had always been far enough away that he figured there was no reason to be particularly worried one way or another, despite the dark air of mystery and awe in which they were shrouded. They seemed all too close, now. Would it have been worse to be slave to the Reamar? A shiver ran up his spine as he thought about how close he had come.

"Well, it's a shame," Argoneis said. "I was going to invite you both to join me this evening for a little refreshment. I've just received the most incredible vintage of Indiran wine. Absolutely superb. Came in with the last shipment. You don't know what you're missing. But we do what we must to keep our neighbors in the Gray Lands happy."

The look on Krige's face told Aric that he did indeed know what he was missing.

According to what Aric had been able to glean over the last couple of years, Daman Argoneis had long since taken over the family fortunes, never seeming to care what his reputation did to him or those who knew him. He was never without his bodyguards, a dark-skinned brother-and-sister team who shared his perverse nature, if not his smiling countenance. The brother, Sabatha, captain of the guard, had the body of a god. The sister, Anice, was deceptively thin, tigerish and fierce. Rumor had it the three of them spent hours amusing themselves with the household slaves. Sometimes the slave would leave shaken, but otherwise undamaged. Others were never seen again.

Whispered reports of strange tortures—compounded by the occasional muffled wailing heard reverberating through the stone halls at night, and the fact that an entire wing of Daman's palatial residence was kept locked off even from household servants—gave rise to the rumor that Lord Argoneis really ran the slave trade just to keep himself in fresh supply of entertainments.

Argoneis turned to Seides. "What say you, Rominan?"

"Well, I hate to disappoint. Perhaps I shall stop by for a few hours, but I find that I wish to retire early tonight."

Daman grinned with a mocking glint in his eye. "Something tells me you want to reward your slave for her grand victory in the arena today."

"Aric," Krige said, "go ready the chariot for departure. I will be along momentarily."

"Yes, my lord." Aric nodded and left. Not often was he allowed to go off on his own, but it wasn't as if escape was an option. Guards stood at every entrance and exit of the arena, and the brief tunic Aric wore was as indicative of his status as the slave brand on his shoulder. While he could temporarily cover the mark, the penalty for removing it was public flogging, and sometimes mutilation.

Two years of looking for Maurin. Two years of watching for any opportunity to escape. Two years of studying every strange face for any sign of the mysterious woman in his dreams, though there was no particular reason to assume she was even here. Aric understood what his cousin meant when he talked about biding his time; sometimes that was all you could do. But he hated sitting and doing nothing while the world rotted around him.

Aric followed the circle of the arena and descended the stairs into the dark passage between the stadium seats. A few people milled about, but for the most part, the hallways were empty. Two matches followed Dania's performance, and most of the audience remained in the arena.

From a corridor on his left emerged a quartet of large men, all heavily armed. One walked in front, one behind, and the two between had chains leading from their waists to the wrists of a fifth person in their midst. Aric stopped to let them pass, recognizing their captive as Dania. Though clean, dressed in a plain tunic, and bandaged on one arm, the Blood Goddess still looked like a viper ready to strike.

Aric guessed that the man walking point carried the keys to her manacles, and the other two were there to keep her from going anywhere. Even if she managed to disable or kill them both, it would be hard to drag their bodies. Her feet were also shackled with a chain long enough to allow her to walk freely, but short enough to cause her to fall flat on her face should she attempt to run.

Taking no chances with you, are they?

As they passed, the woman glanced up and straight at Aric. He took a step back, despite her humbled state. The hostility in her turquoise eyes was palpable.

She stopped short, jerking on the chains. Her lead guard warned her with a scowl, but she ignored him.

"What are you looking at, boy?" Her accent suggested the common tongue spoken here in Caileen was not her natural language, but it didn't sound at all familiar to him. He decided not to try speaking in Aran. The chances of finding someone else from his world were slim at this point, and her guards might take exception to it, anyway.

Aric shrugged. "The winner."

Dania tilted her head and regarded him for a moment, then laughed mirthlessly. She held up her wrists, showing him the manacles. "Winners go home with trophies. Losers go home in shackles. I'm just a slave, boy."

"So am I."

"Your slavery is only as sure as your chains. Where are yours?"

"Let's go," the man in front said. "You don't need to be giving him any ideas."

"Just wait, boy," she called over her shoulder as they led her off. "You may see the victor yet."

Aric stood for a moment, pondering what she had said.

Odd.

Walking past the guards, Aric left the arena. The tattooed crest on his shoulder matched the insignia on the vehicle in its berth. The design identified him as Krige's property just as surely as it did the chariot, but that didn't matter. For the moment, it was a badge of honor, allowing him to move about freely. He allowed himself a tight smile as he approached the vehicle. Most people had to walk or use the waterways, but Lord Krige could afford an airship.

Small but beautiful, it perched like a bird of paradise on the lawn. Its golden metal body and framework gleamed against the white sails and fins. Aric climbed aboard the craft and up into the pilot's seat. He ran a finger over the polished fittings, and pulled the switch engaging the power source.

Krige hired a shipwright once to inspect the vehicle for any malfunctioning parts. Aric had struck up a conversation with the man, asking how the machine worked. Initially, he seemed reluctant to discuss such things with a slave, but Aric's interest eventually won him over. The device inside functioned on a powerful current, a bit like the torches Maurin had been in charge of in the temple back home, albeit on a much more powerful and sophisticated level. Aric wondered at the time if

Maurin would have considered it a sacrilegious use of the power, but as soon as the thought entered his mind, he discovered he really didn't care.

Because now he could fly.

Aric closed his eyes and listened to the growing hum of the charging power source, feeling the now-familiar vibrations of the machine coming to life. He could take off right now. Trouble was, these flying machines weren't so common that he could just make off with one, let alone one bearing Aster Krige's personal seal. He would be a marked man the moment he set down.

Only a few moments passed before he heard Lord Krige boarding the ship, followed by his favorite bodyguard, Leslan Randolf.

Randolf was a surprisingly small man, but wiry and muscular. He kept his ashen hair cropped short, and had the discipline and hardiness born of years spent in off-world military service.

Aric turned to his owner. "That didn't take long."

"I didn't want you getting any notions of flying off without us," Lord Krige said.

"Wouldn't dream of it."

Aric made sure the men were settled, then pushed forward on the lever to his left. He pulled back on the handgrip, and the airship rose off the ground. As always, he felt a slight tingling in his palms when he piloted the craft, but one learned to ignore it. A thrill ran through his body as the ship soared above the arena, turning it into a mere stone bowl filled with insects.

Ten alarm towers were stationed throughout Caileen, each one housing a horn longer than Aric was tall. But none of these came close to rivaling the magnificent spire of Lord Argoneis's palace rising above the rest of the city. Some of the slaves in Krige's household muttered that it was originally meant to be a temple, and Argoneis had usurped it. It certainly surpassed every other mansion in the city in beauty and power. A split white cone ensconced the primary central tower, and six smaller versions punctuated each corner of the hexagonal outer wall. Armed guards strolled in the broad courtyard below.

Aric followed the broadening path out above the waterfall and into the open air. The jagged peaks dropped away, and the land sloped off into a forested area split in two by the Helnrill River.

"This river was originally known as the Baki-bashi," Lord Krige said, leaning forward. "That's the old Maolori word for it. It means something like 'spirits of the waters.'"

"Did Talauna tell you that?" Aric couldn't help baiting him. Why would Krige think he would care, anyway?

Krige looked as if he had bitten into an overripe fruit. "No. Vellis the wine merchant heard one of his Maolori slaves talking about it a while ago with another off-world slave. He told me because he knows I take an interest in everything Maolori."

Aric nodded. *Much to your wife's chagrin.*

"It's a shame; one doesn't get to learn much about the natives. They don't domesticate well."

Which was a nice way of saying they usually died in captivity. "I guess they don't like outsiders much."

Krige eyed him sharply. "You have a dangerous tongue, Aric. Learn to keep it in your head."

"Yes, sir."

"When our ancestors first came, those people were nothing but savages. But we've brought them civilization."

"I'm sure they appreciated that. It's too bad they don't have the sense to know what's good for them."

"I would take those words to heart, if I were you." Krige's consonants were slightly blurred by the wine, the sweetness of it on his breath as he leaned forward in anger, but he was not as drunk as Aric previously suspected. Did Krige simply act that way to keep from having to be too accountable to the others? "I could sell you to Daman—Lord Argoneis—in a heartbeat, if I wanted to."

Aric resolved not to say anything for the rest of the trip.

The sky ahead darkened, but it was not the twilight of evening. A storm was brewing in the south, and they were headed right into it. It didn't seem too serious, but there was nothing funny about piloting these things into the rain.

Aric gritted his teeth as the first blast of cold air buffeted the ship. He kept his hands tightly on the controls and tried to gauge the wind currents. Birds made it all look so easy. The forest sped by beneath him, and the river twisted and slithered like a serpent. Overhead, the clouds grew darker.

"Milord?" Krige's bodyguard didn't speak often, and when he did, his speech was so thick that it was difficult to make out what he said. Still, Aric supposed Krige didn't keep him around for his charm or social graces.

"Yes, Randolf?"

"I don't like you going among them witches," the bodyguard said. "They ain't safe, and you ain't safe dealing with them. Lord Argoneis should do his own dirty work."

"The Reamar respect me." Aric heard the rustling of cloth as Krige shrugged. "A servant must do as his master tells him, and I am Lord Argoneis's servant even as you are mine. Now, I'll hear no more of this talk of superstition, and you certainly are not to speak anymore of Lord Argoneis in that manner. Is that clear?"

"Yes, milord."

"Good."

The cloud cover was so thick that Aric could no longer tell how late it was. He cursed when the first drops of rain started to hit the sandglass shield in front of him. The pane was specially treated to repel water, but rain still made it nearly impossible to see. He reached up and thumbed the tiny lever activating the visor, and it slid into place with a whine. That helped some, but it limited his field of vision to directly ahead and below.

As the water spattered and then poured over the craft, Aric strained to discern the features of the land. He wished for more familiar landmarks, but forest shifted to marsh and back into forest with very little differentiation from the air. Still, he could just see the line the river made in the trees. He had to veer slightly to the east, but hated to lose the assurance of the Helnrill. Well, it couldn't be helped. Several leagues from here, the river took a sharp bend in that direction, anyway. He could follow it all the way to Langfort, but that would mean going well out of their way and wasting energy. No sense taking chances today.

The sky lit up with a brilliant flash as lightning etched a jagged line to the ground. The ship rocked with the force of the thunder. Aric started to sweat in spite of the coolness of the air. Back in the passenger compartment, Krige didn't seem at all concerned. Aric wasn't sure if his owner's confidence was due to his faith in him, or his ignorance of the vulnerability of this craft. Either way, he was determined not to look bad. After all, as long as he was valuable to Krige, he had access to the flying machine.

And as long as he could fly, he could still dream about escape.

If only he knew where Maurin was, or if he was even still alive. He smiled at the image of swooping down out of the sky and snatching his cousin from the noose of slavery. Together they could toss Krige and his lackey out of the chariot and fly off to some distant land.

"What is so funny?" Krige asked.

"Nothing." Aric clamped down on his grin. "Just thinking it won't be long now."

No, it won't be long now, at all.

Now, where had *that* come from?

Aric rolled his shoulders in relief as he saw the trees thinning out, and a white marble structure standing in the midst of a low-lying city. Langfort did not have the elegant tiers and multi-level houses Caileen boasted, but it did have a kind of sheltered solidarity that spoke of home. Though settled in the broad expanse of an ancient river valley, rather than the volcanic uplifts Aric was used to, Langfort also had a thick outer wall to keep the wild lands from encroaching. Walls didn't mean anything to vehicles that could fly, Aric mused as he sailed over it. His smile turned into a scowl as he recalled the day he and Maurin were taken from their world by men who knew exactly that.

Relieved to get out of the driving winds and beating rain, Aric angled the craft down and decelerated, aiming for a courtyard with a grand portico. The great white columns grew nearer, and a wall lined with broad-leafed shrubbery rose to greet them.

"What are you doing?" Krige sounded panicked.

Aric spared a glance at him. His owner's knuckles turned white as he gripped his knees.

"Aric!"

Aric faced forward again and grinned. With inches to spare, he guided the craft between the pillars and leaned on the lever controlling their forward motion. The chariot hovered under the vast roof, the humming of its engine audible again over the rain. Aric eased back on the control holding them in the air, settling the ship to the ground with nary a bump.

Aric smirked. "Didn't want to get you wet, milord."

"You may end up getting me killed."

Several guards came rushing up, but relaxed when they saw Krige exiting the vehicle.

"Milord," one of the men said, "the governor is expecting you."

"Yes, I know. I will need some time to freshen after the trip."

The guard squirmed uncomfortably.

"What is it?" Krige asked, annoyed.

"Well, milord, the governor told me very specifically to bring you to him the moment you arrived." Seeing Krige's scowl, he licked his lips, and gave an apologetic grimace. "He was very adamant about it."

Krige stared at him a moment longer. "Very well. Take me to him."

———————◆———————

Governor Phoecius of Langfort was a fat man with a meticulously trimmed beard and a silken robe. Jeweled rings shone on his fingers, and he wore a close-fitting fur hat. Multiple guards flanked the walls of the reception chamber, standing in the niches between the columns.

Aric stayed in step with his owner as Krige strode forward to greet the governor. Randolf flanked him on the other side, a stride behind.

"What is so urgent that I may not even be allowed the common courtesy of a few moments to refresh myself after my journey?"

Phoecius rose from behind a large stone table. "My dear Lord Krige, I'm so sorry. But I don't know what to do. The whole city is in an uproar."

"What has happened?"

The governor took Krige by the arm and ushered him down the hall. Aric let them get a few steps ahead when he saw the wary look the guards were giving him. He stifled an amused smile at the way Phoecius waved his left hand dramatically as he spoke, jiggling under his robes as he strolled next to Krige.

"Fatamor has disappeared."

"What do you mean 'Fatamor has disappeared?'" Krige said with a laugh. "Cities don't just vanish."

"The entire populace is gone," Phoecius said shakily. "As though they'd been spirited away in the night."

"All of them...?" Krige glanced at Aric, then turned back to Phoecius. "Where would they have gone?"

"You don't understand," the governor said. "Traders and workers from outlying towns say the doors were barred, and the windows shuttered, and still the houses stood empty when morning came."

Krige started visibly. "How? What happened?"

"No one knows. But it's begun a full-scale panic, I can tell you! Fatamor isn't that far from here, and it took only until this morning for the news to reach us. Refugees from the nearby towns have packed up and left already. They've asked us for sanctuary. Those who remain arm themselves to the best of their ability in hopes of fending off any repeats of this mysterious nocturnal invasion."

Krige winced and pinched the skin at the top of his nose.

Aric chewed on the inside of his cheek. Anything capable of making an entire city vanish was enough of a threat that weapons might not be much help. Could someone be stealing people from this world? That would almost be funny.

"Now my own people are getting nervous, and look to me for answers," Phoecius added.

"Well, I'm sure you are doing what you can."

"It gets worse."

"The Reamar?"

"Yes. As I indicated this morning, they seem to have some quarrel with us, but they wouldn't talk about it until Lord Argoneis came. They've sent their Marèse, their man of war, and some spokesman who makes me cold just looking at him. He calls himself Guilan Vail."

Aric shifted his weight from one foot to another. Was there any way not to be in the middle of all this?

"Have you told him Argoneis was not available?"

"No. Better they hear it from you." Phoecius lowered his voice. "Be careful, Krige. The Reamar are dangerous."

"Dangerous how?" Krige asked, his voice full of scorn. "And to whom?"

"In all my contact with the Reamar, never have they sent a *Marèse* to make a point. And it's easy enough to intimidate most people with threats of Lord Argoneis, but you have to be a little more prudent with the other one, this Guilan Vail. The others, you can tell they follow their orders, but him—there's something in his eyes that makes you think he can't be trusted."

"That describes most of the people with whom I come into contact on a regular basis," Krige said dryly. "I'll take it under advisement. I don't believe we have anything to fear from the Reamar. They are few, and have always minded their business, so long as we have minded ours. They ask little more than that we respect their borders."

"You in the northern cities don't have to worry about them," Phoecius growled. "Daman supplies them with a steady shipment of slaves to do the-gods-know-what with. You say they ask that we respect their borders, but the Gray Lands grow every day."

What could that mean? Aric drummed his fingers against his palm as they approached a heavy double door with carved square panels.

Krige's jaw clenched. "Is there anything else I should know?"

"Just be wary." Phoecius nodded to the guards to open the doors.

Uneasy and not keen on sitting and twiddling his thumbs, Aric followed his owner down a half-dozen steps into a long hall. Krige didn't tell him to stay behind, so either he didn't notice or didn't care. A table ran most of the length of the room; this must be the banquet chamber. The light from the current torches flickered and dimmed, threatening to cast the chamber into darkness. At the far end, surrounded by about twenty standing warriors, sat a dark-haired man who wore an open tunic over a muscular chest. This must be the Marèse that Governor Phoecius had been talking about.

To his left was a handsome blond man Aric knew at once to be Guilan Vail. His longish hair was gathered in a tail, and spilled over a short,

hooded cape clasped in front with a sturdy silver brooch. Traces of an indescribable hunger and assurance shone in his dark eyes.

The hatred Aric felt for men like Argoneis and Seides was a visceral, tangible thing. The gaze now focused on him was unsettling in a way he couldn't quite comprehend. It was definitely the eyes, though nothing specifically leapt out as being wrong with them. But somehow, they didn't seem to quite fit; he got the impression of being regarded through a mask.

"You are not Argoneis." Vail lingered a moment wolfishly on Aric, his countenance unruffled.

Aric smoothed down gooseflesh on his arms at the sudden drop in temperature. Was the man talking to him?

Finally, Vail faced Krige directly.

"My name is Aster Krige. I speak for the Lord Regent, and you may be assured anything I say is exactly as if he himself had spoken. On the same token, any message you have for him will be relayed in the utmost confidence to his ears alone."

The cool gaze of Guilan Vail once again turned Aric's way. What was wrong with the man? When the Reamar spoke again, he was still addressing Krige—or was he?—in that calm tone of voice. One might have thought he was discussing the weather. "You have something that belongs to us."

"Oh? And what might that be?"

"One of our own is"—he seemed to struggle with the word—"missing."

Krige spread his hands. "I'm terribly sorry to hear that. Who is it?"

"The young priestess, Siaran Thoud, has been stolen from us. And we demand to have her back."

"I will do whatever I can to see that your priestess is restored to you, but I don't know how Lord Argoneis can help. What makes you believe we know where she is?"

The dark-haired man snarled. "We know where she is not. Your governor of Fatamor turned his disgusting attentions on her the last time we sent her as an envoy to his palace. Yet we have been to Fatamor, and she is not there. Nor is she here."

His owner stiffened at the mention of the vanishing city. Why didn't Krige ask them if they knew anything about the disappearances? Perhaps he feared the Reamar more than he let on.

"With all due respect," Krige said, "how do you know? And what makes you think she has been stolen, and not simply gone off on her own?"

The Marèse leapt out of his chair and started forward in anger. The torches flared into brilliance and waned to pinpricks as he shouted, "She would never leave the Gray Lands of her own accord. She is of the Reamar!"

Krige looked unimpressed. The torches resumed their halfhearted flicker. Aric willed himself to breathe.

"We do not expect mere men to understand the ways of the Reamar." Guilan Vail rose to step in front of the raging Marèse. "Suffice it to say we know she is alive, and we know she is far from us. There are whispers among our followers that she has been seen in Caileen, but I was certain the Lord Regent would not do anything so foolish as to cross us in this manner."

Aric glanced at one of the Reamar warriors next to Vail, but the man dropped his eyes and bowed his head when Aric met his gaze. The next did the same, and the one after that.

If Krige noticed, he did not indicate it in any way. He paused just long enough to let the words of the Reamar hang in the air. "Why don't we all sit down and discuss—"

"We will stand, thank you." It was the first time Guilan's voice rose, and even so, it was calm. "A Reamar slave would be worth a great deal to the foolhardy, but is it worth losing our patronage and our favor, and incurring our wrath?"

Krige was doing his best to remain diplomatic, and no doubt wished he hadn't drunk quite so much wine before coming down. Nevertheless, Aric's owner seemed to have shaken off the worst of the effects. He supposed Krige was in his element now.

"We shall do our best to search for this priestess of yours. Lord Argoneis would never do anything to curry disfavor with his favorite customers, and I'm sure this will all turn out to be an unfortunate misunderstanding."

"We trust you are right." Guilan Vail's voice was cream over wild berries. "If Siaran Thoud is not returned to us in full health within a fortnight, we shall have no other choice than to give you a demonstration of our power. And if she is still not surrendered after that, other cities will suffer the same fate as Fatamor."

Aric flicked his gaze over to Krige. His lips were pursed, but he said nothing at the Reamar's blatant admission

Vail paused, then stepped forward. "Be certain to give Lord Argoneis this message: Should you double-cross us, even your ivory towers will not protect you from the wrath of the Reamar. Your walls will crumble, your strength will fail, and your dead will rise against you."

CHAPTER 6
BLOOD GODDESS

Lean and mean. That was what Seides had said the one time she abased herself enough to ask for more than her usual meager ration of food. *You're my prize fighter, Dania. You need to be lean and mean for the arena.*

Dania looked down at her shackled body, hardened by years of barbarous conflict, forged in the flames of victory after bloody victory in the arena. She considered the thickened thighs and calves, the nearly nonexistent breasts, and the arms like whipcord.

I am lean. I am mean. But I am also hungry.

Dania snarled to herself at the memory.

"I thought you said you weren't hurt." Ruise's voice intruded into her thoughts, and he pointed to the crimson rivulet snaking its way down her side. She took a deep breath and examined the cut on her arm. Certainly not worth a trip to the Healers. Images of pungent antiseptics and wickedly curved stitching needles flashed through her mind, and she ground her teeth together.

The price you paid for fighting distracted. "It's a scratch. Let it be."

Ruise shrugged and handed her a bandage. She wrapped it around her arm—a bit of a trick, with the shackles—and then Ruise and Vaunce took up the chains.

"Think that slave was sweet on you, killer," Vaunce said.

"Shut up."

"You shut up." Vaunce sneered back at her. "You aren't supposed to talk to anyone without permission, remember?"

He gave her chain a sharp tug and chortled. Dania didn't allow herself to stumble. She took the force of the pull with a stifled grunt, determined not to let the pain show. Compared to all her injuries sustained in the pits and the arena over the years, this was nothing. Still, an image of Vaunce's grinning head on a pike brought a smile to Dania's lips.

She flashed him a defiant glare. "Laugh, boy, when you remember the smile I left on Andrus. Would you like to be smiling the same way?"

The grin disappeared in a flash. Vaunce held the chain taut for a few seconds more, just to show her who really had the upper hand, but let it go slack at last, accompanied by a sullen look.

"Would you cut that out?" Ruise said, his feathery tone deceptively soft.

A wave of some unfamiliar feeling—pity, perhaps?—washed over her as she considered what she would do tonight, should all go as planned. She clenched her jaw as they led her to Seides's private coach. Next to it stood a closed-in carriage, drawn by a pair of Alatian oxen. Dania stopped for a moment, sniffing at the air.

"What are you doing?" Corthra, a giant man with a long black braid, held the third chain. His dark face betrayed no sign of hate or interest in her whatsoever; Dania might have supposed him to be without passion, had she not been present when he raped one of the serving girls following one of Seides's after-the-hunt feasts.

"A storm is coming." It couldn't be more perfect. Tonight was the night. And have no doubt, a storm was coming.

A storm was coming, indeed.

"Dania, why don't you close your mouth before I close it for you?" Corthra gave her arm a reminding whack with the short club he carried.

"Beware the silence of a prisoner," Ruise said quietly, giving Dania a weak smile as he stepped into the wagon, "for he who abides in chains abides in fury."

"What?" Vaunce did a double take. "What are you talking about?"

"It's just something from the third book of the Saman Pootkar."

"Well, now, aren't you the faithful one?" The carriage bounced as the fourth guard, Coden, climbed aboard. Of the four, he was the one Dania deemed most dangerous. Quiet, but not in the staid way that Corthra was. Arrogant, but not shallow like Vaunce.

"My son comes of age this month." Ruise tapped the wall of the carriage twice with his club to signal the driver that they were ready. "I have to memorize some things for his rite of manhood."

Pushing aside her pity, Dania closed her eyes as the carriage started off with a jolt. Ignoring the throbbing in her arm, and the musty smell of the men around her, she allowed herself a small smile.

Abides in fury. I like that.

———————◆———————

There once was a famous hunter who sought to kill the most ferocious animal in the forest. A feral boar the size of an ox, the story went, and as mean as a pack of rabid direwolves. But its tusks were worth a fortune, and so the hunter set off to fell the animal.

Tell me more, Dania had said in the near-faded days of her youth. The days of campfires and music, of tales and magic tricks. The songsinger had obliged, filling her ears with all the bloody details. In a spectacularly one-sided battle, the marauder rent the hunter from hip to shoulder. The very prize he sought had been his downfall. A cautionary tale to the men and women of the caravan.

To this day, Dania found the irony exhilarating.

Chained to the damp stone wall in her quarters and smoldering with an inner fire, Dania listened to the shuffling feet of the men coming to fetch her for her master. Staring hard at a point in space, she counted the moments. Distant sheets of rain bathed the mansion in torrents. A blanket of noise on a night of cleansing.

Closer, closer.

The sound of the key in the lock, the door squealing open. The flash of pale light on the first guard, sticking his turbaned head in, grinning lecherously at her.

"Hello, Dania."

Vaunce. Excellent.

Corthra entered the room after him. That wasn't so good, but he could be dealt with. These men knew better than to touch her; she was her master's plaything.

Tonight would be different.

For ages, it seemed, she had been forced to shackle herself before bedding down for the night. When the guards left, she would tug at the chain, pulling at the steel plate bolted to the wall. Just this morning, her efforts paid off; she had managed to work the plate free. She replaced it with care, so as not to arouse suspicion. The heavy chain barely rested in the wall, but it should be enough, in the poor lighting.

Tonight, she would suffer no more.

Leaning over her cot with his great bulk, this scant-bearded fool fumbled with the shackles on her left arm, his hands shaking with lust, his breath coming in quick pants. No doubt he hoped to aid his master in the taming of the Blood Goddess. The other man started to work with the ankle restraints. Within a moment, Corthra had her legs free.

Now was the time.

She wrapped her left arm up and around Vaunce's head, pulling him close. At the same instant, she whipped her right arm free, swinging the loose end of the heavy manacle around and hitting Corthra in the side of the face with it.

Vaunce gasped. "Dania, what...?"

She yanked back his head and lunged, crushing his larynx with her teeth. Eyes bulging and arms flailing, he staggered back, pulling free from Dania's grasp and tearing at his throat. The keys flew against the wall and disappeared down the grate.

Dania swore. She hadn't expected him to have that much strength, but she had already relieved him of the dagger hung at his belt. She swung

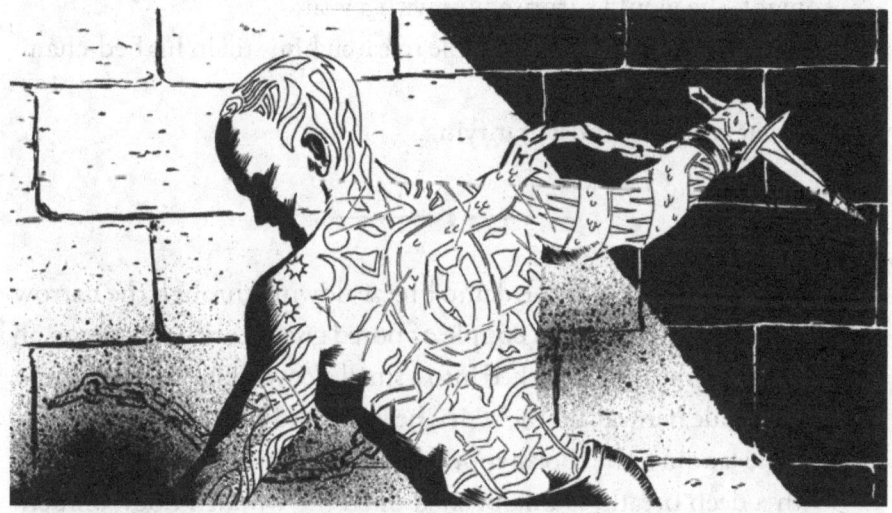

the chain, wrapping it around his wrist, and pulled him back again.

"Smile, Vaunce." She slid the blade across his throat and shielded her eyes against the sudden warm rain that bathed her face. With a gurgle, Vaunce fell to his knees. He reached for her in a final effort, and his body slumped to the floor.

"You should really keep your blade sharper."

Corthra, still dazed, struggled to stand, waving his knife in her direction and pressing his other hand to the side of his bleeding head. She curled her lips into a sneer, grabbed his wrist, and eviscerated the man—almost before he could cry out. Stepping back so she wouldn't slip on his entrails, Dania left him staring at her, mouth working soundlessly. She heard him collapse a moment after she turned her head and dove for the grate.

Mere inches from her fingers, the keys gleamed up from the muck. She tried to prize up the iron, but it was imbedded firmly in the floor. When she realized her efforts were futile, she wasted no more time, but wrapped the chain around her arm. Removing it would just have to wait.

Driven by an exhilarating fury transcending caution, she flung herself out into the hall, padding through the dark corridors on bare, calloused feet. She headed toward the broad, curved stone staircase leading to the third level.

She was tired of being visited by her master.

Tonight, she would surprise *him* with a visit.

If she was lucky, she might be able to catch him still in his bed-chamber.

Yes, that would be most gratifying.

———————— ◆ ————————

The oil torches flickered in the damp breeze flowing through the narrow windows. The low voices of a couple of bored guards drifted through an adjoining corridor. Dania ducked into a small alcove, but they passed and faded. She made her way up the stairs, heart pounding in heady anticipation. At the landing, she took a moment to calm herself.

With a deep breath, Dania pushed open the wooden door, and entered the candlelit chamber. Seides, dressed in a robe, stood there on the skin of one of his many kills. He dropped his glass of wine at the sight of her, and Dania had the satisfaction of seeing his face go completely white.

"Guards!" he shouted at the top of his lungs. *"Guards!"*

With a catlike leap, Dania sprang at him feet first and knocked him to the floor. With one foot at his throat, and another holding down his left arm, she reached under his robe and between his legs. One sharp tug with her stolen dagger, and it was done. Seides made an inhuman screech, and she stomped on his chest, driving his breath out. She tossed the handful of flesh into the blazing fireplace and moved to bar the door. Raised voices grew louder with the rapidly approaching footsteps of the guards.

Seides was curled up on the floor, bleeding all over his prized rug and inching feebly away from her. Dania took a poker from the hearth and ambled over to him, ignoring the guards banging on the door. She prodded Seides onto his back with the poker and clenched her jaw.

"You boast to your friends as you have your way with me. You say you like to look death in the face."

Seides moaned, and she brought the poker down in a vicious arc, breaking his collarbone. He screamed again and pleaded up at her with glazed eyes.

She pointed to herself, imagining her own bloodied and snarling visage. "Look into my face, then, beast, because it is your death you see."

Dania raised her weapon above her head, and brought it down again and again, until Seides's body stopped twitching, and a dark pool spread across the floor.

The door burst open, and Ruise rushed into the room, followed by three other guards.

"Oh, gods, Dania, what have you done?"

She had hoped it would not have to come to this, but she had no choice. With a momentary stab of regret for the only man who had ever spoken gently to her in this place of torment, she swung the poker around, connecting solidly with his head. She drew her blade across his jugular—the sound like the soft whisper of cloth tearing. In a flurry of ringing steel and spraying blood, she dispatched the rest of her attackers. She dropped the poker, grabbed another dagger, and ran out of the room.

If only she could get her armor... but there was no time. She had been sloppy, and the house was on alert. No doubt one of the slaves had been sent to summon the authorities, and the mansion was being shut up. Even now she heard the drawing of bolts across the doors. She ran down the back stairs, toward the servants' quarters and past the alcove.

Without warning, Dania found herself flying forward, rolling to a stop beneath one of the torches. Her neck throbbed, and she saw black spots at the edges of her vision. Shaking her head to clear it, she struggled to get to her feet. Blearily, she recognized Coden Finor descending the stairs after her, swinging his club with an expression of casual smugness.

"Well, now, from the look of things, you have been one naughty little girl," Coden said. "Whose blood is that, I wonder, or do I want to know?"

Dania searched around for her daggers. She must have dropped them when he hit her from behind. They lay on the stairs above, well out of reach.

"Where did you think you were going in such a hurry?"

Dania reached up and tore the torch from the wall, waving it in front of her, causing Coden's face to dance with mad delight. She allowed the manacle chain to fall, and swung it in a whistling circle, daring him to get closer.

"Little girls shouldn't play with fire, you know. They can get burned."

She whipped the chain at him, and he dodged, bringing his club down on her wrist. Dania gasped but didn't let go; the blow had hit her manacle. The next blow fell on her shoulder, reopening her new wound with a burning tear. She blocked his follow-up swing with the torch, ashes and sparks flying as the wood connected. Coden swung his club down with all his might, thankfully missing her wrist this time, connecting instead with the torch. It flew out of her hand and rolled down the stairs.

"Lights out, Dania." Coden slid the club back into his belt and drew a dagger from its sheath. When he lurched toward her, Dania took her opportunity. She grabbed his wrist and fell backwards, tucking into a ball. Caught off-balance, he nearly fell on top of her. She kicked her leg out, catching him under the ribs, and used his momentum to launch him down the stairwell. Coden howled as he sailed over her head, and she rolled after him, bouncing off each stair. She jolted to a painful stop at the next landing, then sat up to see what needed to be done to finish the job.

Coden lay sprawled on the floor, his knife imbedded in his chest, and his neck bent at an improbable angle. His eyes stared sightlessly at the vaulted ceiling. Dania winced as she re-wrapped the chain around her arm; every breath stabbed at her, and her back was a mass of bruises. She heard a shriek from upstairs; that would be Seides's overfed wife.

With a quick glance up and down the corridors, Dania retrieved her daggers. She pulled the satchel off Coden's body, stashed her blades and his coin purse into it, thought for a moment, and took his outer tunic and pants. She stuffed them into the bag as well, drawing it tight. The voices of the other guards grew louder; she had only moments before their search led them to her. She drew the satchel over her shoulder and scrambled up into the window, then kicked open the shutters and peered into the canal below. Several boats were moored along the walkways, but no one was out in the rain. The streetlamps provided just enough illumination for her to estimate at least a thirty-foot drop. Bracing herself, she leapt out and dived, slicing into the canal with hardly a splash.

The cold hit her like a slap, and she had to struggle not to draw a breath at the shock. Plunging deep into the inky silence, Dania swam as far as she dared without coming up for air. The current swept her along, and when she finally surfaced, Seides's mansion already lay far behind her. The icy waters took the pain of her injuries away, replacing them with a fearful ache. She swam until she could swim no longer, and then let the current take her. Rushing past gondolas and skiffs, she was tempted to leave the water for the first room with a fire she could find. Her bones felt frozen, and it was getting difficult to move. She clamped her jaws together to keep her teeth from chattering. But to give in now would be the end of her.

The city walls approached. There were a number of outflows, but she didn't want to go over the falls. Hopefully she remembered right. There it was—a large drainage grate. She grasped at the sides of the canal to slow her approach, skinning her hands and bruising her knees. Somehow she managed to keep from smashing into the iron bars barricading her way. She grabbed them, but only a few inches were above the waterline. She hadn't counted on this, but supposed it was her own fault for not considering the effect the rain would have on the city's main transportation system. Gritting her teeth, she took a deep breath and plunged under again, holding onto the bars with all her might.

Fighting the current pressing her against the grate, Dania turned her head sideways and slipped her arms between the bars, the iron squeezing and bruising her chest. The satchel had slipped around the bar, so she reached back and freed it, making sure it didn't get carried away. She pulled her body through, only to find herself jarred back just when she thought she might actually make it.

Her hips were stuck. If only she had the soft resilience of the women of Caileen. She struggled, wriggling this way and that, trying not to panic. Air was only a few feet away.

I cannot die here.

Slowly, inch by inch, she forced herself through the grate, straining at the effort, when suddenly she was free, tumbling away in the current. Dania swam to the surface and gulped for air. Lightning flashed across the sky, illuminating the outer wall of the city.

She had made it.

Dania was in the river now, being swept along toward the woods. She let the water carry her out of sight of Caileen, then crawled out onto the bank, shivering. Every inch of her body hurt. For just a few moments, she allowed herself to rest, then dragged herself to her feet, slipping in the mud, and cutting her palm on a stone. She could barely even stand, but knew she had to find shelter, and soon.

Dania turned one last time in the direction of the city. The chain clinked as she clenched her fists above her head in defiance. In her mind, she heard the roar of the crowd, calling her name. Inexplicably, she found herself recalling the boy she had met exiting the arena, and bared her teeth in a savage grin.

She shouted into the night: "Behold the victor!"

CHAPTER 7
DARK SOUL OF CAILEEN

"Lord Argoneis? He's the one in charge of all this..." The ragged crone spat, pointing across the street and down the block to an enormous building swarming with people. This was as close as she would come to the slave market; it seemed even beggars had their pride.

Valasand leaned in closer. "Have you ever seen the Lord Regent before?"

"Lord Regent, indeed. They say his nibs sold his own sister into slavery. No, I ain't ever seen him."

"Really?" The Warden arched her eyebrows. "Keeps a low profile, does he?"

"You might say that. He stays in his hole like the pampered swamp-rat he is."

"What else?"

"He bathes in human blood, they say, just like his father, and does things to his slaves I wouldn't repeat to the likes of you, dear, you being so young. It'd fair poison your ears."

"I'm older than I appear, but thank you anyway." Valasand doubted the woman had ten years on her, but she rarely had the inclination to contradict those who guessed her to be younger than she really was. At times, a modestly deceptive appearance had its advantages.

"There's not a soul in the city that don't shudder at the mention of his name, let me tell you. He'd kill his own mother, he would, just so's he could swear on her grave."

Over the course of the morning, Valasand had strolled through the streets of Caileen, stopping periodically to accost a passerby or drop to her knees to talk to a beggar. Several people snubbed her, looking the other way as she passed, or muttering "Woodsman" in spiteful tones

behind her back. "Woodsman" seemed to be a derogatory term for anyone living outside the city limits, outside "civilization."

Interesting, and perhaps not surprising, given the undeveloped wilderness all but engulfing the sparse city-states of this world. This old woman seemed to be one of the more loquacious urbanites, and obviously none too fond of this Lord Argoneis. In just a few hours, Valasand had a glimpse of Argoneis's reputation, and it was as vast, cold, and black as the space between the worlds. If the mutterings she heard were true, Daman's foul appetites had grown to appall even his contemporaries. The way he kept obtaining new slaves implied that the ones he took back to his glistering palace did not live very long. One man told her that in the last few years Argoneis had already taken in enough to populate a small village.

Daman Argoneis, Lord Regent of Caileen, epitomized the vile philosophy behind this hideous business. Argoneis, whose court fountains were said to run red with the blood of his slaughtered enemies. Whose rich, sheltered life allowed him to view anyone not of his station as a mere bauble to be toyed with or discarded at will. And who, from all accounts, was the dark soul of Caileen, the master player in this perverse game. Valasand touched the woman's arm. "Where does he live?"

———◆———

Fifty-foot stone walls ensconced the palatial residence. Massive guards of some indeterminate species patrolled the perimeter, and iron bars blocked the entrances. The towering main gates were no less secure than they were ornate. From where Valasand stood, she could see nothing but the outer fortifications, but when she had made the initial turn at the end of the street, she caught a glimpse of a structure gleaming like a gem above the surrounding splendor—the centerpiece of a coronet.

Valasand's heart burned to see the temple of Yasul barricaded and defiled, now a monument to sensuality, greed, and cruelty. With a resigned sigh, she turned on her heel and headed back into the city.

"So how do I get inside?" she asked under her breath.

The voice answered in her mind, though it always felt as if it came from just over her shoulder. *Request an audience.*

"I'm sure that would go over well."

A chance will present itself.

"I can hardly wait. So, what do I do in the meantime?"

You are searching for someone.

"How am I supposed to recognize this person?"

She will recognize you for what you are.

"Now that's a scary thought." Valasand laughed at the odd stare one of the street vendors gave her as she strode by, apparently deep in conversation with herself. "I just hope this isn't as bad as it seems. I think I've taken on a little more than I can handle this time."

You are never given more than you can handle.

"So you keep telling me. Where is this person I'm supposed to meet?"

Look for her in the market.

"Again, a description would be nice."

No response.

"You know," she said, after a few moments of walking in silence, "for someone not limited by time or space, you're awfully stingy with your answers."

Someday you will see the universe with eyes that are fully open. And when you do, I trust you will not be so ungracious as to begrudge me a little reticence.

"Reticence?" Valasand scoffed. "Compared to you, I'm practically a blabbermouth."

Child, you must learn to trust me.

"Yes, yes," she said. "Always some lesson or another I need to learn. Eternally the student, never the teacher."

Little Flame—there was a sense of quiet laughter—*if anyone could teach me anything, it would be you. But perhaps your chance will come sooner than you think.*

CHAPTER 8
MAURIN

"I know what our masters fear."

Maurin looked up, waving his hand in irritation at the stinging flies swarming around his face. Across the leafy row, the young Maolori slave Coparal focused on gathering grapes.

Natives to this world, the Maolori were sober humanoids with a light covering of hair. Their pointed ears stuck straight out, and a curly mane grew from the tops of their heads to the middle of their backs, like a horse's. After the initial shock of his first encounter just before the auction block, when he'd last seen Aric, Maurin became accustomed to the company of Maolori laborers. Though they didn't say much, what they said was usually worth hearing.

"What do they fear?" Maurin shoved aside the bitter memory of being separated from his cousin, of seeing Aric's face full of the same terror. If only they could have been purchased together. Was Aric all right? Was he even alive? Since that day, the overwhelming pangs of grief, anger and guilt had eventually dulled to a distant ache, but his heart was dead. He woke each day and set about his work with resignation.

The Maolori spoke through the vines. "They say there trouble in cities. They talk free, because they think we not listen, but we do. We hear and understand."

True enough. Slaves were invisible to those raised to believe they were inferior. Thus, the lords and ladies of Caileen did not often take care what they said in front of the servants, any more than they would bother not to utter secrets before their pets.

"What are you talking about?"

Coparal bobbed his head and flicked a fly off his ear with a quick twitch. "The master speak of entire cities that vanish overnight. Talk to other master, and he say dead walk with the living. We know this evil, and it has a name, but these Sacani just laugh, and talk of superstition."

Sacani. The Maolori term for mankind, and generally derogative. Maurin cocked his eyebrow at the younger slave and smiled. The sunlight shone bright on the hills of the vineyard, the air was warm, and the breeze was cool. It was a little difficult to swallow talk like that on a day like this. "Are you saying that this Lord Seides everyone's talking about was murdered by something supernatural?"

Coparal snorted. "Do not mock. Do you not hear? A great fighter slave missing. She murder her master."

"Sorry."

"Others have their lives stolen. The night come on wings, and no one safe. My brother, he believe the Gahna on the move again."

Maurin looked around to make sure no one was watching, then popped a grape into his mouth. The skin was tough, but it burst into sweet coolness when he bit into it. "Gahna, hmm? What are those?"

"You are ignorant, even for a Sacani."

"I'm not from here, remember?"

"You not let me forget if I want to." Coparal's ears rotated in a semi-circle, which Maurin had learned to interpret as their version of a shrug. He supposed he was the only slave in the vineyards who bothered to learn how to speak to the Maolori. The other slaves avoided them. Of course, Coparal mocked his thick accent and stilted way of speaking, but at least he could more or less understand them when they wanted to be understood. When they spoke their own language, however, and not the bastardized common tongue, he was lost. They apparently had no interest in letting him get that close.

Coparal turned his small, earnest face toward Maurin. "In the forest, the Gahna are the spirits of the dead. They walk at night, and feed on the souls of the living, so they might know again what it is to draw breath."

"Dramatic," Maurin murmured in Aran.

"What you say?"

"Nothing." Maurin switched back to Canoine. "So what are you supposed to do about it?"

Coparal rolled his ears again. "Pray to your gods."

Maurin frowned. He couldn't remember the last time he had prayed to Baelon. Probably when he realized that he wasn't going to see Aric again. "I was hoping for something a little more proactive."

The Maolori regarded him strangely.

"Maurin! Come!" Vellis called up to the vineyard. Maurin's master was a short, powerfully built man, nearly as broad across the shoulders as he was tall. His eyes followed Maurin with somber reflection as he sprinted down to meet him. "Well, Maurin, my boy, are you up to some real work today?"

"Yes, sir."

Vellis ran his fingers over his close-cropped beard. "We need to get six barrels of twelve-year Aspos Chavee to one of my best customers this afternoon. You and Ortney load the boat."

"Certainly, Master." Maurin ran through the house and down into the cellar, then out to the overhanging bay where the large gondola was docked. Ortney had already set up the loading ramp and was busy marking off the sale on the inventory.

The large man wiped some crumbs off his dark, droopy mustache, and glanced up at Maurin's approach. "Animal-lover."

Maurin scowled. "Come on; let's just get these things loaded."

"It's about time you did some real work, priest-boy."

Maurin ignored the jibes and struggled to get the barrels onto the boat with Ortney. The other man could roll them single-handed, but Maurin was too light to manage them himself, so he had to endure Ortney's mockery as the man came to his aid.

It's a good thing odors don't kill, or I would be dead several times over working with this ape. Just as well most of Maurin's work kept him outside and well-ventilated. Several minutes and a few splinters later, they were ready. Vellis came down, checked the securing ropes to make certain the slaves hadn't skimped, and nodded his satisfaction.

"All right, boys, let's go."

Maurin untied the mooring line. Ortney, standing near the stern, poled the boat out away from the house. Grabbing the other pole and taking his place at the bow, Maurin drew in a deep breath. The water lapped against the stone sides of the canal, a soft undercurrent to the distant roar of the waterfall. The vineyards were situated on the northern edge of Caileen, which meant outgoing boats could just coast with the currents, and for the most part, they didn't have to go upstream until the gondola was empty.

Another boat passed by, and Maurin recognized one of the slaves poling it as an acolyte from the temple of Baelon. The youth's eyes flickered with recognition, and Maurin forced himself to remain silent for fear of repercussion. His heart ached; this wasn't the first time he'd seen someone from Sangrine, but slaves were not to speak unless spoken to. Oh, to laugh and cry over memories of home with someone from Athure, and most importantly, learn of any news regarding his cousin.

The gondola passed, and Maurin's shoulders slumped. The only true link he still had to his past life was the silken wedding-ribbon he had managed to keep secreted away, a constant reminder of his obligations.

Whatever had become of Kirai? Did she still have hers?

Maurin had anticipated the rule of the two peoples with no small degree of dread. The notion that decisions he made would affect so many others' lives was simultaneously awesome and frightening.

Ironic. No longer would important choices be required of him. All decisions were made for him now. But escape into slavery wasn't exactly what Maurin had in mind. So many freedoms were taken for granted every day.

Just what would have happened that fateful night, had he and Aric gone ahead to run away?

He tried to talk with some of the other slaves about it, but most of them told him to shut up and stop spouting nonsense. The only one who seemed to halfway understand was Coparal, and even then Maurin wasn't sure if the Maolori boy really comprehended, or whether he was just a polite listener. Perhaps he was simply glad not to be bullied and shoved by one of the human slaves.

Slavery.

It wasn't something he really had to deal with in Athure. Some people at home bandied the term about with a kind of flippant disdain. They would talk in melodramatic tones about their own bloody history, and how awful it was, and turn the other way whenever the subject came up. Yet none truly understood why it was so abhorrent, and Maurin believed no one cared to. He knew he had not endured the worst of it. For the past two years, he had been worked hard, but treated fairly—at least, relatively speaking. Yet he had seen it, and lived in the shadow of it, every day.

It wasn't being subject to another; there were always going to be those in higher positions. Maurin supposed those like himself, who believed in the gods, lived their entire lives in willing servitude. It wasn't the work. Work did not rob one of one's own being.

It was the degrading sense that you were deemed less than human. That you were not supposed to look your master in the eye—not because he was truly superior and you were not worthy, but because that might remind your owner that in the long run, he was your equal.

No man likes to truly see himself.

Overhead, the beige and white walls of the city loomed over the canals. Vellis, sitting with his back against the barrels, gave occasional directions. Within a short time, Maurin found himself nosing the craft into the dock of an imposing mansion.

As Ortney tied the mooring rope, Vellis hailed the guards at the dock. He didn't have to show his credentials; apparently, Maurin's master was a familiar sight around this place. Vellis laughed and joked with the guards as he helped Maurin roll the barrels onto the dock and into the wine cellar. Maurin gave a low whistle at the rows upon rows of amphora filled with the finest vintages.

Vellis chuckled. "You know, this guy told me once that he really wanted to be a sommelier, but fell into fortune instead."

Not quite sure what response was expected, Maurin said, "I'm sure he would have made a good one, sir."

Vellis snorted and grinned. "He's the cornerstone of my business. Now come with me; I have some dealings with him."

"Yes, sir." Maurin followed his master up a stone stairway and into a larger pillared hall, the ceiling of which stretched into a vaulted series of arches higher than the roof of the building he lived in. A rich burgundy carpet divided the great hall and offset the stark marble floor. Strange, sad-sounding birds fluttered among the buttressed rafters, calling to one another.

Maurin tried not to gawk at the richness of his surroundings. Here he was in such a beautiful building, dressed in a slave's breechclout and tunic, with sweat making muddy tracks over his dirty arms.

Vellis asked a guard where the master of the house was to be found.

The man pointed to the east wing of the building and said he was in the conservatory.

"Wait here," Vellis said when they reached the entryway. "I won't be long."

Maurin nodded as his master disappeared into a veritable jungle of unusual plants. He leaned against the wall, wishing for someplace he could sit and rest his aching muscles. He closed his eyes for a moment, but opened them again at a soft clinking sound.

Walking down the hall was one of the most captivating women Maurin had ever seen. Vellis had no Maolori females in his household, and this was the closest Maurin had ever been to one. She was a tiny thing, with a sharp, upturned nose. She wore an abbreviated toga, and her body was covered with short, light hair that looked irresistibly soft, just begging to be caressed. Exotic, to be sure, but strangely appealing. She carried a tray of various fruits and cheeses, a decanter of wine, and two stone goblets.

Maurin held her gaze as she regarded him with dark eyes. Long lashes flicked down as she entered the room and swept past him. He couldn't stop staring as the girl glided down the stone path of the greenhouse, her wild mane spilling in dark brown curls down to the small of her bare back. Vellis made some sort of appreciative comment when she stooped to serve the men.

Maurin shook himself. He never knew a Maolori woman could be so pretty.

"Get a good look while you can," a voice said next to his ear. "She's going to be put up for sale soon."

Maurin gasped and found himself against the wall with a hand firmly over his mouth before it even registered that the words were in his native tongue. Strong arms pulled him away from the doorway and into the protection of a supporting pillar. Only then did the grip relax, and the hand lower from his face.

"Guess Krige's wife is tired of having an empty bed while he goes and plows his serving girl," his attacker added, grinning madly.

"Aric?" Maurin had to struggle to whisper when he wanted to shout. Mischievous eyes danced under a curly mop of sandy blond hair, and

Maurin's heart threatened to burst. Every muscle in his body wanted to leap, to dance, to fly.

"Last time I checked." Aric smirked, about as self-satisfied as Maurin had ever seen him.

Maurin lunged forward and grabbed his cousin in a tight embrace. "I thought I would never see you again!"

Aric patted his cousin none too gently to signal he had had enough, and finally Maurin had the strength to let go.

"You're taller!" he choked. "And your voice has changed!"

"Yeah, and your hair grew back. So what's your point?" He was still grinning. "Nice ponytail, by the way."

"Aric... oh, gods, Aric..." Maurin's face hurt from smiling. He pitched his words low and continued to speak in Aran. "What have you been doing here? Have you been treated well? How—"

"Maurin, shut up." Aric gave him an exasperated glare, then checked up and down the halls to make sure they weren't overheard. Then they stared at each other for a long moment.

Two years since they had last seen each other, and here they were, reunited against all odds. Questions welled up and flooded Maurin's mind. "All right, tell me everything that's happened."

Aric scowled and leaned closer. "Two years in just a few seconds? Forget it. I'll fill you in later. We've got to think of a way to get out of here."

"I'll ask my master if he'll buy you. I can work it off..." He trailed off at Aric's incredulous frown.

"Maurin, are you crazy? Do you want to be a slave for the rest of your life?"

He snorted, taken aback. "No, of course not, I just thought..."

"Forget it," Aric said, a strange gleam in his eye. "Now I've found you, we're going to get out of here for good."

"How are we going to do that?" Maurin's voice rose unconsciously. He wrestled down the notion of taking off right then, running down the halls, past the startled guards, and out into the city, where they could lose themselves in the crowds, and figure out what to do once they were sure they hadn't been pursued. "Even without this"—he pointed to his tattooed shoulder—"and even if we could get something to wear besides these"—he indicated their clothing—"we don't look or sound local. We're marked men. Suppose we were somehow able to get out of the city; anyone who found us would turn us in. This isn't like sneaking out of the temple for a midnight snack!"

Aric had that faraway expression, the one that always made him seem as though he hadn't a thought in his mind. It meant quite the opposite. "We're going to have to plan this pretty carefully."

"My master will be coming out in just a few minutes!"

"I know. We'll have to meet again." Aric glanced toward the conservatory. "I might be able to get Krige to send me for the next wine order; he's starting to trust me now. You're in the vineyards to the north, right? Then I can sneak in, and we can plot this out." A wild grin split his face. "This is going to be great!"

"Did you see how much wine we brought in? It could be years before we see each other again!"

"Not the way Krige drinks. Wait—how long has it been since Langfort?" Aric tallied off days on his fingers. "Almost a couple of weeks ago."

"He can go through this in two weeks?"

Aric didn't seem to hear him. "Something's coming."

Maurin whipped his head around, alarmed. "What—?"

"No, I mean... I mean... I'm not sure how to put this... something big is going to happen, and soon."

Maurin's heart skipped a beat. Should he hope or despair? He couldn't read Aric's face, and guessed that meant Aric himself didn't know. "You've been dreaming again?"

"Again? You mean still? More than ever, but that doesn't matter. The Reamar are searching for one of their own that's gone missing, and they've threatened to invade if they don't find her."

"Invade?"

"You know, this is going to take a really long time if you keep repeating everything I say."

"I'm sorry." Maurin stole a glance toward the conservatory. "I'm just having a hard time taking this all in. How would you know about the Reamar, anyway?"

Aric's words came out in a rush. "Krige had me fly him down to

Langfort to talk with the governor about the Reamar. They were there in his mansion, and the whole time I felt like they were watching me."

Curiosity swept all thoughts of escape from Maurin's mind. "You saw them face to face? What were they like?"

"More or less like everyone else." Aric shrugged. "Pale, I guess. Strange accent. Weird eyes."

"I've heard they have some sort of secret dealings with Argoneis..." Maurin stopped at his cousin's annoyed expression.

"Anyway, the whole time I was there, the Reamar kept staring at me. None of them said a word, but I was being watched the whole time. After the meeting was over, and Krige promised he would do everything he could to find this missing Reamar priestess, their spokesman pulled him aside and offered to buy me."

"Why would a Reamar want to buy you?"

"Same reasons as anyone else, I suppose." Aric shrugged again. "Krige said I wasn't for sale—and he told me later how grateful I should be for that, but didn't say why. Then he told this Guilan Vail I was being held aside for Lord Argoneis."

A chill passed through Maurin at that. "Lord Argoneis?" The man might seem weak and effete, but his reputation for barbarism was nearly legendary.

"Relax, will you? It wasn't true. At least, I don't think so." He seemed disturbed, as if considering the notion for the first time. "He's always trying to keep me in my place, and I think he was just making an excuse not to sell me to the Reamar. But I'm a popular guy these days, I guess; Argoneis does keep asking to buy me."

"Gods," Maurin said. "It curdles the blood just hearing you mentioned in the same breath as him. What does he want you for?"

Aric's eyes flitted around the corridor. "Not what you'd guess. At least, not exactly. He wants to put me in this big gladiator circus Lord Seides has planned. So far, Krige has been saying no. I could be imagining things, but lately it seems like he's been thinking about it more before he says it." Aric shrugged. "Guilan Vail told Krige he would call on him again and see if he had changed his mind. The way he said it sounded like a threat."

Maurin nodded. "So then what?"

"So then nothing. When Krige asked why he wanted me, he said it was 'of no consequence.' He told Vail he wasn't selling me, there were any number of other slaves in the Market of Caileen, if he wanted to try his luck there, and he knew for a personal fact Lord Argoneis sent slaves by the drove to the Reamar as it was. What I'd like to know is, who is this Guilan Vail, and why is he so interested in me?"

"Good questions, both." Maurin thought for a moment. "But what does this have to do with us escaping?"

"Oh, right. Sorry." Aric smirked. "Just three more days, and it will have been two weeks. It's perfect, Maurin. Just sit tight. Go back to your vineyards, and don't say anything. Leave it all up to me."

"Don't do anything stupid..."

Aric dashed away almost as quickly as he had appeared. The voices of Krige and Vellis drew near.

"I don't put any stock in this superstitious rubbish," Vellis said. "I'm just a simple man, with a simple trade, but I know when someone is trying to scare me. I suspect this is some ploy of Argoneis's, finding some reason to raise our taxes. He can claim it's for the security of Caileen, and meanwhile, have a drink at our expense out of a new golden cup."

"I'm sure you are right, my friend," Krige said. "Whatever would I do without my favorite wine-merchant?"

"Spend all your time bored and sober, I suppose."

"One and the same, my good man, one and the same." Krige's smile disappeared. "You're doing me a tremendous favor."

"Don't mention it, my lord. I certainly won't. Here, Maurin." Vellis dumped a rolled bundle into his outstretched arms.

Maurin shouldered it with a stifled grunt. Part of the payment must have included an old tapestry. To his surprise, the Maolori girl stepped up to them, looking back and forth between her master and Maurin. Her eyes brimmed, yet no tears fell.

Vellis put his hand on Maurin's shoulder. "This is Talauna. She'll be coming with us. I'll be wanting you to train her in the vineyards."

Maurin swallowed hard, almost regretting that he might not have the chance to do as his master suggested. He couldn't find any words, so he simply nodded and followed his master in a mechanical daze down the hall to the docks.

What a turn of events. Aric, alive! And not too far away! Perhaps Baelon smiled upon him after all. As he took his place at the stern and poled the boat away from the mooring, Maurin offered up another quick prayer of gratitude.

Then he grimaced. Aric attempting an escape now would spoil their chances of establishing a firm ground off of which to make a later stand. Maurin's dream of liberation was sharper and more real than ever. He didn't want to ruin it by having their shackles tightened just when things were looking up. Finally, he had some hope. He needed to talk to Aric again and sort things out. He would work for his freedom and Aric's, and then they could go home.

Home. He'd given up on that possibility. Wait three days? What did that even mean?

He shook his head and took in their new companion, who sat alone on the bench seat behind Vellis. The Maolori girl had not yet said a word.

"I'm sorry. I hope you didn't think I was ignoring you."

The girl started, and regarded him with large brown eyes, but said nothing. If anything, her lips tightened.

"My name is Maurin." He nodded awkwardly in the direction of his companion, who, like him, was poling on the other side of the boat, keeping it clear of the stone edges of the canal. "This is Ortney. He works with us in the vineyards."

Long ringlets dangled on either side of the girl's face and shook as she cocked her head, cervine ears making her seem almost comically alert.

Wary, more likely.

Leaning toward her, Ortney said, "Look, stupid, he ain't gonna hurt you."

The girl shrank away. Ortney broke off as Maurin touched him on the shoulder, gently but firmly pulling him back to his place.

"What?" Ortney retorted, annoyed. He looked as though he would like nothing better than to shove Maurin over the side, but a quick glance at Vellis, lost in thought at the prow, quelled that.

With what he hoped was a reassuring smile, Maurin said, "It's all right. You don't have to say anything if you don't want. We may take a little getting used to, I know. Especially him. He's noisy, but he only picks on people his own size. And me."

Ortney opened his mouth to retort, but Maurin silenced him with a gesture. He grinned again, and this time, the girl seemed to relax a bit. He had hoped for a smile in return, but he'd take what he could get. Maurin reviewed what he had been taught when he was first purchased. He rather looked forward to training this girl in the art of winemaking. And Coparal would be glad to see another Maolori in the vineyards.

Then again, maybe he wouldn't. Another Maolori might simply drive home further the fact that they were not free.

He didn't remember much about the trip home, and the night passed in a tumult. He tossed and turned, too excited to sleep, until at last he dropped off out of sheer exhaustion.

The next morning, Vellis had Talauna waiting for him. Maurin showed her around the vineyards and introduced her to the other Maolori. The girl kept her eyes averted, and still said nothing. Coparal barely reacted to her presence, and didn't speak to Maurin for the rest of the day. Maurin showed Talauna how to inspect the vines for dead branches and the grapes for insect and bird damage. She never acknowledged him in any way, but immediately duplicated his work with long, deft fingers.

Only once did he get a reaction from her, and that was when he tried the few Maolori words he knew. She jerked her head around and stared. Suddenly the rest of his miniscule vocabulary failed him, and he stammered that he could get Coparal to translate if she liked. She shook her head and went back to inspecting the grapes.

His dreams that night left him wishing he had Aric's gift of prescience.

Given how quickly Talauna had picked up his instructions, he didn't hover when she wandered off to work on her own the next day. Though he supervised from a distance, his thoughts kept returning to Aric.

Wait three days.

Wait for what?

On the third night, a voice intruded into his dreams.

Maurin.

"What?" He squinted into the dark. The clouded moons scarcely penetrated the narrow windows. The only sign of life was a white bird perched on the windowsill. It flew away as soon as it heard his voice. No one else seemed to be awake. "What is it?"

There was no answer, so he laid his head back on the hard bundle of rags serving as a pillow and tried to go back to sleep.

Maurin.

He shot straight up in bed, eyes wide open. "Who's calling me? What do you want?"

Again, there was no response, save the soft snoring of one of the

other men. He cat-footed down the aisle, inspecting each of the slaves to determine who was shamming.

"Look," he whispered loudly into the room, "I need my sleep. What is it you want from me?"

The only response he got was an angry oath from Ortney, who wrapped his pillow around his head to drown him out. Maurin approached the window. Was Aric out there, somewhere, escaped despite his warnings? He strained his eyes. Nothing. At long last, he gave a mental shrug. Must have been dreaming. He made his way back to bed.

Maurin. Get up.

That did it. Maurin leapt up and cast about wildly. "What is going *on?*"

Before any of the outraged slaves could answer, an unnatural howl sounded on the wind, coming from the south side of the house.

"What in the seven hells?" Ortney scrambled to his feet. Coparal sat with his eyes closed. His lips moved in a silent mantra as the others tumbled out of their beds and pushed past him in their confusion.

Maurin rushed through the house and out the main doorway. Vellis stood at the gates at the end of the long walk. Talauna and the other women had come out of their quarters, staring in wide-eyed amazement at the scene of pandemonium before them.

Outside the gates, Argoneis's police fired their tined bolt-throwers wildly all around them in what appeared to be blind desperation, streaks of lightning splitting the night in random bursts. Others simply ran. It didn't matter, though, because very few of them got more than a few yards. All around, people were dropping, felled by something unseen in a green-tinged fog. Shouts and screams filled the ozone-charged air.

"What are they doing?" Vellis's wife Latricia shushed her sobbing baby and young daughter.

A distant moan filled the air, as eerie and mournful as the cry of a soul in torment, or perhaps the sound of unfathomable hunger.

"I don't know!" The wind whipped Maurin's hair around his face. All he knew was that it filled him with fear, and he wished to have no part of it.

"Siaran Thoud..." A penetrating voice colder than death whispered on the wind and quested down Maurin's spine. *"Siaran Thoud..."*

At the end of the street, a shadow rushed into view, sweeping over several men, leaving them fallen and twitching in its wake. It sped up the path toward the vineyard.

"Get back in the house!" Vellis shouted. "Everyone inside!"

Maurin barely had time to usher Talauna through the doorway. Vellis was still trying to catch up when it was upon him. He gasped as the specter plunged into his midsection, jerking him to a halt. Then, with a howl, the banshee wind continued through him, exiting with a greenish glow, and a vague winged form faded into the night. Vellis choked and staggered a few steps with the jerky motions of a marionette.

Then he fell to his knees and slumped to the ground, steam rising from his body. His hair turned white, his features aging rapidly, and his dead eyes gazed in horror at Maurin.

Vellis's daughter screamed.

"What is happening?" Latricia shrilled, clutching her infant desperately. "What was that?"

"I have no idea." Had Maurin really just watched his master die? For the space of several heartbeats, he stood in silence, amazed that the thing, whatever it was, hadn't seen them. "But I do think we need to find a place to lie low until this is over."

INTERLUDE
THE ONE

Where are you, my love?

I rise at the soft insistence of the voice. Careful not to wake the others, I move to the bedroom window.

A vision of beauty stands in the gauzy haze of the alley below, a silhouette clad in little more than mist and moonlight. Flowing auburn hair spills over her shoulders. She beckons, amatory hunger reflected in her lovely face.

Heart racing, I leave the window with reluctance. I make sure Pico, the kitchen boy, is still sleeping, and tiptoe out of the room. I find myself already down the stairs and out the front gates. The woman waits at the entrance to the alleyway, gesturing enticingly. Her fathomless eyes lock on mine and never let go.

I have waited for you, Aric. Thick, sensual lips caress the words. *Come to me.*

I move toward her as she backs into the alley, swallowed by the darkness. When I reach the woman, I stand dumb-founded before her.

You are the one, she says in a silvery, ethereal voice. *Your power has called to me from across the empty seas.*

She reaches out and takes my chin in her fingers, drawing me forward into an embrace, kissing me long and hard. An enraptured smile passes over her face, the euphoric expression of one whose hunger has been sated to the point of sleepy bliss.

I feel myself floating away as my soul pours into hers...

CHAPTER 9
STEPPING OUT

Aric cried out and sat bolt upright in the empty room. Another dream. Couldn't he ever just sleep? He collapsed back onto the sweat-dampened bedclothes, drawing a deep breath. Who was this woman, and why did he continue to dream about her?

Then he remembered Maurin, and all thoughts of her vanished. He lay there a long time, staring into the blackness of his quarters.

Wait or act, wait or act.

The Reamar had threatened to make a move in two weeks' time. That meant tonight. It had taken everything in him not to try this the day Maurin showed up. But whatever they intended would surely serve as a distraction while he made his escape.

Krige would be indulging in the new wine, still drinking away his sorrows for having given up his favorite plaything. The night guard was going deaf, and Aric had sneaked past him several times in the past for midnight larder raids. Sedrick, the head servant, should be asleep. No, there would be no better night, regardless of what the Reamar had planned. The time for action was now.

Steeling himself, he pushed off the bed. He could layer all the sets of clothes he had stolen from Krige over the months and secreted away for just such an occasion, but opted to sacrifice them for greater freedom of movement. He chose one dark, simple outfit he hoped would help him blend in with the night, and not draw too much attention. Krige was slightly taller than he, but that couldn't be helped.

Stopping at the kitchen, Aric spread out a cloak on one of the massive counters. He took several chilled hunks of meat, wrapped them in leaf parchment, and arranged them tightly on the cloak. He then folded the edges inward and rolled the whole thing into a bundle, tying it with some barrel-binding cords, and leaving a loop long enough to sling over his shoulder.

He had seen various maps of the city and the countryside, but no one bothered to teach slaves how to read here, so they were nearly useless for finding Maurin. Still, with his many trips over Caileen in his master's airship, it should be no problem to locate his cousin's vineyard.

He picked up a serrated knife and considered it woefully.

Not looking forward to this.

First, he used it to cut one of his old tunics into long, even strips, then pulled a full wineskin off the wall. He set the metal teeth against his skin and scraped them over the identifying slave-brand, grimacing as he willed himself to press harder. Within a few minutes, his shoulder was a mass of raw, bleeding flesh. He picked up a wineskin, undid the stopper with his teeth, and poured the liquid fire over the wound.

It took all his will not to scream. As it was, he couldn't help an agonized gasp, and a few tears escaped his clenched eyes until the shock of the pain receded. He winced as he pulled the clean strips of cloth around his arm, suppressing the flow of blood. Tying them with just the one hand was difficult, but somehow he managed. It might have been smarter to wait until he got clear, but at least this way, he could claim he had some sort of accident, and it just might buy him some time. Otherwise, the

tattoo would be a dead giveaway. He slid his arms into the baggy sleeves of his stolen shirt, grunting as the bandage tugged.

Now for it.

Aric heaved the bundle of food over his undamaged shoulder and walked quietly through the house. Looking in on his master's den, he saw Krige snoring softly in his large chair, several amphorae at his side. Aric smirked. Getting out was going to be the easy part. Getting through the streets was another matter.

Krige's airship? He could steal it and be off before anyone was able to give chase. But the noise would alert the mansion, and anyone in the civilized parts of Argoth would be prepared for his capture by the time he landed. And even on the slim chance he got out of here without being noticed, it was unlikely he could get so lucky twice—landing in the vineyards was bound to wake someone up, and there was no way he was going to get out of here without Maurin.

He would have to hoof it after all.

Aric wandered through the streets of Caileen, hugging the shadows and keeping an eye out for the night patrol. He ducked into an alleyway and paused for a moment. Strange gray vines had grown up from the wall of one building to the next, blanketing the street in between them. Where had he seen something like that before?

"You've come a long way from the Gray Lands."

Aric didn't recognize the man's flat voice, but the accent was unmistakable. He held his breath and hid himself behind a mass of dark creepers grown over a pile of rubble. A blond Reamar male stood reflected in the moonlit alley, his eyes hard and accusing. A severe shell of armor protected his chest, and dark breeches fluttered about his legs in the evening breeze. He carried a strange, braided staff or spear of some sort.

Across the alley, the girl he addressed placed her hands on her hips in defiance. Her white gown hung about her in limp shreds, clearly her sole garment through many hardships.

"What business is it of yours, Vanwè? I seek the Dreaded One, just as you do."

"Yes, but to what purpose? To warn him?"

"I do not wish any to come to destruction. I wish only to prevent unnecessary bloodshed."

The still air of the alley congealed into a cold, hostile blanket around them. "And I cannot allow you to throw away our chances for survival. You are coming with me."

Quicker than thought, the man lunged forward, his body twisting in a nearly animal-like arc toward her. Aric flinched, nearly bolting out of his hiding place. But in a flash, the girl grabbed the man by the collar, spun him around, and flung him to the ground. He struggled, but long white arms pinned him down, and she straddled him in a bizarre parody of passion, grasping his head under the ears, at the base of the neck.

A green mist flowed from the man's body and up the girl's arms, lighting her face with an eerie glow. Her eyes turned to wildfire, and for a few awful moments, the man's body jerked and spasmed. It all happened so fast, Aric hardly had time to register it. Before he could even move, the mist was gone as if the girl had absorbed it. With a slow, deep inhalation, she closed her eyes. When she opened them again, Aric saw a flicker of glowing green. The girl stood up, brushing at the ragged edges of her gown. She stared at the body for a few moments, as if unsure of what to do with it. At length, she took the man's weapon and left, walking within a few feet of Aric's hiding spot.

Aric couldn't hold his breath any longer. He let it out in a long, controlled sigh. He waited until he was sure she was gone, then went to investigate the corpse. He had never seen anyone die like this; what was left of the Reamar lay gray and withered in the street. Aric shuddered. He knelt, placing his hand on the chest. The body was eerily cold, and yet when he picked up the hand by the wrist and let it drop, it was still flexible. Strange.

"Hey! You!"

Aric's gut froze.

"Don't move!"

His first instinct was to run, but he knew whoever it was had a bolt-thrower aimed at his back.

"All right, I'm not going anywhere."

"I'll say you're not, slave," the coarse voice said.

Aric cursed inwardly as two distinct sets of footsteps approached.

"Put your hands on your head, unless you want to lose it."

"My hands?"

"Your head, stupid."

Aric winced as the shackles were put on, and the shorter of the two men ripped his sleeve away from the shoulder, exposing the bloody bandage.

"Runaway. Just like I thought. What'd you do to this man, slave?"

"I didn't do anything," Aric said. "I found him like this."

"I'll bet."

"I did. Look at his purse; he hasn't been robbed."

"He would've been, if we'd come around that corner a minute later." The taller of the two men jerked Aric around and patted him down while the shorter held the tines of his weapon level with his stomach.

As he suspected; members of the local constabulary, their pauldrons emblazoned with the seal of the House of Argoneis.

"Come on, slave. Let's see if you don't feel like talking after a little while in Lord Argoneis's dungeon."

Aric put one foot in front of the other, allowing himself to be led until he could figure a way out of this. He knew he should be frightened, but it all seemed too unreal. This was without doubt one of the most bizarre nights he had ever had. Was it just one long, bad dream?

"Who is your owner, slave?"

Aric didn't say anything, and the shorter man punched him in his wounded arm, causing him to cry out.

"Who owns you?"

"Nobody," he said through gritted teeth. "Nobody owns me. And if you do that again, you're a dead man."

"Oh, really?" The shorter man sneered, and hit him again, even harder this time.

Aric whirled and grabbed the man's weapon, wrenching it out of his grasp. He slid his hands down to the end and wielded it like a club, bringing it up into the man's stomach. The constable's breath went out of him in a rush, and he fell to the ground, clutching at his middle.

Then everything went black for a moment, and Aric found himself lying on the ground, cradling his head. Above him, the stars swam by in blurry streaks, like the firebugs that lit the jungle nights at home. His eyes rolled back, and he could barely make out the wary figure of the senior officer standing over him, poised to strike again.

As Aric tried to clear his head, a long, low tone pierced the night, and he clamped his hands over his ears. One of the city's alarm towers. The two constables looked up, and suddenly the shorter one was bowled over. Through his spinning vision, Aric saw a green-black streak passing through the man, taking with it every last shred of his life.

The taller man swore softly in shock as the spectral glowing darkness fled down the street, merging with the shadows. Distant sounds of chaos, screams of terror and grief. With each passing moment, they grew in intensity.

If Siaran Thoud is not returned to us in full health within a fortnight, we shall have no other choice than to give you a demonstration of our power.

Should've waited. The Reamar were right on schedule.

"Now do you believe me?" Aric asked, scrambling to make some sense of what he'd just seen. "I told you I didn't kill that man."

For a few moments, the stunned constable didn't reply. "Be that as it may, slave, you've still got this mark on your arm to explain." Keeping his weapon trained on Aric, the taller man forced him to his feet. "Let's go."

The constable prodded him along for several blocks, jabbing him when he wanted him to turn left or right. Aric's mind whirled with possibilities; he had only a short time in which to act before he was beyond help. Overpower the man? Maybe, but he would be risking getting flash-burned if he couldn't move fast enough. Still, it seemed he was running out of options. The pinnacle of Daman's palace loomed above the buildings ahead, and he started to sweat in spite of the cool night air.

There's only one man. I can do this. I have to do this. Aric bunched his hands into fists. The shackles were a problem, but not insurmountable.

"Slow down," the constable said.

A solitary figure in a dark cloak stood masked in shadow in the middle of the moonlit street. At their approach, a female voice carried into the night. "Thank you, Constable. I see you have retrieved my wayward servant."

CHAPTER 10
THE MARKET

They waited in a vast underground stable beneath the auction proper, a reeking vault of stale sweat and misery. Gigantic stone columns supported the ceiling at various places around the cavernous room. Maurin and Coparal had come in peaceably, and while all of them wore wrist fetters with a short length of chain between them, the two of them were not shackled to any of the hundreds of iron rings bolted to the wall. The guards tended to get lazy with non-aggressive slaves; Maurin supposed it was too much of a bother to be constantly locking and unlocking the

manacles.

Talauna had simply gone off by herself the moment the guards deposited her in the cage, and now the Maolori girl huddled in the musty corner opposite Maurin in the damp holding cell. The slave-bracelets seemed cruelly huge on her thin wrists. Her large brown eyes stared unseeing at a spot on the wall, and Maurin averted his gaze. He hated the injustice, and worst of all, being impotent to do anything.

Vellis's wife had no interest in running the vineyards, and had opted to sell the chattel and move back home to her family in Sal Dalinde. Maurin's hopes for escape, or at least the comfort of being reunited with Aric, diminished as each of Vellis's slaves were led up the passageways to the auction blocks upstairs. Once upon a time, he would have prayed to Baelon for deliverance, or even for strength. But his faith in such matters had diminished of late.

His moody reverie didn't last long. The presiding guard approached with a heavy tread. He passed among the rows of prisoners, taking the occasional half-hearted swipe at them. Rage welled up in Maurin. Setting his jaw, he scowled at the floor between his bare knees.

The guard opened the door to their cell. He strolled past Maurin and Coparal and a half-dozen other prisoners to the back wall. Talauna gasped as the man grabbed her by the arm and forced her to her feet. She pleaded silently in Maurin's direction.

Maurin sucked in his breath and clenched his teeth. He flashed a hateful glare at the guard, but the shock cudgel the older man carried quelled any impetuous notion of resistance or heroism. His body tensed, energy surging through his veins. His nails dug into his palms as the man leaned over Talauna.

"Come on, sweet thing." The guard dragged her along, gripping her arm so tight he left marks. "You're next."

The Maolori struggled, wild-eyed, terror and betrayal twisting her features. She shook her head vigorously, and dug her bare heels into the stone floor, tugging with all her might to get him to release his grip. She scratched and clawed at him, and the guard let out a yell as she grazed his eye. He raised his arm as if to deal her a blow. He stood only a couple of feet away now...

Do it, brute. Maurin poised to spring. His knuckles turned white on the short chain of his shackles. *Just give me an excuse.*

The guard struck the girl full across the face, rocking her head back. A drop of blood dribbled down her lip, and she moved feebly against the wall, but that didn't stop him from jabbing her in the side with his shock cudgel. Her body jolted once, then lay still. The guard barked a grating laugh as she lost control of herself.

"Stupid wench," he growled. "Ought to know better."

Maurin was on him in an instant, unaware of crossing the few feet between him and the guard. He swung the chain around, sending the stun weapon clattering out of the guard's grasp. Maurin used his locked fists as a club, connecting with the iron jaw of the older man. The chain struck him across the face and ear.

The guard outweighed Maurin by half, but wasn't expecting the attack. He staggered back, his face contorting into a sneering mask of fury. "You're in for it now, maggot!"

A meaty fist whistled toward Maurin's face, clipping his ear as he side-stepped. He scooted away, but the chains on his feet prevented swift movement, and he didn't have much space to dodge.

"You sweet on her or something, boy?" The burly man grinned at Maurin, his face foul and evil under his shaven pate. "Maybe I'll just take this one back home with me for the night, and sell her tomorrow when I'm done with her. What do you say?"

The man swung again. Maurin deflected the blow and looped his chain around the guard's wrist. He climbed up over the man's knee, leapt around, and landed on his back. Maurin pulled the guard's arm up to his shoulder, wrapping it around his neck. He looped the remainder of the chain around the man's throat, then put his head in an arm lock, and squeezed as hard as he could.

The guard's startled roar was cut short and turned into a gurgle. He pulled at Maurin's arm, but Maurin had his neck in a vise grip.

The man beneath him sagged to his knees. Talauna was recovering, blinking in confusion at the melee. Her eyes widened, and she pointed over his shoulder.

"Maurin, behind you!" Coparal's voice sounded distant, surreal.

But the warning came too late. A shock cudgel hit him below the ribs, and he went slack, dropping with the guard onto the damp floor, his useless limbs jumbled into a pile. His muscles would not respond to his commands, and consciousness threatened to desert him. As the other guards disentangled the choking man from his chains, Maurin barely heard the words: "You're dead, slave."

———— ◆ ————

Valasand had chosen this inn for its low profile; certainly there were less humble places to stay, even on the budget she allotted herself. After the events of the other night, well...

She should have picked a place a little more fortified, that's all. At least her time at the Office of Estates had been fruitful, but as long as there was unfinished business, this would be her home.

"I won't be gone long."

Valasand closed the wooden door, which no doubt looked good when it was painted a hundred years ago. She wended her way down the narrow halls and dark stairs. The tables and benches of the long hall lay empty, the air still redolent of ale, bread, and steak. She left the hostelry and readied herself for another fruitless trip to the marketplace.

Nothing but silence the last few days, naturally.

Click, click, click... the staff measured her steps, and she turned down one street and up another until she came to the now-familiar open square of pavilions. A fountain with a spouting statue of some sort of mythical cetacean rose from its center. The usual ambling about and shopping frenzies had been replaced by an edgy focus on the necessities. The handful of people around her grabbed their wares, paid, and left without lingering. Many glanced around as if fearful of another attack.

Today is the day, Little Flame.

"Oh, there you are. Do you know what's been going on here since you've been gone?" She was pushing, yes, but after the last few days, it was difficult to pretend she wasn't in a foul mood. "Do you have any idea what I'm up against?"

I have some idea, yes.

"That's encouraging. Care to elaborate any, or are you going to leave me to guess?"

The voice was suddenly imperative. *Eyes sharp, now, ears open, and mouth closed.*

Valasand's senses came to full alert, and she froze, her question unanswered. A commotion was growing off to her left. Nervous shoppers and pedestrians jumped to make way as a young woman burst into view, an angry mob at her heels. Sweat and grime blurred her gaunt features, her white gown tattered and soiled. She ran past Valasand, cries of "Soulstealer! Kill the Reamar!" hurled after her.

The girl stumbled, sprawling onto the stones of the street. A fresh-faced member of the local constabulary raised a long, forked weapon. Some sort of electric bolt-thrower, Valasand guessed. With a sharp crackle, a jagged blue arc scorched the corner of the wall mere inches from the young woman's head. Wild-eyed, she staggered to her feet. Then, gasping for breath, she sprinted down the alley, the crowd in hot pursuit.

Valasand grimaced and drew in a hissing breath. She did not want to give away her identity, but she was running out of options. She couldn't allow this mob to murder the girl, whatever she had done. More weapons fired. Her lips tightened. But even as she renewed her grip on her staff and moved forward, the cries of outrage abated.

Following a few moments of silence, Valasand waited until the people emerged from the alley, walking away disconsolately and muttering in confusion. Before they could all disperse, she grabbed the shoulder of one of the young men, a greasy type whose clothes reeked of some sort of disreputable-smelling smoke.

"What happened here?"

Resentment burned in his narrow-lidded eyes. For a moment it seemed he would retort, but he jerked his head toward the alley.

"Stinking Reamar witch," he said. "We had her. She ducks behind some crates, and pops right back out again. That's when my man Sinsan hits her, right here." He pointed to his side. "Tore a hole clean through her. But she just keeps running, with nary a burn mark. So Sinsan shoots again, right between her shoulders. Just goes right through, like she isn't even there. Then she turns, all—what's the word? See-through."

"Transparent?"

"Yeah, transparent. Before you know, she's just a green cloud of mist, and disappears in the wind." The young man cursed the girl for a witch again, and his eyes darted about, as if he expected her to reach out of thin air to grab him where he stood. "Getting to be so no one's safe anymore."

"She was clearly a threat to you." Valasand wanted to ask the man what a Reamar was, but at her sarcasm, he snorted, cursed, and bustled off down the street.

She searched the alley for any signs of the girl, but found none. Strange things were happening on this world, and Valasand needed some time to reflect. Was there some connection between this Reamar and the bizarre events of the other night? The city remained in a state of near-panic.

She found a small cafe far enough off the main street that the smell of animal dung and too many people wouldn't overpower what she ate. She drank the astringent Waters of Cleansing before taking a bite of the meat the owner brought out to her. A bit overdone, but it had a hearty flavor she found refreshing. The tangy jelly served with it just made her thirsty. After paying the barkeep, she rejoined the mid-afternoon crowd of the general market.

A few slaves were out buying things for their masters, and several more of the constabulary moved through the crowd, their fingers close to the triggers of their weapons. One of the officers bought a couple of fruits from a vendor and tossed one to his comrade. At least some humanity existed in the city. Valasand leaned for a moment with her back to the wall of a private residence.

"Are you the Dreaded One?"

She whirled to face the speaker. It was the woman chased through the marketplace. No one had been anywhere near; she had just appeared, a child delivered from the womb of another dimension.

"Excuse me?"

"The Dreaded One." Wide-spaced green eyes searched her out from under a veil of tangled hair, and the young woman hugged herself.

Hard not to pity the girl despite the shock. Rips in the young woman's dress encroached on her modesty, and beneath her thin garment, her ribs could easily be counted. Her sunken cheeks spoke of weeks without proper food. Still, she seemed none the worse for wear from her encounter with the mob. Valasand could see no sign of any wounds. She doffed her cloak and reached out to wrap it around the girl's shoulders.

The girl jerked away, fear and distrust in her eyes. Her breathing was shallow and tremulous. "Don't touch me, human!"

Human? Interesting.

Valasand replaced her cloak and stood a respectful distance away, leaning on her staff. "All right, then. Are you hurt?"

The dark-haired girl sniffed. "It would take more than rabble like that to injure the Reamar."

"What are the Reamar?"

"You are a Warden of the Gates and know not the Reamar?" the young woman said incredulously.

Valasand threw her a sharp look. "How did you know I'm a Warden? There are no Wells on this world."

"For ages, the Reamar have looked for the Dreaded One. His coming was foretold."

"*His* coming? I think you have me mistaken for someone else."

"Man or woman, we do not know. A few of the chained still remember how to read the stars, and await the coming of one who will deliver them from bondage. But the Reamar believe the arrival of the liberator is the knell of destruction for us. I give you fair warning: Leave this world immediately, the way you came."

"I appreciate the warning, but I cannot leave."

"You must!"

"Even if I wanted to, I could not. The ship which bore me here has departed."

"Then you will die, for the Reamar know the Dreaded One is coming. When they discover you here, they will send a horde to kill you."

Valasand thought for a moment, then seized the girl's wrist. "Come with me."

"And just where do you think you're taking me?" she said, almond-shaped eyes wide with alarm.

"Somewhere you'll be safe."

The Reamar girl pulled back, twisting out of her grasp with shaky defiance. "No... no! I am free now; I have gotten away from them, and I will not be slave to a human. I would rather die!"

"I do not offer you a life of servitude," Valasand assured, allowing gentle compassion into her voice. "I offer you a new freedom. The choice is yours; I would not force you."

The girl stared at Valasand in growing horror. "Never!" she said, then turned and fled.

Valasand stood gazing in her wake long after she was gone. "I think I just failed horribly."

You will find her in the market, the words came to her again.

"I know. I think I just scared her off."

You will find her in the market.

Her temper started to rise, but then the dread realization hit, and Valasand stopped in her tracks. Not the marketplace, but The Market. The central building of slave trade.

She knew now what she had to do.

Not allowing herself to hesitate at her own reluctance, Valasand stepped to the curb and hailed a large cart pulled by an enormous pachyderm whose front legs were longer than its rear legs. In the driver's seat sat a short, round man with more hair on his face than on his uncovered head, and a floppy sun hat tied around his neck.

How nicely shaded his back must be.

"My name's Padron." A thick cigar never strayed from the corner of the carter's mouth as he grinned at Valasand and gestured to his behemoth of a pack animal. "This here's Poly. Reckon we can get you wherever you need to go. Provided, of course, you gots the money."

"Excellent. Then you and I shall be good friends."

Valasand told the carter where she wanted to go, and the vehicle rattled off. Her mind raced as they made their way through the streets toward that horrible place. She had so much to do.

"After you have dropped me off, I want you to collect a passenger at the hostelry on Jaelsee Street. Then I will need some items picked up."

"Sounds doable."

When they arrived, she gave him more detailed instructions and a list. Valasand handed Padron a number of local coins. "For your trouble." Then she added a larger coin. "For your silence."

The driver eyed the handful joyfully.

"Meet me back here in an hour."

Padron saluted her, and his beast plodded away. Placing her hand on a pillar, Valasand studied the fierce likeness of a tattooed woman painted on a sign. There was intelligence in those eyes, however hidden behind animal fury. The text below the portrait read:

RUNAWAY SLAVE
DANIA "BLOOD GODDESS"
WANTED FOR THE MURDER OF HER MASTER
BARON ROMINAN SEIDES
REWARD OF 5000 BRICA

EXTREMELY DANGEROUS

"I just heard about it this morning," one man nearby said to his female companion. "There was a couple of Argoneis's police talking, and one of them says it was this pit fighter done it. You know, they wasn't even sure it was him for a while—the baron, I mean. They says they couldn't identify what was left of the body except by the rings on his fingers."

"I don't care about her," the woman answered shortly. "If she's out for anyone's blood, it's not going to be ours. I just want to know what's happening with this search for some missing Reamar woman, and if it has anything to do with all those mysterious deaths. If you ask Argoneis's police, they tell you nothing's going on."

"And that you should mind your business," another man said, coming up to them. "But they don't mind asking a bunch of questions people can't answer, trying to scare them into talking."

"They're acting scared themselves. Something isn't right."

The trio moved beyond Valasand's hearing. She considered following them, but she had taken up enough of the day already. She was determined to do this, and do it now. With feet nearly as leaden as her heart, she climbed the steps toward the massive entryway, mustering her resolve as she went. A flood of people boiled through the open doors, and a sickening sense of degradation and shame weighed upon the very walls of the facility. The outer husk of the building was a polished crypt; no persons existed within, just... things.

Upon entering, she was immediately caught up in a din of noise, crowds, and smells. The air was thick and muggy with the presence of hundreds of bodies. Small rectangular openings near the ceiling provided pitifully little ventilation. Dozens of kennels were positioned around the windowless walls, each one housing a variety of slaves. Those not exhibited on the auction blocks were chained to the walls behind great bars or in spike-edged pits allowing no thought of escape. Most of the slaves were human, but some were not so clearly defined. Like these Maolori; according to the archives Valasand had perused, they were indigenous. Certainly she had seen them on no other world. Valasand made out a few large equine-looking creatures toward the back that seemed more like livestock than slave fodder, while a hawker rattled off something about the wild folk of the woods. But she had more pressing things to do than to catalogue new races and listen to merchants' spiels. She mingled with the crowd, peering here and there, searching the cages.

She would know what she was looking for when she found it.

CHAPTER 11
LEAP OF FAITH

"Maurin. Maurin, wake up."

His head throbbed, and every word stabbed into his brain. Maurin squeezed his eyes tighter to shut out the pain. The voice rang in his ears again.

"I no kidding, Maurin. Get up."

"Leave me alone." The ground spun, and he tasted bile. Somewhere in the back of his mind, he realized he must have vomited, but he didn't care.

"We in trouble, Maurin."

Before him, Maurin saw a trio of Coparals sitting cross-legged on the floor, shimmering like Lake Voyen-Dag at home on a hot day. His eyes closed, and he started to slip back again, but felt a strong grip on his shoulder.

"Steady, my friend. You need be awake now."

Maurin rubbed at his temples and took several deep breaths, waiting for his vision to clear. Every muscle in his body hurt. The only light in the cell came from a barred window on a thick iron door. A number of odors assaulted his nose, none of them pleasant. The old straw scattered on the floor poked at his bare skin. Male voices murmured outside.

"What's going on?"

"I not know," Coparal muttered, "but I not like what that guard say."

"What guard?"

"That one." He nodded off to the window on his left, where the guard conversed in hushed tones with another one of the less savory members of their profession. "The one with the big beard. He looking in again."

"What did he say?"

Coparal flicked his ears. "He say, 'So they like to fight?' and the other one say, 'Keep them. They might meet his needs.'"

"Meet whose needs?" Maurin's voice came out a hoarse whisper. He didn't want to speculate, though he suspected anyway. He didn't like hot temper being on anyone's list of requirements in a slave.

"I not know." The small Maolori man gave him a resentful glare. "Be quiet! I cannot hear what they say."

Maurin clamped his mouth shut, but all was silent outside their cell. Coparal was right; they were in trouble, no doubt about it.

Maurin winced, gingerly checking himself for any serious wounds. He was bruised and battered all over. The guards, while careful not to do anything lethal or permanently damaging, had not been above giving him more than a few well-placed kicks and punches. He didn't know what they were waiting for, but he obviously couldn't be sold in the condition he was in. They had somehow avoided summary execution, but he wouldn't be surprised if the guards had persuaded someone to make an example of him and Coparal. Maurin was not eager to die; still, the simplistic finality of that kind of escape held an unnatural appeal.

A few moments passed, and he heard a key turning in the lock. A bald man whose gut hung over his breeches entered, followed by a pair of hefty guards. He motioned to Maurin and Coparal. "They're the ones. Get them up and take them to the northwest stall. Lord Argoneis should be here presently to inspect them."

Maurin felt the bottom drop out of his stomach. Argoneis. It would have been better if they had been killed. Visions of dying a bloody death in a gladiators' arena—or worse, tortured endlessly for the Lord Regent's personal amusement—filled his head, and he struggled to stay on his feet.

The guards escorted them none-too-gently out of the cell, up some broad stairs, and into the bright din of the open market. They led them to a large, barred enclosure toward the back, well away from the main goods. The lead guard told them to keep their eyes down and not to interact with anyone.

"Look," Coparal murmured.

Maurin glanced over at the dozen or so other slaves in the kennel. Desolate, the Maolori girl sat against the wall, somewhat disheveled, her mouth bruised, but otherwise unharmed.

"Are you all right?" Maurin asked, before he remembered he was not supposed to speak. The guard clouted him, then manacled him and Coparal low against the wall.

As soon as they left, Talauna got up and walked over to Maurin. Kneeling, she gazed sadly over his body. She lifted his tangled locks out of his eyes and ran a tentative finger over his bruised cheek and forehead. If her expression was any reflection of what she saw, Maurin figured he must look pretty awful.

He forced a smile. "It's not as bad as it appears."

She didn't respond, but seemed skeptical. After a few moments, she put her back to the wall next to him and sat down. He glanced at her to see if she intended to say anything, but she was already lost in a world of her own.

Maurin tried to look both disinterested and uninteresting. He kept his face blank as he gazed out at the onlookers. The first prayer in months rose unbidden to his lips. "Baelon help us."

Maurin yelped in surprise and pain at a sudden jab in the ribs; Coparal's elbow had found a tender spot. Considering the shape he was in, Maurin would have been surprised if it hadn't.

"What?" he growled, rubbing at his side. "I'm trying to think of a way out of this." Not that anything was coming to him, but being jostled was not conducive to inspiration. Coparal stared intently out into the crowd.

Coming toward them, led by the big-bearded guard from the cell, were two men conversing in hushed tones. One was a slight, graceful man with the darting gaze of a raptor on the hunt. The other was a caramel-skinned giant with long black hair. They walked forward among the rows of slaves. Every tenth one or so, the smaller man would stop and inspect, lifting the head by putting his thumb under his or her chin, or sticking his fingers into the slave's mouth to inspect the teeth. After a moment, he nodded to the muscular man, who drew aside one of the women from the ranks. The slavers took her away, and the men continued walking.

When they were within a few feet of Maurin, the trio stopped. After a few moments of talk, the bearded man gestured to the dais upon which they all sat, and the guard let them into the kennel. No doubt about who the blond man was. Daman Argoneis positively reeked of evil.

A wave of fear washed over him. And he wasn't the only one. Even the toughest slaves quaked as Argoneis approached. Yet the Lord Regent was not reciprocally impressed; if anything, he seemed distracted.

"So what are we going to do about the situation with the Reamar, my lord?" asked the dark-skinned man.

Argoneis yanked down on the lip of the strong male captive standing manacled before him, eliciting an angry groan. One glance at Daman's bodyguard, however, quenched the fire in the man's eyes, and he cast his gaze down in impotent shame.

"Put this one aside for the arena. We shall honor the memory of Lord Seides with a spectacle no one shall forget."

"My lord?"

"Yes, yes... the Reamar. Krige told me they are searching for a missing priestess. I've informed their emissary that I know nothing about her, and they should keep better track of their women. This Vail character had the gall to tell me that I would do well to look more closely after the affairs of my cities. Cheeky, aren't they? It's been a long time since anyone has dared to threaten me." An expression of something that might have been admiration crossed over Argoneis's features. "Still, this little incident shouldn't go unpunished, should it? Tell them the usual shipment will not be forthcoming until suitable recompense has been made for my losses."

"Yes, my lord."

Talauna had her head down, her face buried in her arms. Argoneis did not seem to notice her sitting there. Instead, he headed toward

Coparal. His bodyguard made the young Maolori stand up, and Daman nodded. Coparal shot Maurin a pleading look, and was gone, snatched away for the pleasure of the Lord Regent.

Still deep in conversation with his lieutenant, Argoneis gave Maurin a cursory glance, then moved on. He exited the building with his new acquisitions, leaving queasy terror in his wake. Above, a large bird flapped through the room and out the window. A white feather settled near Maurin's hand.

He sat in stunned disbelief for a long time. Guilt over the loss of Coparal came at him in waves. Hopefully the end would come quickly for him. At the same time, Maurin had just been given a reprieve, and part of him rejoiced.

Suddenly, Talauna's head jerked up. Maurin followed her gaze out across the drove of customers, and focused on a fiery shock of red-gold hair. A woman wearing a long cloak of two-toned gray animal fur wound her way through the crowd with assurance. People seemed to part the way before her. A broad silver necklace fell below the line of her caftan, but she wore no other discernible jewelry. Maurin had seen a total of five woodsmen in Caileen in his two years on Argoth, but this one seemed better kempt, and more decorously situated than those.

The woman with the red hair walked up to the barred edge of the kennel, leaning on a long wooden staff. She glanced over, moved past...

And abruptly stopped, turning back to lock piercing gray eyes with Talauna's. To Maurin's surprise, the Maolori girl got up and reached through the bars, grasping the stranger's hand with desperate strength.

When Talauna let go, the red-haired woman stroked her head. "At last. Poor dear. You have suffered long and searched even longer. Fear not. You will be safe with me."

Talauna motioned her head toward Maurin.

The red-haired woman looked casually through the bars and into Maurin's soul. He flinched and averted his eyes.

"And do you think you are worthy?"

"Worthy?" Maurin stammered and looked up again. Being spoken to by a prospective buyer was unheard of, and her question was as nonsensical as it was unexpected. He cleared his throat. "Worthy of what?"

"Of fulfilling your dreams." The woman smiled disconcertingly, then leaned forward and continued. "You will be tried. You will be forged. You will be conquered, and you will be victorious. Should you choose to go with me, your life will never again be what it was. Make no mistake; the choice is yours, but once you make it, there is no turning back."

Worthy of his dreams? What did she know of his dreams? And what dreams? He didn't have any dreams to be worthy of. Aric, perhaps. His dreams were notorious. But him? Perhaps she was mistaken in choosing him. And what kind of person chose her slaves on the basis of their dreams? This was altogether too strange.

Maurin was on the edge of a precipice, looking out over a new and alien landscape. His face flushed, and his palms began to sweat. He clenched his fists. He had never liked making decisions on the spur of the moment, and he knew he would have to choose his words carefully.

"I don't know what you want of me, or expect me to do." He glanced aside, then back at the woman, whose eyes waited for his through the bars. "But you're obviously not like the rest of these"—he indicated the swarm of so-called humanity about them—"*people*. Take us both out of here"— he gestured to Talauna, who was watching the interaction somberly—"and I promise I won't disappoint you."

The woman smiled. "It is dangerous to make promises that may be difficult to keep." She considered him for another moment. "Very well, then."

She walked off in the direction of one of the traders, leaving Maurin to stare in wonder and growing anticipation.

"I will take those two."

The man cast a scornful glance over the woman's shoulder at her selection and told her she would have to wait. She transfixed him with a look, murmured something Maurin couldn't hear, and the man paled and offered a price immediately.

The red-haired woman didn't say anything, but she must have found the offer unsatisfactory, because she continued to stare at him, and after a few seconds of uncomfortable silence, he flustered, and named a much lower sum. After a few more moments of this odd one-sided haggling, he reached a price the woman must have found acceptable, because she nodded and said, "Have them made ready."

As she turned away, the man's shoulders slumped as though he had just been through a wrestling match. When the woman turned her gray eyes back in Maurin's direction, however, she was smiling pleasantly. She walked back to the cage and leaned as close to Talauna as the bars would allow, addressing the Maolori girl.

"You are worth infinitely more," she said in a conspiratorial tone, her eyes incongruously merry. "But since I am the only one here who seems to have any idea of your true value, I don't see why they should profit from your sale."

Slowly, hesitantly, Talauna smiled.

One of the slavers undid Maurin's shackles, then led him and Talauna out of the kennel to present them to their new mistress.

"Come along." Their new owner left them to walk behind her, exchanging puzzled glances. Chilled by the breeze, Maurin headed out the wide entryway of the Market and into the open streets of the city. All the same, it was good to be breathing something approximating fresh air again.

"My name is Valasand Del Siriné," the woman said at last. "You may call me Valasand."

A large balodont waited at the curb, harnessed to a cart. A man with a cigar sat watching stoically as Valasand ushered her new acquisitions to the back, and Maurin got his second big shock of the day. A cowled figure sat hunched in the cart, looking up at him with an expectant smile.

"*Aric?*"

"Shhhh!" His cousin glanced around worriedly. "You keep asking me that, and it's still me. Hey, Talauna," Aric added, seemingly unsurprised at her presence. He turned back to Maurin. "What happened to you two?"

"Never mind that!" Maurin's shock transformed to elation. What were the odds? Reunited, separated, and reunited again... "What are you doing here?"

"I escaped." Aric shrugged as Maurin helped Talauna into the cart, and then clambered up onto the hard bench opposite him. The cart was stocked with all manner of fruits, vegetables, breads, fresh and dried meats, cheese, honey, spices, and various other foodstuffs, as well as a couple of large casks of water. It was so loaded down that they had to clear small spaces to sit. "I got caught. Twice in one night, as a matter of fact." He grinned at Valasand, who nodded.

"I see you two are acquainted."

"We're cousins," Maurin explained, still reeling.

"Well, that saves me some time," Valasand said cryptically, then limped around to the front and climbed up next to the carter. She conferred briefly with him, he gave the reins a snap, and the cart jolted into motion. The beast pulling the cart didn't seem to be straining in the slightest. Aric gnawed on a strip of jerky, and Talauna munched a cluster of grapes.

Maurin wasn't hungry. To be taken from Aric just after finding him—it was like a cruel tease. But to find each other now; the coincidence was astronomical. Who was this woman, with her large walking stick, her well-stocked purse, and her apparent habit of picking up strays?

They headed back toward the business district, which seemed to distress the Maolori girl. She sat bolt upright, agitated, until, after a few minutes, the driver pulled over to the curb, and Valasand exited.

"Wait for me."

The carter shrugged and nodded amiably.

Valasand entered a low gray stone building, her quick strides punctuated by the tap-tap of her staff on the pavement.

Once she was inside, Maurin turned to Aric. "You escaped?"

"Like I said, not for long."

"Why are you here? Why weren't you returned to Lord Krige?"

"Maurin, would you shut up?" Aric hissed in Aran. "I didn't tell the constable."

"What constable?" Maurin took his cue to switch over, too.

"Just as I was getting out of the mansion, I see a murder—well, a killing, anyway. The strangest thing I've seen; this girl sucks the life right out of this guy who's attacking her."

"The same thing happened to my master!"

"I'm pretty sure they were Reamar. Anyway, while I'm still trying to figure out what I've just seen, Argoneis's goons grab me from behind. One of them is killed by some phantom thing, and the other one is all set to take me to Argoneis, but this woman—Valasand—walks up. She claims I'm her runaway slave, and says she'll take me off his hands. At first, he isn't so sure, but she says something I don't quite catch about the Temple of Yasul, and he lets me go without a peep. So when he's gone, she comes up to me, and asks me what's wrong. Her voice sounds familiar, but I can't quite place it. And I give her this look, like, I'm an escaped slave; what do you think is wrong, you stupid muck-rat?"

Maurin glanced around to see if the carter was listening, but he wouldn't understand Aran anyway.

Aric pressed on: "Anyway, she says she wants to take me with her, and I say I don't mind, but I've got this cousin, and I want to find him."

"Thanks for putting in a good word for me." Maurin reached forward and punched Aric playfully on the arm.

Aric cried out in pain, hissing an oath at him.

"Sorry," Maurin said, startled. "I got carried away."

"Don't mention it." Aric pursed his lips and punched him back on an unbruised shoulder, twice as hard, and raising a knuckle to target a nerve. Aric always knew where someone's sensitive spots lay.

One of his less-missed qualities.

Maurin drew in a deep breath and massaged his abused shoulder.

"What's the matter with you? Did someone beat you too?"

"Not exactly." Aric unstrung his tunic and pulled back a bandage on his bare shoulder. "I had an accident," he said, with an ironic smirk. Where his slave brand should have been was a still-oozing scab. "Kind of stupid, huh? I don't know who I thought I was going to fool."

"That's illegal! You could have been flogged, or killed!"

"I could have been. Who knows what would have happened if Valasand hadn't shown up, pretending to be my owner? Not quite what I had in mind, but..." Aric shrugged.

Euphoria started to well up in Maurin. "But we're finally together again."

Aric scowled. "For all the good it will do us."

"What did Valasand say to you? Do you know who she is?"

"Not really." Aric glanced away. "But she looked familiar."

"She looked familiar?" Maurin nearly fell over. "You agreed to go with this woman because she looked familiar?"

"It was that or go to Argoneis's dungeon. I didn't have to think about it that hard."

"I know, I know. It's just..." He shook his head. "I guess I was hoping it was something more."

"An act of the gods?" Aric rolled his eyes.

"If Baelon has brought us here together after all this time, there must be a reason for it."

"Baelon is a god of another life, Maurin. Another world. Give it up. Give *him* up."

Ignoring him, Maurin glanced over at Talauna and smiled. Her whole countenance lit up, and she flashed a dazzling smile back. His face got hot, and he turned away.

"Besides," Aric said, grinning, "I knew you would be coming along soon enough."

Maurin drew a sharp breath. "Did you dream about this, too? Is this Valasand the woman of your dreams?"

"Not—well, maybe." Aric seemed unsettled. "I just recognized her, that's all. Unless you can figure out where we've met her before and just forgotten, I must have dreamed about her."

"You didn't tell her that, did you?"

Aric crossed his arms over his chest. "I might have mentioned the possibility."

"Oh, no." Maurin felt sick. He could see where this was heading.

"And she gets this funny look, like she's not sure whether to smile or what. Then she says she doesn't believe we've ever met."

"And so naturally, you told her you knew her from your dreams. You know, this isn't like back home, cousin. Being tactless here can get you killed."

Aric ignored him in turn. "Anyway, she says she wouldn't be surprised."

Maurin didn't reply. He leaned back and exhaled slowly through his lips. Talauna watched the interchange with interest, though of course there was no way she could understand Aran.

"She wouldn't be surprised!" Aric repeated. "Nobody's ever said that to me."

"I have."

"Besides you." Aric ran his fingers through his hair. "Anyway, I told her about my plans to go and get you at the vineyards. She says everything is going to be all right, and tells me to stay here—said she was going out to search for someone. But she never did tell me why she saved me from the constable, or what she expects of me—us, now."

Maurin didn't say anything for a moment.

"So what do you make of it?" Aric pressed.

"I don't know. Right now, I'm not even sure it makes any difference. But maybe she can help you interpret your dreams. There's something different about her."

"Here she comes."

Maurin glanced over the edge of the cart. Their new owner had emerged from the building with an armful of parcels. Maurin leapt down to help her get them into the cart, passing them up to Aric and Talauna.

"Thank you, Maurin. Our first order of business was to get all of you some proper clothes."

Talauna leapt up and dug into the parcels until she found a mint-green tunic and a darker pair of pantaloons. With a pleased sigh, she shucked off her filthy toga and tossed it aside.

Maurin's eyes bugged. The carter did a double-take.

The Maolori girl held the garments up, caressing them and letting the fabric slide through her fingers, then holding them against her chest, seeming to enjoy the feel of the cloth.

"Come on, now," their new owner said quietly. "We can't have you distracting the boys."

It was on the tip of Maurin's tongue to object that she wasn't a distraction, but he realized such a statement would be self-contradictory, and so said nothing. Disappointment and relief wrestled in his mind as Talauna slipped into her new clothes.

"You can close your mouth now, Maurin," Aric said.

He gulped. "Sorry."

"It's just Talauna."

"What?"

"Don't think too much of it. That's just her. Don't be surprised if you occasionally have to remind her to get dressed in the mornings."

"Oh. That's, ah... interesting."

Chagrined, Talauna sat down facing away from them.

"She's a Maolori. I don't think they wear much in the forests, and it's not like Krige encouraged her to change that habit."

"I see."

"I trust that you two won't mind waiting until we've arrived at our destination to try on your clothes," Valasand said dryly.

Maurin coughed.

Their new mistress strode toward the carter, handing him what looked like a deed or property title. "Do you know where this is, Padron?"

"Uh, yeah." He seemed somewhat surprised. "But that's outside the city walls. Ain't nobody lives out there, except Woodsmen. Meaning no offense, Ma'am."

"None taken." Valasand hoisted herself into the cart more nimbly than Maurin would have given her credit for and situated herself in the back with her slaves.

The Maolori perched herself on the side of the vehicle as they rode out of the city gates and across one of the causeways. They left Caileen behind and headed down the mountain, plodding down several paths before turning off onto a little-used unpaved byway. They entered a forested region, and Talauna's ears pricked up.

"You know," Padron said, guiding his animal around a fallen tree, "you're the first customer who wanted me to take them anywhere outside the city."

"Hmmmm," Valasand said.

"Not that the city's much safer, now, I suppose," Padron said. "Strange goings-on. Folks around are talking. Shuttering their windows and barring their doors now, let me say."

Valasand's eyes narrowed. "Do you know what's happening?"

"We've got some folk from the outlying cities coming in for sanctuary. They think something bad's coming, and soon. Got some weird tales to tell. Strange talk about whole towns full of walking dead men, and the woods filled with dark spirits. Say the Reamar are on the move."

"Thank you for your concern."

If the dead were walking, Maurin mused, it wouldn't matter how many walls and shutters lay between them and the living.

Aric murmured something that sounded like "your dead will rise against you."

Maurin frowned. "What did you say?"

"Nothing."

"Now I don't really believe all that scat," Padron said, "but still, you never know what manner of beasts might be lurking around out there. And after the other night, ain't nowhere seems safe."

"No," Valasand agreed.

Padron steered the balodont into a glade grown over with broad-leafed plants. Judging from the amount of vegetation, no one had bothered to keep the mountain path up. The sunlight struggled to reach the forest floor.

He maneuvered the cart to a halt, and Maurin gazed at their destination. In the middle of a large clearing stood high stone walls, abutting the mountain on the north side, and obscuring any view of what lay within. The place had clearly been deserted for years, with vines and various other flora growing up the sides of the walls and starting to split the stone.

Aric spat. "Beautiful."

"It's, ah, botanically enhanced," Maurin ventured.

"Very funny," Valasand said.

"You be careful, okay?" Padron cautioned as they exited the cart. The pack-beast strained to reach Talauna. She stroked its neck and muzzle while it drooled over her shoulder.

"We shall."

Aric ran his hand over the wall. "Someone's been here recently. See where the ivy has been pulled away?"

Maurin came over to investigate. Testing the gates, he said, "I think it's deserted."

Valasand shook her head at Padron when he offered to help unload the cart. He looked uncomfortable at being told to stay put while the others did the work. They set the food outside the gate, to be taken inside once he had been dismissed.

"Come back every seven days, saying nothing of our whereabouts," Valasand said, "and I will be faithful to pay you well. We will need further supplies, and occasional transport into the city."

"Thank you, Ma'am. We'll be here, like you say." Padron clicked his tongue at his beast. With a great creak and rattle, the cart turned, and the unlikely duo lumbered back the way they had come.

Two ancient iron rings were driven deep into the wood of the gates. At a nod from Valasand, Maurin and Aric each took one, and pulled with all their might. For a moment, nothing happened, then, with an enormous groan, the doors reluctantly ground open on their unused hinges. Valasand and Talauna went inside, and Maurin and Aric followed, huffing.

"I think someone's just walled off a section of the forest here," Aric said. "Are you sure there's a house somewhere in all this?"

"No doubt you can find it," Valasand said.

Walking on a cobbled path nearly obscured by the growth, they pushed their way through grasses taller in some spots than they were. At last they came to a large, L-shaped structure overlooking the courtyard and integrated with two of the walls. The doors to the mansion opened with surprisingly little difficulty.

"The first thing we need to do," Valasand said upon entering the dark aperture of the massive door frame, "is get some light in here. Then we can bring in the food."

Valasand groped along the corridor for a torch. Maurin left the doors open to illuminate the hall while they explored. The hall branched in three directions, and in the dim light he saw statues, suits of ancient armor, and archaic weapons lining the walls. Before them stood a wider foyer, with a broad stone staircase branching up into both wings of the enormous dwelling.

Valasand stepped forward into the foyer, then held up her hand to stop the others where they were.

"This is a beautiful historical mansion," Maurin said, almost running into her. "Some of these are probably museum pieces. Do you know why it was just left like this?"

"Maurin, hush."

"What?"

An enraged shriek sounded in the echoing confines of the halls. In an instant, Valasand's staff was up, just in time to block a blow coming at her from one of the recesses in the wall.

CHAPTER 12
NO CHAINS

There is a moment when dream and reality intersect, an overlap or echo, when everything comes together, and there's not much more you can do than watch it all play out. Had he dreamed of this? Hard to say, but there's a kind of synchronicity to it anyway, a sense that this was all somehow meant to be.

Aric turned at the scream, but everything flowed in languid motion. Vague impressions of predators—a snarling wolf, a pouncing spider, a striking snake—all coalesced into a tattooed female warrior emerging from the shadows of the foyer, beautiful face twisted into a chilling snarl.

Ah. The Blood Goddess. Wasn't expecting to see her here, but then, so many strange things were happening lately. Aric's eyes flicked over her, head to toe. A pair of mismatched daggers were sheathed at broad hips. She wore an ancient leather breastplate—not the one he was used to seeing in the arena. It seemed ill-fitting, somehow, but she had clearly gathered some other armor for herself. Sandals adorned her feet, and studded leather protected her forearms, one of which still bore a manacle and some links of chain.

Well, this should be interesting.

The tattooed woman swept a halberd at Valasand, but she ducked. The blade smashed into the wall, sending powder and chunks of stone flying.

Aric flinched. Valasand had gone out of her way to keep him safe. She had brought Maurin back into his life. He didn't really want to see her end up as one more stroke mark on Dania's tally, but it was hard to know what to feel. Events just floated around him, searching for some meaning to attach to.

Before her assailant could retrieve her weapon, Valasand rolled up against it, snapping the shaft. The heavy blade clattered to the ground.

Aric huffed. That was unexpected.

The Blood Goddess blinked, but recovered quickly. She spun, thrusting the splintered end of the long handle at Valasand.

Valasand dodged, grabbing her attacker's arm and pulling her forward. Dania appeared to trip, then jumped into a forward roll and came up twirling the broken shaft. She stood back and gauged her opponent. Valasand smiled, holding her staff at the ready.

Aric's heart quickened; this beat the best seats in the arena. He shot a glance at Maurin, who seemed frozen in distress at his inability to defend their new mistress. Aric's mouth quirked up at the corner. Clearly his cousin was more worried about the outcome than Aric was. But for all the times people had fallen to the Blood Goddess, no one had been able to disarm her. The two women circled each other in a kind of dance, the expansive whorl of tattoos gliding over pearl-white skin, the swinging tail of red-gold hair, the fur cloak rippling and sweeping with every move.

Dania flew at Valasand again, bringing the shaft down toward her head in a murderous arc. Valasand deflected the blow and swept her own staff around, striking the other in the back of the knees. The warrior went down with a cry, but leapt to her feet again. Two knives appeared in her hands.

Scarcely limping. Gods, she was tough. Aric caught Maurin's eye, scandalizing him with a grin. Talauna remained at a more-than-safe distance, eyes and mouth wide open.

Valasand herself did not appear upset, or even particularly exerted. Truth be told, their new owner looked like someone enjoying a rousing game. Her smile broadened as she addressed the Blood Goddess. "You're very good."

Dania said nothing, but eyed her with suspicion. Maurin seemed to have stopped fretting. He gave Aric a shrug and tilt of the head as if to say help would be impractical, if not superfluous, at this point.

"I own this house now," Valasand continued, lowering her staff, "but you are welcome to stay with me for as long as you care to."

The Blood Goddess snarled, and the dangling chain clinked as she swung a dagger for effect. "Why would I want to do that?"

Valasand shrugged and gestured toward the gates. "The choice is yours, of course. You are not obligated to remain. But you are a hunted woman, Dania; I saw a reward posted for you in town. If you leave now, you will be on your own."

The warrior furtively searched Valasand and the others for any signs of treachery. Her eyes widened when she saw Aric.

"You!"

"Afraid so." He grinned. "I get that a lot lately."

Giving Aric a wide berth, Dania put away her knives and returned her attention to Valasand. "And how do I know you're not going to turn me in yourself?"

"Let me see your wrist." Valasand beckoned Dania closer.

The warrior hesitated, then slowly offered her right hand, keeping her left near her knife hilt.

Deep gouges scored the lock of the warrior's manacle. Some scratches on her wrist; whatever instrument she used in the attempt to remove it had slipped more than once. Maurin noticed, too; he grimaced, his eyes flicking to Aric's.

"Come outside with me." Over her shoulder, Valasand called out, "Aric, there's another halberd on the wall. Bring it."

Aric reached up to unhook the weapon hanging right behind Maurin's head. "This what you were looking for?" he murmured.

Maurin swiveled and flushed. Together, they followed Valasand into the courtyard. Near the path was a stone fallen from a ruined tower.

"Kneel," Valasand said.

Dania held back, wary.

"You're just going to have to trust me. Put your arm on the stone."

Without a word, the tattooed warrior knelt, stretching forth her arm. Her eyes never left Valasand's. Valasand, without a glance over her shoulder, reached back to Aric, and he silently traded her the halberd for her staff. She grasped the weapon near the end, paused for a moment, and swung it in a long arc straight down. Maurin winced as if he expected Dania's hand to fall away with a soft plop.

A sharp ringing pierced the air, and the shackle clattered to the ground in two empty pieces. Dania's face was an intricate medley of astonishment and disbelief as she stared at Valasand, taking her eyes from her for a split second to look at her wrist, then back up.

Aric released his breath. A grudging respect began to grow for this mysterious woman who had somehow managed to do the impossible. Maurin was back. Talauna was out from under Krige's shadow. And in losing this round, the Blood Goddess was a winner by her own definition.

Yes, things were shaping up nicely.

"Have you had anything to eat?" Valasand asked.

"Not in a few days," Dania said.

"I'm sure everybody's famished by now. You can help us bring the food in. While Talauna and I do something about dinner, you and the boys fetch some firewood, then see about getting this house ready for occupation." Valasand brushed her hands against her cloak, turned her back on the dumbfounded woman, and headed toward the gate.

"No chains," Aric commented as he sauntered past.

Dania silenced him with a nasty look, but followed them outside.

———◆———

The upper levels of the mansion housed the living quarters, and Valasand chose to focus on restoring the wing that seemed in the best repair. She picked a suite at the very end for herself, and to Maurin's further amazement, told them to select their own quarters.

They went through the rooms one by one, evacuating a small family of mammals from one suite and deciding that a nest of birds could stay in the vacant wing until the young were able to fly. Other than those and a small army of spiders, the mansion was remarkably vacant.

A wave of homesickness swept over Maurin, to be replaced with an inexpressible joy. Together again, after so much time of so little hope. Two years of slavery had taught Maurin the art of keeping his mouth shut and doing what he was told. Aric—well, Aric almost had the hang of it. So far, he hadn't gotten them into trouble, but it felt like just a matter of time before his cousin did something rash.

Give him a break. Aric's grown up since you last saw him. Then he noticed Aric's eyes darting over to Dania. Maurin sighed as they entered one of the rooms. *Of course, it is still Aric.*

Maurin stripped the bed and shook the coverlet out the window, sneezing violently. "So"—he nodded toward Dania—"how did you two meet?"

"Just in passing." Aric shrugged. "Seen a few of her matches. How did you escape, anyway?"

Taken aback at being spoken to, Dania answered guardedly, "With much blood."

"Me, too," Aric said.

She straightened up, her tone challenging: "Others', or your own?"

Aric snorted, but didn't answer. He leaned against the wall and watched his cousin work. Maurin had forgotten how quickly Aric could get on one's nerves.

"Outside, you asked if the boy had dreamed of this place. Why?"

The boy? Aric mouthed with a glare. Dania regarded him with somber reflection.

"Because—do you want to give me a hand here, Aric?—because my cousin has a gift."

"Hah!" Aric pounded a pillow in response. Plumes of dust filled the room, causing them all to choke.

"A gift he considers a curse," Maurin amended. "Many of his dreams come to pass. I wouldn't be surprised if he's dreamt of you."

She looked at Aric sharply. "Have you?"

Aric considered long and hard before replying. "Not that I remember."

"Good," she said. "Don't start."

"Now, Valasand is another matter," Aric said.

"Well, regardless of whether or not you dreamt of her, she is our new mistress, and you need to watch what you say around her. I don't care how familiar she may seem; we are still her slaves."

"I'm not an idiot, Maurin."

"You think you're still slaves?" Dania snarled. "You call this slavery? You are idiots." She displayed the narrow raw bands on her wrist where the manacle had been. "Look at your arms." She shook her fists at the ceiling to emphasize her point. "Do you see any shackles? Didn't I tell you, boy, your bondage is only as sure as the chains holding you? Whatever this woman wants you for, it isn't slavery."

———— ◆ ————

Maurin's decision to wash himself before supper turned into a bit of a chore involving multiple trips to the ancient well outside. Unable to find a towel, he mopped himself off with the clothes he wore in the market, then donned the clothing Valasand had bought for him. He tucked the ankles of the loose-fitting pants into high-topped, flexible black boots. Adjusting the wide blue-green sleeves of his tunic, he felt halfway human again.

He rejoined the others just as Valasand called for them. They went down the hall, descended the huge staircase, and followed the light in the corridor off to their left. A low, polished black table sat in the middle of a sunken room. Candles along the mantle and a fire roaring in a broad hearth off to the side provided the illumination. Five padded mats lay on the floor around the table. Valasand and Talauna were putting the finishing touches on dinner, and the unmistakable smells of venison stew and cornbread filled the air. Dania's eyes went wide.

What could have caused the previous occupants of this mansion to abandon it?

I know what it is the masters fear. The night comes on wings, and the dead walk with the living. Entire cities vanish overnight.

The Reamar are on the move.

The flickering flames caused ghostly shadows to dance on the walls, and Maurin flinched when a log popped. A sudden chill raised goose-flesh. He sat down and ate because he was expected to, but somehow, his appetite had gone.

Valasand had Talauna sit beside her, and Aric and Maurin sat across from them. Dania sat to Aric's left at the end of the table. It took a little getting used to, sitting at the same table as their new mistress; even back home, the lower clerics did not eat with the priests. And more unusual yet, Valasand poured their drinks and served the food.

During the course of the meal, Maurin took the opportunity to study his new companions. Valasand was not a large woman, but she had a commanding presence, as well as a mature, intelligent beauty. Clear gray eyes gazed calmly back at her small entourage. The corners of her mouth turned down slightly, giving her a perpetual serious expression that dissolved only in the rare instances when she smiled. Maurin couldn't decide whether the long fur cloak she had finally doffed for the meal was a token nod to a sensual nature from a woman who otherwise denied the flesh, or an effort to enlarge a diminutive frame.

The Maolori girl ate hungrily and in complete silence. She'd not yet spoken a word—or uttered a sound, for that matter—and Maurin was beginning to wonder if she spoke at all. Her disproportionately long fingers, though beautiful in their own right, made using the utensils awkward for her, and she seemed relieved when Valasand told her to just use her hands.

Dania seemed ill at ease as she ate. Her movements were quick and darting, and strong fingers gripped her fork so tightly Maurin thought it would break at any moment. She was totally hairless, so far as he could tell, though it was difficult to say whether it was due to an anomaly of some sort, or rigorous discipline with a razor. Not that she was bad-looking, exactly—in fact, he supposed she was rather attractive, in her own determined and frightening sort of way. Certainly Aric seemed to think so.

Maurin glanced over to the bowl resting beside Aric's plate. "Aric, have you offered those to Dania?"

"No," Aric said. "She doesn't like mushrooms."

"Oh?" Maurin raised his eyebrows. "How do you know?"

Aric shrugged and continued to eat.

"Have you asked?" Maurin put a warning edge in his voice.

Aric picked up the bowl and proffered it to Dania with exaggerated politeness. "Oh, I'm so terribly sorry; did you want any of these?"

"No." She eyed him guardedly, then turned to glare at Maurin. "The boy is right. I don't eat fungus."

Aric mouthed her words to himself again, scowling.

"My mistake." It was hard to tell, sometimes, where Aric's rudeness ended and precognition began.

"I thought you said you hadn't dreamed of me." Dania's eyes narrowed to slits.

Aric shrugged. "I haven't. I just sense things, somehow."

Valasand wiped her mouth and set down her napkin. "Tomorrow morning, you will begin clearing out the courtyard."

"I knew it," Aric muttered.

"Aric!" Maurin prepared to apologize to their new owner, but she didn't seem upset. He made a mental note to rein in his cousin as soon as possible, before he got them into trouble.

After dinner, they spent a few hours cleaning the rooms, until Valasand told them to get some sleep, for they would need their strength tomorrow.

Seeing light from Talauna's room, Maurin touched Aric on the shoulder. "I'll catch up with you in a minute."

The girl's eccentricities intrigued him, her perpetual silence an interesting puzzle to solve. Would she emerge from her shell once she felt safe, among friends? Cautiously, he approached the open door and peeked in.

Talauna stood alone in the middle of the room, turning slowly. She walked around inspecting the knick-knacks, picking them up and setting them down again. She seemed a bit surprised to see Maurin.

"Hi," he said. "Is everything okay?"

The Maolori girl cocked her head and turned her back on him. She pulled back the covers of the bed, then replaced them hurriedly, as if afraid of being caught. Talauna peered over her shoulder again and caught Maurin's inquisitive look. When she seemed satisfied he wasn't going to come in, she went on to inspect the rest of the room, leaving the door open, but seemingly paying no more attention to his presence. She returned to the bed and removed the blankets and sheets in a single wad. Walking over to the corner farthest from the door, she tossed them down onto the floor and started unlacing her tunic. Maurin whirled around to face the stone wall opposite, breathing fast. Once his face had cooled and he heard nothing else behind him, he risked a peek back into her room. Talauna had fully wrapped herself in the bedclothes and nestled deep into their musty warmth. Her new clothes lay in a wad beside the bed.

"Nice to have our own rooms, isn't it?" His voice cracked a bit in his attempt to sound casual, and he cleared his throat. Talauna peered at him from under her cocoon.

He closed her door, taking a deep breath before heading back to Aric's suite, where his cousin already lay sprawled facedown on the bed. Maurin seated himself in a nearby chair and steepled his fingers in thought.

"So what do you think of our new owner?"

"Hnmmm?" The sound coming from Aric's bed suggested that he had been more than halfway asleep already.

"Valasand. What do you think of her?"

"I don't know." Aric's voice came muffled and a bit cross from the pillows. "She hasn't exactly given us much to go on, has she? Part of me thinks we should just leave and see how far we can get."

Sangrine was farther away than Maurin could imagine. He allowed himself a brief sojourn back home. Kirai. The temple of Baelon taking its proud place among the lush green peaks. The familiar stars bestowing their wisdom from the ages. The ancient scrolls, filled with knowledge and mystery.

The promise he had made the woman who had ransomed them.

"I think this is where we need to be," Maurin said. "With Valasand. At least for now."

Aric rolled over onto his back and stared out through the window, as if listening to something only he could hear. "I don't," he said softly.

"Where would you go? Assuming you could go anywhere, of course? Home?"

"It's a big world, Maurin." Aric spread his hands. "Maybe even just one big world out of dozens, even hundreds. When you realized we weren't alone, didn't it ever occur to you there might be better places to live? No, I suppose not. You were happy stuck right where you were, with a wife you didn't know and a duty to your father and his god. That's just not good enough for me, Maurin. I want to live. I want to find—to see what's out there."

"I can understand that. Don't think I'm not tempted. But we aren't exactly emancipated."

"She leaves the door unlocked," Aric said in an ominous tone.

"She treats us well. She brought us together."

"Whatever. I say we're wasting our time here."

"Biding time isn't the same as wasting it," Maurin reassured him. "Be patient. Something good will come of this."

Aric didn't answer, and after a few moments, it was clear he didn't intend to.

"Are you awake?"

Aric turned his head just enough that he could be heard without the pillows getting in the way. His eyes were still closed. "Leave me alone, Maurin."

He was about to object, but decided against it. "Of course. It's been a long day. I'll let you get some rest. Sleep well, cousin."

Aric paused, then softly said, "Don't I wish."

Maurin closed the door behind him, stepped out into the hall, and returned to his own room. He spent a long time trying to make himself go to sleep, but his mind was in rebellion these days, it seemed, and wouldn't shut off. Too many unanswered questions. After a while, he gave up and decided to explore. He lit the old oil lamp he found in his room and, feeling almost sneaky, stepped out into the hall. One wing of the mansion had fallen into near ruin, and had an empty tower with a parapet that dropped off sharply. On the ground floor, however, he found a library. Ancient scrolls lined all four walls to the ceiling. He grabbed several that looked interesting, took a seat in the chair near the hearth, and spread a blanket over his lap. He didn't dare light a fire, but he kept his lamp on a small table near the chair. He unwound the scrolls, taking care not to crack them. If only he were more proficient in reading the common tongue! He could pick out a few words here and there, but that was about it. The historian in him ached to know what they said.

As it stood, he found himself admiring the artwork and the calligraphy. Were any of these considered sacred? Would sacred texts on one world be profane on another? Father would have been fascinated by them. Maurin was absorbed in a pictorial depicting an ancient race facing a great disaster, when he heard a shout.

"Maurin!" Aric's voice, even muted by the thick door, carried and echoed through the halls. "They're not men! Not... men..."

He gritted his teeth and leapt up, dragging the blanket off his lap and dumping the scrolls to the side. Maybe he could wake his cousin before he roused the whole house. He bolted up the stairs toward Aric's room, skidding to a halt when he saw Valasand standing stoically at the end of the hall, still dressed. Aric was muttering away about something, but at least he wasn't yelling anymore.

"Does he do this often?"

Maurin nodded miserably.

"I begin to see." Valasand favored him with a grim smile. "Go back to bed, Maurin. Everything will be all right."

He hesitated. "My lady?"

"Yes?"

"You—you asked me when you purchased me if I thought I was worthy of my dreams. I don't dream. Not like my cousin. What did you mean?"

"I sense in your spirit something that sleeps, waiting to be wakened." Valasand opened the door to her suite, and turned to enter. "When you are roused from your slumber, you will know what I meant."

"I see. Is there anything you need?"

She nodded. "You can douse the hall lamps."

"Um," he said, "all right, then. Good night, my lady."

"Good night. And Maurin?"

"Yes, my lady?"

"It's *Valasand*."

INTERLUDE
DARK ANGEL

Come to me, Aric. You are mine.

I open my eyes to see her gazing back at me. Her face is the purest beauty I've ever known, reflecting a love and yearning I never imagined. Upon my lips lingers the taste of her unspoken promise. She rises and turns her back to me. Her violet cloak becomes black ink against the moonlight, her draped form a beautifully rendered caryatid supporting the arch. She stops before the window, and turns once more, silhouetted against the portal. Her eyes beckon to me.

Come, my love, my intended. All my life, it is you I have sought.

In one grand, sweeping movement, she throws up her arms, and the sandglass shatters, exploding outward in a tinkling spray of crystalline shrapnel. The cast-off skin of her cloak flies from her shoulders and flutters away, disappearing into the night. Her arms are no longer arms, but wings, the fingers elongated to form the spindly supports between pale membranes. A dark angel remains, the wind whipping her hair about her face as she waits for me to follow.

Through the open window, the deafening refrain of hateful screams and howling wafts past her, piercing my soul. I want to cover my ears. She doesn't seem to notice.

Then she turns away and draws her wingtips together, standing on the edge of the balcony, teetering on the precipice. With a graceful billowing of gossamer wings, she launches herself into the night.

I cry out, and rush to the edge, not wanting to lose her, but afraid to jump. She is one of the bat-like creatures from before, but somehow a woman, too, whole and unblemished. There is no way she can be both at once, yet in the odd logic of dreams, it all seems to make sense.

She calls to me. I make up my mind, and leap.

This time, I am caught up in my own power, and cavort and soar as I please. I catch sight of my siren lover and start after her. As I near her, the shrieking howl becomes more harmonious, the horrible screech distills into a darksome melody, almost like singing. The sky becomes brighter, and the demon chorus is now an angelic choir.

Come to me, Aric. Find me. I have loved you forever.

No fear now, just trust: simple, complete, and utter trust. It feels so right. I catch her, and enfold her in my arms, and we stand on a blissful plain, where nothing else exists but the two of us, and bright, warm sunlight. She smiles at me, and all my problems melt away.

I promise you, I will find you. Wait for me.

CHAPTER 13
REGRETS

Lord Aster Krige slumped uncomfortably in his favorite chair. He brooded in solitude, the light globes in his study dimmed to match his mood. He scowled at an eight-century-old family tapestry, running his fingers absently through his hair.

Lord Aster Krige.

Lord Krige.

Lord of nothing. Certainly not lord of himself.

Krige swirled the liquid in his glass and took another gulp, indulging in a drink he reserved for bouts of depression and self-pity. He reached for the call-trumpet and keyed the valve that opened one of the myriad of tubes leading to the other rooms of the house.

"Sedrick, come in here." Krige focused on his pronunciation, forcing himself not to slur. "I need to talk to you immediately."

Krige stared out over his fingertips, tapping them together idly until a courtly steward entered the wooden doors at the end of the room. Sedrick straightened his lapels with a practiced flick of the fingers, his steps echoing off the walls and ceiling. He had been with the family for

years, and his hair was beginning to gray in testament to that fact. He was the highest ranking servant, and prided himself that his was the most respected opinion.

"What can I do for you, sir?" he asked as he approached Krige's side, beady eyes shining.

"I want you to go back to the Market," Krige said, speaking with difficulty, "and, ah, see if you can find Talauna."

"Sir?" Sedrick's eyebrows furrowed. "You made a deal with the wine merchant."

"He's dead."

"Dead, sir?"

"What happened the other night was a warning. A message." Krige chewed on his lip. "But it's a message out of my power to answer. I told Argoneis we needed to take the Reamar seriously, but he never listens."

"I see, sir."

"I want her back." Krige attempted to control his voice, to sound matter-of-fact. He couldn't.

Confusion registered on the steward's face. "I thought the girl had found, ah, disfavor with your wife, sir," he said guardedly. "Might I ask what caused you to change your mind?"

"Just get her back, damn you!" Krige shouted, pounding the chair arm. "This is none of your business!" He slumped back, then, and his head spun. Apparently the man thought his tenure allowed him to breach protocol.

Sedrick hesitated, then nodded. "Very well, then. And what price would you be willing to pay, sir?"

"I don't care," Krige said in exasperation.

After a few moments of silence, Sedrick said, "If I may suggest, sir, Lord Argoneis has made a standing offer for any of your, ah, lower stock. It's possible he has already gone through the selections. Mightn't we forgo the unpleasantness of the Mar—"

"NO!" Krige launched himself out of his chair. "That's what I'm trying to avoid! He's not going to get any of my slaves... especially Talauna! Why do you think I gave the girl to Vellis in the first place? Argoneis laughed when he heard about Baron Seides! He ordered me to post the bounty for his killer at five times the usual price—he wants to tame her and put her in his circus. There's no way I want him to get his hands on..."

Krige stopped abruptly, cursing himself for his tirade, for saying too much to a mere servant. Must be the drink. He had to look foolish for reneging on his prior orders. He ran his hands through his hair, moaning and rocking back and forth.

Sedrick frowned. "Sir...?"

"That is not how I wished to be rid of her," Krige whispered, turning his back on his steward, and gritting his teeth in exasperation. "She does not deserve that."

"You are, of course, correct, sir."

Krige looked up, his eyes no doubt red-rimmed from lack of sleep and composure. "Argoneis plans to honor Seides's memory by going ahead with that damned circus of his. I don't want him buying up all of the slaves just so he can have his fun killing them."

"I will do what I can, sir." Sedrick pressed thin lips together.

Krige collapsed back into his chair and stared at the floor, listening to the echoes of Sedrick's footfalls fading away. He took a long, mournful drink from his glass.

Hours passed, and the decanter on the tray next to him was empty long before he heard the sound of the servant's return. Shaking himself awake, he struggled to focus on the man walking toward him. Sedrick's expression was grim.

"Well?" Krige demanded. "Where is she?"

"She's already been sold, sir," Sedrick said apologetically.

Krige's heart seized in his chest. "Argoneis didn't get her, did he?"

"No, sir. The gentleman told me she had been sold to a woman just this morning."

"A woman?" That was a bit of a relief, anyway. "Who?"

"An outsider, apparently." Sedrick held out a copy of the proof of purchase. "One Valasand Del Siriné by name, sir." He paused, and looked searchingly at his master. "Perhaps I should tell you about it later."

"I'm not drunk. Not too drunk, anyway. What is it I need to know?"

Sedrick took a deep breath. "I took the liberty of tracking down this newcomer's activity, as much as I could. It seems she was interrogating a local merchant before two of Argoneis's police caught up with him. When they asked him what the woman wanted, he informed them she was asking after Lord Argoneis."

"Lord Argoneis? What did she want with him?" Krige reached for the bottle, only to be reminded of its disconcerting emptiness.

"She wanted to know who he was, where he lived. That sort of thing." Sedrick bit his lip. "Surely Lord Argoneis must be informed of this?"

Krige thought for a moment. "I will deal with the situation. In the meantime, I want you to find out where this woman is living."

His servant nodded. "One more thing: It seems she showed a badge of authority to one of the clerks at the Hall of Records."

Krige looked up sharply. "What kind of badge?"

CHAPTER 14
STIRRINGS

Sunlight streamed through Aric's window, and for once his dreams seemed distant and irrelevant. No one had come to fetch him for over-sleeping. He dressed, then seeing no signs of life from the other rooms, sauntered downstairs. "Hello?"

"You're finally awake." Maurin was already up and eating breakfast with Talauna. "There's some bread and cheese, and tea."

Aric nodded, slumping into a cushion across from them. The Maolori girl, he noted, sat rather close to his cousin.

"Where's Dania?" he asked.

Maurin shrugged and gestured towards the window. "Outside, doing some sort of exercises involving knives."

Aric grabbed a couple of slices of bread and sauntered over as casually as he could muster. Dania had found a tiny spot in the midst of the veg-etation, and was taking full advantage of it. Her skin glistened as she ducked and spun, then drew her wiry arm back to thrust a dagger at an imaginary foe.

"Valasand said she would be down in an hour or so."

Aric raised his eyebrows. "Trusting, isn't she?"

Dania leaned to one side and kicked out above her head. She remained balanced on the one leg, flexing the other at the knee with slow precision.

"She must not have owned any slaves before, or she would be taking greater precautions." Maurin took a sip from his mug. "Laxity of this magnitude can get you killed."

Dania pivoted and repeated the exercise with the other leg.

"Or at least out a lot of money." Aric turned back and chewed thoughtfully, hardly tasting the bread.

Krige never took any such chances with Aric or Talauna. He had always been afraid to let her too far out of his sight, lest she fall into one of the bouts of melancholy for which her race was notorious, or perhaps even work up the nerve to escape. Not that there was much chance of that happening now, Aric supposed, noting Talauna's face as she gazed at Maurin, oblivious to everything else.

Aric finished his breakfast, and Maurin insisted on checking his wound. Amazingly, it didn't seem to be infected. Maurin found some material to use as a new bandage. Talauna took the strips of cloth from him, and bound Aric's shoulder with dexterous fingers. She fixed him with a scolding glare.

"Don't look at me like that." He checked the dressing when she was done, then leaned out the window again. Dania had wrapped up her katas and was headed towards the house, daggers held loosely at her sides. Her eyes met his, and he ducked back until she was out of sight.

The woman of his dreams. What did she want? Who was she? Part of him dreaded the meeting, and yet his heart raced every time he recalled those eyes—oh, those eyes—those lips, and the silken tresses of her hair. He would be lying to himself if he didn't admit that in some way, regardless of her strange words, he badly wanted to meet her in the flesh.

Talauna made a strange face and hastened out of the room.

"Where's she going?" Maurin asked, throwing away the old bandage and taking a seat against the wall.

Aric shrugged. "Privy?"

"Oh." Maurin's fingers tapped a staccato rhythm on the floor. "Does Talauna talk?"

"Hmmm?"

"You knew the Maolori girl from your last household. Have you ever heard her talk?"

"Nope. Not once."

"Do you think she does?"

"She doesn't," Aric said. "That's obvious enough."

"That wasn't what I asked," Maurin said, annoyed. "Well," he conceded, after a moment, "maybe it was. What I meant was..."

"Can she?" Aric finished, turning back from the window. "I knew what you meant. I think she can. I don't know why," he qualified, before Maurin could ask. "It just seems that way."

"I wonder what happened." Maurin folded his hands and rested the tips of his index fingers against pursed lips.

Aric groaned. "I hope you don't expect me to answer that."

"No. It just seems there's a lot going on in her head that she doesn't say."

"Of course she doesn't say. She doesn't talk."

Maurin scowled. "Why do I have the impression this conversation is going around in circles?"

"Pointless chat has a way of doing that."

"Sorry," he snapped, rising stiffly from the floor. "I just wish I knew what to say to her."

"You like her, don't you?"

Maurin blushed. "What?"

"You heard me. You like her."

"No, I don't!" Maurin said defensively. "Well, I don't dislike her, but I don't know her, and..."

Aric chuckled. "Maurin, just shut up and admit it. You've been at her side and soaking up every look she gives you ever since you laid eyes on her back at Krige's mansion."

Maurin waved his hands as he paced. "It would be nice to know something about her. That's all I was saying."

"She was with Krige when he bought me." Aric shrugged. "He told me her name meant beauty in old Mao. 'With a feminine diminutive implied.' I don't know if he gave her the name, or if it was on her papers at the Market."

"Hmmm." Maurin tugged at his lip. "What else?"

"He didn't make her do any hard work. She was his plaything, and his wife finally had enough of it, I guess, because he ended up trading her to the wine merchant. 'Course, you know that."

"Yes."

The door opened, and Talauna padded in. Her hair was damp and detangled, and her cheeks rosy. Aric glanced over at Maurin.

And just like that, I'm invisible. He chuckled and turned back to the window.

Within a few minutes, Valasand came downstairs and summoned them all to the hall armories, where she had them glean some strange weapons from the wall. Each one looked like a short sword fastened to the end of a six-foot pole.

"We're clearing the courtyard with these?" Aric asked incredulously as they followed her out the door. The others' faces mirrored his skepticism. These glaives didn't seem especially practical for cutting down weeds and small trees. Come to think of it, they didn't seem especially practical for anything, save perhaps stabbing someone six feet away.

He quickly pushed that thought aside.

"Yes." Valasand nodded. "Spread out and keep out of each other's way. Don't overexert yourselves; push until it begins to hurt, no further. Take the smaller saplings and toss them outside the gates. The softer weeds and vines I want you to leave in piles by any trees too large to remove. I will tell you what to do with them later."

Aric and Maurin exchanged glances as Valasand went back inside. They waited until they heard the clang of the front doors before speaking.

"How pointless can you get?" Aric tugged off his shirt and tossed it onto the threshold.

Maurin bit his lip. "Her instructions may be odd, but the task is simple. Just do as you're told."

Aric gave his cousin a withering scowl. "Aren't you the one always lecturing me about the difference between 'simple' and 'easy'?"

They all headed in different directions, giving each other plenty of space. Dania adapted quickly, cutting a straight swath in the center of the courtyard, making a direct path to the opposite wall. She obviously enjoyed the activity, but Talauna, trying her best, still had to make frequent stops, sitting down and gasping, slicked down by sweat, until she regained enough energy to continue. Aric was better equipped than he would have been prior to his kidnapping, but his hands were still getting tenderized.

Under the outer wall of the compound, the courtyard was filled with grass, shrubs, and trees. Aric encountered some resilient weeds thick enough to be saplings. They didn't want to go down. He hacked at them, swore at them, and used every bit of his strength to cut the plants, but couldn't find a good point of leverage.

"This is insane!" He threw down the weapon in disgust. "It's impossible to cut down a tree with this thing!"

Aric stalked back toward the mansion and ran directly into Valasand. Apparently his shouting had drowned out the sound of her coming up behind him. An eternity passed as she stared at him, then she handed him her staff. She picked Aric's glaive up off the ground, held it by the end in both hands, and spun with it.

The blade cut through the air with a whoosh, then impacted with a thunk. The green stalk shuddered and toppled.

"Really." Valasand traded him his weapon for her staff, arched an eyebrow at him, and shuffled away.

For the rest of the morning, Aric worked as he had not worked in— well, ever. He wanted to quit, but Maurin made him keep going. His cousin was determined to make some progress on the courtyard, to have something to show Valasand when the day was over. At this rate, all they would have to show for it was bruises and blisters.

After a seemingly endless stretch of hacking and bashing at the weeds, Aric came close to breaking his weapon on a shattered fountain hidden in the shrubs. His hands could take no more. Winded and frustrated, he went to draw some water from the well by the mansion wall.

Sitting with his back against the stone, Aric stewed in silence as the other three swiped at the miniature jungle, sweating and grunting. The Maolori's movements were becoming weak and jerky. Her swings were not even cutting the grass anymore. Plainly, Talauna was wearing herself out.

"Um..." He stood up, but of course Maurin had already noticed. His cousin threw down his weapon and rushed over just in time to catch her before she collapsed. He helped her to a seated position as Aric jogged over. Her face was flushed, and her breath came in shallow pants.

"What happened?" Dania asked.

"She's overworked herself."

Valasand had apparently seen the whole thing from one of the windows; she hurried toward them from the mansion. She placed her hand on Talauna's forehead, then checked her pulse. "I think you've had enough for one day," she said, mildly stern.

Talauna took a deep, shivering breath, and her eyelids fluttered. She glanced wearily at Valasand, then back at Maurin.

"Are you all right?" he asked.

"She'll be fine. Bring her inside."

Maurin nodded. When Talauna had difficulty standing, he knelt and gently eased his arms under her knees and shoulders. He planted one foot on the ground for support, then raised her in one motion. Her cheek came to rest on his shoulder. He shot Aric a glance and bit his lip as he swept past the thick wooden door and into the foyer. Aric and Dania left their glaives and followed them.

"Aric, get me a basin of water and a sponge. And a separate glass of water." Valasand motioned for Dania to put some cushions out on the floor.

Aric rolled his eyes, but complied. When he returned to the sunken great room, Talauna was reclining against the cushions. Valasand tossed her hair back from her eyes and indicated for Aric to set the tray with all the items down beside her. She loosened Talauna's garment somewhat and dipped the sponge in the water. Wringing it out, she applied it gently to the girl's forehead, cheeks, neck, chest, and arms. Valasand slipped a small pinch of salt between the Maolori girl's dry lips, then placed the glass to her mouth. Talauna drained it with greedy abandon.

Maurin squatted beside them, watching Valasand minister to the Maolori girl. Aric shook his head and glanced at Dania, who steadfastly avoided his gaze. Talauna reached for Maurin's hand, but he quickly stood, his face turning crimson.

"Let me see your hands," Valasand said.

Maurin hesitated, then held them out, palms up. Valasand made a disapproving sound when she saw the mass of blisters.

"And you?"

Aric and Dania followed suit. Her hands were in nowhere near as bad of shape as his. He ground his teeth.

Valasand sighed. "Well, since none of you listened to me when I said to push until it began to hurt and no further, I think I'm going to change your itinerary."

Before she could say any more, a rapping sounded at the door.

Shock flashed over Valasand's face, then her austere mask fell like a curtain. She pulled herself up with her staff and limped up the stairs toward the foyer. "Stay here."

Maurin murmured in Aran, "Visitors?"

Aric shook his head. "I don't think so. Something's wrong." Voices echoed from the corridor, but he couldn't make out the words.

"I can't stand it anymore. I have to know what's going on." Aric opened the door as quietly as he could and crept through the hallway, adopting the Maolori girl's cat-footed walk. Maurin followed. As they approached the foyer, Aric could hear someone talking with Valasand, and motioned for Maurin to stay back. He edged as close as he dared to the corner.

He's found me! Aric fought to calm the sudden fear gripping his heart at the sight of the formal attire of a high-ranking Caileenian servant. He turned away, hoping Sedrick hadn't seen him.

"What's going on?" Maurin whispered, crowding next to him. Talauna staggered in from the great room. She peeked around the corner and gasped when she saw Sedrick. They ducked back against the wall with Aric. Dania watched them from a distance, staying where she could bolt out of sight at a moment's notice.

"Who is he?" Maurin asked.

"Krige's steward."

"Maybe he's not here for you."

"Don't be an idiot, Maurin. Do you know what these people do to escaped slaves? He's probably going to have me taken to Argoneis." Aric listened for a moment, frowning.

"I don't see why you won't sell," Sedrick whined from the corridor. "My master's offer is more than generous, and I've been authorized to compensate you for your troubles."

Valasand's response was terse, but polite. "I am simply not interested in selling her."

Aric almost passed out from relief. Maurin and Dania turned to stare at Talauna, who quaked beside them, large eyes filled with fearful tears.

"Don't worry," Maurin whispered low into her ear. *"We won't let him take you away."*

Sedrick's voice sounded again. "You could buy five slaves for the amount my master is prepared to pay. What is so special about this girl?"

Valasand's tone remained cool. "If you could not see what is special about her while she was under your master's roof, what makes you think you would be able to see it now?"

"This girl cannot mean that much to you."

"On the contrary; she cannot mean all that much to your master. If she had, he would never have sold her."

"I believe I have been more than reasonable," Sedrick said, and Aric could picture him stiffening with wounded pride. "Lord Krige will not be refused. He will have the girl one way or another."

To Aric's shock, Maurin strode past him and into the entryway. The heat of his rage radiated from him as he stood in full view of Krige's man-servant. Talauna gasped, and Sedrick glanced over. Aric cursed inwardly; the man had seen him. And recognized him.

"I think she wants to stay," Maurin said, his voice authoritative. His muscles twitched with barely restrained fury. The last two years had chiseled Maurin's body into rock.

It took Sedrick a moment to find his composure. "I see you are harboring a fugitive here, as well."

Might as well join them now. Aric stepped forward, helping Maurin block the way to Talauna.

"Your master is no longer theirs," Valasand said. "And the only way he's getting them back is over my corpse."

"That can be arranged," Sedrick said coolly. "The next time I come, it will be with Lord Argoneis's security force."

"There won't be a next time," Aric growled, taking a menacing step forward. "You know as well as I do that Krige—how did he put it?—will never allow the Lord Regent to put his filthy paws on her."

Krige's steward gaped back at Valasand, not accustomed to having his master's influence so casually dismissed, and clearly expecting her to do something about her recalcitrant slaves. "You haven't seen the last of me. Lord Krige will be most displeased."

"The door's behind you," Maurin said, his face a hardened scowl. Aric was a little surprised to hear his cousin add a highly uncomplimentary epithet in Aran; Sedrick wouldn't know what it meant, but the emotion behind it was unmistakable.

The steward hesitated, then, without another word, minced out of the foyer.

Dania sidled up to them, remaining out of their visitor's line of sight. "Do you want me to kill him?"

Valasand shook her head emphatically.

The outer doors slammed, and Aric expected a rebuke, at the least, and very likely severe punishment. Valasand merely seemed bemused, and said nothing for a few moments.

"How did he find us?" Aric asked.

"It would seem your old master is very determined." She made her way back to the great room.

"He didn't want to get rid of Talauna in the first place," Aric said. "He'll try again."

"It will be all right," she said, looking around at them. "I am under no obligation to sell her back. I may do anything I like with my slaves— even free them, if I so choose."

Maurin nodded hesitantly.

"Granted, I may be branded an eccentric," she added, with a wry twist to her mouth, "but something tells me I already lay claim to that distinction."

———— ◆ ————

"You know," Maurin said through the door of Aric's bathing room, "it's not as though we're being treated cruelly. She feeds us, clothes us, gives us our own living quarters... We could be a lot worse off. A little hard work won't kill us."

"Ha!" Aric snarled. He toweled off and got dressed, then opened the door and threw himself onto the bed. With an irritated sigh, he flexed his hands and grimaced as he examined his battered palms. He supposed he should put something on them before retiring for the night, but he wasn't thrilled about the idea of rummaging around this enormous house for ancient medical supplies. "Whatever, Maurin. I still say it reeks. She didn't even give us decent tools to do her gardening with."

"Understood," Maurin said, placating. "My hands are killing me."

Aric snorted his opinion of Maurin's endurance.

"You aren't exactly impervious to pain, cousin, regardless of what you like other people to think," Maurin shot back.

Aric just seethed for a few minutes and willed his blood pressure to go down.

Maurin was right about one thing: The fact that Valasand gave them weapons at all indicated some degree of trust. Not many masters would have been so daring. Of course, not many of them could have held their own against the gladiatrix in hand-to-hand combat, either.

Aric, for one, didn't feel like starting any revolts anytime soon. And Maurin was too curious to leave. Still, the sense of urgency grew. Shadows lurked in the recesses of Aric's mind, growing more distinct with the dawn of each passing day. If they didn't get out of here soon, the nightmares would invade his waking world. He could sense them closing in. His only hope lay in finding the mysterious woman whose whispers haunted his dreams.

CHAPTER 15
COUNCIL

"It would seem we have a Warden of the Gates in our midst." Countess Lauran Dalinde sat forward, tucking an errant blonde hair back into her perfect coiffure. Of the four nobles seated around the oblong table in Aster Krige's meeting room, she seemed the most unaffected by the news of Sedrick's discovery. "I knew this was going to happen. I told you this was going to happen."

"Quiet, Lauran." Hargin Dalinde had the look of a man whose world was coming apart, and who was trying desperately to hold it together with his bare hands.

Krige had summoned the "slattern daughter of a nobleman," as Argoneis had called her, as well as her father, and Arvin Phoecius, governor of Langfort, in the hopes that they could decide on an appropriate course of action. Though Sedrick had come back rebuffed from his first attempt at contacting the Warden, Krige had not given up. He knew she was not going to be easily persuaded, but due to her choice of habitation, she could be easily watched.

"Perhaps the Warden's coming has nothing to do with us," Phoecius suggested. "There is the incident of the other night. She may be here to investigate that."

"Unlikely," Krige replied. "From what I gather, she was here before the Reamar's little... demonstration. And she couldn't have gotten here so quickly on a ship."

"It doesn't matter why the Warden is here. The fact remains that she is, and we must act accordingly." Hargin Dalinde stroked his chin again.

"So what do we do?" Phoecius asked sullenly. "Are we supposed to tell Argoneis about this?"

"Hardly," Krige said. "I propose we do nothing at all."

"Agreed," the countess said. "Argoneis is bringing about his own downfall. We had a civilized society, a society that worked, and his brutish antics are simply coming back to haunt him. Give it enough time, and he will be his own ruin."

"Yes, daughter, but what of us?" Hargin fidgeted with his signet ring. "If the Wardens are here, they will hold all of us accountable. We will be perceived as accomplices to Argoneis's crimes. Someone has to go and talk to him, tell him he endangers us all."

"Do you remember what happened to the last person who told him he couldn't do what he wanted?" A spray of spittle flew unheeded from Phoecius's mouth. "Daman had a set of his favorite books bound in his hide!"

"Rumors, nothing more," Krige said.

"Nevertheless," Lauran said, "I think we are all in agreement that Lord Argoneis is a dangerous man. He is unbalanced, and his slaving

raids are soiling our world. Our native slaves can buy their own freedom, but these wretches taken from other worlds want none of that. They want blood. You can't give them their freedom, or they will destroy you. With each new shipment coming in, Daman runs a greater risk of a slave revolt."

"And I've seen more and more come through of late," Phoecius said. "Why is that? What is he stockpiling them for?"

"Haven't you been paying attention?" Hargin Dalinde asked. "It was supposed to be this great secret, but there've been whispers among the lower caste. Daman never could keep his mouth shut around his servants, and now the news is spreading. Argoneis and Baron Seides masterminded some bloody farce involving gladiators, and so forth. He's been billing some 'new kind of game,' a circus of sorts, and is keeping track of the slaves in all the cities. He buys and pulls aside those he thinks would put on the most interesting show."

Lauran shuddered. "I've heard what sorts of things Argoneis thinks of as an interesting show. Does he really think that will appeal to anyone not suffering from his own warped sensibilities?"

"I don't think that's it," Hargin said. "Seides was behind this, and he's always been more interested in battles and hunts. No mere reenactment or theater for him. He likes to see real blood fly when swords are drawn."

"Seides is dead," Phoecius reminded him.

"Lord Argoneis likes bloodsport, too, though he generally prefers to keep it more personal." Krige paused. "But there's nothing he loves more than a good show. He likes to flaunt his power, and it wouldn't surprise me if he chose to honor Seides's memory by presenting the circus more or less as they had originally intended."

"Honor?" Lauran Dalinde snorted, accepting a drink from a slender Maolori slave—ostensibly Talauna's replacement, but no one could take her place. "What does he know of honor?"

"All this is beside the point. We need to decide what to do about the Warden." Krige looked around the room.

"Couldn't we just get rid of her?" Phoecius asked. "One woman can be disposed of fairly quietly, I should think..."

Krige and the Dalindes shared a collective gasp.

"Kill a Warden?"

Phoecius shrugged. "It was just a suggestion."

"Even supposing," Krige's icy tone bit out across the dark veneer of the table, "such a feat was possible, just what do you think that would do? Do you want to guarantee all the might of the forces of the Temple come down straight upon our heads? Because that's what killing a Warden would mean: suicide."

"All right, all right, I get the point. But we don't need anybody nosing around, least of all this Warden. So, do any of you have any better ideas?"

Several moments of consternated silence went by before anyone spoke. Lauran Dalinde finally broke the tension, and this time, her father did not interrupt her.

"Perhaps we can use this to our advantage. Argoneis is powerful, yes, but we outnumber him. We should send a delegate to tell him he has attracted the attention of the Temple."

"So what if he kills the woman?" Phoecius said. "I know you think the Wardens are invincible, but I assure you, they are not."

"That's true," Hargin Dalinde said. "And if anyone had the power or gall to kill one, it would be Argoneis. But then the Temple, as you say, would be bound to investigate. Even if the blood were on his hands, there's no way we would be found guiltless in all of this. We're back to where we started."

Lauran tapped her fingertips on the table. "We need to tell him. If we don't, the Warden is bound to cause trouble, regardless, and Argoneis will start looking for someone to blame. Test the waters with a delegate. We have no wish to go to battle over something like this; the whole point of this coalition is to prevent loss of life, and the preservation of our culture. He must know in what danger he puts us all, and perhaps it will be more likely to register with him if he can see the danger to himself."

"He won't see the danger in a single Warden's presence," Hargin put in. "The man thinks he's above the law."

"He is." Krige pinched the bridge of his nose. "Argoneis is the law here, and lets no one forget it. But perhaps even one such as he can be scared into paying attention."

"So who is going to go?"

"It shouldn't be someone local," Krige said. Awful enough he was even thinking of actively opposing Daman, even if merely in word. Bad news was always unwelcome in the House of Argoneis, regardless of its source. "I think a delegation from one of the forest cities would be more effective in demonstrating how widespread this problem is. But you must remain silent regarding the source of this information. Rumors overheard in distant towns will carry more weight and implicate none of us in his eyes."

"Especially you." Lauren rang the goblet in front of her with a painted fingernail. "Convenient."

"Are you forgetting that it was not Argoneis to whom I first came with these tidings? Do you not suppose he would reward my faithfulness in informing him of this? It is my wish that we all benefit from this intelligence."

"Well?" Phoecius asked.

Krige took a sip of his drink, watching each of Lauran Dalinde's thoughts playing as legible as a scroll across her face. She no doubt vacillated between the natural horror of having to face Daman Argoneis, and the chance to prove herself worthy—both in her father's eyes, and those of other nobles. As the heir apparent to Sal Dalinde, the family estate, she must show her strength before her father left her in control. She tried harder than her father ever had to demonstrate her leadership.

"Very well." The countess nodded. "I'll go."

"What?" her father roared.

"She's right," Krige said. "I believe it should be the one who first gave the suggestion."

"Why her?"

"Countess Dalinde, you have been the most vocal in your opposition of Lord Argoneis's practices. Your skills at negotiation are without compare. You might be able to appeal to Daman's sensibilities as none of us could." Krige ignored the building retort waiting to explode from her father's lips the moment he stopped talking. "Go back home and send a message to Argoneis stamped with your personal seal. Tell him you wish an audience with him, to discuss a matter of great importance. If I know Argoneis, he won't be interested in what you have to tell him, and will neglect to answer your correspondence for as long as he can put it off. However, he may take up your case on a whim, and the prospect of being visited by one as beautiful as yourself might strike his fancy."

"That's what concerns me, Krige," Hargin Dalinde said, unable to contain himself any longer. "You want my daughter to expose herself to that kind of danger, while you sit here comfortably and pull the strings?"

Krige nodded, amused at the sudden protective streak in the nobleman who was primarily concerned that his female offspring have no say in matters of politics.

"You just have to know how to negotiate with the man. Take an entourage of bodyguards adorned as your house slaves. Wear the signet of Sal Dalinde to show you have the authority to speak for the city. And most important of all"—Krige emphasized his words with a waggling finger—"when you get there, never let him close the doors behind you until you have gone."

INTERLUDE
SOULLESS

I'm going to die here.

Random gouts of green plasma billow from the gray arterial walls of the corridor. They ebb and flow with an unseen tide. A strange resonance pulses in the air, causing my head to throb. My veins swell with electric lightness.

The further I go, the more I feel I'm being driven into the bowels of this place. I'm so confused; all these channels and arteries look alike. The thrumming is getting so strong I can feel it, pounding my soul in sympathetic cadence. I am a foreign body in a single gigantic organism.

My mincing steps stir the glowing mist around my feet. It's getting darker, and the hair on the back of my neck stands up. I reach out to steady myself, running my hands along the ribbed surface. If stone could be made flesh, this is how it would feel.

Dear gods, this whole place is alive.

I find myself in a cathedral of organic rock, a vault large enough to hold the gladiatorial arena with room to spare. A knotted mass of convolutions rises like a sundial from the floor, connected at an odd angle to the ceiling and walls by tendon-like pillars. From these, branched ribs spread in every direction. A grayish residue coats the floor, and sickly light seeps from the thin sheets of green mist.

Thrum, thrum, thrum.

I see a movement toward one of the walls, a flash of corpse-pale white. I breathe as quietly as my jangled nerves allow, and strain to catch another glimpse of it.

The darkness swallows me in silence, and the pulse of this place is as the beating of my heart.

A hand grasps my shoulder.

I whirl. Cold as frost, the grip is like a steel pincer. I shiver in horror at black-on-black eyes, abnormally huge in their lidless sockets. Pallid and shrunken, the creature seems little more than skin stretched taut over misshapen bones. The thin black gash of a mouth opens in a silent hiss.

I look into those soulless eyes and see myself.

Help me. Oh, help me...

What have I done?

CHAPTER 16
VOICES

Aric jolted awake, rolled out of bed, and vomited on the floor. He cleaned up his mess, then reeled down the hallway.

"Lace up," he said as he pushed past Talauna and into the privy, closing the door behind him. A pitcher of water sat in a bowl on a stand. He tipped it back and drank, then poured the rest into the basin and splashed it over his face and neck.

I've got to get out of here. Somehow he had to convince Maurin that staying was not the "right thing to do." That was going to be tricky; his cousin clearly trusted their new owner.

He walked back down the hall, scratching at the insect bites covering his lower arms and calves. He paused at the thick wooden door of Valasand's suite. Was that talking he heard inside? A male voice came through, soft but resonant. Perhaps Maurin had decided to confront her about her plans. Aric drew closer.

"What will you do now, Little Flame?"

That was not Maurin.

"I'm moving to the next phase. I think they're ready."

"Do you intend to tell them?"

"I'm not sure yet."

For a moment, all Aric could hear was the pulse thrumming in his ears.

"Someone is listening."

Aric leapt away from the door and sprinted down the hall on tiptoe. Who was that, and how had they heard him? He slid into the recessed stone entry to Maurin's suite, pressing himself flat. A squeal from the end of the corridor told him Valasand had opened her door.

Just look around, he willed her, sweating, *see no one's there, and go back in. I'm going to feel really stupid if you see me squashed against Maurin's door.*

He listened for the tap of Valasand's staff, and the shuffle of her limping gait. His heart pounded in his ears, and he struggled to keep his breath from betraying him.

Nothing. The door closed again, and no one walked past asking what he was doing. He waited for several minutes more, then turned around to open the door.

Of course his cousin had barred it.

"Maurin!" he whispered. He thumped as softly as he could with the heel of his hand. "Maurin, wake up!"

Aric popped his head out into the hall to see if he had been heard, then ducked back in and tried again.

So his cousin was still a late sleeper. "Since when do you bar your door, Maurin? You afraid of Talauna or something?"

Aric turned his body to the side and battered the door with his upper arm and shoulder. One last subdued whack and he was going to give up. This hurt too much, and he was bound to attract attention. He stepped back for some momentum, and threw his weight into it—

And found himself sprawling on the floor as the door flew open.

"Ouch. Ugh. Maurin—oh!"

The Blood Goddess stood above him, scowling. "Whom did you expect to find in my room?"

"Sorry, wrong door." Aric picked himself up off the floor and gave Dania an apologetic wince. He backed away and pushed at the door across the hall.

That one opened. Throwing a sheepish grin in Dania's direction, he closed it behind him and went to shake the snoring lump under the covers.

"Maurin! Would you wake up?"

"Erghmph."

"We're not alone here." Aric shook him again.

"What?"

"I heard Valasand talking to somebody."

Maurin sat up and rubbed his eyes. "Calm down a moment. What are you talking about? When was this?"

"Just now. I was walking by her room, and I heard a man's voice say something like, 'So what do you plan to do with them?' and Valasand said something about moving to the next phase, and she didn't know if she was going to tell us."

"Tell us what?"

"I don't know," Aric said. "They stopped talking."

Maurin swung his legs over the bed and shook his hair back. "This doesn't bode well."

"You think? Someone else is in this house, someone who knows more about what's going on than we do."

Maurin frowned. "I never saw anyone come in, and we did a pretty thorough sweep after we found Dania lurking around. I think we'd know if we weren't alone. Are you sure you weren't dreaming?"

"I'm telling you, there's someone here!"

"All right, we'll take a look."

"Now?"

"Of course, now." Maurin pulled on his work clothes.

"What, are you just gonna walk up and knock while they're sitting there?"

"Best way to see who she's talking to."

"Ah—I guess so."

"You hide in the privy. If I don't see the stranger when she answers the door, I'll draw her out. Wait until we're gone, and then check out her room."

Aric grinned, and rushed off to comply. He held the door almost closed and peered out. On his cue, Maurin strode boldly down the corridor, walked up to Valasand's suite, and knocked. Aric heard a fluttering noise.

"Come in."

His cousin opened the door and stood in the frame.

"Yes, Maurin?"

"Um." He cleared his throat. "Since we're getting close to finishing the courtyard, I wondered what you'd like us to do today?"

"Come with me." Her voice faded into the distance over the tap of her staff.

After they were out of hearing range, Aric slipped out of the privy and over to Valasand's room. He pushed open the door.

Nothing.

He went through her entire suite. No signs of anybody else living there, or even visiting. Not so much as a jar of mouth soap or a pair of men's slippers. A small trunk sat by the window, but it was locked. He left her rooms and started into the empty wing.

ARIC.

"What?" His heart hammered against his rib cage, and he backed against the cold stone wall. "Who are you?"

HEED MY VOICE.

Aric ground his fists into his ears. *This is another dream, this is another dream.*

COME. FIND THE FREEDOM YOU SEEK.

Aric dashed down the stairs and careened down the hall.

WHY DO YOU RUN FROM ME?

He skidded to a halt in the foyer. Valasand was waiting for him at the doors.

"Did you get lost?"

"I, ah—I thought I heard something." That was true enough. *And I never want to hear it again.*

She scrutinized him for a moment in silence. "And did you find anything?"

"No."

"Old houses are full of noises."

But this one is full of voices. Aric nodded, and followed her to where the others waited in the crisp morning air. He gave his cousin a slight shake of the head.

"Aric has decided to join us after all." Valasand came to a stop beside a large pile of mown vegetation. "This should be easier on your hands, as long as you take care with the grasses. Today I want you to make scarecrows."

"Scarecrows?" Aric echoed.

"I'm glad your hearing is top-notch. Yes, scarecrows. Life-size, if you please."

Valasand pulled a length of vine out and knelt beside the weeds. She took two forked branches and tied them together with a length of vine. Then she laid out a bundle of weeds, wrapped it around a branch, and tied it at the top, middle, and bottom. Valasand repeated the procedure until the branches, forming a rough skeleton, were covered. She poked a third stick in at the top and wound a ball of grasses around it for a head.

"Be creative as you like, but make them durable. They need to hold together. I want as many as you can make. Lean them against the trees when you're done. Any left over, line them up by the wall."

Aric saw a myriad of unspoken words behind Dania's eyes.

"Don't forget to eat and take breaks," Valasand called over her shoulder as she headed back to the mansion.

"Scarecrows?" he said again.

Dania grabbed a fistful of weeds. "Just do as you're told."

Maurin waited until Valasand was gone to come over to Aric. "Well?"

Talauna hovered at a distance. Aric stared at her, but she didn't go away. He pulled Maurin aside and started speaking in Aran. "Thanks for keeping Valasand outside until I was done."

"No complaints, cousin; I bought you as much time as I could. What did you find?"

Aric told Maurin everything he had seen. He left out the voice in the hall. His cousin worked on his grass effigy as he listened.

"Was that trunk big enough to hide a person in?"

"No, and it wasn't on a trap door, or anything, either. I checked."

"You would." Maurin seemed impressed. "I trust you put everything back where it was?"

Aric snorted. "What do you think I am, anyway? Of course I did. You don't ransack someone's room when you're looking for something the size of a full-grown man."

"Maybe it was a midget."

"Come on, Maurin. Think of a better one."

"Talking to herself?" Maurin suggested. "I don't know, genius; you're the one who thinks he heard all this."

"I didn't think I heard it, Maurin. I heard it. Wherever this guy's gone, he's quick."

"Sounds to me as though he's more than quick. It's a sheer drop from Valasand's window. Anyone jumping would break every bone from his toes to his sternum. And no one's been through those doors but us. Unless there's a secret exit from the mansion, your mystery man disappeared into thin air."

Aric cursed. "I'm not kidding about this, Maurin!"

"All right," Maurin soothed, as Dania looked their way. "Keep your voice down. I'm not saying you're making it up. But there's no one in the house, and nowhere he could have gone. What conclusion do you draw from that?"

"So... what, then?"

Maurin shrugged. "Maybe she has some sort of long-range communication system. Some of the nobles have those. I would have loved to see what Father thought of them."

"I didn't see one in her room. Besides, it didn't sound like one."

"The door was closed, for Baelon's sake!" Maurin said hotly. "How could you tell?"

Aric glowered.

"I believe you, but I risked my neck so you could search our mistress's rooms. When you show me the physical evidence that someone else is in the mansion, I will do something about it—I'll have to. In the meantime, we're going to have to assume she was communicating through some sort of device, because there is no way anyone could have gotten past us. Am I right?"

Aric slowly nodded. "I guess so."

"Good. Then get to work. I've had enough close calls for one day."

The mansion loomed over Aric as he created another dummy. In the sunlight, he could pretend he'd never heard anything. But sleep was an enemy these days, and going back inside felt like entering hostile territory.

What do you plan to do now, Little Flame? Do you intend to tell them?

Aric wasn't looking forward to another night in this house. The last thing he needed was a haunted mansion.

Unless...

Unless it's not the house that's haunted.

It's me.

The hours slipped away, and the stiff-limbed grass regiment grew. Across the path, Maurin worked steadily at his effigy, and kept stealing glances at Talauna.

"Did I ever tell you about the first time Maurin saw a Maolori?" Aric said in Canoine. Dania turned toward him, and Talauna looked up.

Maurin scowled. "I'd appreciate it if you didn't bring that up."

"What did he do?" Dania set aside her labors and walked over. Talauna followed suit.

"Well, we're still in the holding pit in the slave market, and it's dark. Maurin's still trying to get over the shock that we're on a different world."

"As was everyone there. Seriously, do we need to talk about this?"

"They open the door and let in some other captives. And Maurin can't see them very well, and he's trying to communicate with them."

Talauna smiled.

Maurin's face showed red behind green-stained fingers. "Just bear in mind it was very dark."

"I mentioned that. Anyway, a cloud slips away from the moon just as Maurin's asking if these new people came from Sangrine, like us."

"Aric, I'm warning you..."

"And?" Dania tilted her tattooed head at him.

"He screamed."

Dania chortled. "Screamed?"

"I hadn't seen anyone like you before," Maurin explained to Talauna. "I couldn't take it all in."

She twisted her face up at him.

"He did try to apologize to the poor Maolori guy, but I told Maurin he'd scared him enough already."

"I'd scared him? Right."

Talauna feigned a pounce at Maurin, then grinned ear to ear.

"Very funny. Thanks, cousin."

"Don't mention it. Anyway, you've come a long way. Now you can't take your eyes off—"

Maurin launched himself at him and clamped his hand over his mouth. With a smothered laugh, Aric grabbed Maurin's arm and spun him onto the ground. Maurin pulled him down with him and rolled over. He grinned as he grasped Aric's wrists and pinned him face-down.

"Yield?"

"Never!" Aric twisted and snaked away from him, throwing his cousin off and flipping him over on his back.

"Just like old times, hmm?"

"Except now I can beat you."

"In your dreams, cousin, in your..." Maurin's smirk disappeared as his attention was drawn over Aric's shoulder.

Aric turned to see Valasand standing behind him. In her right hand, she held her staff. In her left, she held two more. From the discoloration and tapered ends, he gathered they were spears that had lost their tips.

"I see you are no strangers to violence."

Maurin flushed. "We were just playing!"

"I know. But I recognized some martial training."

"I wouldn't exactly say that."

Valasand cocked her head. "Explain."

"Fighting wasn't allowed at the temple where we grew up." Maurin sniffed and ran his fingers through hair gone stringy with perspiration. "But that didn't stop Aric from teaching me the rudiments of some of what he learned in his woodscout training. When the other priests weren't watching, of course. Wrestling, archery, a bit of quarterstaff defense. That sort of thing."

"Show me." Valasand handed each of them a staff. "Fight it out properly."

"My lady?"

"It's *Valasand*, and you heard me. Show us what you know."

Aric and Maurin drew apart from the rest of the group. Maurin slung his staff off his shoulder and held it out in a relaxed defensive position. Aric whipped his around and likewise stood on guard.

Maurin smiled. "Whenever you're ready."

Aric grinned back, and swung his staff around in a side sweep, which Maurin easily blocked. The loud clack of wood against wood echoed through the courtyard, and several birds took startled flight from the roof of the mansion.

"Don't strain yourself," Aric said, bringing his staff down toward his cousin's skull. Maurin parried the blow again, then spun with a clumsy flourish, his stave whistling. Aric countered, locking the two of them in a frenzy of whirling billets.

Maurin turned red, but kept up his grin as he blocked Aric's onslaught. "Do you remember when you taught me how to use a bow and arrow?"

"Yeah." Sweat started to soak Aric's back and drip down his face. He feigned nostalgia. "Those were the days."

"And how I couldn't figure out why I kept missing the target," Maurin huffed. "It took me forever to realize the problem."

"It's not my fault I'm left-handed," Aric retorted, laughing, pressing

Maurin back toward the trees.

"You never told me I had to hold it different than you did."

"It didn't occur to me until later," Aric explained. "I'd only learned that day."

"But once I figured out which hand you were supposed to hold the bow in—"

Aric slipped his staff in under Maurin's guard and struck him squarely in the side.

"Ow!" Maurin woofed with surprise and held up his hand. He leaned on his staff and panted for a moment, clutching his bruised side. "Damnation!"

"I still beat you flat out."

Maurin nodded grimly and raised his staff again. "But I was pretty good. I think I could have gotten as good as you, if Regin hadn't caught us and made us stop." Sadness flickered across his face.

Aric lashed out again and again, before his cousin could get lost in grief. Maurin deflected the attack and struck with a vengeance, driving Aric back for a few paces. Then Aric gained the upper ground, raining down blows in furious succession. He smacked Maurin on the thigh and laughed at his cousin's annoyed grimace.

"All right, boys," Valasand said, "that's enough."

Dania stared at Aric with hard-bitten approval, and he was suddenly aware of how grimy he must be.

"You both show potential," Valasand said with an affable smile. "I think you had better quit, though, before you kill each other."

"Spoilsport." Dania's smile was rapacious.

"Come." Valasand turned and walked on toward the mansion, leaning into her staff. Aric and Maurin followed her and Dania. "You are both fairly adept young men. I think it's time I taught you how to prepare dinner."

"Dinner?" Aric said.

"After you've bathed, of course."

"I used to prepare meals for the priests back home," Maurin said. "Nothing fancy, of course. I wouldn't let Aric near the kitchen, though."

"Why is that?"

"Let's just say I hope you like your meals burned..."

Aric replied with an Aran curse that satisfactorily shocked Maurin.

"None of that," Valasand said. "I may not know your tongue, but I don't tolerate that kind of behavior."

"Sorry," Maurin said.

"And don't apologize for Aric."

"I'm sor—all right."

Valasand and Dania headed in. Aric lingered just long enough behind to walk in with Maurin.

"Where is Talauna?" Maurin asked.

Aric hadn't seen the Maolori girl since they started fighting, but had a sneaking suspicion he knew where she was. He bit back a smirk. "She probably went inside to take a bath."

Maurin exhaled loudly. "I'm not looking forward to lugging up all those buckets."

"Maybe you don't have to."

"What do you mean?"

Aric coughed into his hand. "There's a mountain stream a little distance away outside the walls. Save yourself some time."

Maurin stopped and graced him with a sour look. "Wouldn't that be cold?"

"Not much colder than the well water, I'd think. Might feel pretty good right now."

Maurin gnawed on his lip. "Right. That's not a bad idea. What about you?"

Aric smiled. "I'll put the staffs away and be along."

———————◆———————

The gates hung open slightly, so Maurin pushed past and walked out into the woods. The air was fresh and cool, without being cold, and rich with the odors of vegetation. The tinkle of distant water off to the left of his path mingled with the sigh of the breeze through the trees. This part of Argoth was in its late summer months, approaching autumn, and the greenery gave way in some places to the varicolored suffusion of leaves. The warm light shone through them, giving the place a living glow that invigorated him with every breath he took. Maurin loved it here, away from the bustle of the city, and could feel himself relaxing as he traipsed through the woods toward the brook.

It almost felt like home.

He heard quiet splashing up ahead, not quite rhythmic enough to be the stream itself. Maurin approached quietly, hoping to get a glimpse of the local wildlife. Parting the ferns at the bank, he looked out.

Talauna faced away from him, bathing in the stream. The water flowed languidly around her hips, sparkling in the sunlight. She turned abruptly at Maurin's surprised gasp.

When the Maolori girl saw who it was, a broad smile set her face aglow, and she splashed out onto the bank to greet him. With a squawk, Maurin backpedaled and tripped on a stone. He crashed into the rushes, landing on his head.

"I'm all right, I'm all right," he assured her hastily as she rushed up to him in concern, water droplets flying. Maurin covered his eyes with one hand while waving her away with the other. "Ah, sorry—I didn't know it was you." He winced. Brilliant. Just brilliant. "I mean, I didn't mean to interrupt your bath." He staggered to his feet and turned around. "I'm really sorry. I'll leave you alone now."

He didn't hear any response, so he glanced back. She watched him over her shoulder with the strangest expression as she gathered her clothing and tugged her breeches up.

Idiot. What response did you expect? Since when has she responded to anything? He couldn't believe he had allowed himself to stare. *And you call yourself a gentleman.*

He tried to look away, but couldn't. He was a little surprised he hadn't noticed it before, but under the slave-brand on the girl's shoulder, several long, pale scars marked Talauna's back, one of which curved around almost to the velvet swell of her breast. He recognized the pattern, all too well: whip lines; old, long since healed over, but still present, still visible. Like those scars, the pain of the hate it took to treat someone like that lasted much longer than the actual physical damage.

There was only a short list of crimes this girl could possibly have committed, he thought, a sour taste rising in his mouth, and rejection of a master's advances was probably at the top. She certainly didn't give the impression of being a thief, and seemed incapable of any serious mischief. How could anyone misuse a creature of such obvious frailty?

In a rush of fury, Maurin wished to purge the world—all worlds—of slavers. To forever halt the traffickers of souls. It eclipsed every other desire—his promise to Valasand, his constant longing for home. He hated those who thrived off the humiliation and degradation of others, and his heart burned with the desire to liberate the dwindling spirits kept chained to this world.

"What happened?"

Talauna whirled, clutching her blouse to her chest.

Maurin bit back a frown and averted his eyes. "I saw your back. Who did that to you?"

She hung her head.

"Nothing like this is ever going to happen to you again." He stepped closer. "I promise."

She looked at him with something like wonder, then threw her arms around his neck and pressed herself against him.

Maurin's mouth went completely dry. Stunned and flustered, he didn't move, but he didn't embrace her, either.

"I cannot touch you," he said, his voice husky.

Hurt and confusion played over Talauna's features as she pulled away.

He tried to reason with her. "It's forbidden."

She glanced down at herself and donned her blouse with an exasperated sigh. Then she grabbed his wrists and pulled his arms around her. She wrapped her own around his middle and rested her head against his chest.

I don't know you. Why are you doing this? Part of him just wanted to relent, to simply melt into her warm, accepting innocence, to envelop her in his embrace. The other part would not let him. Don't get close. Don't become attached.

Visions of Kirai, paralyzed with fear under the slavers' ship, flashed unbidden through his mind. He wasn't sure how binding the ceremony was, considering it had been interrupted two years ago; nevertheless, he suspected he was a married man, and wondered how he might need to go about finding his bride.

He was a little disturbed to realize that the notion wasn't as pleasant as he might once have thought.

A lump formed in his throat, but he closed his eyes, and unconsciously started doing what he had wanted to do since he first laid eyes on Talauna; he ran his fingers through the thick, dark curls of her mane, and massaged her neck and shoulders. Tried not to think too much, tried not to feel her relaxing under his touch. She started to shake, and he shushed her, telling her everything would be all right.

"Am I interrupting anything?" Aric stood a few feet away, eyes sparkling.

Maurin broke away from Talauna, his face suddenly hot. "Uh, no."

The Maolori girl frowned and strode off.

"It's not what you think."

"S-u-u-u-re, Maurin," Aric drawled.

"I didn't do anything, I swear! She just..." He stopped. Just what? Needed a hug? That was silly.

"I know," Aric said, his expression the soul of innocence. "Hey, it happens to me all the time."

"In your dreams." Oh, now, that was mature, Maurin. You're such a wonderful example for him.

"You'd be surprised what happens in my dreams."

"You did that on purpose, didn't you? You knew she would be there."

Aric shrugged and smiled.

"That was wrong, and you know it."

"She didn't seem to mind." Aric smirked. "It's time you got over this bizarre obsession with Kirai anyway."

"Even if that were true, I don't need your help."

"Could have fooled me."

Maurin no longer felt like arguing the point. Aric's teasing grin disappeared as they walked into a clearing, and he stopped dead in his tracks.

Below, the forest dropped away, forming a rough green valley. In the distance, up north, Maurin could make out some features of the city, and beyond that, the white outlines of the peaks protecting Caileen.

"It's something, isn't it?" Maurin said. "From a distance, you'd hardly know what sorts of things go on there."

Aric didn't respond.

When Maurin glanced back over at his cousin, a violent chill seized him. Aric had gone rigid and pale, his eyes fixed on some unknown point in the distance.

"What is it?" Maurin whispered.

Aric shook himself. "No matter how bad things are," he said in a hollow voice, "it's nothing compared to what's coming."

———— ◆ ————

The town of Glenyss writhed in its death-throes. A green mist swirled around the buildings, tendrils stretching up into the clouds. Sickly green lightning flickered in response to the shrieks of the damned. The Reamar warriors leapt like shadows cast by a flame. Krige was glad for the distance; he couldn't see the faces of the people, but he could still hear their screams.

"None of them have seen Siaran Thoud." Marèse Shavad was most displeased that they still had not found their priestess. The Reamar man of war surveyed the activity below, his features jagged as the sheer cliffs in the distance.

"How unfortunate," Governor Phoecius growled. "I told you we didn't know where she was."

"Still, a good harvest." Guilan Vail flashed a predatory grin at him.

Randolf's eyes flicked over at Krige. He didn't have to say anything. Everything the man had cautioned about the Reamar was vindicated.

Krige had been summoned again by Phoecius, whose latest folly included a treaty of sorts with the Marèse. Since the missing priestess was not in Langfort, and nobody wanted a war, Shavad had suggested the governor should gain from his campaign. The outlying towns under Phoecius's jurisdiction would be the Reamar's to inspect and raid without question or interference, and most importantly, no one would raise the alarm among any of the other cities. As a reward, Langfort was to be left alone, and Phoecius himself would receive a fair compensation of the booty, which was by no means inconsiderable.

Everybody wins. Everyone important, that is.

"This wasn't exactly what I had in mind when you spoke of raids," Phoecius said. "You said you would just take things of value."

"The lives of your people have great value," Guilan Vail said, dark eyes mocking. "Do you just now realize this?"

"This is slaughter," Krige said. They were systematically wiping out town after town, ostensibly in the search for this Siaran Thoud. Yet Krige had heard mutterings of another, a Dreaded One they hunted with as much diligence as they did their missing priestess. Though the Reamar were proud and boastful, he sensed a growing tension, even as they gloried in the deaths of thousands.

"Slaughter—is that not what you call it when animals are prepared for a feast? An appropriate term." Guilan Vail reclined on an ancient battlement, adjusting the silver serpent brooch adorning his cape. "Tell me: what became of the slave you had with you when first we met?"

"He ran away," Krige said. "And he would have done the same to you, so at least you haven't wasted your money."

"He would not have escaped from us," Vail said.

"Your priestess did," Krige retorted.

He knew at once it was the wrong thing to say.

"She did not run away!" Marèse Shavad whirled, ice-blue eyes tinged with green fire. "No one leaves the Reamar!"

Leslan Randolf, to his credit, placed himself between the Reamar and his master. Sweat popped out on Krige's brow, but he held his ground. "Very well, then, have it your way. That doesn't interest me so much as the reason you are killing our people."

Guilan Vail smiled. "You have among you someone very dangerous. We are simply making this world safe for all of us."

"By eliminating everyone who might be a threat?"

"Exactly."

Krige watched the courtyard below in horror as the ever-expanding aura passed over and through every last man, woman, and child in the town. Their cries rose in pitch as, one by one, they dropped in their tracks, collapsing even as they tried to escape the main gates of the city—barred against threats from the outside.

Far above it as he was, even Krige felt the prickly cold invasion of the green fog. Soon, none moved below. The corpses lay covered with frost. The Reamar stood with arms outstretched, absorbing the glowing haze into their bodies. They moved as one to gather at the base of the tower, and hundreds of luminous green eyes gazed up at Marèse Shavad, who smiled with approval.

"It is finished," Vail said. "The Dreaded One was not among them."

Phoecius looked white in the moonlight.

When he could speak, Krige asked, "Why have you shown me this?"

Guilan Vail's eyes curdled the marrow in Krige's bones. "Life has come anew to the gods of the Gray Lands, and we will not have it threatened by anyone. The Reamar will not diminish, and the glory of our dominion shall be restored. Too long have we languished in injured slumber. It is time to bid the gods arise."

CHAPTER 17

MESSENGER

In the hallway leading into the protected arena seats, Krige worked up the nerve to join his lord and master. The screams of Glenyss echoed in his soul, and he pinched the bridge of his nose. Leslan Randolf gave him a questioning nod, but Krige waved him away.

So exhausted. Constantly torn between Phoecius and the Reamar, Daman and the other nobles. Couldn't a man just be left in peace? Daman had invited Krige to join him as he went through a pre-game selection of contestants for the circus. Voices echoed ahead, and Krige crept closer to listen, just in case he couldn't go through with it and had to turn back. He recognized one-half of Daman's favorite bodyguard team: Sabatha, captain of the guard.

"My lord," Sabatha said in the strangely modulated accent of a domesticated offworlder, "there is a matter that needs discussing."

"What is it?"

"It's the Reamar, my lord. They've been too silent about our cutting off the slave shipments after that blatant attack. That should have provoked some message of protest or defiance. But there has been no word from Darkhorn Fell."

"They never have been especially chatty, have they?"

"No, but this is not a good sign. We should be wary."

Daman's voice turned speculative. "Do you remember hearing of the Reamar when you were young?"

"No, my lord," Sabatha said. "I was not raised on this world."

"Of course you weren't," Daman said absently. "Well, the Reamar are reputed to kill in order to live. They take life in order to prolong their own. There is a transfer of essence upon the physical consummation of death. Some believe the one who takes the life also consumes the essence. Hence, the more blood on your hands, the longer your life."

"No one lives forever, my lord." Krige could hear the smile in Sabatha's tone. "Not even you."

"My father thought he would try."

Krige had seen Daman's father only a handful of times—a sallow-faced, bearded man with wild eyes. Uneasy didn't even begin to describe the feeling he evoked. Did Krige really have the energy for this today? His mind and body ached.

"It was he who started the dealings with the Reamar. He rather worshipped them, I fear. Believed they were gods."

So it was true. Krige edged closer. Randolf gave him a half-smile of vindication.

"Indeed," Sabatha said.

"I think *they* believe they're gods. At any rate, my father wanted to learn their secrets. Thought there was power in blood, and attempted to restore his youth. Went through countless slaves before he realized it wasn't helping."

"I see."

So did Krige. Perhaps Daman's hobbies had their origin in his father's misguided quest for eternal life. Much as he ached to go in and ask if that was what was behind Argoneis's penchant for torture, one never actually broached the subject with Daman. If Daman wanted to talk, fine, but you never, never asked. Besides, he suspected what the father began with purpose, the son carried on for mere sport.

"Yes, well... it didn't work, obviously."

Krige decided it was time he announced himself. Eventually, his presence would have been missed, and he didn't feel like thinking up excuses this time. Better to endure, as he had always done. He nodded to Randolf and coughed politely. The two men glanced up as Krige shuffled in to sit beside Argoneis. Krige nodded briefly to the powerful man who sat on the other side. Inscrutable dark eyes peered at him over an aquiline nose. He didn't see the sister, Anice, anywhere.

"Ah, my dear Krige," Argoneis said. "Good of you to join us."

Sabatha stared pointedly at Krige.

"Oh, you can say anything you like in front of him. He's my loyal friend."

"I am your man," Krige said.

"There, you see? Come, join us. We were just about to discuss our games with Farel, here." He indicated a hardy-looking man walking up to meet them. "Have you met Farel before?"

Krige shook his head wearily.

"Ah. Well, allow me to introduce you. Bodar Farel, this is Lord Aster Krige, one of my closest personal friends. Bodar is an artisan of the pits; his preliators have gained recognition across the land. It was he who trained that pit-fighter-turned-gladiatrix who used all of her skill on Lord Seides. I've hired him to work with the circus trainees."

Krige ignored the fact that Daman had just breached protocol by introducing him to the arena master, rather than the other way around. Right now, he couldn't care less. More than anything, he just wanted to be somewhere other than here. Sighing, he asked, "What are we doing here, my lord?"

Daman's eyes danced with glee. "We are training. See that fellow there? He has spunk. He's sent five separate slaves to medical. Old Rominan would have paid a good hundred marks just to see him fight once. This one could well be our star attraction; unless, of course, we can find Seides's runaway. Any word on her yet?"

"Nothing, my lord," Krige watched with Daman as the combatants below fought for the right to prolong their lives by another day. Some time passed before Argoneis spoke again, and when he did, it was with a tone Krige didn't much care for.

"My friend," he said, "there is another reason I asked you here today."

"Oh?" Krige's tongue cleaved to the roof of his mouth. "What is that?"

"You have made several trips to Langfort lately. Is there something going on that I should know about?"

More than you can imagine. Krige hesitated. "Actually, my lord, I'm not certain. Governor Phoecius may be hiding something."

"What do you mean?" Daman asked sharply.

"Well..." Krige swallowed. Something approximating the truth should keep Daman's eyes off him. Of course, the governor of Langfort might suffer for it, but that was his own problem. "He has a fear of invaders."

"From the Temple?" Daman frowned. "I've been informed that a Warden of the Gates may be nosing around."

So the Countess had gotten to visit him after all. No word one way or the other from Sal Dalinde, so it couldn't have been that long ago. Daman tended to kill the messenger, but if she managed to make it sound in Daman's best interests, perhaps it hadn't gone over as badly as Krige feared.

"Really? I hadn't heard anything about that. No, the danger he fears is from our own world."

"Ludicrous," Daman scoffed. "Who would dare?"

"Who indeed, my lord?"

After a moment passed, Daman gestured by way of inducement to continue, and said quietly, "Who?"

Krige licked his lips tentatively, scanning the crowd, praying the eyes of the Gray Lands did not extend this far north. "He mentioned the Reamar, my lord."

"I see." Daman was silent for a few minutes. "What do you know of the Reamar?"

I know you've been dealing with them quietly on the side for years, and you send them all manner of off-world captives. I know that if you'd seen what I just saw, you'd be taking them a lot more seriously. But I also know that I'm a dead man if I say anything.

"Not much," he said, smiling. "Nothing substantial, anyway—more in the vein of legend. I was taught to stay away from the borders of the Gray Lands, and to always lock my doors and windows at night, lest the Reamar come to steal my soul."

Daman laughed. "We wouldn't want that, now, would we?"

"No, my lord."

"Well," Daman said, "it would appear our gray neighbors have become quite the subject of the hour. Perhaps it would behoove us to have a little chat with our dear governor, and find out just what it is they're doing that's troubling him so much."

Krige swallowed hard. "I'm sure he would welcome the chance to have an audience with you."

The rest of the afternoon passed in a red mist, and Krige looked forward to spending the night forgetting it. He mulled over his options. Phoecius had contacted him directly about the situation with the

Reamar. Perhaps the governor thought after that first time that Krige would be quicker to act than Argoneis, but that seemed improbable. It wasn't as if any kind of force was Krige's to command, and what could one do against an army of soul-drinking immortals?

Hiding something, indeed. That was a laugh. Everyone on this world could be hiding something. But might Phoecius have sympathies with Argoneis? He had mentioned that possibility to Sedrick, who replied, *With all due respect, I don't think that's likely, sir. He doesn't seem to have the, shall we say, stomach for the kind of friendship that Lord Argoneis requires.*

Nonetheless, money could be a powerful motivator, and greed could override the governor's sensibilities, in which case Phoecius was setting Krige up for a fall. Yet he didn't think that to be the case. The events in Glenyss had shown the man to be a coward caught in a web spun by his own avarice.

Meanwhile, the Warden still had two of Krige's slaves, and he wasn't eager to advertise that fact to Argoneis unless he had to. He knew where she lived, but not what she was doing. He had a spy watching her movements, but so far, the man had nothing terribly interesting to report.

On top of that, could the council have made a grave error by allowing Lauran Dalinde to confront the Lord Regent? Like it or not, they were all in this mess together. Perhaps it was not Argoneis to whom they should have sent the envoy, but the Warden of the Gates. If the countess was correct, and the Temple wished to charge guilt by association, he had to make certain they understood just how much of the blame lay squarely on Lord Argoneis's shoulders.

———— ◆ ————

A messenger awaited Krige when he arrived back at his mansion. The boy, dressed in a page's attire, could not have been more than fourteen years of age.

"I bear a message from Darkhorn Fell." He spoke with a proud, measured tone. "I am to deliver it in person to Lord Krige of Caileen."

"A messenger from...?" Krige paled. "Let me have it, boy."

"It is for you alone."

"Very well." Krige waved his bodyguard out. "Go. Leave us alone." The boy waited until Randolf had left the room.

"Well?" Krige pressed nervously, lowering himself into the chair by the fire. "What is it?"

"I do not know, my lord," the boy admitted.

"Just give it to me, then." Krige held out his hand expectantly, but no scroll was dropped into it. The boy simply stood there.

"It is not written down, my lord."

"Randolf!" Krige shouted. "Come take this impudent young scamp out of my sight. He is wasting my time!"

"Just a moment, my lord." The boy closed his eyes and took a deep breath. His teeth clenched, and his body went rigid. Randolf opened the door and took one step inside before Krige waved him away.

The youth's eyes rolled up into his head for a moment, and back. He stared blankly through Krige. For an agonizing eternity of a second, there was silence. Then the boy spoke in a clear, distinct voice:

"Krige." But it was not the boy's voice. It was the harmonious voice of a grown woman. And his countenance had altered, too. The direct and disapproving gaze sent chills down Krige's spine. The boy's face had an attitude of superiority now, a confidence born of power. He crossed his arms in deliberate scorn.

"You have betrayed us." The eyes, pupils dilated unnaturally, now

screamed accusation at him, and the voice took on a deadly tone. *"That was unwise."*

"Be... betrayed?" Krige squeaked. "Whatever do you mean?"

"You reported our activities to Daman Argoneis, self-styled Lord Regent of Caileen."

"No! No!" A cold sweat popped out on his forehead. "You misunderstand! I was compelled to mention you, but I did not tell him what you were doing, I swear it! Argoneis is upset about the attack on our city, and his advisors blame you! They do not know why you have not responded to the arrest of the slave shipments."

"We are aware of his actions," came the voice again, scaldingly cool. *"Just as we are aware of your duplicity in this matter. Prepare for the day of your doom, for it is at hand."*

Krige slumped down out of his seat, barely keeping himself upright as he hooked one arm over the arm of his chair, grasping at his chest with the other. *Yasul,* he thought, with sickening dread, *they must have eyes everywhere!*

"Please... I told him nothing! Just ask your sources, whoever they are. They'll tell you, or they can find out. Believe me!"

After a disconcerting stretch of silence, the voice finally answered. *"Very well. I shall look into the matter. But I shall not forget this, Krige, and should I find you have been lying to me, you will rue the day of your birth."*

"Thank you, my lady," Krige breathed, too terrified to be relieved. "I would never betray you."

"Let us hope not."

The boy's eyes de-focused again, and he reverted to his former youthful stance, his arms smartly behind his back.

"Did you get the...?" he started to ask in his own voice, before noticing Krige half-lying on the floor.

Krige could barely find the strength to move. He forced himself back into his chair. The decanter clanged against the glass like the clapper of a bell as he poured himself a drink.

"I see that you did," the boy said. "Thank you, milord. I'll find my own way out."

CHAPTER 18
STRAW MEN

"This is a gamble." Valasand paced the halls, perusing the ancient weaponry suspended in ornamental uselessness over her head.

Obedience is never a gamble.

"Still, I'm not comfortable with this whole situation."

Comfort will come later.

"I know, I know. Don't remind me."

Hadn't she already done all the hard work, searching for all that time, finally pinpointing the odious source of the evil? Nevertheless, the decision was made. She would do what she had sworn to do, and follow through with it, wherever it led. Jashara had faith in her ability; she should too, right? She wished she could just hand the whole situation over to him—or her, or it, or whatever Jashara was. Human terminology didn't work very well with the Vigilant.

You'll make it, Little Flame.

Steeling herself, she strode out into the foyer and climbed the stairs.

Unsurprisingly, Aric was up already. Of the four, he was, perhaps, the most attuned to the waking of the world. "Aric, come here."

The youth frowned as he turned toward her. "What?"

"Don't be so surly. You'll enjoy this." She didn't give him a chance to retort. "We're going to the east wing."

"The east wing?" he repeated dully.

"Where all the swords are hanging on the walls."

"The swords?" Aric's surprise quickly changed into a grin.

Valasand nodded. The last few weeks had been good for him.

"Yes! I knew it!" Aric ran down the hall and knocked on his cousin's door. "Hey, Maurin! Are you ready? What's taking you so long?"

A muffled yawn came through the door. "What do you want?"

"Come on. Something new today."

There was a pause, followed by an inarticulate mumble. Valasand stifled a smile as Aric kicked at the base of the door. "Aren't you up yet?"

"All right, all right." The door creaked open, and Maurin nearly got

a fist in the nose as Aric raised his arm to knock again. Maurin's hair was still not brushed and fell in wild strings around his face. He rubbed at his eyes. "What's going on?"

Aric immediately turned and trotted down the stairs, carrying his stocky frame lightly, with the grace of a natural athlete. Conversely, this early in the morning, Maurin moved as though he were much heavier than he actually was.

"We're going to the armory," Aric said, as he bounced on ahead of Maurin, who would have had to jog in order to keep up with him, and was obviously disinclined to make any such effort. "Come on! She's going to teach us how to use the swords today!"

"Oh." Maurin nodded sleepily. Then he stood still in his tracks. "Oh!" he said again, suddenly alert. He glanced back at Valasand. "What?"

She nodded. "It's time."

Dania and Talauna joined them, and they all gathered in the east wing and waited for her to speak. Let them wait. It would heighten their interest, and make them pay closer attention when she broke her silence.

Valasand ran an evaluating finger along one of the swords on the wall. It was lightweight and well-balanced, with a two-handed grip, and a blade that came to a razor point. This one reminded her of Aric; edgy, precise, and subtly lethal. Aric bore a temper; that much was obvious, but there was a strong sense of justice in him, too.

This sword, she thought, moving to another, was like Maurin. Beautiful, strong, built with principle, but almost too weighty and rigid to wield. Being close to Maurin was like walking by a broad, quiet river. The water might appear calm on the surface, but the currents ran deep, and if one were to dip into the river at just the wrong place, one could get swept away before realizing the danger.

She reached up and took the weapons from the wall, handing them to the boys. Aric examined his with hungry excitement, and Maurin studied the edge of his blade, balancing his sword and turning it from side to side. Valasand marked the sly smile spreading across his face. It would be easy enough to teach them how to fight, she supposed. But being a Warden was about controlling chaos, not causing it. She was

tapping into some potential danger with these four. It was such a fine line to walk.

Another sword looked as if it might snap between her fingers, but when she tried it, the slender blade had a quiet strength and resilience. Talauna was the only one of the new recruits who bore no such apparent anger or resentment, but her silence and strange behaviors were an enigma, and her emotions, while strong and directed, were always difficult to read. Yet the Breath had whispered in Valasand's ear of this girl's importance; an importance that might even eclipse the others'.

Talauna looked at her sword as if she had been handed a dead rodent.

Dania remained coolly unreadable. "What about me?"

"What about you?" Valasand asked.

"Why did you not give me a sword?"

"You already know how to fight."

"Teach me what you will. I can still learn."

Valasand nodded and considered another one. It had a short, brutal blade with an ugly bite. There was nothing decorative or fancy about it; like Dania, it was clearly an instrument of death. The warrior's anger was intense; more potent, in many ways, than Aric's or Maurin's, but as easily reached as it was deep-rooted. Constantly scowling, her features twisted into a raw, bitter visage, she wore her hatred like a badge of honor. But Dania contained the capability to rise above her emotions, should she be properly motivated.

"What are we doing?" Maurin squinted at the sun as they passed through the doors to the courtyard, where the scarecrows awaited them.

"What does it look as though we're doing?" Valasand regarded him with one eyebrow raised.

"I mean, why?"

"If for no other reason, because I want you to do so. Ask me no more questions now."

"I'm sorry," Maurin said, taken aback.

"I want you to attack them," Valasand went on, "and make what would be a fatal blow on a human." She motioned to Aric, who unhesitatingly rushed up to the straw man and ran it through with a straight thrust. Valasand nodded approval. "What were you aiming for?"

"The heart," Aric said, clearly proud of himself.

"Missed it, by a good four inches," Valasand said, deflating his self-satisfied smile. "Still, that was a fatal blow. You pierced the left lung. Very good."

She motioned to Maurin. He made an attacking slash that went down the shoulder of the straw man and on through the chest.

"Good, but impractical. On a live person, you would meet resistance from bones, and often from armor. Go between them, rather than through them, whenever possible."

She gestured to Talauna. The Maolori hesitated, then made a short stab.

The boys' eyes widened, and Valasand tried not to smile. "That would definitely be incapacitating, but if you're aiming for the heart, go up about a foot and a half." She approached Talauna. "Here, hold the grip firmly in both hands, like this, see? You don't have a man's advantage of weight and strength, so you may have to use your palm to drive the point home. Later, we'll work on how to use your enemy's size to your advantage."

Aric, smirking, muttered to Maurin that she seemed to be doing just fine driving the point home, and maybe Talauna was more dangerous than she seemed. With a choked laugh, Maurin agreed.

Valasand pretended she hadn't heard. "Dania?"

Dania, who had been looking at her sword very carefully throughout the duration of the practice, gave a cat-like scream, and set upon the straw opponent with a vengeance. The first blow was a stab to the chest; the second blow was a hack downward, spilling the unfortunate thing's straw guts. The third blow cleanly whacked off the dummy's head.

She hit it again, and as she prepared for the fifth fatal blow, Valasand grabbed her wrist on the backswing.

Dania turned and snarled, fury blazing in her eyes, but she couldn't break Valasand's grip.

"The first one was sufficient," Valasand said. She let Dania go, replaced her devastated straw man, then ordered a second round.

Aric plunged his sword directly into the "heart" of the dummy, and Valasand nodded in satisfaction. Maurin managed to do the same.

"That'll do."

On her next turn, Talauna put the sword through the straw mannequin's throat.

"Very good," Valasand praised.

Silence.

"Were you aiming for the throat?" she asked.

Eyes downcast, Talauna shook her head.

"The heart?"

Still looking at the ground, the Maolori nodded yes.

Valasand closed her eyes. *I suppose this is to be an exercise in my patience, as well? I know you sent me to her. But she's going to be a liability in battle. I'm sure your reasons will become clear.* She reconsidered. *Then again, maybe not.*

She gave the girl a few more tips about stance and grip. "Keep practicing. Now, Dania. All right. One fatal blow."

Dania moved to the next straw man, wound up for a big two-handed swing, and severed the head again. As she swung around, she didn't stop, and she slashed the dummy's chest. Then she screamed and lost control, hacking until she reduced the poor target to a pile of loose, shredded straw. She stood breathing heavily and staring at the sorry remains. The others all watched, eyes wide and mouths open. Aric wore a half-smile, a mixture of disbelief, awe and admiration.

"Dania, come with me. The rest of you, continue to practice by your-selves for a while." They moved some distance away, just out of earshot of the others. Valasand turned and scrutinized her. The gladiatrix stood there, heaving. "Dania, look at me."

She glanced up, seemingly against her will.

Valasand considered her next words carefully. Dania was too good at what she did to lose control like this. The training was there. Reliving, or fantasizing? Something—or someone—had clearly pushed her over the edge. "What were you searching for?"

"The blood... there is always blood when you kill them." Dania shook her head at the ground again. "Stupid. They're only straw men."

Valasand nodded. "Tell me, how would you attack someone if you did not wish to kill him?"

"What do you mean?"

"How would you attack someone if you did not wish to kill him?" she repeated, her gaze unwavering.

Dania didn't respond.

Valasand took her over to a fresh target, away from the rest of the group. Maurin was trying to mind his own business and not pay any at-tention to them. Talauna kept stealing concerned glances in their direc-tion, and Aric stared unabashedly.

"I want you to attack this one; I don't want you to kill it."

Dania looked at Valasand as if she had lost her mind.

"I want you to deliver a non-fatal blow," she reiterated. "Proceed."

Dania stared at the dummy for a moment, seemingly mystified.

"Where can you hit someone, and not kill him?" Valasand prompted, her voice calm.

Three more times, Dania prepared to strike, and each time, she stopped short of beginning the swing. Then something changed in her eyes. Dania dropped to one hand and swept her blade across the back of the straw leg, hamstringing it. With a returning arc she plunged the tip of the sword into the side of what would have been the dummy's gluteal muscle. A quick thrust, and the blade pierced a couple of inches into what would have been the junction of the shoulder blade and spine. She lopped off the straw man's "hand," then plunged the sword through its calf and left it there.

"Still alive," she spat, turning to Valasand in fury. "Why would you want to attack somebody and not kill him? Fools' talk!"

Valasand didn't allow herself to be disturbed by the outburst. "The others need to learn how to kill. You are already adept at that. We need to teach you how *not* to kill. As it stands, you have no choice; whenever you fight, you believe you must kill. You have effectiveness, but as you demonstrated even now, you do not have control."

"Control produces losers," Dania retorted, "and gets you killed."

"Truly?" Valasand raised her eyebrows. "When you attacked me, I had the choice of whether or not to kill you. You are alive due to my control."

"If you do not kill, you die!" Dania pleaded desperately.

"Who told you that?" Valasand asked.

"The Pit Master."

Valasand sat in silence for a moment. "Tell me how you came to be here."

Dania's eyes flashed defiance. "It has been many years."

"That's all right. Tell me what you remember."

Dania took a deep breath and squared her shoulders. "I was raised in a caravan by a man who was not my father. He taught me to steal, and to perform tricks for the crowds. We were very poor, and I was always dressed in rags. One day, some men in uniforms I did not recognize walked in my direction. They were not Enforcers, so I paid them no heed. What could they have to do with me? Then I heard one of the men say, 'That one will do.' Before I knew what was happening, strong hands grabbed me."

Valasand waited as Dania struggled with the pain of the memory.

"I remember being walked to the ship. Once aboard, I saw many other castaways like myself. I do not know how long I was there. It could have been a day, or a year. When we arrived, I was bathed and sold at an auction in the Market." Dania laughed. "The woman of the house returned me right away. She complained that I would not do anything, no matter how much she beat me. Lady Vician said I attacked the other servants for no reason whatsoever." She straightened with defensive pride.

"But there was a reason. There was always a reason."

Valasand regarded the strong, noble structure of the young woman's face, and the deep, penetrating eyes. Behind the mask of tattoos, Dania had come from a truly beautiful people. "Yes. I'm sure there was."

"She said I was a waste of money, and to get rid of me, and get her a new one. So two big men came and took me to a place I had never been. The slaver was talking with a stranger. When he saw me, he said, 'I think she's perfect for you, Farel.' The man called Farel said 'We'll see,' and told the men to let me go. He walked over and stood in front of the door, opening it a crack. I watched him closely. He said, 'If you can get past me, you're free. That's all you have to do, girl. Think you're up to it?'"

Dania fell silent. When she spoke again, there was a hint of a smile on her lips.

"I flew upon him. I hit him, I scratched him, I bit him. His fists were enormous and covered with hair. One blow sent me flying across the room." She punctuated her sentence by smacking her fist into her palm. "When I got up, my mouth was bleeding, but I tried again. He hit me again. I got up again. He hit me again. After five times, I could fight no more. He looked at me much as the man who called himself my father used to, and I got sick. Then he said, 'She'll do,' and asked what the slaver wanted for me."

"Was Farel the Pit Master?"

"Yes. He started training me in the ways of pit combat. He trained me first against animals. He threw me into the ring with no clothes or armor. They had a spear set up in the ground in the middle of the pit, and I had to get to it before the loder-cat got to me. I killed it, but just barely. After I showed Farel I could kill anything he sent out to kill me, he put me in with humans. He taught me to love my fury, to feed on it."

"Go on," Valasand said.

Dania cast her eyes down. "One night, when I had grown, he seduced me. He caught me staring at him in his bathstream. He asked what I was looking at. When I could not answer, he told me to come closer. 'I've shown you how to be a fighter,' he said. 'Come here, and I'll show you how to be a woman.'"

Dania gritted her teeth.

"After that night, we were lovers. I was never given a choice. He was rough, and he was demanding, but he was always there. It was a part of my life, just like the fights. And I was good at fighting. I never lost. Sometimes I was set out with a team, but he liked to see me fight alone. Many important lords of the city came to watch. Lord Argoneis himself sat in the place of honor at several matches. He was smiling, always smiling."

Dania's visage clouded as the power of her recollection overcame her. Valasand could feel the hostility crackling in the air like current. "Then what happened, Dania?"

"It was the day Baron Seides came to the pits. The Baron thought himself a connoisseur, and loved to watch me. After the fight was over, he came down into the stalls under the arena to speak to Farel about moving me from the pits to the gladiators' arena. I heard them haggling over me like a piece of meat. I couldn't believe Farel talked about me like that, had even considered selling me. But, I reasoned, he sounded as though he were trying to discourage the sale. Maybe it was just show talk. I wouldn't really be sold. I meant too much to Farel, as a fighter, as a lover... I was a *valuable asset*, he said. Then this Seides said, 'I must have her! Name your price, Farel; she's a gem!' My master looked at me, and said, 'You give her half a chance, she'll rip you to shreds.' I knew then he had already decided to sell me. The other man said again, 'I must have her.' I would have killed him for the look in his eyes alone, but I was chained."

Dania choked. She looked away, but tears were evidently an unwelcome visitor to her. Valasand's own vision began to shimmer, and it took everything in her not to reach out and embrace her.

"When the medics came, they gave me something for the pain," Dania continued, her voice strong again. "But it was different. The next thing I knew, I was cold. I couldn't move. As I came to, I saw the reason: I was tied down to a metal table, my arms and legs bound with leather. I knew I had been betrayed when I saw the face of my new owner leering over me. 'I will have you,' he said."

A stray tear managed to escape, but her face was proud, her jaw and fists clenched. "I always told him—every time I told him—that if ever I got free, I would kill him. So one day, I did." Dania gave a casual shrug, defying Valasand to rebuke her.

"Yes," she said softly. "He is dead, but are you free? You hated him, and you killed him. He is no more, but your hate did not die with him."

Dania looked stricken.

"As long as your hate still lives," she continued, "you will never be free."

CHAPTER 19
DESPERATE MEASURES

"Good day to you, Lord Krige, and welcome to Daes Yasul. Your visit is most pleasing to the Lord Regent. Won't you come this way?"

"Thank you," Krige said stiffly.

Sabatha escorted him under a sweeping arch and through a broad hallway. Burly Talormine guards stood at loose attention, spaced every fifty feet or so. The Talormines were a mysterious people native to the northern regions of Argoth, a kind of sister race to the Maolori, if primitive records were to be believed. They had the same dark skin and curly hair, but there the resemblance ended. While the Maolori were, on the whole, small, quiet, and lithe, the Talormines were known for their mass and strength; each one taller and heavier than any man, with broad shoulders and backswept skulls. Small mad eyes glared out from under thick brows, and wide nostrils flared on a broad snout. Often called Horseheads by locals, they bore no known relation to any equine species. But the Talormines' strength, speed, and size lent them the wild and warlike reputation attached to horses, and so the misnomer stuck. The fact that Daman had been able to tame the Talormines was impressive. He must have gotten these when they were just cubs.

"This way, please," Sabatha repeated, gesturing toward a giant column fashioned to look like a white tree with a serpent spiraling down its massive trunk. Krige glanced over and saw its twin on the far side of the vast hall. Each serpent was actually a stairwell whose functionality was disguised by the angle of the viewer on the floor. The carved white branches of the trees buttressed the ceiling. The temple had been built as a tribute to the god Yasul, and every part of its construction was meant to tell a story, but Krige was not a religious man. No doubt it was very pretty, but any meaning escaped him.

He had wanted to send Sedrick on this mission, and felt reasonably confident Argoneis wouldn't do anything to his trusted manservant, but no sense taking chances. Better to talk to the man himself than risk losing a good slave.

Too much time had passed. The situation with the Reamar was escalating, and nothing had come of the countess's visit. If the bubble was to burst, perhaps it was best that Krige be the one to do it. And more than anything, he burned for Talauna. He had given in to Mirian too easily. Selling the girl had been a mistake; he could see that now.

Krige's small retinue of bodyguards followed Sabatha and two of those wretched Talormine guards up the stairway on the right, climbing to the uppermost levels of the temple. Krige had to breathe shallowly to avoid the stench. Not only did they reek in the enclosed space, but the creatures could never stand straight up, so they took up an uncomfortable amount of room, lurking in their primal crouch, and snuffling like animals. Krige distanced himself as much as possible, and didn't look at them. He imagined he saw amusement on the face of the captain of the guard.

By the time they reached the top, Krige was nearly winded. If Daman climbed these every day to his quarters, it was no wonder the man stayed so slim and youthful. Sabatha ushered Krige to a private suite and announced him with a nominal amount of pomp. Krige's bodyguards were made to stand outside. Sabatha left the room, but did not close the doors behind him.

Argoneis reclined against purple satin pillows on a bed big enough for a dozen full-grown men. His bare feet jutted out lazily at Krige from under a loose-fitting silken gown, and in his hand a small coffer put forth an aromatic steam. From the look on Argoneis's face, it must have been some sort of drug. Krige took care not to breathe too deeply.

Four unhappy young slaves reclined on the bed beside Daman. One tended to his bare feet, and a couple fed him bits of fruit and cheese, carefully holding a flagon of wine to his lips when he gestured for it. The fourth was apparently there just for Argoneis to lean on to keep from keeling over in his excess.

"Lord Argoneis"—Krige tried to ignore the decadence and pretend he was addressing the man in a more formal setting—"thank you for granting me audience."

"Anytime, my friend," Daman said blearily. "You know my house is yours. I never see you here these days."

He was drugged, all right. "My apologies, my lord. Your invitations have all been most welcome, and I would have joined you for more of your banquets if it were not for pressing business I simply had to attend to."

Daman waved off any further comments. "Not a problem. What can I do for you?" He gestured lazily. "Wine? A girl? A boy?"

"No, thank you." Krige took a breath and stepped forward. "I have news, my lord."

"News?" Daman gave his slave a halfhearted squeeze and sat up a little straighter in bed. The movement, however, caused his eyes to roll back, and he just as quickly fell onto the cushions with a moan. "What kind of news?" he asked. "Is it good?"

Krige smiled. "I have reason to believe that a certain outsider is harboring dangerous criminals. After some effort, I discovered that the murderer of Baron Seides is living in a mansion outside the city limits."

"Really?" Argoneis's eyes, returned now to their natural position, shone with interest, but Krige was dismayed to see how hazed they were. Just how much of this was getting through?

"Yes, my lord," Krige said. "The gladiatrix, Dania."

"Excellent." Daman's face brightened. "The circus would not have been the same without her."

Krige nodded politely. "This outsider and some runaway slaves come into the city often for supplies, leaving the preliator behind, lest she be recognized. With your permission, my lord, on the outlander's next excursion, I will arrange for some bounty hunters to grab the criminal and deliver her to you. It took some time, but I was finally able to get some interested in the job. For some reason, no one seemed interested in turning her in."

"Her reputation, no doubt," Argoneis said dryly.

"Perhaps. Meanwhile, the outsider also will be arrested and brought to you. I request only that the slaves are delivered to me."

Argoneis glanced up in surprise. "Why?"

Krige started pacing, which made Daman's Talormine bodyguards nervous. He wasn't worried, though, because his own retinue stood just outside the open door. "One of them used to belong to me." Two, in truth, but he saw no need to mention Talauna. He had a feeling Argoneis would be less than forgiving if he managed to find out Krige had gone ahead to sell her to Vellis. This seemed the most advantageous way to retrieve her.

Daman scrutinized Krige. "Who? Not that devastating little Maolori? I seem to recall that I offered to buy her from you at one time, but you had something of an itch for her. That's not the one, is it?"

Krige felt the hair rising on the back of his neck. "No, my lord. Just one of my lesser slaves, not worth a tenth of a mark. He used to be my pilot."

Daman sat back and stewed in his own inebriated juices for a few moments. A sudden malicious glitter appeared in the corner of his eye as he watched for Krige's reaction.

"I want the arena warrior brought to me, of course," he said. "As for the outlander, when she comes into the city, we will be ready for her. I will break her arms and her legs, and set her on a pole for all to see. Then there will be no doubt about what happens to those who disregard the law. And all of the outlander's slaves will be flayed alive and set on shorter stakes in a circle around her as an example."

Krige blanched. "My lord, isn't that a bit drastic? Surely the woman alone deserves your justice. But the slaves could be resold…"

"No, Aster," Daman said in a fatherly tone. He was smiling, but his expression remained hard as stone as he absently drummed his fingers on the scalp of the slave next to him. "We must not show weakness to the masses. There have been stirrings of discontent among the slaves, or so my friends from Sal Dalinde would have me believe. What better way to quiet those rumblings than to have a full-fledged demonstration of our power?"

"None, my lord," Krige quavered, numb to the core.

"Very well, then," Daman said with glee. "You have my thanks for informing me of this shocking and flagrant disregard of the law. We will see to it that justice prevails once more in this city."

"Yes, my lord."

"Cheer up," Argoneis added. "You've been an active part in enforcing the law. I won't forget your help in this matter."

The frightening thing about that was, he wouldn't.

As he left, Krige tried to control the frantic angst threatening to overwhelm him. By going to Argoneis, he had unwittingly sealed Talauna's doom.

CHAPTER 20
SIMMERING

"Something very extraordinary is happening here." Valasand had gathered them all in the library. "Events are transpiring that are beyond even me. I don't know where it will end, but I believe we are being prepared for something specific; something powerful. Each of you has a gift unique to bringing about the purpose of the one who sent me."

Aric's innards clawed at him to escape as he stirred the logs with a poker, trying to drown out her words.

"Who is that?" Maurin asked, foolishly intrigued. Talauna's leg casually grazed his hip as she lounged next to him.

Aric kicked Maurin's foot as he returned to his seat. His cousin was far too trusting.

"My god, Yasul. The Source."

Aric blinked. "What?"

"Valasand," Maurin said hesitantly, "I don't mean to forget my place, but... who are you?"

She gazed at him evenly. "You and Aric are not from this world, are you?"

"No, my lady. We were brought here. We didn't even know there were places like this."

And if I had my way, we'd be gone in a heartbeat. Aric watched the intricate dance of shadows the crackling fire cast on Dania's marked skin. *Something darker than a winter's night here, and it's not Argoneis.*

"I thought not." Valasand glanced away. "There are many worlds, Maurin, of which this is just one small and seemingly insignificant example. I come from a place where the cities are grander, cleaner."

"You must think us primitive."

"Not at all." She smiled and took a sip of her wine. "When the worlds were young, we all came from a place of great beauty... and of great evil. Holy men lived there who worshiped the Source and feared for their lives, because that world had become so corrupt. Some believed the land would not sustain such evil, and would rise against mankind to purge itself. But these holy men discovered the secret of the Wells of the Worlds, the gateways between one world and the next."

An animal howled in the night, and Valasand paused. When no other sound followed, she seemed to relax somewhat, but her eyes did not lose their wariness.

"So men began to leave their original home, and come to live on other worlds. Some believe the land we came from no longer exists. Others believe it has been cleansed, and we may someday find a way back to live our lives as the Source intended. I don't know." She swirled the wine in her glass and looked in Aric's direction.

For some reason, he couldn't meet her gaze.

"I am a Warden of the Gates. Through the centuries, the Yasulite Temple has kept the embers of knowledge glowing, and trained us in the mysteries of the creation and the arts of war and defense. It has allowed some of us to travel from world to world to do the work of our god. I have found some worlds like yours, where the people know little of their past save that which legend tells them. I have visited worlds in which the people have all but forgotten they are human, and have reverted to the evil barbarian ways our ancestors so feared. I have seen worlds whose peoples have advanced far, whose technologies surpass even what you see here."

"So what brings you to this place?" Dania asked.

"I came to this world to track down the ringleader of this slave trade. I found him." Valasand's laugh was bitter. "This was a colony under the auspices of the Temple, a chance to bring the light of our faith to the people of this world. Daman Argoneis has taken over the holiest of missions and turned it into a market of flesh. We should have known about this much earlier. But the colonies have little contact with the Temple, and inspections are more and more infrequent. Too much space between worlds, too much time between visits, and too much corruption in the soul of man."

"What's all this to do with us?" Aric asked. *Or my dreams?*

"I am here to put right these wrongs, and have gathered all of you to help me do so. The Breath of Yasul has been stirring in our lives, moving us toward a certain end."

Does it whisper to you in quiet halls? Things had been uneventful since that last experience, but Maurin told Aric to keep his door barred at night, just in case.

As if he needed the warning.

Maurin picked up on Aric's irritation, and spoke before he could. "So what is this end, to which we are all being shaped?"

"The utter eradication of Daman Argoneis and his foul slave trade."

Aric went cold. Enough was enough. Their mistress was insane. Eradicate the slave trade? Even he didn't have dreams that big. Kidnapped, sold as a slave, reunited with Maurin... only to have this madwoman get them killed playing the hero at the whim of her mad god.

No, thank you.

It was time to leave. Tonight, if possible. He would convince Maurin to go with him. He didn't know how, but he would do it. There was only so much one should be expected to take in a lifetime. An angry shrieking at the back of his mind fought to drown out the nonsense she spewed. Maurin?

His cousin was smiling and nodding.

No, Maurin. No.

"Why us?" Aric asked, not even trying to hide the disdain from his voice.

Valasand answered, but her attention was on Maurin. "Because you are special, every one of you. Our meeting was no coincidence. The Breath spoke to me of each of you before I ever laid eyes on you. I knew from the moment I stepped through the gates of Caileen that I would meet the ones selected for this task."

"But I never had any special talents," Maurin said. "How am I different from anyone else?"

"You have heard the whisperings of the Breath. Don't give me that look; I know you have. I can see it in your eyes. No one can hear the voice of Yasul and remain unchanged."

"But I'm a priest of Baelon," Maurin said; "I don't follow your god."

"It makes no difference. You have been chosen by the god of gods, and Yasul does not make mistakes. You ask, Maurin, how you are different. What differs from person to person is strength of spirit. In short"— she looked pointedly at him—"your will determines much of your ability to be used by your Creator. But you will have an edge, should you choose to stop bending the knee to a lesser god. Your ear was created to hear the voice of Yasul, and when you hear the Breath of the Source whisper, you will know what to do."

Maurin bristled, most likely at the insult to Baelon, and Aric smirked, thankful the Warden had given him some leverage.

Valasand smiled tenderly. "You have a formidable strength, Maurin, but you have hidden it deep within yourself for years. What is it you fear?"

Maurin seemed to shrink at her words.

"I have known you since the moment I first laid eyes on you at the slave auction," Valasand continued, her voice stern. "You claim to fear no one, but that is not strictly true. You fear yourself, and what would happen if your untapped potential were to be set loose."

Maurin glanced down, ashamed.

He respects her. Great. Just great.

"The choice of what to do with it is yours. You may choose to allow me to forge it into a weapon, to be wielded by you with strength and wisdom, or you may choose to let it stagnate within you. It is true that if you choose the latter, you will reduce the possibility of harm to others, but you will also decrease your chances of doing good. It is also true that with strength comes responsibility, but I would not give you this responsibility if I did not firmly believe you have the capacity to know what is right, and follow through with it."

"Are you saying that knowing right from wrong just comes naturally?" Aric asked, with more than a little sarcasm.

"To a certain extent," Valasand said, turning to him, "everyone is aware of what is right and wrong, and how their own actions fit in those categories. This is universal, transcending even the most alien of cultures. Even very young children know—again, to a degree—when they have done something they should not. This is the reason I hold Daman Argoneis fully accountable for what he does. He is not insane, and he has not been wronged. He is simply spiteful and cruel—a weak, petty man who enjoys inflicting pain on others."

She regarded Maurin again. "You have been driven ever since you were taken from your home. You have waited, watching, all the time wanting to abolish this plague of slavery once and for all. And you are right; it is an evil institution that needs to be expunged. But in this quest, you must never lose sight of the fact that you want to serve what is right. When you are so bent on punishing evil that you forget why you follow those ideals in the first place, you are in danger. Though you have a great heart, I sense in you a tremendous potential for ruthlessness."

Maurin frowned, apparently unsure of what to say.

"Talauna, my dear," Valasand said, turning to the Maolori. "I was told of you long before I found you. You contain a treasure beyond price." She shifted, regarding the Blood Goddess. "Dania, you are a warrior whose heart and spirit have remained hidden, guarded and defended for years by your physical strength and ability. In time, they may be brought to work for you, instead of against you. And Aric"—she held his gaze—"you have the gift of foresight; your dreams may well hold the key to the fate of worlds. But oh, Aric, you must take great care you do not fall prey to your own power."

"What's that supposed to mean?" No wonder she favored Maurin. They were so much alike.

"I will teach you, if you let me. In the meantime," Valasand said with a sigh, "you are no longer slaves. You have known that, deep in your hearts, from the moment I first ransomed you from the Market. You are free to go at any time."

Excellent. Now leaving wouldn't go against Maurin's sense of obligation.

Maurin stared hard at her. "And should we choose to stay?"

Aric bit back a furious curse.

"Then you must prepare yourselves for what lies ahead," she said. "Aric first informed me about the circus Argoneis is planning, a grandiose debut at the end of the season. All kinds of spectacles. Reenactments, one-on-one fights, animals, every-man-for-himself—all of which will end in death."

"I thought the circus would die with Seides." The quiet pain in Dania's voice jerked Aric out of his thoughts, but she glanced away.

"I have been devising a plan. On the first day of the circus, we will infiltrate the arena disguised as guards, and then free the gladiators, who, if all goes as planned, will join us. United, we will have the numbers and the power to overthrow Argoneis."

"This is why you've been training us?" Maurin nodded, lips set in a thin line. "If you're going to take down Argoneis, I want to be a part of it."

Aric fought to quell the rage roiling within. He had to break this spell the Warden had cast on his cousin.

"You will be," Valasand answered. "And we must do what we can to see that you are ready."

———————◆———————

Maurin looked smug and thoughtful as they headed up to their rooms. Valasand's talk had obviously lit a fire in him. There would be no getting him out of here; at least not tonight. Aric screamed inwardly as he trudged up the stairs.

It's not our fight! The five of them, trying to win over some gladiators and overthrow Argoneis's forces? Madness! Aric distracted himself with the callipygian sway of Dania's hips as she ascended ahead of him. She glanced over her shoulder and caught him staring. He blushed and averted his gaze.

Maurin noticed, and motioned to Aric to step inside his room.

"What was Dania doing in your room earlier?" he said, making sure she was out of earshot. "I saw her leaving before Valasand called us into the library."

News to Aric, but he didn't feel like giving Maurin the satisfaction. This wasn't the conversation he expected to have right now. "Borrowing a comb?"

"Very funny. Really, what was she doing?"

"How should I know?" Aric scowled. "Don't be so paranoid."

"Don't give me reason to be."

Aric rolled his eyes.

"She's dangerous." Maurin held up a hand to forestall a retort. "I know you're young, and she excites you, but you'd better stay away. She's a killer, and she's not stable."

"She's dangerous? Valasand is the one who's going to get us all killed!" Aric spat. "And at least Dania's not some stupid Maolori doe who's never going to talk."

"Hey!" Maurin snapped. "Talauna isn't stupid. Who knows why she doesn't speak? Those scars on her back didn't just grow there!"

Aric's pulse raced and throbbed through his temples. "You just like her because you know she won't run away."

Maurin looked angrier and more hurt than he had ever seen him. "Why are you saying this?"

Aric pretended not to care. "You know, Maurin, between you and Valasand, I've had enough lectures this evening to last a lifetime. I'm sick of this place, and sick of waiting for things to turn around. I'm going."

"Going?" Maurin stood with arms folded. "Going where?"

"To bed. I'm tired." Aric slammed the door behind him. Perhaps by the morning he would have his thoughts sorted out better, and he would be able to convince Maurin of the folly of Valasand's plans.

Before Aric could stalk down the hall toward his quarters, a voice from the shadows surprised him.

"Aric, I wish to speak with you." Even as Dania said the words, she headed back into her room.

"What?" It caught up with his brain a few seconds later that he was supposed to be following.

She turned on him and frowned. "Are you busy?"

"No, not particularly." Aric shrugged. He could barely make out her features, but she seemed relieved by his reply. Once they were both inside her room, she shut and barred the door behind them. Aric's stomach fluttered.

"I have a question I wish to ask you." Dania hesitated, and glanced down for a moment, seeming shy, of all things. Of course, that could have been a trick of the light. Shy was not a term Aric would normally have used to describe Dania. But something was very definitely different about her. Uncomfortable, maybe. When she looked back up, there was determination in her eyes.

"Sure. Go ahead." What if Maurin was right? Was she out of her mind? Come to think of it, maybe he was out of his mind, just being here.

She riveted him with an iron gaze. "I have seen you watching me."

His heart stopped. He hoped to all the gods it wouldn't be permanent. *This is it; I am going to die now.*

After a moment of excruciating silence, she continued. "Do you find me"—she glanced down again, and frowned, as if searching for the word she wanted—"desirable?"

Aric swallowed around the lump in his throat. "Y-yeah. I guess so."

"That's good," she said, grasping him by the shirt and breathing harshly into his ear, "because I want you, Aric."

"To...?"

She threw him to the floor. "Now."

Whose eyes am I looking through? I can't tell. Daman Argoneis stares at me, fascinated by this exquisite treasure he's captured. Chained between two columns in a white stone room, I am surrounded by cruel men and a handful of those horse-headed Talormines.

I dare him to make a move toward me. Argoneis circles around and lays a hand between my shoulder blades. I endure his touch with rage, quaking in fury and cold revulsion as the man runs his hand down my spine, from my neck to the small of my back. My jaw tightens, my fists clench.

"You know," Argoneis says, "I can set you free."

"I don't want freedom," I snarl, my voice high and raspy. "Not from you."

He is taken aback. "You don't want to be free?"

"I know the price for your freedom. I would rather be a prisoner, or a slave."

"Either can be arranged, you know," Argoneis says, angry now. "You would fetch quite the price on the Market."

"Better to die than to whore my way to freedom, you filth."

He slaps me, but I barely flinch.

"Why don't you just kill me?" I mean to sound defiant, but my voice sounds weak and strangled.

"We'll get around to it," Daman replies pleasantly.

"What?"

"You're assuming quite a bit when you say you know what price I would exact for your freedom."

His smile chills me to the core.

"It's a belief universally held in noble and commoner circles alike that I am a man obsessed with death, driven by a desire to subjugate, and eventually wipe out, all inferior life forms." He pinches me hard, and laughs.

"Nothing could be further from the truth. Death and eradication, in and of themselves, do not particularly interest me. Death is merely an unfortunate consequence of my hobbies. My true love is the art of suffering. Pain fascinates me, you see. I am intrigued by the degree to which a soul can be broken before it can be considered utterly destroyed. I am an explorer in a vast realm, and I am determined to reach uncharted territory."

I squeeze my eyes shut. I do everything I can to escape this nightmare. But I cannot. Argoneis gestures with a look of manic hatred and glee. His two bodyguards approach with shock cudgels. One leans toward my side.

I hear a loud crackle, and my body jolts. Burning pain rakes through every fiber of my being.

CHAPTER 21
FLIGHT FROM FREEDOM

Dania woke to a blurred impression of the Maolori girl hitting the wall. Focusing on the frightened face before her, Dania relaxed.

"Oh, it's only you, girl." Her body still racing with adrenalin, she rose off the rug and approached the Maolori, her initial primal fear turning into shame. She recalled a vague impression of someone laying a hand on her shoulder; she must have reflexively thrown Talauna before she even awoke.

She could have sworn she had barred the door last night. Oh, right. Aric had returned to his quarters to get another blanket. He must have forgotten to replace the lock on his way back.

Wide-eyed and trembling, the girl stared apprehensively. Soft. Wouldn't have lasted a day in Farel's compound. Dania grasped her by the arms and straightened her up. Turning her to the light, she gave the damage a quick inspection. The girl's shoulder was bruised, the skin slightly broken. A slow trickle of blood seeped from the wound.

"You should not touch me while I sleep." Dania's voice sounded brusque even to her. She let her go forcibly. "I could have killed you before I woke. What were you doing in here?"

It's morning, and time to get up, Dania cursed herself. *She was just fetching you for the day.*

Something inside her wanted to apologize, but she didn't know how. Instead, she turned away to get dressed. She could still feel the girl's eyes on her, and finally whirled with a scowl. Talauna shook herself off, pity gradually replacing the fear in her eyes. With a slight nod in Dania's direction, she left the room. Dania gazed after her.

After Aric had gone to sleep in her bed, Dania slept on the floor in the main room of the suite. It was just too uncomfortable with him right there. She couldn't close her eyes. Yet, eventually, close her eyes she did, and slept as she could not recall having slept since her youth in the caravan; peacefully, with no dreams, and no fear of being wakened in the middle of the night for a rendezvous with her master. Unbelievably, Aric was still snoring softly off in the bedroom. She tiptoed in to take one last look at him. His hair shone gold in the early morning light. Her eyes dropped to the bruised and scratched curve of his shoulders and back.

Still green as a sapling.

Dania went outside to sit on the woodpile in the northeastern corner of the grounds. She slowly dissected the branches of the trees, then shredded the leaves into narrow strips.

Too close. She had let them get too close. What was she thinking? A tumble of faces filled her mind's eye.

Aric.

Seides.

Farel.

Aric.

Her stomach roiled, and she tasted bile. Though disjointed, shuffling steps warned her that someone was approaching, Dania did not look up. She glared instead at the growing pile of organic confetti at her feet.

Aric laid a hand on her shoulder, but she shrugged him off.

"Hey...!" he started.

Dania cut him off with a sharp gesture, warding him away with the palm of her hand.

"Don't."

"What did I do?" Aric said in disbelief.

She remained silent for a moment before answering. Her voice choked with restraint. "If you ever think about telling anybody, I'll kill you."

The indignation on Aric's face flared into anger. "What is it you want from me?" he bit out. "Don't forget, you're the one who came to me. You can't just come in and then leave and pretend it didn't happen." He jabbed his chest with his thumb and took a step forward. "I was there for you, and I didn't have to be. Whatever game it is you're playing, I don't want to be any part of it. You said what you wanted. Fine. I can handle that. I wanted it, too, or I wouldn't have gone along with you. But now you feel—what, guilty?—and make out like it's all my fault? I'm at least due some respect and... and... decency. After all, I gave up something because of you. But if you can't see that, well, then, to the Flames with you."

Dania turned, her quaking gut a potpourri of fury and shame. She drew her dagger, and raised her arm as if to throw it at him.

Aric didn't flinch.

She brought it down into the rock beside her, shattering the blade, and let out a scream of pure fury and frustration that echoed through the glades.

Aric just shook his head in disgust, and stalked back into the mansion.

The decision she had been mulling over since her loss of control last night had just been made for her. She would leave. She would not kill this Valasand or her slaves, although she probably should. They knew who she was, after all, and could turn her in. But for some reason, she did not believe they would.

Valasand seemed like a woman of honor, though Dania had known so few people of honor in her life that the concept in and of itself was a little nebulous. Still, she got an odd feeling every time she looked into those gray eyes. A feeling of—what?—trust? Was it possible that Dania, the killer, the Blood Goddess, could actually trust someone?

Then why was she running away?

It was because she wanted to be free, she told herself, as she loped through the woods, the branches scraping past her arms and face. She ducked under a lower limb and dodged another tree. Save for the road that led to Caileen, there was only one way to leave the mansion: through the path in the trees. She soon passed the stream where Talauna liked to bathe, and was well into the woods. The leaves rustled underfoot in a *hiss-hiss* sound. She wanted to no longer be a slave. Was that not why she had escaped in the first place? What was the point of escaping one form of slavery only to enter yet another?

Valasand did not want slaves. She had just said so last night. But it didn't matter. Though Dania knew she could wait till they left for the city after breakfast, just to find her gone upon their return, she couldn't stand facing them again. Her tumult of emotions insisted she leave now.

The Blood Goddess would not become a pity-case for this woman's personal crusade. It was obvious what she was doing; Valasand gathered people she felt sorry for, perhaps was going to give them all a comfortable home as her way of caring for the poor of the world. To be a surrogate mother to the dregs of Caileen's slave population, to ease her conscience...

The cuirass she pilfered from the mansion's armory was restrictive, and did not allow her to breathe deeply, and yet she ran without ceasing, too angry to tire.

Valasand was right; Dania was dangerous. She shouldn't be around others; only on her own could she make certain what happened this morning did not happen again. The Maolori could have been killed by a pit fighter's reflexes.

Had the girl gone looking for Dania again after she left? What would her reaction have been at that moment of realization? A sigh of relief? Or simply an indifferent shrug? Dania would not be a burden on anyone. She would owe no one. And yet, as the image of the Maolori girl lingered in her mind, she could not escape the distinct impression that her expression would not have been one of apathy, but rather disappointment, maybe even hurt. Dania scoffed. The girl couldn't possibly want to be friends with a killer?

Dania pulled up short and squeezed her eyes tight to block out the image of that sorrowful countenance. So what if Talauna—that girl, she corrected herself—would miss her? She was only a stupid little mute, anyway, with all the fighting instincts of a lump of pudding.

Until this morning, Aric had borne her no ill will, but now—how could she face him again? What was this shame? And his cousin—she read dislike in his eyes every time they met hers. This would not improve things.

Dania sat down roughly on the ground, hugging her legs painfully to her chest, and tucking her knees up under her chin. The image persisted, and suddenly, it was replaced by another, a vision of all of the others, walking... somewhere, eyes facing forward in a common goal. Dania was not with them, and there was a definite sense of something wrong, something missing. Could it be because she was not part of the picture? Nonsense. She had never been a part of anything in her life. There had always been Dania, and only Dania. Worlds and people would come and go, but Dania would abide, and abide alone.

Alone.

Alone.

Alone.

The refrain stayed with her as she got back to her feet and ran deeper into the forest. Too many wrongs had been allowed to stand unavenged. Seides was dead, but Farel yet lived, and that had to change. Last she heard, he still presided at the training compound.

Dania came to a halt, squeezing her eyes shut at the pain that constricted her heart. Too much blood. Too many ghosts. Her nostrils flared and contracted as she struggled to control her breathing.

A rustle off to her right broke the rigid silence, and in a flash, her remaining knife was in her hand. She took a tentative step forward...

And was knocked off her feet.

Arms pinned to her sides.

Dania struggled to right herself, but couldn't move. Her entire body was enmeshed in a rope net, weighted with stones and thrown from a distance.

Dania would drown in their blood before she allowed herself to be carried away. She tried to retrieve her dagger.

"I wouldn't bother with that, princess."

A hairy bear of a man, who easily outweighed her by two hundred pounds, came lumbering forward, surrounded by nine other scruffy, jeering faces. Dania's eyes narrowed into slits.

"I should thank you. You've saved us a little trouble, coming out into the open like this. I hope you're dressed in your best, because Lord Argoneis is dying to meet you."

CHAPTER 22
UNWELCOME GUESTS

"Is everything all right? What was that scream?"

When Aric returned, sullen and angry, everyone was up and eating, and Maurin wore an expression Aric had always hated—he felt like a little boy when his cousin looked at him like that.

Aric shot him a scalding glance, skewered a roll with his fork and slammed it onto a plate.

"O-kaaaay." Maurin bit his lower lip, subdued. Talauna gazed sympathetically at Aric, but seemed to realize that he didn't want comforting. Valasand watched in silence.

He didn't get far. His roiling stomach wouldn't let him eat. Aric pushed away from the table and went back to his room.

Do you find me desirable?

Of course.

It was true enough, although he had never seriously envisioned himself with her in any sense. At least, not more than fleeting fancies of curiosity. Yet he had almost feared to refuse her.

He swallowed, a flood of memory overflowing his senses. He heard her purr of pleasure so deep and throaty it was nearly a growl. He could feel the cool firmness of her pale, tattooed skin on his, and smell the brindlewood soap from her recent bath. A tapestry of beautiful, enigmatic markings of dark blue ornamented her entire body. He had looked for some recognizable patterns beyond the stylized animals and such, but could not discern any—not that he had much time to study in depth. Whipcord muscle moved in sinewy concert as she pulled him to her in an embrace that was almost an attack.

After the initial shock, he had relaxed a bit, and allowed himself to fall into the familiar motion. Every touch a thing remembered, every new sensation something he knew. So odd, so familiar, so... good.

And yet, somehow, not right. Instinctive—natural, even—but not right. Still, he ignored that inner voice telling him to stop.

I can make my own decisions, Maurin.

Upon waking, he had found himself once again lying in a pool of sweat. Embarrassed, he had cast about to see if Dania had seen him, but she was gone. He hoped he hadn't been talking in his sleep again, or worse yet, screaming. A dream about his father, this time. Memories were worse than visions sometimes. Flashes of terror, compounded with guilt—*How could you know, you little monster? Did you make it happen?*—vague faces he supposed were his brothers and mother. Father, so angry, so scared, tearing apart the house. Blood. Aric hiding, curled up in a ball under the counter.

You're not him. You're not him. Maurin says it—does that even count?—but it's got to be true.

Make it not be true.

Still, he'd shaken it off. He always did. Dania's absence had troubled him too much to dwell too much on it. He wasn't quite sure what he expected when he woke up, but this certainly wasn't it.

Kill me if I tell, will you?

A soft knock at the door roused him from his musing.

Wonderful. Maurin. Just what he needed.

"Where were you last night? I came to your room, but I couldn't find you. I wanted to apologize for arguing..."

Aric grunted something inarticulate and gestured vaguely at Maurin as he pushed past him. He took the stairs two at a time. Talauna and Valasand were cleaning up from breakfast, and glanced up as he went by, but Dania was nowhere in sight. Aric walked outside without greeting them, making a beeline for the open gates.

Where did she go, anyway?

He searched the path outside the walls and started to follow the trail. He should be glad she had left. But he wasn't. Something was terribly wrong. A kind of nervousness he could not identify loomed over the horizon. He closed his eyes and stood as straight as he could. He felt the way the land breathed, the flow of energy, even from the mountains.

Experimentally, almost without effort, he extended forth his senses and feelings, drawing off the ambiance of the dawn. He took a moment to concentrate and found himself caught up in a waking vision. He soared above the frosted peaks, seeing a city from above. Caileen! It seemed so beautiful, so peaceful from up here. He could barely hear the bustling sounds of the street vendors setting up for their morning sales as people milled through the byways of the city.

Aric recognized the Market and skimmed over it, not allowing it to break his concentration. A dazzling palace, like something out of a fairy tale, stood out above the squalor of Caileen. It was the hub of the city, the residence of the Lord Regent Daman Argoneis.

Dania...?

The vision was gone, and Aric was gasping, doubled over and clutching at his sides, where a spasm had struck him. After a moment, the initial pain subsided, replaced by a kind of phantom tingling in his ribs. His anger faded, and a creeping horror overtook him.

He'd dreamed this. He didn't want to admit it, but he knew what happened. She was gone, and it was his fault.

Again.

Before the vision could take him again, he fled back to the mansion, scarcely aware of turning around or covering the returning ground. He hurtled into the kitchen. "Dania's been captured by Argoneis!"

"What?" Maurin turned pale and set aside the bowl he was washing. Talauna sat down so fast it seemed her legs had turned to putty.

"I can't explain how I know. I just do. She's going to die if we don't do something, and do it quick!"

"It would seem my hand has been forced." Valasand's lips tightened into a hard line. She grasped her staff and stood up. "I think it is high time I paid Lord Argoneis a visit. It's been long overdue."

———————◆———————

Valasand Del Siriné strode briskly through the columned corridors of Lord Argoneis's palatial estate, flanked by Maurin and Aric. They had instructions to remain absolutely silent and let her do all the talking. She hoped they were up for the challenge. Valasand left Talauna outside with Padron and Poly, for Aric had warned her of Argoneis's interest in her, and she had no wish to endanger any of them with her presence. She would have preferred to leave the Maolori girl at the mansion, but something in her spirit had warned her against it.

Two enormous horse-headed guards opened the towering mahogany doors leading to Daman's audience chamber, which he no doubt used strictly for show. He had no more genuine respect for propriety than he had love for his fellow man.

There he sat, the pompous ass, on a throne set upon a low dais at the end of a long hall. A blood-red carpet led to the pedestal, the only covering on the marble floor. Candelabras lined the spacious passage, and weapons of varying degrees of ornamentality decorated the walls under a balcony encircling the room.

A good place for an ambush.

To Lord Argoneis's right stood a breathtakingly handsome man; dark-skinned, with the sculpted muscles of a professional athlete, black eyes, and straight black hair falling to the middle of his back. To Argoneis's left was a slender woman who could have been the other guard's sister. Probably was. She stared inscrutably at Valasand, her high cheekbones and regal bearing giving her a haughty demeanor. Each of them held a spear out to the side, resting the butt caps on the ground. They looked more like nobles than guards; how did they end up serving under someone like Argoneis?

Daman himself was of unremarkable height and build. His shaggy blond hair didn't quite touch his shoulders. He wore a loose white tunic open at the chest. His lips might have been considered sensual, had they not been hardened with that cruel smirk.

Valasand steeled her spine, forcing herself to gaze unwaveringly into those mocking eyes. She came to a halt several feet before his seat of power, Maurin and Aric standing protectively beside her.

"Do you know why I have come?" she asked through stiff lips.

Daman gave a look of mock perplexity, then sat up straight with feigned surprise and gratitude. "Are you inviting me to a party?"

"Lord Argoneis, you are guilty of crimes unspeakable..."

"Then why speak of them?" he said with a warm smile. "It's such a lovely day, and you're such a lovely woman; perhaps you would like to join me for a stroll through my gardens? I'm sure we could find something pleasant to discuss. For instance, how you got past my patrols. There is a warrant out for your arrest, you know."

"How ironic," she said, once again grateful for Aric's precognitive warning to enter the city by an alternate route. "It is for your arrest that I come."

Argoneis relaxed on the throne. "Is that so?"

"It has come to my attention that you are responsible for the wholesale trade of flesh. You have stolen people from their homeworlds for labor and vice."

"How else were these unfortunate folks going to get out and around? Show people some culture, and you're branded a whoremonger and a slaver."

"Lord Argoneis," Valasand said, "I hold you and your ilk in the highest contempt. Your vile trade is a plague on all the worlds. Moreover, you have defiled the seat of authority upon which you reside and befouled the Temple of the Source with the blood of innocents."

Argoneis looked bored. "And what would you have me do? Give up my businesses? Free all of my slaves—retire to a monastery, perhaps? Hmmm? Tell me, my dear, are you opposed to slavery? I've heard it said—perhaps you have, too—that some men are only fit to be slaves."

"That may well be. But I know of none fit to be masters."

His smile slipped a notch. "I see."

"My opinions are of little consequence." Valasand pulled her amulet from her robes. "What is more important is that your trade has come under the scrutiny of the Temple, whom I represent."

"All joking about arrests aside, what do you want from me?" Argoneis no longer smiled.

Valasand stepped forward. "I am a Warden of the Gates on a mission from Yasul, and I have come to tell you that your days are numbered."

Daman laughed once through his nose. "Do you have any idea what happened to the last person who threatened me?"

"I can well imagine. But you will not stand against the authority of the Temple." Valasand felt the two young men bristling beside her, ready to fight. *Stay calm. Give them patience.* "You have taken captive a person under my charge. You will return her now."

"Who might that be?"

"Dania the gladiatrix."

"Dania the criminal. Dania the escaped slave. Dania the murderess. Do you honestly believe I am going to allow this dangerous creature to go free?"

"I do."

"My dear Warden, I have had plans for you since the moment I heard of your arrival. I never dreamed you would simply show up on my doorstep." Daman gestured to his two bodyguards.

The door creaked and slammed as the horseheads closed it behind Valasand. She stepped forward to meet the advancing dark warriors. Mercifully, Maurin and Aric were a step behind her; she would need her space. The man and woman lowered their spears and moved to the sides.

"I will give you one last warning," Valasand said as they moved closer. "I am protected by an unseen host, and to challenge me is to challenge a force greater than you can comprehend."

Daman chuckled, and his guards' expressions never changed.

"So be it." Valasand grasped her staff in both hands and whirled, allowing it to slide under her palms until she had reached the end, then held it tight. Using the momentum of her spin, she carried through and struck the male on the side of the head, causing him to drop his spear and fall flat on his back, dazed and bleeding.

The woman cried out in rage and alarm, lunging forward in an attempt to skewer Valasand. The Warden swept the end of her staff around and brought it down with all of her might on the dark woman's wrist. The spear flew from her grasp with a snap of bone.

Without wasting a second, Valasand whipped her staff around. It whooshed through the air and connected with the woman's stomach, doubling her over. The male staggered to his feet and retrieved his spear, but Valasand already had the woman on the floor. She placed her foot on the bodyguard's broken wrist, then pinned her to the ground by jamming the end of her staff against the base of the woman's throat.

"Care to reconsider?" Valasand asked.

Daman stood in fury. "Kill her!"

"One step forward," Valasand warned, "and she dies."

The dark man didn't move.

"Sabatha!" Daman stamped his foot.

"I'm not going to put my sister in danger, Daman."

Argoneis's jaw dropped. Clearly, he was not accustomed to being disobeyed.

"I propose an exchange," Valasand said.

Argoneis's eyes glittered in spite, but he nodded. "Very well, then. Bring the Blood Goddess."

The one called Sabatha regarded Valasand with a hatred she could practically taste. "You harm my sister, and you will die."

"Do as you are told, and no one need die," Valasand said.

Sabatha called out for the Talormine guards to open the doors, then strode out, clutching his bleeding head. They ran forward at the sight of Valasand and the woman on the ground, but he stopped them and told them to come with him.

As soon as she could no longer hear the receding footsteps of the guards, Valasand motioned to Maurin with her chin. "Keep your sword at her throat." She gauged the likelihood of resistance from the woman, but saw feral hatred, and nothing more, in her gaze. "What is your name?"

"Anice," she said with a sneer.

"Get to your knees, Anice. Aric, bind her hands behind her back. Be careful with her wrist; it's broken."

Aric leaned over and cut the sash from the woman's hip, then tied it firmly around her arms. For a moment it seemed he might be tempted to tweak Anice's wrist, but Valasand gave him a stern look quelling any notions of cruelty.

Stern looks had always been her specialty.

Aric spoke softly to his cousin in their native language. Maurin nodded and addressed the woman in Canoine. "Get up slowly." He kept his sword-point at her throat as she complied.

Screwing up his face, Aric cut the sash from the other side of Anice's hip, then used it to tie one ankle and then the other. Leaving some space between, he connected the two sashes and held the slack.

He's a smart one. Aric had formed a crude shackle; Anice would be able to walk, but not run, and any overextension of her legs would pull on her arms. After another exchange in the tongue of their homeworld, Aric took over the main duty of guarding the woman; he placed his dagger at her throat with his left hand while holding the sash with his right. Maurin retreated a step, but kept his sword out and ready.

Argoneis seemed almost amused at the whole situation.

"I trust you have a plan to get out of here?" he asked.

"She goes with us to the gates. You stay here. Any other arrangement will end in her death."

"You think that will keep me from doing what I must to stop you?"

"I think you fear Sabatha, and would be a fool to do anything to incur his wrath. If you were to be responsible for this one's death, I have no doubt your own would follow."

"I fear no one." But Daman made no further reply. She had scored a point.

The next several minutes were excruciating; Maurin and Aric were doing better than she expected, given the circumstances, but she could tell Anice was contemplating an escape attempt. The longer Sabatha took getting back, the greater the odds the woman would try something.

Valasand was just about to ask Daman what was taking so long when Sabatha returned with several horse-headed guards. They walked behind a manacled Dania, shock cudgels pointed at her back. It wasn't as bad as Aric had described—dreams and visions could be notoriously interpretive, and she had told him so—but it was bad enough. Dania was bruised, shaky, and limping. Her eyes bulged when she saw Valasand.

"So this is how you treat those who displease you," Valasand said bitterly.

"Not at all." Daman shrugged. "This is how it pleases me to treat those who reject my authority. She was fortunate. I was letting her recuperate before starting in earnest."

"Unchain her."

"Absolutely not," Sabatha said.

The hunger in Dania's face was unmistakable.

"Dania, they are going to release you now. You will come with us. No heroics. No revenge. Do you understand?"

The gladiatrix hesitated a long moment before nodding. The dark-skinned man glared, but acquiesced.

"We're leaving now. Come here, Dania." Valasand turned to Anice. "We're going outside. We have a cart by the gates. You"—she nodded to Sabatha—"stay."

"Like fires I will." Sabatha's voice was pure venom.

"Like fires you won't." Aric pressed his dagger close to Anice's jugular.

"We will let her go when we are safely away. So long as you stay here, and do not attempt to follow, she shall remain unharmed." Valasand did not wait for any further discussion, but turned and walked out of the room. Maurin and Aric followed, leading Anice awkwardly along. Then came Dania.

The walk back through the palace was horrible. At nearly every junction, Talormine guards snorted and lurched forward, blocking their way. When they did this, Aric gently tugged the cloth close to Anice's wrist, causing her to gasp in pain. His smile was disconcerting, but Valasand said nothing; they needed every bit of good fortune and protection they had to get out of here alive. By the time they reached the outer doors, the procession had grown quite a bit; over a dozen guards, both human and Talormine, walked behind them, waiting for an opportunity to storm the intruders.

Valasand scarcely noticed the courtyard, or the opening of the gates. She just hoped nothing had happened to Talauna while they were inside. A quick glance told her all was well; a pudgy cart driver and a tiny Maolori ragamuffin were not enough to draw the attention of the local populace.

"I'm not going with you!" Anice screeched. "You'll just have to kill me!"

"Don't tempt me," Aric said. Maurin's face remained unreadable, and Valasand was glad.

"Stay back, all of you!" She gestured to the crowd of Argoneis's men circling the cart. "Your master will not want to lose this one." One guard rushed forward, and she rewarded him with a broken nose. He fell back, blood gushing down his face. "I do not wish to harm anyone, but we will not hesitate to kill Anice if we must. Now stay back!"

To her surprise and relief, they did. Daman must have put the fear of death upon all of his servants, if they were more afraid of him than they were of a single woman with a staff and a couple of novice lads with swords. Maurin and Aric each took a side, and lifted Anice into the cart with some difficulty; she squirmed and fought, but once she was in the hay, Aric leapt upon her and held his dagger firmly across her throat. She went still immediately.

"Pull away slowly." Still watching the guards, Valasand climbed into the seat next to Padron, whose eyes seemed liable to pop out of his skull. "Stay calm."

Valasand kept her gaze on Argoneis's force as they receded all too slowly from her sight. The cart rattled and bumped along.

"You came for me?" Dania's voice was raspy and incredulous. "Why...?"

"You are one of us," Valasand said. "And the Source makes no mistakes choosing its own."

"Aric..." Dania turned to him. "How...?"

"I dreamed of you." He shrugged. "It was bound to happen sometime."

Valasand saw it coming, but didn't have a chance to say anything. The moment Aric's eyes were off Anice, the woman twisted like a snake and rolled out from under his knife. She threw herself out of the cart and somehow managed to land on her feet. Instantly, she went into a crouch and pulled her arms under her, so her hands were in front. Dania leapt forward, but Valasand grabbed her arm.

"Let her go." The dark-skinned woman immediately began pulling at the knotted sashes with her teeth. It wouldn't be long before she was free. Turning to Padron, Valasand asked, "Exactly how fast can this animal go?"

CHAPTER 23
LEAVING CAILEEN

"I don't think Poly was built for speed," Maurin called out as they made their way as quickly as they could down a side street.

Aric swore.

"The mansion is the other way." Maurin indicated the road.

"It is. We're in trouble." Without further comment or explanation, Valasand took the reins from Padron, and urged the animal through the darker passageways and tight corridors between buildings. Maurin kept his hand on his sword as she steered the cart into yet another alley. Would it even fit? Somehow she managed to navigate the narrow space. Soon, though, they came to a dead end. It would take too long to maneuver back around; Argoneis's men would be on them soon. Maurin bit his lips and tightened the grip on the hilt of his sword.

"We'll have to leave the cart," Valasand said.

"Go on," Padron responded. "We'll be all right. It's you they want."

Valasand regarded him for a moment, then handed him the reins.

"Before you go…" Padron's face screwed up. "Hit me."

"What?" Maurin did a double-take.

"It's got to look like you made me do this. Somebody hit me."

A dozen possibilities flitted through Valasand's mind, and she glanced at each of the others. Maurin obviously wouldn't do it; Aric would probably enjoy it, and, well, Dania...

Better do it herself. "I'm so sorry." She whipped her staff around and dealt him a light rap on the forehead. Just enough to give him a good-sized lump, not enough to give him a concussion. "Go with the blessings of Yasul."

Hissing through his teeth and clutching his head, he nodded and waved them away. Then he slumped over, pretending to be unconscious.

With the cart acting as a temporary shield from Daman's men, they put as much distance as possible between themselves and their pursuers. Maurin risked a glance back to see about the fate of the carter, but there was no sign of him. Argoneis must be in a state of apoplexy by now. Talauna sprinted ahead, lithe limbs carrying her faster than he would have thought possible. At the corner, she dropped to the ground and flipped her head into the alley. With a gesture he assumed meant *all clear*, she headed off to the left.

They passed a couple of alleys, and Maurin was no longer certain which way they had come. Talauna continued scurrying forth, and Valasand seemed confident as she followed, carrying her staff off the ground. Within a few moments, Maurin found himself in the corner of an L-shaped alley.

"Give me one of your knives," Dania said.

Aric hesitated to part with one of his weapons, but handed it to her hilt-first. She stood for a moment, just breathing, and looking at each of the group in turn.

"You came for me," she said again.

"We will never forsake you," Valasand said, her voice warm.

"There they are!"

Maurin whipped his head around toward the voice at the end of the alley. Argoneis's men had found them. They started to run toward the group, brandishing their weapons.

They ran, but their mad dash lasted only a moment, because a whole herd of Talormine guards barred their way.

Argoneis must have pulled out all the stops. Talauna had turned back yet again; they were trapped between the advancing troops in the one alley and the massive, loping creatures in the other. They had only seconds to act before the two forces converged on them. Talauna's eyes were round and panicked. Maurin swallowed, tense and alert. Valasand placed a small, dark pouch next to the wall.

"Great," Aric said. "Now what?"

As if in response to Aric's question, a bright flame crackled and hissed from the pouch. "Get back," the Warden ordered, her tone leaving no question of disobedience. She backed away quickly, shielding her eyes. Maurin followed her example.

"What are we do—"

A sound like a lightning crash split the air, and Maurin's ears rang. A portion of the stone barrier had been reduced to rubble. As the uniformed men came around the corner, Valasand ran forward and kicked what was left of the wall inward.

Aric smirked. "You're just full of surprises."

"Get in."

Talauna scrambled through, and Dania crawled after her. In a matter of a few seconds, they were all inside. Fortunately, the Talormines made it to the opening first. Despite their speed, they were not especially flexible, and, apparently, not too bright. The horse-headed creatures clustered around the hole were too stiffly armored and bulky to fit through, and so intent on following the escapees that the human pursuers lost precious seconds in persuading them to move out of the way.

Maurin found himself running with the others after Valasand through an obstacle course of scrumptious-smelling pastries and astonished workers.

Dania snatched a tartlet as they ran through the store, pushing customers aside and tipping over a couple of tables. Within moments, they burst through the front of the bakery, trailing flour and dribbles of jelly. An irate little man came running after them, yelling, "Stop, stop! Who's going to pay for this?"

"Sorry," Maurin tossed over his shoulder as he ran. As an apology it was a little lacking, but what could he do? They hurried away, drawing curious stares from the people on the street. Valasand veered off to the right.

"But the gate's this way!" Maurin yelled.

"I know!" Valasand shouted back, between breaths. Dania and Talauna were ahead of them; the Maolori held one arm close to her middle as she ran. Was she cramping, too? Dania ran lopsidedly, stumbling a couple of times, but otherwise seemed to be all right. Definitely a tough woman. They ducked into another alley and made several twists and turns. They rounded a corner...

And ran directly into a patrol.

Dania's knife flashed once, and the man who had been reaching for his weapon grabbed instead for the side of his throat. As he collapsed on the ground, Aric grabbed another officer by the head and jerked sharply. Maurin winced as he heard the man's spine snap. Valasand's training had apparently paid off, he thought with some sadness.

Aric hurled the limp form bodily at another man, knocking him down. Dania, meanwhile, had done something unspeakably gruesome to the last guard, and Maurin was glad he wasn't close enough to get a good look. He turned Talauna away from the sight.

Aric ran up to the end of the alley and poked his head around the corner. "More are coming!" he said, running back to join the others.

"We should be able to circumvent the main patrols this way," Valasand said as they passed through a small gate leading to one of the lesser causeways. She pointed at the mountain. "See that road? That's where we're headed."

Maurin strained to see through sandglass rendered nearly opaque by the clouds of mist sent up by the falls. He could barely make out the slender path leading around the peak.

"I saw some airships berthed up here when I first arrived," she said. "We're going to attempt to steal one."

"Attempt?" Maurin coughed. "What happens if we can't?"

Valasand said nothing, but Dania voiced the answer already all too clear in his mind. "Then we die."

Maurin resolved not to waste energy wondering what would happen if they were caught, and Lord Argoneis got to mete out his peculiar brand of justice.

The walkway led into the cliff face itself. A natural cave had been carved into something more serviceable, and Maurin found himself in an empty, dimly-lit corridor leading directly under the landing pads several hundred feet above them. They made their way past several halls, and Talauna found a stairway. Holding their weapons at the ready, they climbed as fast as their legs would carry them.

When they came upon the doors, Valasand nodded to Dania, who seemed to know what she had in mind. "Talauna, Maurin, when I give you the signal, throw the doors open, and hold them back."

Maurin quickly positioned himself, taking a firm grip on the door's handle. Talauna aped his movements on the other side. Together, Valasand and Dania found the best hold on their weapons, and Aric followed suit, staying just a couple of steps behind them. Valasand held up her open palm, folding down her fingers one by one. When she had made a fist, she nodded, and Maurin and Talauna burst through.

Maurin shivered as he was greeted by a stiff, cold breeze. Two startled enforcers went for their bolt-throwers, but Valasand struck first with her staff. One man flew backwards, his weapon skidding across the stone. He moaned, but did not get up. Dania brought the other down with a single dagger thrust under the ear.

Aric made his way across the expanse of the landing pad between several small ships. "Come on!" he exclaimed. "I can fly this one!" He climbed inside almost before Maurin saw where he had gone.

It looked like a general transport shuttle of some kind, with large buoyancy modules on the top, and a passenger gondola underneath. A sudden humming from the machine caused Maurin to jump. Aric must have already activated it from the inside. Valasand stormed aboard, the others right on her heels.

"Sit down, everyone," Aric said, his voice exuberant.

The transport lifted magically off the paved stone, and Maurin's stomach leapt into his throat. He was flying! Then the ground was a story or so below them, and Aric pulled back on a lever. The ship streaked away. Whatever else their getaway might be, it would be fast. Maurin watched out the window as the port shrank behind them.

"That was close," Aric said.

Dania nodded fractionally. Valasand slumped back into her seat.

Aric brought the shuttle back down into the mountains, weaving an intricate path through the peaks. They sped northwest, along the range.

"Is it necessary to fly this close?" Maurin asked as Aric took a sharp right turn past the rock face.

"Trying to keep a low profile until we get out of the mountains. It'll be harder for them to track us."

Leveling out the craft, Aric turned south, away from the range. Their mansion shot by underneath, small as a child's building block. The peaks and valleys of the Secoras fell away in a pair of heartbeats, and the green carpet of the forest streaked by.

"See anyone following us?" Aric called.

Valasand scanned the air behind them, and Maurin joined her at the window, forcing himself not to look down. Talauna gripped the cloth of her seat as if holding the craft together with sheer will.

"Not so far," Valasand said. "Well done, Aric."

"I'll feel better when we've put some leagues between us and Caileen."

The Warden sighed. "As will I."

Maurin felt his tension easing as the minutes passed, but he couldn't take his eyes off the rippling forest and the river.

"Quite a view, isn't it?" Valasand asked.

"I've never been in one of these," Maurin said. "I could never have imagined that's what the world looks like from so far away."

The Warden smiled. "Some things do improve with distance."

After some time, Maurin relaxed enough to sit back, and contented himself with watching the clouds. He had almost dozed off when he heard Aric say something about coming up on Langfort.

"Is that a friendly place to land?" Maurin asked, noting the city directly below them.

"Not really," Aric said. "Krige was pretty chummy with Governor Phoecius. I'll take us past the swamps; there should be a couple of places where we can set down."

Then the humming sound of the shuttle went abruptly silent.

"Uh-oh." Aric started to shake the steering yoke and slap at various levers.

"What happened?" Valasand asked.

"I don't know! I've lost the power!"

The craft shuddered and nosed downward. Shouts of surprise and screams of terror merged with one another and were nearly lost in the shrieking howl of the wind as they plummeted, the interior of the shuttle a flurry of chaos and confusion. A spinning eternity went by in the blink of an eye as, with an incredible impact, the ship rolled over, sending up a massive plume of water. Maurin wrapped himself around Talauna, but they were thrown across the passenger section, hitting the bulkhead hard. A deafening explosion rocked the craft. Sparks and bits of metal flew everywhere, and Aric howled out a curse.

After a series of jolts and tumbles, at last the ship came to rest. The interior of the shuttle was pitch black, with the exception of the sparking of ruined conduits. All around him, Maurin heard groans of pain. He could hardly stand, but somehow dizzily made it to his feet. He stumbled, and his hand landed with a splash. Gasping, he smelled the unmistakable tadpoles-and-moss scent of stagnant swamp water.

"We're sinking!"

CHAPTER 24
WELCOME TO FATAMOR

Aric felt his way in the dark. Every step sent a jolt of pain through his collarbone. Dania and Valasand were already up. "Maurin?" he shouted. "Maurin, are you alive?"

"For the moment." The weak tone of his cousin's answer left it a little unclear as to whether that was a good or a bad thing. "How're the others?"

"I'm fine," Valasand said. "Dania?"

"Didn't you say you piloted Krige's chariot?" the gladiatrix snapped. "How many of those did he have?"

"Funny." Someone brushed up against Aric, and he started. A shower of sparks illuminated the interior of the vehicle for a second, and he saw Talauna looking up at him, small and frightened. The shuttle began to sway and shift.

Everyone was more or less intact, but it was getting a little soggy for Aric's taste. Already he was up to his knees in brackish water, and the shuttle was listing. He and Maurin went over to the release, but Aric soon realized he couldn't help. "I think my collarbone is broken."

Valasand came over and pushed up against the side hatch with all her strength along with Maurin, but it wouldn't budge. The door was caved in, no doubt crushed by a collision with a tree in the fall.

The shuttle creaked and groaned, and the sound of popping bolts reverberated throughout the cabin. The stern slipped further. It wouldn't be long before the vessel stood on end in the water.

Valasand climbed up to the pilot's area. She jabbed hard at the sandglass window with her staff.

"It won't do any good. That stuff is unbreakable."

She ignored him, and kept striking with all her might. At first, nothing happened, but a crack appeared, and then a hole. Aric winced as the vacuum broke with a sucking sound, and the water rushed up in earnest. Within seconds, she had smashed out the front window.

"Grab your weapons and hurry!"

Aric scrambled up over the pilot's seat and through the frame. Once outside, standing shakily on the hull of the shuttle, he took a quick glance back. A huge gash had been carved in the swampland, trees and plants mown down in a muddy path leading to the shuttle. Water kicked up by the force of the splash rained from the surrounding trees.

"Come on! Get up here!"

Talauna raised her arms to Aric in a gesture for help, but she was too short to reach his outstretched hands. The shuttle was sinking fast. Maurin bent down, planted both hands under her bottom, and boosted her up in one heave. Aric caught her, crying out as a white-hot jolt of pain lanced through his shoulder. Gritting his teeth, he pulled her up beside him.

Dania clambered onto the surface of the shuttle. Aric held out his hand, but Valasand was right behind her in the water, and helped her up. For his shoulder's sake, he was grateful. Maurin brought up the rear.

"We're going to have to swim to shore," Valasand said.

Dania jumped in with an oath, then swam with untrained but powerful strokes toward the spot Valasand indicated. Aric and Maurin glanced at each other, shrugged, and followed suit. He instantly regretted his decision; hitting the water caused a fresh wave of pain, and swimming was agony. He started to panic, but then remembered his survival lessons from years ago. He didn't need his arms to swim. Aric rolled over onto his back, attempted to relax, and floated, kicking his feet. Valasand and Talauna swam right behind him.

Aric found himself at the base of a vine-wrapped tree, sitting on some spongy material only marginally less wet than what he had just swum through. He turned at a slurping sound just in time to see the shuttle disappear beneath the surface of the water.

"Oh, boy," Maurin said.

"Do you know this area at all, Aric?" Valasand asked, bedraggled and wringing out her fur cloak.

He nodded. "Usually we didn't go this far south, but I've flown over the swamps a couple of times. We were forced to fly pretty low once due to the weather, but had to be careful around this area. The chariot tended to agitate the animals, so we powered down until we passed through their territory."

"Animals? What animals?" Maurin asked.

"Well, like that, for example." Aric pointed to a tree jutting starkly out of the swamp.

"I don't see—oh!" His cousin gulped. "I was looking for something a little smaller."

The creature hung suspended upside-down from a thick branch, gripping the stygian tree with clawed feet. Its vaguely cetacean head led directly into a thick body ending in a stumpy tail. Moss covered the amphibian skin and ridges on its back. The massive beast reached one of its long arms forward, getting a better purchase, opened its mouth wide, and closed it again. In the interim, Aric caught a glimpse of a long, coiled tongue.

"It doesn't look too dangerous," Dania observed.

"They aren't, particularly," Aric said. "But you still don't want to get them upset. A whole knot of those things attacking—well, I'd rather not be around when that happened."

Talauna grabbed Maurin's sleeve and pointed to a log or a bit of debris floating in the marsh only a short distance away. Then Aric saw it move, and realized he was seeing a blow-hole and the top of another creature's head, submerged past the eyeballs. How many others lay camouflaged in the swamp?

"What are they called?" Maurin asked quietly.

"Don't know. Some sort of marsh-wallows, I'm guessing." Aric pointed off to the west. "I'm pretty sure the river and some towns are off in that direction. If we can stick to the shallows, we should be out of their territory shortly."

Talauna started to peel her soggy blouse up, but stopped when the Warden cleared her throat. The Maolori's face twisted into a moue of displeasure, while Maurin fixed his gaze studiously on the animal in the tree.

"Let's get moving, shall we?" Valasand tested the ground with her staff before taking a step, keeping progress through the reedy pools slow. Talauna slogged along after her, tugging at her clothing and looking miserable.

Aric ground his teeth at the searing pain in his shoulder, listening to the sounds of the swamp over the panting and rustling of the others. While some of the animals eyed the group with suspicion, they all kept their distance. One of them submerged a few yards away, sending eddies of water swirling around Aric's ankles.

"I don't believe this." He shook his head. "Stuck in the swamp with no vehicle and nowhere to go."

"Why do you suppose the shuttle lost power?" Valasand asked. "Were there any indications it was having difficulty?"

"No," Aric said. "I've never seen anything like that before. It was like all the energy was just sucked out of it."

"Don't be upset," the Warden said. "There was nothing you could have done, and you kept your head under extraordinary pressure.

Overall, I'd say our first engagement was a success."

"Success?" Maurin said, incredulous.

"Absolutely. We achieved our goal"—she smiled at Dania—"and the only casualty we suffered was a stolen vehicle."

"And a broken shoulder," Aric muttered. The thin slate covering of clouds, combined with the bleak tones and ripe odor of the swamp, did nothing for his mood.

Talauna sloshed over to him and ran her fingers over his collarbone, pressing gently along the length of it. He winced at the touch and uttered Aran curses under his breath. The Maolori shook her head at Valasand.

The Warden examined him for a moment. "It's just cracked; not broken straight through. Be careful with it, and it should heal well enough."

A long stretch of black water stood between them and the next clump of vegetation. The group slogged through the knee-deep muck, and Aric could feel the mud oozing down into his boots and around his toes. Nothing indicated that they were in any danger of being sucked under. All the same, Valasand continued to poke ahead with her staff.

A huge surge of water nearly knocked them over. Aric froze in his tracks. All his instincts said to run, but in this sort of terrain that would not only be counterproductive, but possibly fatal.

Stay calm, stay calm.

Aric scoured the dark waters for whatever had just swum by them. A rounded snout surfaced, and Aric had the impression of a powerful tail. Then it submerged again.

Maurin turned white. "Where did it go?"

After a few seconds, the worm-like creature emerged at the base of another tree growing out of the water. It pulled itself up with two stubby limbs, wrapping its tail around the trunk and ascending in a spiral. The animal crawled halfway onto an outstretched limb and arched its back. It opened its mouth and took a deep breath, causing its upper body and the skin under the jaw to swell up. A basso cross between a howl and a roar reverberated across the still surface of the swamp. After a moment, the creature repeated the process, altering some of the patterns of the sound.

"What is it doing?" Dania asked.

Another bellow answered from a great distance. It went on for several seconds, followed by silence. Only then did the strange worm seem to be satisfied. It turned, placed its forelimbs flat against its sides, and dove into the water from where it sat.

"Calling for others, apparently," Aric said.

"Think we look like food to it?" Maurin asked.

"Rather not find out," Valasand said. "Move along."

Aric tensed every time he heard one of them call in the distance. Every flinch caused his shoulder to flare with agony, so he echoed each bellow with an imprecation. They got further away, though, and finally receded behind the group. Aric counted himself lucky.

After they reached a sizable patch of dry grasses and earth, Dania cursed softly, and started picking at her legs.

"What's wrong?" Maurin asked.

She held up a small snail-like creature for his scrutiny.

"Bloodsuckers," Aric said, attempting nonchalance as he examined his own legs. Maurin scrabbled all over, frantically scraping at his clothing, trying to explore all possible areas of parasitical refuge on his body at once while at the same time attempting to maintain a modicum of dignity—not an easy task, by any means.

"The sooner we get out of the swamp," Valasand said, "the sooner we can find a town, and put some steroline in our baths. That should kill off any leftover hitchhikers."

"Gah," Maurin said, cringing. "Give me any large predatory animal over a bloodsucker any day."

"You're so squeamish." Aric refused to get sick. He waved off a cloud of insects he suspected had the same staple diet. "Everything has to live off of something."

Dania plodded steadfastly through the marsh, avoiding Aric's eyes. No one felt like talking, and it was just as well. What was there to say? They were lost. He had begun to despair of ever finding land when Valasand pointed off into the distance. "Do you know what those are?"

A herd of reptiles grazed in the distance. Some of them glanced up at the group's approach, but they didn't seem particularly threatened, or, for that matter, interested. Each one was marginally larger than an average horse, carrying its sleek long neck, back, and tapered tail high above the ground. The mouth curved down at the ends before rising to meet the hinge of the jaw. The underside of the creatures was pale, almost white, contrasting with the blue-gray dappling of the flanks and nearly solid backs. The feet were not quite hooves, but rather three thick toes, the middlemost being the thickest and strongest, and bearing most of the weight. A short, rounded spur was set just a few inches above the foot of each animal.

Aric grinned. "Those are a good sign."

Maurin waited expectantly, too tired to ask.

"Don't know what they're called, but I do know they don't go very deep into the swamp. Shows we're coming to the end of it."

"Thank Yasul," Valasand murmured.

The amphibious equines must have decided they had gotten close enough, because one snorted, and the lot of them bolted, scattering away from the group in great loping strides. The creatures had a serpentine grace, nickering and wheezing like a nest of vipers.

"Go the opposite direction," Aric said. "They'll be headed for deeper water for protection."

Maurin nodded. Dania stumbled, but dragged herself back up before anyone could offer assistance. Soon they were climbing out of the bogs and onto a grassy bank. Aric's feet rubbed raw in his soggy boots, and his shoulder throbbed.

"Which way now?" Dania asked no one in particular.

Aric bit his lip and frowned as he scanned from horizon to horizon.

"South," he said at last. "I'm pretty sure there are some towns south of here."

"Be sure," Valasand said softly.

"I have to admit I'm not feeling very optimistic about the greeting we're going to get," Maurin said.

"It's a chance we're going to have to take."

Dania made a point of straightening up and walking ahead of them. Within a few moments, Maurin let out an exultant yell in Aran.

"What is it?" Valasand asked.

"Road!"

Valasand closed her eyes, bowed her head, and drew in a deep breath. Even Dania looked relieved.

The sun was on its downward curve when at last a town rose from the plain, virtually unsheltered save for a few low hills. Aric smiled, entertaining thoughts of a meal.

"Stay back a bit. Something is strange here." Valasand stepped ahead of the group, narrowing her eyes and staring so hard that Aric wondered if she was trying to see through the houses. The others stayed close. Aric found himself in the rear again.

There was no one in sight. The buildings lay in sparse clumps, and a gray pall hung over the town, a weighty sense of oppression transcending the murky twilight. A sign hung on a post, marked with large, weathered letters.

"What does that say?" Maurin asked.

"*Welcome to Fatamor,*" Valasand said.

"Funny," Aric said, gazing out into the empty streets, "I don't feel very welcome."

"Is anyone here?" Dania's throaty voice echoed through the town, the last traces of her call dying away without reply.

Aric went up to the darkened window of the transport station. "Hello?" he called, tapping on the pane. There was no answer. The door swung easily on its hinges. Inside, ledgers and timetables were left out, half-drunk containers of liquid sat on tables, and what were obviously pieces of luggage and parcels still waited to be picked up.

Strange voices, echoes of dreams, perhaps, sounded in his head.

It begins here. The Dreaded One will not escape us.

Maurin frowned. "What is it, Aric?"

"Something... awful happened here." He offered no further explanation. Their footsteps crunched in his ears as they wandered through the streets. "This place is dead."

The wind whistled between the low stone buildings with a kind of melancholy lament. Otherwise, the place was totally devoid of any signs of life. The few carts he saw were abandoned in the road. A few animals lay about dead, but no carrion-eaters were in sight, and no insects buzzed about. The carcasses were gray and withered, and smelled odd.

"Gods, what is that?" Maurin said.

Aric followed his gaze and felt a sudden chill. The wall of the building ahead of them had been cracked open by what looked like a giant root made of stone. Whatever it was had thrust up suddenly, because the ground was broken and crumbled at its base, and the rock of the wall was likewise freshly damaged. It was taller than all of them, with one main thick structure terminating in what appeared to be a burst seed pod, and a few minor tendrils probing around the area where it had torn through the ground.

"Have you ever seen anything like this before?" Valasand asked.

"No," Aric lied. The memories of the bizarre killing in that alley in Caileen were all too fresh, and all too vivid. He didn't know why, but he could barely speak. "Never."

Come to me. Come, my love.

"You look really strange."

Aric's pulse throbbed in his ears. "We're not going to find anyone. The Reamar have been and gone."

"How do you know?"

He shrugged.

"What now, Valasand?" Maurin asked.

She considered in silence a moment before answering. "I think the danger here has passed. We need to find a safe place to stay, and Dania, I should probably examine you."

"I'm fine."

"Probably so," Valasand said, "but we should be sure. Now let us go to the sentry station. It should be reasonably well-defended, and give us a better viewpoint than any of the other buildings. We need to find as much as we can in the way of food, blankets, medical supplies, water, weapons, and anything else useful you come across."

"How long do you think we're going to be here, anyway?" Aric hated this place. It was too empty, too... familiar.

"I'm not certain, but it's best that we keep a low profile until we're sure Argoneis isn't searching for us."

When they had situated themselves as much as possible, stocking the larder from various houses, and barring all the entrances to the sentry station, Valasand and Talauna took Dania behind a screen to examine her and give her whatever medical aid they could.

Aric listened uncomfortably to her protest. No, Dania had not been broken; that much was clear. But she had been humbled, and that was perhaps worse in her eyes. He caught her gaze over the partition, and saw shame reflected there. He closed the door, and let the women work.

Maurin seemed lost; he kept twiddling with his hair and gnawing at the sides of his fingers as he paced back and forth. When Aric asked him what his problem was, Maurin muttered something about never feeling as though he could keep a home, then went back to his pacing. Eventually, Aric left him alone and went to find a place to lie down.

The first night was a terror. The wind howled across the plains, and the gusts rattled shutters and banged doors throughout the entire town. Aric resolved to secure as many as he could the following morning. Demons of the dark and ghastly creatures haunted his dreams and tormented his sleep.

He went on a self-imposed reconnaissance mission the next morning. Maurin and Talauna were still asleep, Valasand was nowhere in sight, and Dania's mat was empty. After several minutes of going from house to house and making sure doors were closed, Aric went back to the site of the strange tree-root structure. He wasn't sure, but the smaller roots around the base might have grown some overnight.

No doubt about it; he wanted out of here as soon as possible.

This place is dead.

Yes. Yes, it was.

He climbed to the open air of the sentry tower to ruminate alone. Some time later, he heard a soft tapping on the trap door in the floor. When he opened it, to his surprise, Dania was on the ladder.

No words from the moment she came to him to the moment she left. No apologies, no explanations. Aric didn't pursue or question her. But he was more confused than ever. Was that "thank you for coming after me," or just Dania being inscrutable?

Though he could hardly complain at the attention, he was starting to feel ashamed. He knew he did not love her. True, she had not asked for his love, his kindness, or his tender affections. But they were using each other, and that unsettled him. He started to wish he'd never said yes in the first place.

He wanted to find the woman in his dreams.

She would help him find meaning in all this.

INTERLUDE
SERPENTINE

Thunder crashes, and lightning casts a strobing aura, silhouetting her statuesque figure in night against a cobalt and sapphire storm. Lit with an eternal flickering glow, her eyes swallow me alive. Her lips move in supplication. Her every feature is as familiar to me as my own. Her beauty follows me everywhere, the melodious tones of her voice thrown into sharp relief by the howling, tormented winds.

I love you, Aric.

I love you, I answer automatically. *Who are you?*

I am waiting for you. You need only come to me.

I'm coming... I'm coming...

I struggle, drawn once more into the inevitable conclusion of the dream. I know what lies ahead. The vision rushes closer. Blue-green eyes flood me with memories of things not yet happened. She draws me into her arms and opens her mouth for a kiss. Her eyes creep open when we part, the dark, fathomless pupils elongating vertically, becoming mere reptilian slits. The agonized chorus of the dead sings louder as the loving embrace turns into a lethal strain. Her limbs are massive serpentine coils, tenaciously entwined about my body. My ribs creak as she begins to squeeze. Her eyes glow with an unnatural fire. In a bizarre admixture of pain and ecstasy, I scream as I feel my life drawn away...

CHAPTER 25
BACCHANAL

The annual feast of Shang Perralt proceeded with all the sybaritic posturing the nobles had come to expect of Lord Daman Argoneis. Only the conspicuous absence of Rominan Seides marred the occasion that celebrated the beginning of autumn. The man's jovial manner and endless stories about his excursions into the wilds had provided Daman's guests with hours of entertainment, and were sorely missed. Missed by all but Aster Krige, at any rate. He gnawed at a chunk of oil-dipped bread, all the while slumped down in his chair, wishing he could just disappear. He hated making appearances at these get-togethers of Daman's; they always ended on a horrible note.

"Death comes to us all," Daman mused without preamble.

"So it does, my lord," Krige said. All around the long table, hapless servants attended to the nobles' needs; pouring wine and distributing food. Seeing the slaves made Krige thank whatever powers existed that Talauna had not been sold to the man. Was she still alive? Where was she? Was she thinking of him? Of course she was. Why wouldn't she be?

"Then why does it trouble us so?"

"I don't know. It troubles some, I think, more than others."

"Tell me, my friend, are you afraid of death?"

Krige considered carefully before answering. "I don't believe I fear the moment of my death," he said at last. "But I do not wish to hasten it, either."

Daman smiled. "A good answer."

"A truthful one."

"Yet Lord Seides used to thrill from the idea that death was only a heartbeat away. Does the idea of imminent danger excite you?" Daman appeared genuinely curious.

"Not particularly, my lord."

"Hmmm." Daman frowned. "Nor does it me. Sometimes I think old Rominan would have liked to be a gladiator himself, in the arena or even the underground pits throughout Caileen, fighting with the slaves."

Sabatha laughed softly. "I suspect that is so."

"Why would he want such a thing?"

"I believe it was his way of controlling death, of making it more personal." Sabatha shrugged. "Maybe even less frightening. If he could face it and live, he was immortal."

"I see." Daman mulled this over for a moment, then brightened. "Didn't work, did it?"

"It never does, my lord," Krige said. "Speaking of Seides, are we any closer to apprehending his killer?"

Daman's eyes flashed for a moment. Then he stood suddenly, and raised his voice along with his glass. "I give you a toast: To the late, lamented Lord Seides, who spent his life hunting game almost as wild as... as..."

"As wild as one of our dear Lord Argoneis's parties!" a reveler interjected.

Daman smiled wanly at the compliment. General guffaws sounded all around the room. Krige didn't much like the look in Argoneis's eye; he had imbibed far too much already, and was clearly beginning to get bored. A bored Daman was a dangerous Daman.

"On a serious note," Argoneis said, wobbling ever so slightly, "I would like to point out that the way Lord Seides met his demise was, quite literally, the pits."

A few uncertain titters met his remark. Once his little joke had run its course, and he was certain of the audience's undivided attention, he continued:

"Seides made a fatal mistake. He was done in by a dangerous off-world woman he brought into his own household. He believed he could control her, and was taken off guard. The treacherous wench killed him as he slept."

General murmurs of outrage swept across the table.

"I think it is clear from what happened to Lord Seides what these creatures are capable of. This very thing could happen to you, should you let your guard down. Yet despite the fact that impositions on the slaves are made for your very safety, I've been criticized for not giving the slaves more freedoms. Indeed, recently there have been some who had the audacity to come to me and tell me they didn't like the way I run things. They even threatened to turn me in to the Temple."

Daman's testy expression turned into an all-out sneer. "It seems, gentlemen, there are those who believe I am no longer free to do what I wish in my own world."

A youth poured wine into Daman's decanter as he spoke. Without warning, Daman drew back his arm and smashed his fist into the boy's jaw, sending him sprawling across the table. A glass broke under his body, mingling blood with the wine running freely over the white cloth and spilling over the hands and laps of the nobles. He moaned and slid off to the floor. Daman put his foot down on the boy's unconscious form, and held up both hands with an incredulous expression. "Can you believe the temerity?"

It was all Krige could do to keep from retching. He winced at the sight of the boy under Daman's sandaled foot. Things could turn ugly so quickly with Argoneis.

Daman took something small and slender from a fold in his cloak, and tossed it onto the table. It landed next to the plate of one of the nearest nobles, who recoiled in horror. The signet ring adorning the severed finger was instantly recognizable as having belonged to Lord Hargin Dalinde.

Argoneis proceeded to tell his guests about the visit he had received from Lauran Dalinde. He'd then summoned her parents, Hargin and Maula, and brought them all together into one room. Daman told Hargin his punishment for sending Lauran was to choose whether his wife or his daughter would go through the excruciation. Hargin offered himself, if only Daman would let the two women go. Daman told him it was a noble thought. Ordinarily, it would have been the right choice, as he was the main offender for sending his daughter to do his dirty work. However, Daman told Dalinde, he preferred people learn something, and you can't teach a dead man. This lesson he would always remember.

Hargin had pleaded with Daman, saying he couldn't choose, and when Daman said he must, he chose his wife. After it was all over, and Lauran Dalinde no doubt hated her father almost as much as she hated Argoneis, Daman had Hargin's finger removed as a reminder to him and any other nobles—as if they would forget. All this Krige had heard from Daman's own mouth, and to hear him tell it, it was the most reasonable, compassionate thing ever done.

"I know," Argoneis continued, waggling the ringed phalange, "not one of you would ever, ever, think of pointing your finger at me in condemnation and betrayal."

Certainly not now. Krige forced himself not to wipe away the sweat at his collar.

Daman gave the boy at his feet a kick, and two slaves came to take him away. Argoneis, meanwhile, glared at each of the nobles in turn. The gaiety of the room had turned to solemn fear, and no one knew quite what to say. Several of the men were sweating, their eyes bulging slightly in a vain attempt to appear calm. They avoided direct eye contact with one another, not wanting to be implicated by a misinterpreted gesture. The atmosphere grew stifling. Suddenly, Daman brightened, a strange hunger in his eyes. He smiled, and clapped his hands together twice, startling several with the sound.

"But fortunately, I know who my friends are, and have no cause for concern regarding your loyalties."

From somewhere down an adjoining hall came a horrified shriek of protest, followed by a distant scuffling.

"Now," Daman said, turning to the source of the sound with an expression of rapturous glee, "let's have a little fun."

Krige managed to make his excuses and leave before the session began; he had attended far too many of Argoneis's parties not to know what happened next, and he had no stomach for it. He wanted to go home, but Daman would be insulted. Instead, he spent a few hours in the library. Impressive, though he doubted the Lord Regent had actually read any of the books in it. He poured himself a glass of wine Argoneis had imported from off-world. Daman himself didn't care for the rare and exceedingly expensive stuff; he mostly kept it around to impress people.

Krige found a small scholarly work on the Maolori people, and whiled away the time reading about the explorers who first came to this world and studied them. It was amazing how little they'd discovered since the colonies were centuries old. But then, the Maolori were elusive creatures. Ironic. The Temple put forth tendrils of itself into other worlds so that the natives might know the Source; cities and communities were established for the sake of a people who would not be seen within leagues of a civilized area.

Krige sighed, unable to keep his mind from Daman's speech. The raiding of other nations and worlds for slaves alone was a relatively new concept. Never would he forget how the trade of flesh had gotten started, when Daman took over the offices of the Temple over two decades ago.

It had begun with the overcrowding of prisons. The Shoan Dynasty endorsed capital punishment for certain crimes, but laxity among various worlds in carrying out the letter of the law meant some of the institutions were overburdened and undermanned. Some housed nearly three times the number of inmates each facility was equipped to deal with. It got to the point where many cities did not have the resources to keep funding these institutions at the rate they were filling up. Then came charges that the common man was being taxed to oblivion to feed and house the criminals. Sometimes these convicts lived better than the people whose taxes kept them in prison. The general mood of the people was ugly; they'd had enough of freeloading men and women leeching the livelihood of the law-abiding citizen.

Enter Daman Argoneis. Young Daman and his sister had sat silently in the halls of the general assemblies on the world of Tarace, listening to the discourse about the crisis. Krige was there, and though it had been years, the day was still freshly imprinted on his mind. Krige recalled Daman's sister, Uva, was also blond, and attractive, though consanguinity gave her the same slightly hard-edged appearance. Daman's slender face was clean shaven, and his hair stylishly trimmed in the traditional royal Argoneis manner. His robes had been simple but elegant, creating a noble but approachable impression. He exuded a youthful tranquility, like a eunuch priest of a Taracine monastery.

"May I offer a suggestion?" he had asked after one particularly grueling day in the High Court. "Daman Argoneis, of Argoth," he identified himself, when all eyes turned toward him. "The House of Argoneis would like to make a statement."

Judge Yawara seemed to consider for a moment. "Come forward,

Lord Argoneis," he intoned somberly. "Perhaps a fresh voice is what this hearing needs."

Daman had smiled graciously and inclined his head in a modest bow. He stepped out into the midst of the assembly. Not actually a member of the courts, Daman represented his family in his father's stead, ever since his death only a few months prior. At the time, Krige recalled, Daman was one of the youngest men there.

"Your Honor," Daman said, "might I suggest we are going about this in the wrong way? The main purpose of penal institutions is punishment, of course. But punishment without rehabilitation is without merit."

"Most of the prisons in question have a strong rehabilitation program."

"True, but how effective is it? How much can those people learn about how to live a normal life while inside the walls of a prison?"

"What do you suggest, then, Lord Argoneis?"

Daman refreshed that placid smile of his, sending shivers up Krige's back, though at the time he had no idea why he should react that way.

"I propose a system of work outside the prison. Put these people in a program allowing them to be useful to themselves and others and learn the value of a productive life." He spread his arms wide in a grand, visionary gesture. "I suggest we give these people the opportunity to give something back, to make themselves a part of the very societies they currently hamper. I have a tentative itinerary of supervised labor under minimum security. Those convicts who have proven to be the most dangerous, of course, would go to more physical jobs under stricter supervision. However, they would all be able to prove themselves worthy of becoming members of society again."

"It sounds suspiciously like conscripted labor," the judge said.

"Not at all, Your Honor," Daman said smoothly. "Why, on my own world of Argoth—we're one of the Temple's colonies, you know—our servants rise through the ranks to become titled gentlemen and ladies of property. And what I propose would be voluntary; anyone not interested would of course remain in the penal colonies and prisons. However, I would think the chance to earn a second chance in life would appeal to

millions of those souls currently languishing away on your poor taxpay-
ers' hard-earned salaries."

"And do you have a course of action in mind?"

Daman's eyes had glimmered in triumph at that moment.

"Naturally, Your Honor. First of all, we would want to get these people off their home planets, away from the environments that helped nur-
ture the dysfunction in the first place. This helps engender the feeling of
a fresh start. We would start small, with a number of trial groups, and
monitor them closely. If the program seems to be working, we could ex-
pand into other territories, gaining the cooperation of those businesses
and guilds that could use the help."

"Your idea intrigues me, Lord Argoneis," Judge Yawara admitted. "I
would like to hear more before presenting it formally to this body and
putting it to the vote."

A slow, thin smile spread across Daman's lips. "Certainly, Your
Honor."

As it happened, the idea was most timely, and most welcome. Glad
to get rid of the surplus prisoners from thousands of prisons across the
Shoan Dynasty, the members of the High Court agreed almost unani-
mously to put Daman's plan into action. Shipload after shipload of in-
carcerated people were farmed out from one end of the ocean of stars to
the other, and the monitoring program put into effect. But Daman's program was multifold and deceptive. Several of the prisoners were sold on
the black market, and though their records said they were alive and working diligently in their rehabilitation programs, they were never heard
from again. Others were paraded in front of a review board several times,
demonstrating how successfully Daman's plan of reform was working.
Soon the prisons gave up thousands of inmates at a time, eager to get the
wrongdoers off their hands and into someone else's.

After a while, the High Court became more and more confident in
Argoneis's brilliance and charitable disposition and requested fewer and
fewer updates. Trips between worlds without gates were, after all, time-
consuming and expensive.

The time eventually came that his enterprise was not looked after at
all, with the exception of a routine, perfunctory checkup done by one

person, whose loyalty, it turned out, was easily bought. The High Court, naturally, had other concerns, and didn't care to throw loose cogs into what were obviously smoothly working gears.

Daman continued to grow in popularity, amassing a great deal of wealth in addition to that which he naturally inherited as an heir of the prestigious House of Argoneis. It was not until he was the most powerful person in Caileen that the people of Argoth began to realize that this young wonder had a dark side.

In spite of rumors that Argoneis's father had been a clandestine Reamar-worshiper, and that Daman himself was developing a taste for creative cruelty, he had somehow ingratiated himself over the years with the residing priest at the Temple of the Source on Argoth. These whispers never made it to the ears of the High Court or the Temple proper; dissenters had a habit of disappearing. When the priest died, Daman declared that he would stand as regent until the Temple appointed a replacement. Months passed, and finally years, before it became apparent that no replacement was coming.

"I thought I might find you here."

Krige started; he must have dozed off. He set aside the volume that had slid from his hands, then brushed his knees. "My lord."

"Are you well?" Daman walked over and sat in a chair facing him. His bodyguards stood silent just inside the door, Anice wearing a splint on her wrist.

"Oh, yes," Krige said. "Sometimes my stomach gives me a bit of trouble, that's all."

"Too much drink, my friend."

Not enough, actually. Krige nodded and managed a smile. "No doubt. Yet who can refuse to indulge on a night like tonight? The feast of Shang Perralt comes but once a year."

"Indeed." Daman frowned, and stared into the fireplace, where the flames had gone low.

"You seem troubled tonight, my lord."

"Oh." Daman dismissed the comment with an overly casual wave of the hand. "This whole business with the Warden has been giving me fits."

"The Warden?" Krige's throat went dry. "What Warden?"

"Oh, I didn't tell you? That outlander you discovered turned out to be the rumored Warden of the Gates."

"Really? How did you discover this?" Krige tried to sound calm, but wasn't sure he succeeded. Surely if Daman had sensed duplicity in him, he would be dead—or worse—by now.

"She told me herself." Daman said. "She had the gall to march right into my throne room. Even more incredible, she took Anice hostage in order to free that gladiatrix."

Krige coughed. "Did she have slaves with her?"

Daman shook his head. "A couple of young men—one of whom was your runaway pilot. The other I didn't recognize, but he was nobody remarkable. I hate to admit it, but she caught us all a little off-guard. Didn't she, Anice, dear?"

Anice snarled an ear-blistering reply. Sabatha shushed her, and Daman laughed wistfully.

"What happened?" Krige could scarcely breathe. No mention of Talauna. Had she been with them? Had she stayed back at the mansion? Where had she been?

"They managed to escape, more through luck than skill. They somehow made it to the port, took off in a shuttle, and according to some witnesses in Langfort, ended up crashing in the swamps." Daman shrugged.

"Dead?" Surely Talauna couldn't have been with them. Yet Krige couldn't keep from sweating.

"Who knows? I have people looking for them, combing the area just in case. I can't have a Warden running around loose on the planet."

"No, I suppose you can't." If he had felt sick before, Krige thought he might pass out now. The idea of Talauna lying twisted and broken in a pile of wreckage out in the southern swamplands was too much to bear. On the other hand, if she were dead, she would be out of Daman's grasp forever.

Now that was a thought with considerable appeal.

"My friend, are you certain you're feeling well?" The genuine concern in Daman's eyes would have been gratifying, coming from anyone else.

"Yes... no, actually." Krige shook his head. "As you know, my wife has been ailing these past few weeks." She wasn't, but it was as good an excuse as any for her not to appear tonight. "I may have a touch of her illness." He managed a wan smile.

"Do you need a physician?" Daman stood. "I can get you the best."

"Oh, no," Krige said hurriedly. "I'm sure it's nothing a little rest won't cure."

Daman nodded. "In that case, I'll get my coachman to take you home."

"Thank you, my lord."

Mirian was already asleep when Krige got home, so he simply crawled into bed and lay with his eyes open for some time.

Oh, little one, I hope you're still alive.

INTERLUDE
THE CAVE

Trapped. The bear-wolves have penetrated the cavern. Their unholy howls mingle with the screams of the dying. A young mother shrieks at her daughter, begging her to run, to get away, but she is abruptly silenced, and a scarlet fountain slicks the cave floor. A thick brown fog casts the scene of hell below in sepia tones. I clamber up the rock toward the mouth of the cave, ignoring cries for help. All that matters now is survival. Freedom is just a few yards away.

Then I see them. Shadows stirring the mists, resolving into mighty men. I know why they are here, and an arrow of fear pierces my heart. The animals are not wild, after all. They are sent by someone, sent for someone. Sent to hunt me. The leader comes forward, his great cloak swirling about him, the rounded horns of his helm reaching nearly to his shoulders. The others level their weapons. Then, slowly, the leader reaches up and lifts his helmet...

This can't be real, this can't be real. Wake up, Aric. It's just another dream.

The man steps forward, and the gleaming eyes skewer my soul.
IT'S JUST A DREAM!

CHAPTER 26
STRAINED

"You want to leave?" Dania stopped her ritual katas with a look as sharp as any dagger. "What do you mean, leave?"

"I want to get off this world." Cold waves of nausea swept over Aric at the intensity of her emotions. "You want that as much as I do, and you know it."

"And you would abandon your cousin like this?" Dania snarled. "Leave him here to fight Argoneis alone?"

"I'd make him come along, somehow."

"He wants to stay."

"He's not thinking straight," Aric argued. "He's too stuck on Talauna. He just won't admit it yet."

"She is not the only reason." Dania poked Aric in the chest with a hard index finger. "Maurin wishes to end this slavery. He stays because he believes it is right to do so. I thought you did, too. But perhaps you are afraid."

"Afraid to fight?" Aric scoffed. "Dania, I could burn this world to ashes and never look back. I just don't care."

"You don't care?" Fire flashed in her eyes. "You don't care? Then you don't care about what you know to be right and true? You don't care that people die here? You don't care about..." She waved her hand, letting the unspoken words hang in the air.

"Aw, come on. This is stupid."

"No, Aric," Dania said. "This is wrong."

Aric seethed for a moment. "All right. You want to know the truth? I am afraid. I'm running away, Dania. It's that simple. I'm being a coward. There is something here, something bad, that I don't want to be a part of. It doesn't have anything to do with you, and it doesn't have anything to do with the slave ring. It only has to do with me. You happy now?"

Her eyes did not let him escape. "If it is a danger, we will face it together. And we will defeat it."

"It's a danger." Aric turned away. "But I'll have to face it alone."

"Then you choose to be alone." Dania stalked off.

Aric sat brooding in silence for a few moments before he heard someone approach. Talauna.

"So you were listening. That figures."

She nodded.

"I wouldn't really leave him, you know."

Talauna frowned and sat beside him.

"I just don't know what to do."

Talauna put a sympathetic hand on his shoulder, which he promptly shrugged off.

"You know," he said, laughing ironically and poking at the dirt with a stick, "he's always kind of been my hero. Do you know how long it took me to even have an opinion that was different from his?"

Talauna shook her head.

"Used to be I wouldn't even take a drink without finding out what Maurin was having first."

She started to reach toward him again, then apparently thought better of it.

"What's funny is that here Dania thinks I'm being an ass for not wanting to bring everyone in on this, and she's the one who never lets anyone do anything for her. And all the time I don't know what to do, because all I have is a bad feeling, and who pays attention to bad feelings?"

A moment passed in silence. Aric felt Talauna staring at him, and he turned and glared back at her, his contemplative mood gone as quickly as if he had been dropped into a mountain stream. "What?"

She glanced down again with a hurt expression.

"Oh, don't give me that." Aric was mortally tired of this charade. "You can talk. Why don't you?"

Talauna looked back up at him, stubborn and defensive. His cousin might find those shining eyes compelling, but Aric thought them puer-ile. That little-girl-lost quality so endearing to Maurin was wearing a bit thin.

"Let me guess," he said, "you don't talk for just anyone, right?" He laughed harshly at her confused and wounded expression.

"You know, Maurin really likes you." Bit of an understatement. His cousin thought flowers bloomed where the girl's feet had passed. It was rather sickening, really. "It wouldn't hurt you to let him know you like him, too."

Aric could read her face as easily as if she had spoken: Was Maurin angry at her? Talauna no doubt thought she had let him know. She was an open book to those who had eyes to see. Talauna turned away in dis-tress, and he dismissed her with an exasperated wave.

"Forget it," Aric said. "I couldn't care less. But believe me, one of these days, he's going to get tired of talking to you, and having you not answer. He gets bored with people who can't speak for themselves, and mad when he thinks you don't care what he's saying. Eventually, he may get over those big brown eyes of yours, and just decide to go get someone who will talk back to him."

Talauna rose abruptly and hurried off.

Aric stared aimlessly into the trees. How much did Maurin know about him and Dania? How would he react if he were to tell him what had been going on? No doubt he would chastise him for getting in over his head and tell him *I told you so*. It seemed ages since Aric had talked to Maurin of the things weighing on his heart, and even longer since he asked him for advice. His cousin would not approve of this. Aric had not even been of the traditional marrying age when they were taken from Sangrine, and even though he was technically responsible for himself now, he was still just barely into manhood.

None of that mattered at the moment, though. None of it was im-portant enough to bother with. Relatives and Wardens and lovers could go to all the various hells of the universe, for all he cared. All that con-cerned him was the dark vision dominating his mind's eye when he went to bed.

———————•◆•———————

The following morning, Valasand said it was time to head out. No one had any objections; all were eager to be quit of this forsaken place. They had gathered all the salted meat and dried fruit they could carry, and the Warden had procured dark brown traveling cloaks for them. Aric had scrounged some rugged all-purpose packs to put it all in. Dania had already found daggers that suited her—or at least would make do until she found better ones.

Aric had searched in vain for some sort of airship, but as Maurin pointed out, this was a pretty small, out-of-the-way town. The chariots were more or less the exclusive domain of the rich, and this didn't seem like the kind of place that warranted extravagances. More legwork, then. Funny how quickly things like that could spoil you. Still, it wasn't so much that he minded walking as it was that he craved flight. Oh, to soar again above the mountains...

Valasand had found a map, a yellowed scroll the others couldn't read, but she seemed to have figured out where they were, and where they should go next. "We'll head to Mor Tespir, north of here."

"North is not on the way," Aric said.

"That depends on one's destination, doesn't it?"

Maurin nodded passively.

Aric didn't answer.

Come to me. The voice pulled him south, and he rubbed at his temples. "You're going back, aren't you?"

"It's why I'm here," she said. "Nothing will deter me from eradicating Argoneis and preventing his circus."

Maurin had that same aggravating expression Aric remembered from before the wedding. That stubborn damned-if-I-don't-do-right look he always got when he was trying to make a point.

Aric shook his head. "I don't suppose there's any other way off this world?"

Valasand raised an eyebrow at him, then spun on her heel and headed toward the edge of town. "Not that I'm aware of."

CHAPTER 27
SUMMONING

"Does something seem a little odd here," Maurin asked, "or is it just me?"

The streets of Mor Tespir, while not exactly bustling, were active enough. But there was something off-kilter about the people. Perhaps it was that they moved a little too much in unison, their wanderings a bit too precise. There almost appeared to be some sort of internal rhythm to their steps as they walked down the pathways, each person's foot hitting the ground at approximately the same time as the others'.

"No." Valasand eyed the too-steady stream of humanity uneasily. "It's not you. They're like automatons, aren't they?"

"Exactly." Maurin's brow furrowed. "I thought it was just my imagination."

The hand that slipped into Maurin's was almost like a child's; small and slender, with long, pointed fingers and delicately formed bones. He did not shy away this time, but merely glanced at Talauna and gently squeezed, trying out a tentative smile. Her eyes softened, and she smiled back. But the butterflies in his stomach just increased at her unsettled expression.

"This place is strange." The Warden rubbed at her temples. "Something here troubles my spirit."

Maurin passed several dock workers going about their jobs, eyes vacant and staring. Mor Tespir must have had some regular influx of traffic from the other cities to justify a port this busy. He still couldn't get used to the notion of inland ports and ships that flew through the air. Strangely, though he saw several berthed vehicles, none were active.

"Excuse me," he said, trying to catch the attention of a muscular, shirtless man carrying a heavy bundle over one shoulder. "Could you tell us where we might find a hostelry?"

The man walked past without acknowledging Maurin's presence in any way. He tried again with another passing dock worker, but got the same results.

"What are we, invisible?" Aric said.

"Hey!" Maurin shouted in the direction of the departing men. "I'm talking to you!"

Talauna tugged at his sleeve and shook her head at him, telling him to let it go. He threw one last spiteful glare at the man's back, and allowed himself to be pulled away.

Valasand's eyes focused somewhere else, while her body merely occupied space here. "She's right, Maurin; it won't do any good to get angry with them. This is not the place to start a fight."

"I wasn't going to," he objected, still fuming slightly. "I just hate being ignored, that's all." Poor hearing he could excuse, but snobbery rankled him sorely. Though he might be more sensitive than usual. He couldn't believe that they had come so close to Argoneis and had to flee with their tails between their legs. This world just kept getting stranger, and home seemed farther away than ever.

"I don't think they were ignoring you intentionally. I'm not even sure they're aware of us. Something has happened here. We must be careful."

"My shoulder hurts," Aric put in, apparently feeling a lack of attention in his own right.

"Don't be such an infant," Dania rejoindered.

Talauna headed toward an open market with several stands of fresh fruit and a few merchants selling clothing and various wares. The people moved around the group without seeming to notice their existence. Something was wrong, Maurin thought; Valasand might wear a thick cloak, but a woman of her distinctive qualities should never fail to turn a few heads here and there.

"It stinks here," Dania said.

"Could be us." Maurin tripped and swore. Another one of those gray vines. It pushed its way through the stones of the city and climbed up the walls of the various buildings, more like veins than a plant. "What is with this stuff? It's everywhere."

Aric's expression turned somber as he kicked at it. "Hard as rock, too."

They continued through the town, everyone around them absorbed in his own business. No conversations, no haggling among merchants and customers. Many wandered the streets or huddled in corners, gazing at nothing in particular.

"That's weird," Aric said.

"What?" Maurin asked.

"Have you noticed that none of these people actually seem to be buying anything? They're just going through the motions of shopping."

"Oh, gods," Dania said.

"What?" Maurin followed her eyes, then felt the color rise to his cheeks.

"Talauna...!" Valasand rushed over to where the Maolori girl stood examining a colorful dress. Talauna's blouse and breeches lay pooled around her ankles. "What have I told you about that?"

Valasand tugged Talauna's breeches back up over her hips, pressed the other garments to her chest, and ushered her around the corner, reminding her that there were partitions specially designed for changing behind, and it wasn't customary or proper to try something on in the middle of the open air market.

Aric snickered. "You can take the girl out of the forest, but you can't take the forest out of the girl."

It wasn't very funny. But perhaps even more disconcerting was the fact that no one had reacted in the slightest. The clothing merchant stared straight ahead, unblinking, as if nothing at all had happened. People continued to flow around them like water over stones; no one had slowed, no one had objected—no one had even gawked. Maurin found it vaguely insulting.

Valasand came around the corner with Talauna in tow, fully dressed and properly contrite. She hung the dress back on the rack. "Sorry about that."

Maurin watched for a reaction on the part of the merchant. There was none.

Valasand pressed on. "We have recently come from Fatamor. The city was totally deserted. Do you know what happened there?"

Still the steady, empty expression.

Maurin squirmed. Dania radiated irritation.

"Nothing has happened," the man said at last, with a slightly glazed look. "Everything is perfectly normal."

"Right." Aric dripped with sarcasm. "No problem."

"Yes," the older man said, visibly relieved that someone had understood. "No problems."

Aric's expression mirrored Maurin's quizzical glance.

"Come on." He slapped Maurin on the back. "Let's go. I don't know about you, but I've had enough of this place."

"I see," Valasand said to the merchant. "Thank you for your help."

Aric whistled as they left the market. "I'm glad he told us everything was normal. Otherwise I might be worried."

"I'm don't relish the idea of spending a night in this creepy city," Maurin said. "Better to take our chances in the wild."

"I agree," Dania said.

"The nearest city is more than a day's journey through the swamps." Valasand raised her eyebrow at them. "If we take the shortcut, that is. We should see about getting some food and lodging for the night."

"Yeah," Aric said. "Especially the part about food."

Maurin shoved down his foreboding. It didn't do much good to argue when you knew the other person was right. Fortunately, it didn't take them long to find a hostelry. It was a quaint old place, a larger version of the other houses in the town, with rough brown wooden beams framing the windows—all shuttered and locked.

According to Valasand, the sign on the door said matson's house of rest. Flowers lined the window boxes along the outside of the hotel, but they had not been tended to for a few days. All the plants seemed to be dying. Talauna ran her fingers over one particularly sad-looking shrub, then frowned at Maurin. Valasand rapped on the door with the end of her staff.

No one was in sight.

"Is it abandoned?"

Valasand's voice sounded weary and careworn. "No, I don't think so. Someone's here."

"Where?" Aric asked.

"I think they're hiding." She pointed. "You see? There's a man peeking out the window, watching us."

Dania scowled. "So what does he have to hide from?"

Maurin bit his tongue. The sight of her scowling would be enough to send any reasonably sane man packing. At length, he heard a shuffling from inside.

"*What do you want?*"

"We have traveled a long way, and are all weary," Valasand called through the door. "A room and some supper would be most welcome."

"*You aren't Graylanders, are you?*"

She raised her eyebrows. "No, just weary travelers seeking shelter for the night. Do you have room for us, or not?"

The door unlatched, and an older, broad-faced man leveled an archaic hunting weapon at them, its long, tarnished barrel boasting a proud history. The man—presumably Matson—was evidently taken aback by the motley crew standing on his threshold.

"Do you have any rooms available?"

"All of them," Matson said gruffly. "We're empty at the moment."

"Excellent." Valasand brushed past. "Then you can help us."

Dania glowered at the innkeeper, who drew his hand over a sweaty brow, brushing back strands of thin white hair.

"We don't usually allow her kind in here." He indicated Talauna, who was closely examining the weave work on a small basket. "Bad for business."

Hard to imagine under what circumstances a Maolori would enter a human city and ask for a room in the first place.

"It seems these are not typical times for anyone, then," Valasand said. "She is a member of our party, and if she goes, we all go."

Aric looked as dismayed as Maurin felt at the prospect of spending the night outside, but the innkeeper shrugged.

"It don't make no difference to me. Still," he said with a sigh, "you're paying customers, and since nobody else's here to object, I guess it'll be okay. Not like I have people griping about the riffraff."

"We're not riffraff!" Aric fumed.

"We look it," Maurin said quietly. Had it been his own inn, would he be disinclined to admit such a ragtag party?

Probably.

"I'll be serving up supper in a few minutes, if you'll follow me into the dining room. Lately I'm the only one eating it, but I have some leftovers that won't take me long to get ready. How long are you staying?"

"For the night, then we plan to go on to Caileen, if we can get a transport."

"That might be a little hard to come by." Matson put away his firearm and turned back to the group.

"Why is that?" Dania asked.

"Haven't you heard?" the innkeeper asked incredulously. "Ain't none of our transports working. Not for some time now."

"We just got into town," Valasand said. "The last one we encountered, Fatamor, was deserted."

"You've picked a bad time to be traveling, and a bad place to stay." He started rummaging around with his kitchen, throwing together some odds and ends of food and stoking the fire in the grate. "There's been a lot of strange goings-on of late."

"What kind?" Maurin prompted as the innkeeper led them into another room with a long wooden table.

"Unnatural things. Over in Birn Aloi, they found Darland the blacksmith looking like he'd aged fifty years, been scared to death."

"Really?" Valasand's eyebrows arched. "That's very odd. What do you think could have caused that?"

"Those blasted godlings, the Reamar!" The man's eyes grew wide, and he leaned forward conspiratorially. "They're soul-stealers!"

The Reamar. Maurin smoothed the hair on his arms and took a seat with the others.

"Ah." The Warden kept her face expressionless.

"No one wants to leave their homes. Cities and towns all around us, people are disappearing, and dying." However much this man might have wanted to talk, he was genuinely frightened. Matson's lips quivered nervously as he said, "Everyone's been thinking we're next."

"Have you had problems with these beings in the past?"

"There's always been stories. Legends, I suppose. Nobody used to believe them. Now"—the grim owner of the inn shrugged—"now nobody doesn't. At first we thought people was dying from the plague.

Only they don't stay dead."

Talauna's eyebrows just about disappeared under her scalp. Not that Maurin could blame her.

"I'd always assumed death was permanent," Aric muttered, unsmiling.

"Hear tell, they come back. But they aren't... who they were. They come back in the night to take the living." He took a lamp from the wall and lit it, adjusting the illuminating panel to medium intensity. "There're those who've took to blocking the tombs, but they say that don't guarantee nothing. There's still dozens unaccounted for."

"Your dead will rise against you."

"What's that?" Valasand asked.

"Nothing," Aric said, not meeting her eyes.

Maurin frowned at him. "What is going on with you lately?"

Aric shook his head, and looked away.

"So you believe these Reamar are responsible for all of these deaths and... strange occurrences?" Valasand said as Matson ladled out a heavy broth over some unidentifiable meat and tubers, and put them in the middle of the table.

"Only ones who could be. Towns going missing, or put under a curse. Now everybody here hides out in their own houses and goes out only if they has to."

"Who are the Reamar?" Valasand asked.

"No one knows, exactly." He set out a loaf of steaming bread covered with butter, and Maurin's mouth watered at the aroma. "Some say they come from another world. The Graylanders been here longer than the colonies. And I was always thinking they was a myth. All I know is what my parents told me and my sisters back when I was a boy: You're never supposed to go out at night, because the Reamar would get you."

"Get you?" Maurin asked.

"It was said they live in a faraway land, and come out only to feed." Matson said in a sepulchral whisper. "They drink human souls."

"Human... souls. Dead coming back to life." Maurin sat back in his chair. "I'm sorry. This is all just a little too much for me."

"Don't laugh," the proprietor warned, raising his voice to be heard as he shuffled around the corner and into the other room. "Them they don't kill, they turn into their slaves, to live in that temple of theirs forever, with no mind of their own. Everywhere the Reamar go, death follows. They say the ghosts of Darkhorn Fell stalk outside the boundaries of the city, roaming the woods in search of prey."

"The ghosts of...?" Valasand asked.

"Darkhorn Fell." Matson returned with a pitcher of wine. "That's the name of it. The heart of the Graylanders' world."

Maurin leaned over to Aric and whispered in his ear, "I'm not quite sure which to be more impressed by: the stories, or the fact that they're being taken seriously."

Aric didn't respond. In truth, he looked a little sick.

"Do you have any idea what the Reamar want?" Valasand broke off a piece of bread.

The innkeeper shook his head. "But there might be someone who would. The old man of the woods. Lives in the outskirts of Heth Erlire, been around forever."

"Where is this Heth Erlire?"

"It's a city of ruins some ways south. That's all I know."

Valasand made an exasperated sound. "Unfortunately, we're headed north. Back to Caileen."

"So you said. I can't say as I'm going that direction, but best to get out of here one way or another. Some of us are leaving as soon as we can. Mor Tespir's under a curse, too."

"Is that why people are acting so bizarre here?" Aric asked.

"Reamar worshipers." Matson nodded and spat off to the side in contempt. "Think the Graylanders are gods."

———— ◆ ————

Maurin crossed his arms and leaned expectantly against the candlelit wall outside Aric's room.

"Aric, look at me." Valasand touched his uninjured shoulder. "Do you know something about what is going on here?"

"Not really." Aric squirmed under the scrutiny. "Before you came, a

Reamar in Langfort wanted to buy me. I have no idea why. They were looking for one of their priestesses at the time."

Valasand nodded slowly. "I wonder..."

"Wonder what?" Maurin asked, placing his hands on his hips.

"A girl—she claimed to be a Reamar—approached me in the streets of Caileen shortly before I found you. Could she be this missing priestess?"

"What did she want?" Dania asked.

"To warn me away." Valasand stroked the end of her staff. "She somehow knew I was a Warden of the Gates, and told me the Reamar were afraid of a Dreaded One, and waiting for some sort of liberator to come, but I couldn't tell if they were one and the same... I'm afraid I don't know what she was talking about."

Maurin shuddered. How much darkness could one world sustain?

"Perhaps you are the liberator," Dania said.

Valasand smiled. "Never mind. Go refresh yourselves and get some sleep. One way or another, we shall discover the meaning of these mysteries."

Each of them picked a separate room, though Talauna lingered a bit at Maurin's door with a wistful expression, before going one over. He glanced across the hall to see if Aric was going to make a snide comment, but his cousin pretended not to notice.

Despite his fatigue, Maurin didn't fall asleep. He couldn't get his mind off the conversation of the evening. Even if most of it was simply scary tales meant for children, the Reamar were real; that much he knew for a fact. And there was the matter of the empty city to consider, lending some weight to Matson's words, far-fetched as they sounded. Scoff as one might at the notion of beings that could animate the dead, a few years ago, Maurin would never have believed it was possible to travel to another world.

And here he was.

Maurin's pillow felt as though someone had pounded it flat with a hammer, and no amount of fluffing softened it. The rope bed creaked, and the straw mattress poked him throughout the night. Every groan of the inn, every bang of the wind at the shutter, had him seeing ghoulish invaders ready to pounce on him the moment he drifted off. He even imagined he could hear chanting voices on the wind.

"Matson's House of Rest, indeed," he muttered, listening to the squeak of a door opening across from his, and footsteps heading down the corridor. Aric, heading to the privy, no doubt.

But that was at the other end of the hall. The stairs creaked, and moments later, the door of the hostelry opened.

Maurin leapt up and flung open the shutters, shivering at the burst of cool night air. Aric, dressed only in his breeches, walked slowly on the street below.

"Aric?"

His cousin didn't stop. Perhaps Maurin would have to add sleep-walking to Aric's list of eccentricities. Someone told him once it wasn't good to wake a somnambulist, but in this place, it seemed more dangerous not to.

"Aric, wake up! You're dreaming again!"

Valasand's voice came through the door. "What's wrong?"

Maurin threw it open to see the Warden standing in the doorway with Dania and Talauna. "He's gone outside, and he's not responding. I have to go after him."

"I'll go. Grab your weapons and catch up."

Maurin tugged his boots on with an oath, slipped into his tunic, and slung his sword over his shoulder. Of all things. What was happening with Aric? He joined the other two in the hall and rushed down the stairs.

"Is anything the matter?" Matson asked, his voice deep with recent sleep.

"No, sir." Maurin swept past. "My cousin's just sleep-walking, that's all."

"You'd better hope that's all," the innkeeper muttered.

Maurin blinked, but didn't have time to stop and ask what he meant. Dania had already rushed outside, and Talauna was waiting for him.

Dania pointed. "This way."

Talauna sprinted ahead.

"How does she move so fast on those short legs?" Dania asked as they ran, hard-pressed to keep up.

Maurin saw Valasand and Aric at the end of the street, and caught up within moments. He ran around to block his cousin's path. Aric's eyes stared through him, pale blue in the moonlight. "Hey, what are you doing?"

Aric didn't break stride. "She's here..."

"Who's here?"

"Voices." There was something not quite right about his tone. "They're calling my name."

Maurin grabbed his bare shoulders and shook him. "Wake up! No one is calling your name! You're dreaming!"

Aric pushed past him, unseeing.

"Let him go, Maurin," Valasand said softly.

"What?"

"I want to see where he is going."

"It has begun." Aric's lips twisted into a sneer, and his voice didn't sound like his own.

"What has begun, Aric?" the Warden asked.

He just kept walking. They stayed close as he led them across a broad avenue and toward a pillared building standing far above the rest. He climbed the steps and opened the huge wooden door without hesitation.

"Interesting," Valasand said, following him in.

Talauna balked.

"What's the matter?" Maurin whispered.

Talauna shook her head and looked uncertain, but after a moment, she slipped into the dark corridor with him. When his eyes adjusted to the dim light, Maurin saw the faint flicker of torches ahead.

Aric moved steadily toward the glow. Talauna walked beside Maurin through the narrow hallway, her hand grasping his with fervent intensity.

MAURIN.

"What?"

"Is something wrong?" Valasand sounded perplexed.

"Didn't you just call me?"

"No. Be quiet, now. I want to watch what he does."

MAURIN, BE STILL.

This time, it struck him: he wasn't hearing the voice with his ears. For some reason, he felt calmer. He followed the sound of Valasand's movements, and while the hall was chilly, he somehow felt warm. *Who are you?*

MAURIN. COME TO ME. HEED MY VOICE.

Was this some sort of trick? Somehow, he didn't think so. But who was calling him?

"What's that?" Dania asked.

"You hear it too?" It took Maurin a moment to realize she wasn't talking about the voice in his head.

Valasand listened hard for a moment. "It sounds like chanting."

Ahead, the low monotone chorus of voices grew louder. Aric left the hallway and stepped into a much larger room, stopping at the edge of a stone balcony that ran the circumference of the room; evidently the building extended underground. The others took up places in the shadows nearby.

Below a small pilgrimage headed toward the central area of a massive chamber, where several hundred robed figures stood in a semicircle, preparing for a ceremony of some sort. Equidistantly placed braziers lit the tiers of the amphitheater-like room. The chanting reached a crescendo:

Vi me sindre reyamarya
Lan de becwe velanala
Dorusela na ba kulinor
Kan me vi reyusor

"We're in a temple," Maurin said.

Valasand's lips were a tight line, and she stared straight ahead. Soon she murmured something clearly not meant for him. Probably praying.

Below, a bearded priest at the front raised his arms, and a hush fell on the crowd. "Tonight, we invite the gods to bear witness to our love and devotion. We ask them to live within us, so we might live forever with them. *Vi au sindre reyamarya.*"

"*Vi au sindre reyamarya,*" the crowd repeated in unison.

Dania looked grim. "The Reamar worshipers."

Maurin's head went light, and his stomach churned. His flesh prickled in response to a cold that wasn't physical. He squeezed Talauna's shoulder.

"Will the chosen come forward?"

"I will."

The adherents parted to allow a pubescent girl wearing a plain white dress to make her way on bare feet to the center of the arena. A garland of flowers adorned her brow, and her straight black hair hung down her back.

"Sacrificial virgin?" Dania whispered.

"Looks that way." Maurin gritted his teeth, defenses alert. Any sign of danger to the girl, and he would interrupt the ceremony.

"Be careful." Valasand sidled up between them. "We are not in a position to give ourselves away."

"You can't mean for us to just stand here and let them kill her!" Maurin said incredulously.

"No..." Valasand's face reflected some internal struggle. "But wait until I give the word before you act. That goes for all of you," she said, staring pointedly at Dania. "We don't know that they mean to kill her."

The young girl began to recite some words in an arcane language, while the priest presided stolidly. Drums played in the background, but Maurin couldn't identify the source. The chorus began again, this time at a lower volume.

"This girl has been found acceptable," the priest said. "Are you willing to be joined with your gods, Mayal?"

"I am willing," she answered.

"I don't like the sound of this," Dania murmured, taut as a bowstring. Aric hadn't moved since he touched the stone barrier.

"The joining has been accepted," the priest said. The drums continued to gain in intensity. "The chosen is worthy. Shall they be joined?"

"*They shall be joined,*" the congregation chanted.

Maurin frowned, riveted on the pair at the front. "Is this some weird kind of marriage ceremony?"

"I don't think so," Dania said. "Where's the groom?"

Once again Talauna's fingers gripped at Maurin's arm. She pointed to a greenish light growing in intensity above the heads of the priest and the girl.

"Come unto us!" the priest cried. "Show us thy divine love! Show us thy power and give us everlasting life! Come forth unto this vessel, chosen for thy pleasure, O Glorious One!"

The light above them grew larger and brighter, and Maurin thought he saw miasmic shadows moving within.

"Do you want us to put an end to this madness?" Dania asked quietly.

Valasand considered for a moment, shaking her head. "I don't think we can. This is something they have done of their own will. This whole city is given over."

Disgusted, Dania turned her attention back to the ceremony. Maurin bristled for attack.

"Enter this vessel, my lord," the girl, Mayal, called in rapturous tones. "Cleave unto my flesh, and we shall be one!"

The drums became louder, and deeper, and seemed to resonate like a heartbeat in the chamber as she moved forward with slow, deliberate steps, turned, and faced the audience. The drums reached a climax, then ceased altogether.

Maurin's heart started to pound faster. He watched in horrified fascination as the green, misty aura began to swirl and glow around the girl. "They're killing her!"

"I don't think so," Valasand said, a grim set to her jaw.

The mist began to descend. Its greenish radiance floated down in tendrils of living flame, wrapping around Mayal's body at the front of the sanctuary. She raised her arms in ecstasy. For a few moments, she shone brightly, burning in a pale, cold fire. Then the aura began to recede.

The glow, dimming once more to a green mist, shrank and coalesced into the body of the girl. Within a few seconds, the last of the smoky substance passed into her small frame.

"We are one," she said. With that, Mayal collapsed into a spent heap on the floor. She wasn't breathing. For several moments, nothing happened. One voice began singing, and then another. Soon, the entire chamber was filled with a lilting, joyful song.

Maurin watched in stunned disbelief as the girl rose from the ground—she did not get to her feet so much as appear to be lifted by unseen hands. Her head lolled forward, and she continued to rise until her limp body hovered several feet off the ground. She took a deep, shuddering breath—almost like an infant just emerged from the womb—and opened her eyes.

Maurin nearly fell backward. They were glowing green.

"How fare you, Mayal?" the priest asked with quiet respect.

The expression did not belong on a girl's face. Wisdom and experience shone in her eyes. And when she answered, the voice resonated through the now-silent temple with age and cunning.

"*I continue.*" The girl descended slowly to the floor. Row by row, the congregants knelt before her.

Aric flung his arms out, shouting, "*Ulora Vailorscha! Eh tsa reyamarya! Kammata meh!*"

As one, the worshipers looked up at the sound.

The girl below snapped her head around and immediately fixed her gaze on Aric. Maurin thought he saw recognition and fear in her eyes, swiftly displaced by anger. He wrestled his cousin to the ground and slapped him repeatedly in the face. "Come out of it!"

Aric shook his head and blinked in perplexity. "Where are we?"

"Aric," Dania said, "I'm going to murder you."

"I don't think you'll have to," Maurin said.

"He's here!" Dozens of voices took up a cry of alarm. "Kill him! Kill them all!"

CHAPTER 28
NIGHT TERRORS

Why am I afraid? This is not like me.

Dania was the first down the corridor, but as she reached the end, a chorus of unearthly wails went up outside. The door banged and creaked inward.

"Whoa," Maurin said softly, pulling Aric to a halt. Though disoriented, at least he'd had the sense to run when prompted.

Valasand maintained a death grip on her staff. "We'll have to find another way out."

Talauna slipped ahead of Dania and into the shadows of the temple. She ran down hallways in seemingly random order, while the others did their best to keep up. The furious voices of the worshipers followed—too close. Soon, however, they came to a doorway that looked just like the one they had come through. Dania drew the bolt back and flung open the door.

A fog billowed in unnaturally fast, flowing through the dark streets and alleyways. It came from all directions, encircling the city. Dania swore. Within moments, the mist had reached them, and she could barely see the buildings around her. Strange voices muttered dark words in the distance, and sound became muted. Even the figures of Aric and the others grew dim.

A scream pierced the night, and Valasand's head jerked up.

"Fright's a human emotion," Maurin said. "There must be some normal people left here."

Normal people had filled Dania's life with blood and misery, and the terror of the damned did not bring her much comfort. With the coming of the fog was a chill that gnawed at the bones and caused flesh to crawl. Maurin grasped for Talauna's hand and did not let go.

Dania raised her knife. "We need to get back to the hostelry."

Then the screams started again, harsh and horrified.

"Shhhhh..." Valasand, this time.

For a moment, things went deadly silent. Dania could just make out a wailing sound on the borders of hearing. She shifted the knife in her grasp.

"I hear them..." Aric's voice sounded farther away.

"Aric, get back here!" Maurin said angrily. "I don't know what's going on with you lately, but we're going to have a serious talk when we get out of this."

Aric didn't say anything. Dania listened hard, but heard nothing besides the crunching of gravel on the stone street as they walked and the sound of their own breathing, still and close in the impenetrable fog. Maurin muttered about not having a torch, but no one responded. Time seemed to freeze just as surely as the air around them; distance and sound were meaningless in the murk.

Soul-drinkers, came a voice from her childhood. *Demons that haunt the southern wilds.*

Dania swallowed the lump in her throat. A flesh-and-blood enemy she could deal with; certainly she had experience enough in the arena that she shouldn't be nervous. But these Reamar—flesh, blood, spirit—no one seemed to know what they were. And it terrified her to the core.

Never show fear.

A howling sounded, like a great wind over a valley, but there was no wind. Her blood ran cold. The night took on a sickly greenish glow, and all around voices raised in terror, blended with cries of anger and predatory shrieks. Shadowy figures cavorted at the edge of Dania's vision. Talauna slipped out of Maurin's grip and set out at a rapid pace down an alley. He called after her.

"Get behind me, girl," Dania said. "You're going to get hurt."

Annoyed, Talauna pointed off to the east with a fervent gesture, but stayed back. Dania nodded. She spied a short length of rusted pipe, and scooped it up without breaking pace.

A shout of rage and a blow to the side greeted Dania as soon as she left the alley. More by reflex than skill, she whipped around, tossing off her assailant. He hit a pile of refuse. It was a young man roughly Aric's age. Her attacker was on his feet again in an instant, snarling and howling like an animal. His eyes glowed green, and darkness seemed to follow him as he moved.

Dania pivoted on her heel and extended her leg, allowing the man's momentum to trip him and carry him past. As she did so, she swung the pipe as hard as she could. He bowled over, unconscious or dead, rolling to a stop several feet away.

"There's one."

Running footsteps grew louder.

"And here come more," Maurin said. "Must be the send-off committee."

"Shut up." Dania felt weak; not only did she not look forward to the fight; she rather dreaded it. What had the Warden done to her? She gritted her teeth as she closed on one of the approaching figures. The man slid a knife from his belt. Dania swung, the pipe whooshed, and the knife spun out of the man's hand. She swung again, connecting with his gut.

Dania struck the man between the shoulder blades as he fell. She checked to make sure he wouldn't be getting up again, then scanned warily for her next target. Wraiths and phantoms whirled through the fog in the streets all around them, stirring the air and raising gooseflesh.

"Find the Dreaded One!" a voice cried in the night. *"Kill him!"*

Here was a new thought—the Reamar were afraid of someone? If so, that gave her an edge. Not much of one, maybe, but an edge nonetheless.

The mist resolved itself into a wild-eyed figure darting at her with an axe. She rolled out of the way, and with a quick sweep of her leg, knocked his feet out from under him. With something akin to remorse, she slashed his neck with her knife.

Green eyes glowed all around them.

"Yasul, give me strength," Valasand said as she joined Dania. The Warden stepped forward into the mists, twirling her staff. She made a swift motion and connected solidly with a man aiming the prongs of a bolt-thrower at her head. The energy weapon flew off into the bushes. She drew back, holding onto her staff with both hands, wound up, and swung it in a horizontal arc toward another approaching man. He went down, and Valasand continued to spin and twist through her assailants, sending a hail of weapons sailing out of their grips. Most people would at least have been wringing their hands from the pain, but these just kept coming with the same blank, unseeing faces. Not one of them said a word. All at once, several of them let out an inhuman shriek, and Dania's blood curdled.

She didn't have time to be impressed with the Warden's skills, however. A dark figure armed with an ancient curved sword had targeted Talauna as easy prey. He backed her down into the alley from which they had just emerged.

Maurin ran toward the attacker. His angry shout reverberated through the streets. He brought his sword down on the back of the man's neck, and several screams of rage sounded throughout the city. It was as if they all felt the killing blow.

What manner of people were these?

Those not under the thrall of the Reamar had taken up their meager arms and were fighting back. Apparently, they were making a last stand against these unholy servants of shadow. Shouts of rage and cries of pain rose throughout the city, chaotic but blessedly human. It was the first truly comforting sound Dania had heard since they first set foot in this accursed place.

In contrast, the followers of the Reamar fought in unified silence. Dania struggled against the tide of attackers to reach her comrades. Nebulous shapes came at her from the mist, and she was lost in blood and angry shrieks. She ducked at the flapping of unseen wings, and claw-like hands reached for her. She had an impression of a gray death's head floating just on the edge of her vision, watching her fight.

Dania bashed in the skull of a man, and another started toward her, but Talauna leapt upon his back, wrapping her legs around his upper thighs. She grabbed his head with both hands, digging her fingers into his eyes with a determined expression. The man screamed in agony and dropped his sword, trying to pry her off. He grasped her by the wrists, and with a heave and a snarl, flung her over his shoulder to land squarely on her back.

Dania tapped the man's arm. He whirled, ducking just in time to catch her pipe crashing into his nose. She snarled, ground her teeth together, and put all of her force behind a thrust into his eye. The man went down and did not get up. Dania left the pipe in his head and retrieved his sword.

"Now this is more like it." In a melee like this, Dania couldn't dispute the clear advantage of a sword's length and weight against multiple armed enemies. But she preferred the balance of a pair of good knives; in the arena, they seemed like extensions of her own body. But Shadows lurked and darted at her from every angle, and she swung her new weapon deftly, inflicting a vertical slash on one's abdomen as soon as it resolved, and opening another's throat.

Shrieks and howls of rage sounded all around her. Many of the attackers were just too fast for her, though; she would swing her sword at one of the vague forms only to find herself meeting empty air. She couldn't tell where they were coming from, or where they went when they disappeared. One moment they were there, the next, they weren't.

How fared Maurin? She glanced over, and something shimmered in her vision. She squeezed her eyes shut for a moment, and when she opened them again, a figure came abruptly into focus. Although evidently human, he did not look like the townspeople or the worshipers in the temple. His face was painted in shades of gray, the area around the eyes and lips darkened to give him the aura of the walking dead. He wore strange armor, and the weapon he raised was equally foreign. A wicked-

looking braided spear seemed to writhe and twist in his gray hand. He bore down on Maurin, dark cloak billowing around his armor.

Was this a Reamar? Unlike the people of the city, this man seemed resolute of purpose, and his glowing eyes were full—too full—of life.

Dania raced toward them. The trouble with fighting against spears was that the opponent with the longer weapon usually wins.

Maurin was taking no chances on this one. The Reamar thrust his weapon at his midsection. Maurin dodged, and with a swooping rush of steel, brought his sword down on the Reamar's elbow. The stroke hit the armor, and for a second, Dania thought it had glanced off. Then dark blood poured from the joint, and the spear fell to the ground.

Not bad for an amateur.

Dania expected a shout, a scream... something. But with a simple expression of angry surprise, the injured man reached down and picked up the spear with the other arm. Maurin stood in stunned silence as the Reamar once more advanced on him with a bestial growl.

Dania ran toward them. The attacker put all his force into an overhand thrust designed to skewer Maurin through the neck.

That was the Reamar's mistake. By aiming high, he was taking a bigger chance than if he had simply struck at Maurin's center, for Maurin instinctively ducked. The spear caught his shirt and pinned him to a tree. With a grunt, the Reamar let go of the spear, rushed forward, and grasped Maurin's throat in his one good hand, pushing him up against the tree. The Reamar's glowing eyes focused on his kill, his teeth clenched. Maurin's body went rigid, as if the gaze of the Reamar had paralyzed him. Then his face drained of color. His legs twitched. A tingling sensation crawled along Dania's scalp when she saw the look in his glazed-over eyes.

Despite herself, she grinned. She finally had an open shot.

"Oh, gods, Maurin," she said with mock reproach, "just kill him." She ran up and around, then planted her foot in the Reamar's chest to tear away his grip. His trailing hair flew about his bizarre battle-painted face as he staggered back, and she drew the sword in a flashing arc across his throat. His eyes grew wide, and he coughed, reaching for his ruined neck. Blood flowed in a river over his chest.

But he did not fall. He stumbled once and wrenched the spear free of the tree with a single smooth motion. He reeled forward again, this time toward her, grasping the spear in one blood-soaked hand. Dania slashed at the Reamar again once he was within reach, but he still did not go down.

"Would you just die!"

A blue-white blade flashed from behind, cleanly severing the Reamar's head. A green light exploded from the falling body with a hideous demonic shriek. Greenish-black flame wailed and streaked out and away into the night even before the withered and smoking portions of the Reamar hit the ground.

"That was a strong one," Valasand said in the moment of shocked silence that followed, lowering the strange blade.

"Oh? You think so?" Maurin coughed and shook on the verge of hysteria. His hair had started to go white at the temples. Talauna put her arms around him. Dania and Valasand joined them. Valasand knelt by Maurin's side, pressing tenderly around the spreading bruise on his shoulder. He winced, but nothing appeared to be broken.

"Where did you get the sword?" Dania asked.

"It was one of theirs." Valasand wiped it off with distaste.

"Where did they go?"

"I don't know." Dania looked around. "When that one died, the rest disappeared."

It had all happened in a few minutes. Apart from the strangely blasted corpse of the Reamar, bodies littered the streets—mostly her own work, of course. Some people yet lived; a few moved in a state of shock while others cast about warily, ready for another attack. A few wept over the dead. Some wilted gray forms lay in the ditches moving feebly.

That was no glorious way to die.

The fog stirred and roiled. Softly at first, and growing with steady intensity, a howling wind unlike any Dania had ever heard before moved through the streets of the city. Talauna's eyes grew huge, and she grabbed Maurin and pulled him after her.

"Follow her," Valasand said in a voice that brooked no argument. They ran into an alley and under an overhanging stone stairway. Talauna squeezed herself in as far as she could get, and Maurin shielded her with his body. Dania and Valasand crowded in next to them. "Yasul, protect us."

The screams of the dying joined the lamentation of the wind, and the fog swept through the streets like a green lightning storm. The wind died down and the fog rolled away to reveal a starlit night and a city as empty as a pauper's cupboard.

All was silent. Several stunned moments went by before Dania spoke up: "Where is Aric?"

CHAPTER 29
DEMONSTRATION

"Someone is holding out on me."

"My lord?" Krige's footsteps echoed down the marbled expanse of the hallway along with those of Argoneis and his guards.

"There's no way a Warden of the Gates just shows up on this world without someone noticing. I should have heard of this long before news reached Sal Dalinde. I must have a traitor in my midst; someone who wishes me harm."

Krige refrained from asking why anyone would wish him harm. Daman was many things, but an idiot he was not. "It could be that no one knew what they were looking at. Unless she was foolish enough to give some indication of who she was, there would be no way of knowing."

"I'm glad I have you." Argoneis squeezed Krige's shoulder. "I don't know what I would do otherwise. Sometimes I feel utterly alone in this world."

"I am your servant, milord." He smiled. *And if you don't kill me, the irony will.*

"My friend," Daman reminded him, smiling back. "I think you may be right; Governor Phoecius has been acting strangely. I asked him what he feared from the Reamar, and he pretended not to know what I was talking about. I could tell he was lying."

"Really?" It didn't matter whether or not Daman could actually tell if someone was lying; all he had to do was suspect it, and the suspicion became fact. Krige supposed he should be relieved that, to date, Argoneis couldn't tell when he was lying, but somehow, it was impossible to feel any kind of relief when faced regularly with Daman's misgivings. "What has he said?"

"He said he had some dispute with them, and not to concern myself about it."

"Incredible." Sweat popped out on his brow at the recollection of the messenger from the Reamar. "And how did you respond?"

Daman's eyes flashed with ire. He turned around and leaned in dangerously. "I told him anything that has to do with Warden interference on this planet concerns me, and he would do well to remember that answering my questions directly is the easiest way to make me happy."

"Surely he would never betray you."

"I'd like to think that is so. In the interests of making sure, I've invited him up here." A smile, somehow more unsettling than overt anger, spread over Daman's features.

"The governor is here?" Krige didn't like the idea of that overweight weasel directly in contact with Argoneis; he could get nervous and talk. He had, after all, been part of the committee that sent Lauran Dalinde to talk with Daman, and that hadn't gone so well. And if Phoecius let it spill that the Reamar had taken to attacking the outlying towns of Langfort, and Krige was aware of it, well—the game would be over, as his bodyguard was wont to say.

"Yes, he's waiting for us in the anteroom." Daman gestured, and two guards opened the doors for him. He strode in, all too pleased with himself.

"Lord Argoneis!" The governor stood abruptly and removed his hat, then used it to shield his shaking hands. "Ah, how kind of you to invite me to visit; I'm always pleased to..."

Daman cut him off with a gesture. "This is not a social call, my dear Governor. I have questions I feel need answering."

"Q-questions?"

"You weren't here at the feast of Shang Parralt, were you? Well, let me tell you something: I have never had anyone not tell me what I want to know. How long it takes, and in how many pieces you want to leave Caileen, are up to you."

Phoecius nodded submissively and swallowed. "No need for that, my lord. I will answer any questions you might have for me, and gladly."

Krige caught the governor's eye, and shook his head, ever so slightly. He couldn't tell if the man intended to keep his silence, or even if he understood.

"Answer me this: Do you know anything of how it is a Warden of the Gates showed up on my doorstep, despite the fact that there is no Well on this planet?"

To his credit, Phoecius didn't confess. Of course, for this, he didn't have to lie.

"No, Lord Argoneis. I have no idea how that could be. Unless he was smuggled in on one of the supply ships."

He. Nice touch. Maybe this wouldn't be as bad as he expected. Daman gazed at the man searchingly, and finally nodded. Krige couldn't help but breathe a sigh of relief.

"I suppose that's possible," Argoneis admitted. "Tell me about the Reamar. They had the gall to attack our city for no apparent reason, and then go silent. They do not say why, and they have not even asked for their routine shipment. Moreover, I hear you are concerned they might invade."

"Rumors, really," Phoecius said uncomfortably. "There's talk they seek a missing priestess, and fear they might retaliate if she isn't found."

"Lord Krige informed me of this when he first returned from Langfort, and indeed they did make a small but noticeable demonstration, for which they have been sanctioned. I have nothing to hide, and no interest in this missing priestess of theirs. Why would they hold any of us accountable for their loss?"

Krige was glad Daman's eyes remained on the governor. He flushed, then hoped Anice and Sabatha hadn't noticed.

"You know the Reamar, Lord Argoneis. They have their own way about them; they don't think the way we do. They don't even believe they're human." Phoecius made a sickly attempt at a smile.

"Indeed." Daman looked thoughtful for a moment. "My dear Governor, come with me. I have something I want to show you."

He turned on his heel, and Daman's two bodyguards fell into step with the noblemen.

"Where are we going?" Phoecius asked.

"It's a surprise," Daman replied, with a disconcerting smile. "Just something I think you'll find stimulating, and hopefully educational, as well. I've been meaning to do this for a while, but it seems so long since I've been able to entertain a guest that I'm glad I never got around to it."

Krige didn't like being caught in the middle of this. On the one hand,

Guilan Vail had made it quite clear what would happen to Phoecius, and to the entire city of Langfort, should the governor choose to refuse cooperation with the Reamar. And, of course, there was the message from Darkhorn Fell to consider. On the other hand, he literally risked life and limb by not telling Daman about the Warden, but it was too late now to admit that he knew about it. Was there no way to rid himself of these twin vipers, ready to strike the moment he didn't do their bidding? And now, he had Phoecius to worry about.

Krige noted with unease that they were headed toward parts of the palace obviously not meant for show. Daman led them down a damp stairway and dark hall lined with thick, ancient doors. The storage rooms below the temple had been converted into a dungeon. An indefinable organic stench lingered about the place, but Krige was no stranger to these rumors of macabre relics privately displayed in Argoneis's palace. He clenched his fists as Daman walked up to a thick wooden door and opened the lock with an enormous, old-fashioned key. He stood back in wonder when Argoneis turned to him with a playful smile, then stuck his head into the tiny stone room. Rancid air wafted out.

"Oh, Countess." Daman's voice cut mockingly into the lightless cell. He smiled at a moan and shuffling sound. "You have visitors."

"Go to the Fires, Argoneis."

"I've brought you something to remember me by, Countess." He stood framed in the doorway by Anice and Sabatha. Krige stayed back, hoping to avoid being seen. Phoecius did the same, although Krige suspected he just wanted to stay clear of the filth of the dungeon.

"I don't want anything from you, murderer," sulked the bitter voice from the dark.

"Oh, come now," Daman said, his tone taking on an amused, injured quality. "It hasn't been that bad, has it?"

There was a rattling of chains, and a spitting sound. "You tortured my mother to death in front of me, you monster! What have you done with my father? Let me out of here! When the Temple finds out what you've made of their colony, your life is forfeit!"

Krige flinched. All it would take now would be for her to notice his presence. *Don't say anything, don't say anything, don't say anything...*

He knew the Lord Regent was making a point to Phoecius: No one crosses Daman Argoneis and gets away with it. It was fitting Krige should be here, as the message was unknowingly intended for him, as well. He was glad for the dark; no doubt the countess' eyes were sensitive by now, and he and the governor would be silhouetted in the hallway by the light of the torches.

"And I thought we were friends." Daman shook his head in mock sorrow. "Maybe this will cheer you up. Your father sent you a present."

Daman held forth a thin chain with something dangling at the end, shaking it tantalizingly. It took Krige a moment to recognize the signet ring of Sal Dalinde, complete with what he supposed was Hargin's finger, bronzed and mounted on a necklace. The countess's eyes grew wide in horror as realization hit her.

"No!" she shrieked, flailing and twisting at her bonds. "Let me out of here! Daman, please!"

Daman slipped it over her neck. "If I ever come back and find you aren't wearing it, I promise you, I shall make nine more just like it."

The countess dissolved into tears.

Lord Argoneis merely smiled and closed the door.

CHAPTER 30
LOSS AND LEGEND

Aric was gone, no doubt about it. A quick glance around the newly cleared streets spoke plainly enough.

"Aric!" Maurin called out, his heart racing. *"Aric!"*

"Quiet!" Valasand said. "Maurin, stay. Think for a moment. Do you know when he was separated from the group?"

"No," he said bitterly. "The last time I remember seeing anything of him was when he thought he heard someone call his name. Maybe it was Aric's hand I should have been holding. Something's been wrong for a long time, and I've been too stupid to see it."

"It will do you no good to blame yourself."

"If Aric is dead," Maurin said, "I will hunt down his killer, and one of us will die." He turned his back on the group and stamped down the empty street.

"All right, Maurin," Valasand began, "you're upset..."

"Upset? Upset? You'd better believe I'm upset!" Maurin stalked toward her with a rigid, loping gait, clenching and unclenching his fists. "Aric was my only remaining relative. From the time he was brought to the temple, we were raised as brothers. He's my only friend! 'Upset' doesn't even come close!"

"He's alive," Valasand said.

"How do you know?" Maurin whirled around.

She bit her lip and cocked her head as if listening for something. "I have heard no whispers of his death."

He shook his head. That made no sense.

"I am telling you, even if we find some fallen remaining—you will not find him here."

Dread settled on him like an icy embrace. "You mean... he's been taken by *them*?"

Valasand placed her hand on his shoulder. "I fear so, yes."

Maurin turned his back on the Warden and threw his arms up in the air. He paced aimlessly, eyes darting here and there as his jaw muscles worked in constant, grinding tension. Even Talauna did not dare come near him. Then all his strength left him at once. He slumped onto a wooden bench and buried his face in his hands.

"I can't let my cousin be carried off by these things! I should have looked out for him! I lost him once; I don't want to lose him again!" He gasped for breath. Talauna knelt behind him and laid her head on his back.

Valasand said nothing.

At last, Maurin looked up. "If you're right, and he's alive, I have to go after him."

"Do you remember your promise to me?" the Warden asked quietly.

It came to him, taunting: His words at the slave auction, spoken so long ago, it seemed, but in earnest. His vow to never disappoint her, should she remove them from that place. Was that what held him to her?

His rugged determination to fulfill a vow made to a woman he did not know?

"Yes," he bit out. "I remember."

"Please don't disappoint me, Maurin."

"What are you saying?" Maurin rose to his feet, and Talauna backed away. "That you don't want me to go?"

Valasand wrapped her hands tightly around her staff. "I must do as Yasul wills, Maurin."

"Uuuuuraaggh!" Dania snarled, slashing her knife against the nearby door jamb and carving out a hefty slice of wood. "We are wasting time! If Aric is alive, we must go find him!"

"We cannot afford this delay," Valasand said.

"Delay!"

"I did not come to this world to do battle with creatures of the dark. I had hoped to remove Lord Argoneis from power before he could even begin preparing for this circus."

Maurin ground his teeth and pointed to the wilderness. "My cousin is out there somewhere, at the mercy of a strange and sinister race. I don't know or care what lies ahead. If they've hurt him, they will pay dearly, and at my hand."

"Maurin."

He glared at Valasand. "What?"

"You have death on your heart."

"You'd better believe it," Maurin snapped.

"Don't be hasty in your actions. Your anger could cloud your judgment."

"My judgment," Maurin said through gritted teeth, "is just fine."

"Just, yes. Fine, no. I have never seen you so angry. Your thoughts seethe and boil like a storm at sea."

"And how do you know what I'm thinking?" He glanced over to Talauna, who watched the interchange with wide eyes.

"Talauna can feel it in your spirit, and I can read it on your face. If you think it is easy to hide your dark purposes, you are mistaken. You will not accomplish anything useful by going into a berserker rage or walking into an ambush. That is not the way of Yasul."

"Damn you and your Yasul," he snarled. "I'm not a Warden, and I don't worship your god."

Valasand's lips tightened. Maurin regretted his outburst, but did not apologize.

At last he hung his head. Obviously, there was no reason the loss of Aric should mean as much to her as it did to him. She was here to cripple the slave ring, after all. "I want to honor my promise to you. And I want as much as you do to bring down Argoneis. But I cannot leave my cousin. I have to find him and bring him back."

The Warden sighed and closed her eyes. "I understand."

Maurin's heartbeat counted off the silent minutes that followed. Dania seethed with fury. Why did she care so much about finding Aric? He suspected he knew, and wished he didn't. Talauna gripped Maurin's arm and gazed hopefully at the Warden. Every moment allowed Aric's abductors to get that much further away. Would he even be able to reach them in time? And what would he do when he found them?

"Very well," Valasand said at last, still not opening her eyes. "We shall find him."

Maurin exhaled in relief. "Thank you," he whispered.

Valasand strode off toward the center of town. "I did not anticipate this, nor do I welcome it. Even now, I wonder if this is the wise choice. But I am called to deal with it, and so I must. Come. Let us see if there is anyone left. Perhaps we can find some answers."

They searched the town, but the only living creature they came across was a wandering balodont, no doubt set free to escape as it could. Larger than the pack-beasts used in Caileen, it was clearly fretting, probably searching for its owner. Talauna took it by the bridle and greeted it with a kiss on the nose. She stroked its tiny ears, eliciting grunts of pleasure. Once the animal stopped shaking, Talauna didn't even take the reins to lead the beast away. She simply beckoned, and it followed. Amazing that she could do that without saying a word.

She has the same power over you, you rutting ox. Maurin imagined Aric's voice. "So, what do we do now?"

"I think," Valasand said, considering the question carefully, "given the circumstances, we should head on to Langfort to get some help. If we are going to rescue Aric from the Reamar, we are going to need more resources than we alone can muster."

"That's quite a jaunt from here, you know?" Maurin said, remembering the map in Fatamor.

"Well, we have transportation." Valasand nodded in the direction of the animal. "You don't have to walk unless you want to."

Talauna approached the balodont with handfuls of grass and flowers. It slurped up one side of her face with a long, mobile tongue. She grinned at Maurin and patted the animal's nose.

"I don't like it. We need to be looking for Aric."

"I don't like it either, Maurin. But you saw what we were up against. We made it through the night only with the help of Yasul."

He bit back a retort. "How will we know where to look?"

"The Breath will lead us," she said, perfectly confident and exasperatingly calm. "There's a large wagon two streets down. I don't think the owner will need it anymore. Talauna, bring the animal, and we'll hitch it up."

On their way over, they raided houses for supplies. Maurin still felt like a thief doing that, but he supposed there was nothing else to be done. Besides, as Dania pointed out, they could be certain nothing would be missed. He returned to the inn to gather what little they had left behind.

One good thing: we won't have to carry all this on our backs for a while.

The balodont patiently allowed itself to be harnessed. Maurin took the reins, and Talauna sat next to him on the driver's bench. Valasand and Dania rode in a bed of hay behind them. He turned the animal around, clamped his mouth tight, and kept his eyes straight ahead as the cart rumbled out of Mor Tespir.

They traveled past the dawn and through the day with only short breaks to relieve themselves, and to let the animal rest and graze, until Valasand decreed they should stop for the night. Maurin pulled the cart off to the side of the road. Talauna took the harness off the balodont and led the animal over to the water. The animal gulped greedily, smacking its lips. When it was done, it went over to a hollow in the ground, where it immediately knelt and rolled over.

"There aren't any trees here," Maurin said. "Should we tie the animal to the wagon?"

"I don't think we'll have to," Valasand replied, climbing up into the back of the cart and nodding toward Talauna.

They all joined her as she broke a loaf of bread amongst them. Dania procured dried meat of some sort, and they shared a round of cheese Maurin found in one of the houses. He supposed one of his former master's wines would have set the meal off perfectly, but as it was, it still tasted wonderful. To have any appetite at all surprised him.

Valasand and Dania wrapped themselves in blankets, though it seemed the Warden was going to sit up and keep watch for a while.

Maurin lay down beside Talauna and pulled the blanket up over his chin. He couldn't sleep, though. He had heard people talk about being sick with worry, but never truly known what it meant until now. His stomach tied itself in knots. Would he ever be able to think straight again? For a while, he tried not to speculate about what might have happened to Aric, but that didn't work, so he focused on the events of the previous night, trying to piece them together in a way that made sense. No success there, either. He wished he had Valasand's certainty.

The chill of the night began to settle in, and even with the blanket, he shivered. He heard a rustling next to him. Talauna placed her own blanket over his, doubling the thickness. Maurin started to protest, but stopped when she crawled in under both blankets. She slid her arm around his waist and snuggled in. Within minutes, the combined weight of the blankets and the heat of her body had him pleasantly warm. Now he couldn't concentrate on anything. Yet fatigue finally won out, and Maurin dreamed of exploring the forests around the city on his homeworld with Aric, when they didn't have any worries, and certainly hadn't heard of this place.

After a quick breakfast, Valasand took the reins. Maurin sat in the back with Talauna and Dania, trying to relax. That was a little difficult, because the gladiatrix took an inordinate amount of time inspecting every inch of her knives, turning them over and over and looking for chips or flaws in the blades, cursing that she didn't have a whetstone to sharpen them. Valasand finally called back that she was certain they could find one in the city, and Dania put the weapons away with reluctance.

Valasand, for her part, spent much of the journey talking quietly to herself. Or so it seemed, anyway. She never spoke loudly enough for Maurin to hear what she was saying.

Small, gentle hills swelled from the relative flatness of the countryside on the road to Langfort. The sparse woods thickened off to their left toward the swamplands and the Helnrill River. Talauna seemed jittery and Dania listened intently. When his nerves could take no more, Maurin asked what was wrong.

"No birds singing," the gladiatrix responded. "No animals rustling in the thicket. No insects. Nothing."

She was right. Maurin shuddered. In an instant, the peace of the country transformed into the silence of the grave.

The city of Langfort, when they finally came upon it, was like a giant castle set upon a hill. Only slightly smaller than Caileen, it was built along similar lines, with tall stone walls. Its massive outer wall led into a sharp incline, at the base of which was a deep moat. A bridge led from the road into the city, and while the gates were open, they had heavy bars on them, presumably used at night. For the first time in several days, he felt secure... until he noticed the jagged web of the pervasive gray vines creeping up the base of the walls. They looked dead and slick in the overcast light, like polished stone.

As they passed through the main gates, Maurin saw that the vines did not reach inside; for some reason, they stopped at the outer wall. Buildings adjacent to the wall were integral with it, and the inner ones abutted against each other, forming tight alleyways and sharp corners. The city was as noisy and bustling as the outside was still.

Valasand tied the animal's reins to it found a hitching post near a courtyard full of restaurants and market booths. They left the confiscated Reamar sword under the hay in the back. Maurin, Dania, and Talauna followed her as she began searching for a place to buy some food. Then, without warning, Valasand halted, staring straight ahead.

"What's wrong?" Maurin asked.

"Someone I know is here," she said, blinking and squinting for a better view through the crowds. "No, it couldn't be..."

Smack! Maurin heard the unmistakable crack of the palm of a hand across someone's face.

"It is." Valasand sighed and started forward again.

A tall, lean, dark-haired man about her age rubbed his cheek and looked in disappointment after the angrily retreating figure of one of the local women. He wasn't exactly handsome, but striking, with slightly dark, hawkish features and evocative eyes. Dressed all in black, with a sword strapped between his shoulders. Here was a man, Maurin mused, who would be impossible to ignore.

As they approached, recognition lit up the stranger's face. "Wait a minute," he said, "don't tell me..." He scanned Valasand up and down with the eyes of a connoisseur. "Vals!" he exclaimed after a moment, snapping long fingers. "I never forget a face."

Already, Maurin didn't like him.

"Be careful, Masalla," Valasand reproved gently. "You still bear the marks of your last greeting."

The man's hand moved to the lingering pink outline of fingers traced on his angular jaw. "You haven't changed a bit," he said, without embarrassment.

"Neither, apparently, have you."

"How many years has it been, anyway?"

"Not enough," Valasand said, but she smiled as she said it.

"And what brings you to this lovely place?" Masalla gestured like a goods seller.

"That's a longer story than I have time for at the moment. We have lost a member of our group to a race of dark Powers. I believe him to be alive, and so we are here to request help from the local governor before proceeding. And what are you doing here? Did the Temple put you on 'special assignment' again?"

"Ha, ha," Masalla replied dryly, his joking demeanor gone in an instant, replaced with a brisk, businesslike efficiency. "Actually, I'm here on much the same business. I've been following rumors of a growing threat on this world, one that may hearken back to the Wars of Dominion."

"Perhaps you would care to accompany us? We could use the help of another Warden."

"Won't you introduce me to your companions?" he said, leaving her invitation unanswered.

Valasand sighed. "Maurin, Dania, Talauna, meet Penelo Masalla, a man of noble ideals and questionable morals."

The man grinned broadly.

"He is also a Warden of the Gates, and an old acquaintance of mine."

"We'd guessed." Dania greeted the newcomer with an indifferent nod.

"Hello, little one," Masalla said to Talauna, and kissed her hand.

She pulled it away with a gasp and hugged it close as though he had burned her. Talauna stared at the newcomer with wide eyes and an open mouth.

Maurin's frown did not go unnoticed.

Dania looked as hostile as Maurin had ever seen her, and Masalla wisely decided to forego the kiss on the hand, opting instead for a polite "Good morning, my lady," and a slight bow.

"Right," Dania said caustically, her hands on her hips, her fingertips nearly brushing her daggers.

"And Maurin, was it? A true pleasure."

Maurin opened his mouth, inhaled, and closed it again.

"Let's get something to eat," Valasand said. "Then we need to see the governor."

"Good idea," Masalla said. In short order, they settled around a low stone table and partook in a plain but suitable lunch.

"So just how did you get here?" Valasand asked. "I didn't see you on the supply ship, so either you were on the one ahead of me, or you somehow managed to get private transportation."

"Better still," Masalla said; "there's an open Well on this planet."

Valasand's sandwich stopped halfway to her mouth. "An open Well?"

Masalla nodded. "I'd been checking out some of the old routes, and mapping those that had gone dormant, when I found this one. It took me a while to realize I'd reached a colony world; it's been so long since the Temple has had any real contact with this place that I think they've more or less forgotten it's here."

"That figures," Valasand said, setting the sandwich down again. "I searched for over three exhausting years to track down the perpetrators of this slave ring. I went from one world to another, spending most of my waking moments searching for any clues that might point to the ringleader. It seemed I was following cold trails, though, for a while. I was looking for a slaver, not a nobleman." She shook her head in disgust.

"If Argoneis can even be called that," Maurin said bitterly.

"Who?" Masalla raised dark eyebrows at Valasand.

"I'll tell you about him later." She sighed, and the weight and personal cost of those years showed on her face. After a moment, Valasand continued: "I was able to narrow down my options, until at last I came across a lead that sent me here to Argoth. I went through all the transit schedules and found a ship bringing supplies to the colonies. I told the captain who I was, and that I would need passage, and here I am. I could have saved myself months if I'd known this place had an open Well."

"Don't feel bad," he said. "It's not in any of the records. From what I can tell, it's been abandoned for centuries. It's in an old ruined city some leagues southeast of here."

"I'm sorry," Maurin said. As if it wasn't hard enough having one Warden making enigmatic remarks; now these two were going to hold entire conversations above his head. Keeping up was going to be a challenge. "Can we just pretend for a minute that I'm from a backward world, and I have no idea what you're saying?"

"Pretend what?" Masalla said, surprised.

Maurin bristled.

Valasand quickly stepped in. "You remember what I told you about the Wells of the Worlds? We are custodians of the old gateways, and use them to keep an eye on the interests of the Temple. The Shoan Dynasty holds power over most of the known worlds, and we act as a kind of counterbalance to that power. A single person, or even an army, might be able to go through a planetary gateway, but a ship is required to push through the ethereal rivers in space. Such travel can take weeks or months, whereas stepping through a Well takes the blink of an eye."

Too much to process. "I don't understand."

"That's not surprising," Masalla said. "No, don't get offended, young one. It's a difficult concept, and it doesn't fit well in even the wisest of brains that there are actually shorter ways between two points than a straight line."

Maurin frowned. "How can that be?"

"You eliminate the line." Masalla held his sash out straight between his thumbs and forefingers, then brought the tips together. "You literally step into another realm in which the distance is not so far."

Maurin reeled for a few moments, trying to wrap his mind around that. "Okay, never mind. Go on."

"These dark Powers you mentioned... you're talking about the Reamar, right?" Masalla said.

With a surge of relief, Maurin sat up and forgot his food. Perhaps this man could be of some help finding Aric.

"I've been doing a little investigating on my own. After some reconnaissance, I was coming here to get supplies and gather more people to set out for their temple."

"Then you will be a great help to us. These Reamar have been emptying entire cities of their inhabitants."

"They're expanding their territory, possibly even their numbers." Masalla shrugged, watching a waitress pass by. "It seems they've always been part of the history and legends of this planet, but they're just now crawling out of the woodwork and making tremendous nuisances of themselves. One woman I was questioning about the Reamar shrieked something about the coming of the Dreaded One, then shriveled up and died even as I stood there. It was as if the life was just drawn out of her as I watched."

"The Dreaded One," Valasand mused. "That's interesting. We witnessed a vile ritual just before losing Aric, and during the skirmish that followed, we heard that term called out. And one of the Reamar approached me in Caileen, thinking I was this Dreaded One."

"They're afraid of someone," Dania said.

"Clearly. And they've been looking for whoever it might be."

"So what is it, exactly, we're dealing with here?" Maurin said.

Masalla collected his thoughts for a moment. "Ages ago, the Urey'la, once known as the Glorious, were immortal, and freely sailed the oceans of space, becoming masters of the worlds. But they were arrogant, and sought to overthrow their celestial rulers, the Anaian—we call them the Vigilant—servants of the Source, and higher beings than they. Long wars were fought, and the Urey'la were vanquished."

Stunned, Maurin said, "We have similar tales in our histories and holy scrolls. On my world, there were generations where the visitors from the stars came down and ruled and guided mankind. We even marked the anniversary on our holy day calendar as the Eve of Descent."

Masalla nodded. "I'm not surprised; there are comparable legends on nearly every world I've visited. To this day, the Vigilant act as instructors to the Wardens of the Gates. The Glorious—the Urey'la—were envious of their exalted position."

"Is that what you think the Reamar are?"

"Something like them, at any rate. From what I have been able to glean, after the wars with the Vigilant, the Glorious were cursed with mortality as punishment for their rebellion. Fearing death, they sought to prolong their lives, and even attempted to once again achieve their god-like status. They did so by drawing off the life-force of humans, draining and killing them, and thereby increasing their own power."

"They can actually do that?" Valasand asked skeptically.

"Oh, absolutely. Leeching the life from other beings is a nasty trick, but energy is energy. You just have to know the art of channeling it. Of course, whether or not one can achieve immortality is open to debate, since the power gained is both limited and temporary—at least to the best of my knowledge."

Maurin put a finger to his lips, simultaneously fascinated and re-pulsed. "Then it isn't for nothing the old man in Mor Tespir called them soul-stealers. And I thought Argoneis was a parasite."

"So tell me about this Argoneis," Masalla said. "That's the second time you've mentioned him."

"We'll fill you in as we go." Valasand paid for the meal, and together they headed for the governor's mansion. Masalla had a long, easy gait, and had to keep slowing down for Valasand's sake. She told Masalla about Daman Argoneis, and his reputation. She briefly sketched out their adventures, including the run-in with the likely Reamar priestess, their escape from Caileen, the dark rite, and the loss of Aric.

Masalla, for his part, seemed confident they could take care of the Reamar problem—or "infestation," as he called it, as if the gods of the Gray Lands were some sort of tropical parasite or pesky kitchen nuisance—without too much trouble. Though the Warden might just be trying to bolster everyone's spirits.

The governor's mansion seemed a little too showy for its drab surroundings. They were escorted by armed guards through a wrought-iron gate, then through the mansion itself, ending up in the governor's audience chamber.

"It would be good to look like our proper selves again," Maurin murmured, ruing his outfit. "It's been a long time since I've worn anything appropriate to my position."

"Slave?" Dania jibed.

Maurin's eyes turned to slivers. "Son of the high priest of Baelon."

"Above no one, and below many," Dania said. "Rank livery is a jester's cap."

Maurin resolved never to voice that particular vanity again. But he wished his other clothes weren't still at the mansion. The things they had raided from Fatamor were pretty plain fare by comparison, and travel hadn't improved their condition much. For that matter, his own state left something to be desired, and blending in was out of the question.

Then again... He considered their eclectic group. *I can't think of where we would look at home.*

Masalla and Valasand appeared to take no notice of these things, however, and strode into the hall with dignity. Masalla explained the situation to the governor while the others stood back and tried to remain inconspicuous. Valasand stood beside the taller Warden, ready to back him up.

Statues and fountains lined the governor's spacious reception room. Clearly a man used to comfort and power, Governor Phoecius of Langfort had not been particularly pleased to grant this little audience in the first place, and the order of business did not improve his disposition any. He seemed eager to be rid of his unwelcome guests as soon as possible.

"What we are talking about here, my lord," Masalla explained, "is an indeterminate number of creatures with the apparent ability to invade the consciousness of living beings, siphon off their life-essence, and possibly even reanimate dead flesh. These Reamar are no less dangerous than they are mysterious; for whatever reason, they have raided several smaller villages and towns nearby, and I wouldn't be surprised if they struck here soon. They're getting bolder, moving north, and hitting larger targets..."

"What do you want me to do about it?" the governor snapped, pacing irritably in front of them.

Maurin's heart sank.

"Well, sir," Masalla said, hands on narrow hips, "you have the authority to alert the city to possible danger, and the responsibility to protect it, am I right?"

"Don't talk to me about responsibility," the man snarled. "You say you're Wardens of the Gates. You take care of it."

"You fool!" Dania hissed, striding forward, fists clenched. "Don't you realize you're in peril here? Care you nothing for your own life?"

"You ought to keep your slave on a tighter leash," Phoecius said reproachfully. "She seems to have forgotten her place."

In an instant, the governor was on his back, a wickedly curved blade at his throat. Guards all around the room gasped and drew their weapons, poising them for a clear shot at the tattooed warrior.

"If you ever even think that again..." Dania's voice shook with pain and rage, her face a contorted mask of fury.

Phoecius silently begged for help with wide, terrified eyes. If ever Maurin had hoped for assistance from Langfort, those hopes were dead and buried now.

"Dania!" Valasand barked.

She looked up reluctantly, her mouth twisted into an ugly snarl.

"Let him go," Valasand said, in a quieter voice.

After a moment's hesitation, Dania rose and backed away, taking several grudging steps away from the magistrate. The Warden's gaze never left her. Valasand's expression suggested a stern lecture would follow at another time.

"Lower your weapons!" Masalla commanded.

The guards glanced uncertainly at the pasty-faced governor, who rose shakily from the floor with help from a couple of his council members.

He glared at Dania in spiteful fear and fury. He seemed on the verge of giving the order for his guards to attack, when he saw Masalla's sharp eyes burning into him.

"Lower your weapons in the name of the Temple."

Whatever cavalier facade this Warden wore, he was a force to be reckoned with. Maurin also made a vow to himself to be very, very careful to watch what he said around Dania. She had referred to herself as a slave more than once; surely that couldn't have been what set her off.

The leash...

Maurin shuddered. Perhaps it was more than a metaphor for her.

"Order your men to stand down, Phoecius." Masalla had still not drawn his sword. "Order it now."

The governor's eyes darted from the guards to Dania, who still panted with restrained anger, then from Dania to Masalla, and back to Valasand. Phoecius finally waved his men to comply.

"We're leaving now." Valasand said, gathering the group, and ushering them toward the exit. The guards parted to let them through. "I can see asking you for help in our quest is a waste of time. But you are shirking your responsibility to the people of Langfort—and indeed this world—by your inaction. Be warned: the blood of this city is on your head."

CHAPTER 31
REFUGEES

Aric awoke in terrible pain from his head to his toes. Well, perhaps not quite that far. From his shoulder to his toes. His collarbone still hurt, and lying on cold rock for hours was bound to be bad for the body.

"Drink some of this; you'll feel better." The woman looking after him brushed stringy red hair away from a dirty face. What was her name again? Ah, yes. Holis. Seemed to be in her thirties, though it was hard to tell with that many missing teeth. Her husband, Gade, stood guard at the entrance to the cave. Aric winced as he sat up. His blanket smelled as if it had been used in a stable.

"Where are we?"

"In a safe place."

Aric took a scalding swig of some sort of broth. He wasn't sure whether to compliment her on it or not; after that first drink, he could scarcely taste it. He'd burned most of the sensation out of his mouth. They must be made of tough stuff here.

"And where is that?"

"A cave. We're not too far from Mor Tespir now. Some of the men-folk found it a while back and cleared the bears out, thinking this might be a good place to shelter our horses and all. But with the Reamar wor-shipers taking over, we started bringing our own out of the city. It was only a matter of time before the Graylanders came, and we was doing everything we could to have everyone who didn't love them gone by then. You're lucky. When Matson, there, saw you out there wandering through the fog with the moon in your eyes, and the others all around attacking anyone who wasn't of them, well..."

Aric glanced over and recognized the innkeeper. "I don't know what happened."

"You come from good people," the man growled. "Otherwise I'd have left you. If you hadn't just showed up in town, I'da sworn you was one of *them*."

Aric nodded, unsure of what to say. "Did you see my cousin?"

"I don't know. I heard some fighting and grabbed you before it was too late."

"Poppi, come back here!" A young mother chased her girl away from a sleeping elder and gathered her up, shrieking and giggling. "You leave him alone."

Aric felt as if he had just heard an echo, an unpleasant aftertaste in his memory. He shook his head, then regretted it. "I can't stay here."

"You'll have to," Holis said. "You can't just go back. The town's empty, you know, and your shoulder ain't going to get any better if you keep moving it around like that."

"I'll be fine." Aric stood, grinding his teeth at the stabbing pain. In the dim candlelight he could make out several dozen people around him. They all seemed to be in a state of agitation.

"How long have we been here?" a man asked.

"I don't like it," a woman said before anyone could respond. "They'll find us here, sure as they found all the others."

Aric shuffled over to a group of fair-skinned people sitting off to themselves. He raised his eyebrows at the nearest, a thin girl in her teens with a mark peeking out from under the brown strap of her top. "You're slaves."

"What's it to you?" One of the larger men with a curly blond beard and a slightly crazy demeanor stood up, leaning toward him with menace in his eye.

Aric was unimpressed. "Not a thing." His tunic was already loose, so he just shrugged one shoulder out of it, and turned it toward the man, showing him the scar where his brand had been. "What are you doing here?"

"What's your name, lad?" The large man held out his hand.

Aric stared at it, puzzled. "Aric."

"Samran." He grasped Aric's wrist and squeezed. "Sit with us."

Aric chose a place not too far from the girl he had first noticed.

"We were all being sent to the Reamar," she said. "We were set upon by the wildlings of the forest and made our escape while the ones delivering us to the Gray Lands were being slaughtered." She made a face. "I think they ate them."

"Serves them right if they did," Samran said. "Any rate, we comes across these people here, and they don't take slaves. 'Course, we couldn't go into the city, 'cause someone might get the idea to turn us in to Argoneis, and we all know what that means."

A general murmur of horror and disgust went up around the slaves.

"You can't stay here forever," Aric said when the commotion ceased.

"Try us," said another young man about his age.

"No—Aric, was it?—Aric's right," Samran said. "I've been trying to figure out what to do. We've got to get back home somehow."

"There's no going back home," Aric said.

"Says who?" the girl screamed and gave him a shove. "I've got a mother and father, and I'm supposed to be married next season. I can't live in this cave for the rest of my life!"

"No one's saying you should." Aric gingerly stood again, not wanting to risk another jar to his aching shoulder. "The more of us there are, the better chance we have of survival."

"That's mighty big talk for such a young guy," Samran said. "Where are you from, lad?"

"From a world called Sangrine," Aric said. "My cousin is the son of the high priest of Athure. And I don't care if I ever get home. But I'll be damned if I stay here."

Samran crossed his arms over his chest and looked at the girl. "We're all damned if we don't."

"Speak for yourselves." Aric paced around the group. "You have to have some sort of plan. Does anyone here know how to get off this world?"

There was silence for a minute as he looked around. He had gathered quite an audience.

"Yes," a man sitting in an alcove high above said. "The slave ship visits Caileen every eight months, roughly. And there's a supply galleon that comes every so often."

Aric smiled. "All right. Then we start heading north to Caileen. We go by way of cities that don't keep slaves and find what help we can. Maybe there are enough people who are sick of Argoneis that they would be willing to fight. My cousin—he's still alive, I'm sure of it—he'll be looking for me. We can rendezvous with him. I know a mansion outside the city where we could all hole up until the slave ship comes in. When it does, we go into the city by night, take over the ship, and get off this slimy world."

Everyone in the cave was listening to him now. He scanned the faces for some kind of reaction. Many jaws had dropped, and it was quiet for some time before Samran stood up.

"Lad," the blond-bearded man said, "You're either a moon-eyed dreamer, or a born leader."

"No," Aric said. "I'm a survivor. You just have a choice of whether you want to survive with me or not."

———◆———

After their confrontation with the governor, Masalla informed them they would have to get rid of the balodont. Where they were going, they would not be able to travel far with a cart. That had not endeared him at all to Talauna, who spent the rest of the evening furiously avoiding the entire party. After they spent a restless night in one of the local hostelries, she scrutinized dozens of animals—and their owners, as well, Maurin supposed, as she finally pointed Valasand in the direction of a couple that took good care of their livestock.

Some distance down the road, Valasand looked over her shoulder at the receding city, and then spun around. "Look at that."

"What?" Maurin frowned. Purple and black clouds loomed over Langfort. The shadowy billows fluoresced with lightning, yet there was no thunder.

"Look at it." Valasand nodded in the direction of the sky. "Just look."

Talauna gasped. Maurin squinted and stared. And then he saw it. The contours of the clouds and the deep violet shadows formed an image.

A face.

The visage of a man blanketed the whole city of Langfort. Though the features were indistinct, high cheekbones and a lean, chiseled jaw stood out under angry skull-like pits of eyes.

"Dear gods." Maurin's skin crawled. "I've never seen anything like that."

Masalla shook his head. "Neither have I."

As the gathering storm shifted the clouds, the illusion gradually dispersed. But the sensation of being watched lingered long after Langfort was out of sight.

The country they traveled was low and hilly. Still on the borders of the wetlands, they happened across several small streams and tributaries running out of the Secora mountains. They were approaching the Danir range now, heading south and slightly east of Langfort on a seldom-used path Masalla assured them would soon give way to woodlands. The foothills of the Secoras were blanketed in a primeval forest. Even in their escape from Caileen and the subsequent travel across the country, they had not been subject long to the laws of the wilderness. Now they were truly setting foot out of civilization.

"Woodsmen's realm." Valasand leaned into her staff. "I'm glad to have you along."

"The ruined city is over a week's journey away," Masalla said. "But I haven't been able to find the Gray Lands on any local maps. Charted country ends not too far south of here. We'll need a guide to get to the heart of the Reamar territory, assuming your companion is alive."

"He is," Maurin growled. *He has to be.*

"Too bad we couldn't have obtained an air-chariot," Valasand mused.

"The governor's would have done nicely," Dania agreed.

Masalla nodded. "Definitely would have been convenient. At least for getting us closer to the Gray Lands. We probably would have had to leave it at the borders, though."

"Oh? Why is that?"

"From what I hear, no airships work anywhere near Reamar territory."

"That's strange." Maurin recalled the innkeeper saying the vehicles of Mor Tespir were dead, and the sudden loss of power the shuttle had experienced before crashing into the swamp. "Is Langfort near the Gray Lands?"

"Not that I know of," Masalla said.

"Seides did not speak of the Reamar often," Dania said, "but I heard him say once the Gray Lands were growing. What does that mean? A land's borders may be changed, but land does not grow."

"The people I talked to say that where the Reamar go, the Gray Lands follow," Masalla said, his mouth set in a grim line. "I'm not quite sure what to make of it, frankly."

"Perhaps we'll know when we get there," Valasand said. "It could well be we are on the mere skirts of a problem that could easily mean the subjugation or death of everyone on this planet."

Maurin swallowed. "Why do you say that?"

"These Reamar are powerful and treacherous, Maurin." Her face screwed up. "It also concerns me that this world has an open Well; that is a very dangerous vulnerability for a planet harboring dark Powers. And though it does not give me pleasure to assign second priority to the matter of Argoneis and the slave arena, I see no choice but to follow the road where it leads. Nevertheless, I have faith that we can take care of this brushfire before it becomes a full conflagration. And, assuming there are no complications—which is always a dangerous thing to assume—we should still be able to get back to Caileen in time to stop the circus."

They walked for several hours before pausing to eat, then continued into the late afternoon. Valasand relied on her staff more as the days wore on. She believed in stopping before exhaustion, so they had plenty of free time in the evenings to relax and cool down from the day. Maurin asked her whether they weren't wasting time by not walking into the late hours of the evening, but Valasand replied that in the wilds, you needed to prepare for the night as much as you needed to travel during the day. She was probably right; it sounded like something Aric would have said during his woodscout training. Still, not making better progress made him edgy.

You don't even know where he is. He tried not to despair.

Valasand sat on a log at a distance from the others, her eyes closed. While Masalla tended the flames with an ornate green tinder box, coaxing them into a nice blaze, Valasand summoned Maurin with a subtle flick of her fingers. "Something about your cousin is troubling me."

Maurin raised his eyebrow as he sat beside her. "You mean besides the fact that he's missing?"

"For some time, he has been holding back some great secret, but I do not know why." Valasand opened her eyes and regarded Maurin gravely. "You have seen it, as well. I think Aric is an integral part of what is happening with the Reamar, though in what way, I cannot even guess."

That was impossible. Wasn't it? But then...

"Aric told me a Reamar man had tried to buy him." Maurin whispered. "What would the Reamar want with him?"

"Your cousin is a dreamer. To dream is to walk with one foot in the physical world and the other in the realm of the spirit. Aric's stride takes him on that path in his waking moments and in his sleep. This is why he is so dangerous—and so desirable—to the Reamar. He is the perfect bridge between their world and ours."

"So the Reamar are spirit? What about the one we fought in Mor Tespir?"

"I'm not entirely sure I would define them as spirit in the truest sense," Valasand said. "But I don't believe their substance is strictly material, either. Remember the ritual we observed?"

Masalla coughed as he joined them uninvited.

"I take it you have a different theory," Maurin said dryly.

The Warden shrugged. "I've talked with Valasand a great deal about what you've seen, coupled with what I know about the Reamar, and we think we know what we're dealing with now, at least generally speaking. Of course, as always, you have to separate the fact from the legend."

Maurin spread his palms. "So what have you come up with?"

"The Reamar seem to hold to a notion of cosmic unity, that life is all interconnected by a power they call the Lifestream. I believe these creatures are, on the whole, predators, draining the life force from weaker beings to survive. However, my guess is that they also have the urge to seek after bigger game, those whose spirits are particularly strong." Masalla sniffed. "In their belief, assuming their own power increases in proportion to the strength of spirit in an individual, the more powerful the prey, the better."

"In that case," Maurin said, "weak-willed people might actually be better off."

Dania eyed them from across the fire. Talauna might or might not have been listening; it was a little hard to tell with her.

"Right—or at least less tempting. Then again, they are more easily subjugated and destroyed. But here's the interesting part: The exchange of life-energies may have to be consensual, to a degree, so with the tempting power and strength of a person's essence comes a proportionate increase in resistance."

"So... the more strong-willed you are, the less likely you are to be susceptible to these creatures, is that right?" At least Aric stood a chance. A stronger will Maurin could not imagine.

"Theoretically," Masalla said. "Therefore, since a strong-spirited person can't be forced to give up his life, he would have to be tricked or seduced into it."

Now that was a scary thought. So either they wanted to use Aric for some unimaginable purpose, or they wanted to consume him. The options did not look particularly hopeful in either case. "And my cousin is at the mercy of these leeches?"

"Many cultures believe in the existence of a power created by life," Valasand explained. "Devotees to such religions believe they draw their strength from this life energy. Life feeds and nourishes this"—she waved her hand in the air, searching for the word—"what did they call it?"

"Lifestream," Masalla said.

"The difference, however, lies in the methods. The Reamar, if we understand aright, draw their strength directly from a network of living beings. The more powerful among them siphon off the lesser in a kind of pyramidal web. Through this Lifestream, each Reamar is connected, linked inextricably with the others. I believe they have a mental—or perhaps, spiritual—connection with their victims, as well as with each other."

"Do you believe this Lifestream exists?"

"No, Maurin, I do not," Valasand said. "At least, not in the sense the Reamar do. But dark forces are at work in the worlds, and most of them are not fully understood, even by their adherents. There is another possibility, one I almost hesitate to mention."

"What is that?"

"They may be using him as bait."

"Bait for whom?"

Valasand didn't answer.

CHAPTER 32
BAD NEWS

"They're alive?" Sabatha leaned against the wall, massive arms crossed over his chest in an attitude of casual repose.

"I'm afraid so." In a quiet alcove in Daman's palace, in a corridor adjoining the main foyer, Krige conversed in hushed tones with Argoneis's captain of the guard. "Governor Phoecius sent word that she showed up in Langfort. To make matters worse, she was in the company of another Warden of the Gates."

"Another Warden?" That put a frown on Sabatha's hand-some face. At least something was capable of ruffling this man's feathers.

"For years, we don't hear a thing from the Temple. Now, all of a sudden, we have two Wardens appearing on our doorstep; no indication of how they got here, or whether there might be more of them, or what they want—though I imagine you can guess. This morning, the group headed south."

Sabatha considered this. "South? But there's no civilization south of Langfort."

"Not worth speaking of. Just woodsmen, wildmen, and, of course, the Gray Lands—Reamar territory."

"Reamar..." Sabatha swept a curtain of long black hair back from his shoulder. "Why would they go there?"

"I'm merely telling you what I know." Krige stiffened. *And damned for it, no doubt.*

"You don't suppose they're going to strike up some sort of alliance, do you?"

"I don't know, Captain." It hadn't occurred to him, but it made sense, after a fashion. Why else would anyone willingly head into the Gray Lands?

"It seems significant to me that we have not heard from the Reamar for some time now. No emissaries have come looking for more slaves; no one has asked again about that missing priestess of theirs. It's as if they've lost interest in us altogether."

"I would suggest the opposite is true," Krige said grimly. "It's when the Reamar are quiet that they are the most dangerous."

Sabatha nodded his agreement. "When you first came to us with news of this stranger in Caileen, I told Daman he should act immediately, that there was something suspicious about her. He dismissed me completely; said she was only one woman."

"Yes, that sounds like our Lord Argoneis."

"We should have dealt with her before she became a problem," Sabatha said, troubled and angry.

Could it be you question your loyalties? Krige scrutinized the man. He would have to be careful; Sabatha was too much like Daman to just turn on him without good reason. But he was arguably more intelligent than his master. Perhaps his own self-interest might take priority over his devotion to Argoneis? No one was in a better position to get rid of him; from what Krige gathered, Anice and Sabatha frequently shared Daman's bed as well as his bloodlust. There were no closer allies to have. On the other hand, he didn't want to see Argoneis deposed just to have someone equally dangerous and cruel put in his place. If, however, Krige could convince Sabatha that he was genuinely concerned about his well-being and had the best solutions for their problems, perhaps the stage would be set for Krige himself to fill Argoneis's shoes.

And then the Temple would have no reason to be interested in us, and we could live in peace. He pitched his voice with just enough sympathetic inflection as he said, "I'm sorry. I know you did your best. It is unfortunate, is it not, that Lord Argoneis didn't see the wisdom of your counsel?"

"He will see." Sabatha gritted his teeth. "He must see. Come, we will tell him now."

No! Of all the things he wanted to do today, relaying bad news to Daman was not anywhere near the top of his list. But already the captain of the guard strode purposefully toward the grand stairways. Krige forced himself to stay calm. "You know, you could receive a commendation for this."

Sabatha didn't reply. That last remark might have been miscalculated. Should have known better. This one was too bright to be swayed by glitzy promises of meaningless recognition.

Daman was in a playful mood when they finally found him. According to Sabatha, he'd ordered a young Taracine slave drowned just this morning, watching her frantic, thrashing struggles in the viewing tank as he ate breakfast.

Argoneis stood in front of his pet castocs as the four-limbed avians sniffed eagerly in anticipation. Their sharp yellow eyes followed his every move, and jet-black pupils dilated in the shadowy confines of their stony holding pen. Several large slabs of meat lay at their feet, but the animals did not budge. Finally, Daman snapped his fingers. Their brown-furred bodies sprang into motion, beaks and talons ripping voraciously into the meat.

Daman's face reflected casual admiration as the castocs devoured their meal, dividing it with blood-spattered claws, their slender tails twitching back and forth. One of them snapped at the other, which responded with a rasping hiss, the fur on the nape of its neck rising.

"You know," Daman said absently, "for a while, I toyed with the notion of feeding the Countess Dalinde to them, but I've decided against it. I'm still considering selling her at the Market—the ultimate humiliation for the ultimate pest." He smiled to himself at the thought. "Later on, I'll check to see how she's enjoying her new necklace."

Krige had heard it said that misery loved company, and making people miserable was what Daman did best. He had expected a more gruesome demonstration for the governor's benefit, but Daman must have decided psychological torture was enough. For once, he hadn't done anything physically damaging, though his little sessions with the countess left her in mental anguish.

"My lord," Sabatha said, "we have news."

"News?"

Sabatha repeated everything Krige had told him, minus the veiled criticism, of course. Daman's eyes narrowed into slits.

"I want them found." Argoneis's voice was acid and murderous.

"My lord?"

Daman paced. Sabatha stood up straighter, clasping his hands behind his back. Krige wished he could dissolve into the shadows the way the Reamar were reputed to do.

"You heard me." Daman's usual smiling countenance was anything but smiling now. He snarled with pure hatred. "Send out a contingent. I want them scouring the countryside. Search every last room in every last city, town and village from here to Birn Aloi. I want their heads on stakes. No one makes me look like a fool in my own house!" Daman punctuated each word with a fist on the pillar. "I want... them... found!"

———————◆———————

"Long ago, when Firstworld was young, and the sun shone brightly on the newly-formed land, when Khadas and Kudan, the mother and father of all humankind, wandered the forests with impunity..."

Massala, with his pleasant voice, crisp diction, and air of sleazy competence, would have made a fine actor. The Warden leaned back at the campfire, lanky legs out in front, crossing his ankles and warming his feet. He related a tale eerily similar to the holy writ of Maurin's own home-world. He told of a young human race guided—and sometimes molested—by the gods who descended on the land, and of the mass exodus that occurred before a colossal destruction. Maurin recalled the caverns of Balfor back on Sangrine, and the divine visitants painted there. Stunning, and baffling, that two completely different worlds should have such similar—almost parallel— histories. If only he could compare the ancient texts from home with whatever existed on other worlds! Still, it was hard to see where Masalla was leading with this.

Dania clearly thought so, too, because she interrupted the Warden. "So what's your point?"

"I want you to have some idea what we're up against," Masalla said.

"We can't fight the gods!" Dania objected.

"I'm not asking you to," Masalla said. "What I was leading to is the fact that many believe these gods are nothing more than extra-planar beings; probably very like the Vigilant."

"Extra-planar beings?" Maurin tossed a sliver of bone from his meat ration into the fire. "What do you mean?"

Masalla steepled his fingers. "Maurin, you know that reality consists of the seen and the unseen, right?"

Maurin shrugged. "You can't see the wind, but you know it is there, because it moves the trees."

Dania nodded.

"Exactly. The same holds true for life. Some you can see and touch, and some is too small to see with the naked eye. And some"—he pulled a bowl from behind the log on which he sat, and set it on the ground where they could all see it—"lives in another environment, and you can't interact with it except on special occasions."

Maurin screwed up his face at the little dark shape swimming around in the bowl. "How long have you had that?"

"I fetched it before dinner. There's a nice little stream back that way where you can wash the dishes later."

"I'm not washing that," Dania said. "Why do you have a fish in a bowl?"

"I wanted to illustrate a point." The Warden held up a finger. "You can't really interact with a creature of the water unless you can learn to breathe underwater."

"Okayyy..." Maurin said.

"All right. There are some creatures that are invisible to us, not because they can't be seen, but because they are made of different stuff."

"Right."

"Only their whole world is like that. We can't see it, but it's all around us. But sometimes, you feel their presence all the same. Just like the wind."

"I think I understand."

"Okay, now pretend you're this fish." Masalla stuck his finger into the bowl. "What do I look like?"

"You look like a finger."

"Ah-ha! But is that all I am?"

"Um, no..."

"But you don't know that, because that's all you see."

Maurin nodded uncertainly.

"The finger is just a part of the whole, but it's the only part interacting with the fish's environment."

"I'm following you... so far."

"Let's say I'm the Vigilant. You're... you. When we see the Vigilant, it's because they choose to interact with our environment. They can't go all the way into the bowl, because they can't breathe water."

"Breathe water?"

"Metaphorically speaking, Maurin."

"Oh."

"But they can put in a finger, or a toe, or a hand. They can interact, but only on a limited basis, because they literally won't fit in our world."

"Now you're losing me."

"Look. When you do see the Vigilant, and that won't be often—it's the same as the fish in the bowl here."

"The one trying to eat your finger?" Dania piped up. Some of Aric's mouthiness seemed to have rubbed off on her.

"Yes. Forget that and pay attention. What we see is just like my finger is to the fish."

"Food."

"Don't be smart. It's just a part of the whole, but it's not me. It's just the only part that the fish can comprehend, the only part it can see— ouch!" Masalla pulled his hand back.

"Or eat," Dania said.

"So, how do the Vigilant fit into all of this?" Maurin asked.

"The Reamar are the gods of legend in this world. If they are what I think they are, they are similar to the Vigilant in substance and nature."

"So you're saying the Reamar are too big to fit into our world, so all we see is just a puppet, a physical extension of a much larger creature, whose world we can't see or comprehend?"

Masalla sat back, apparently satisfied. "You're a good student, Maurin."

"Years of practice."

Dania scowled. "What does this have to do with anything?"

"It's just an illustration. Back on Isture, another world I've visited, there are whole seas full of frozen mountains, floating like ships on the waves. These mountains extend much farther under the water than they do above the surface; a ship passing by might be fooled into getting too close, because they appear to be much smaller than they really are. I'm just saying we all need to be on our guard, because I believe these Reamar are much more than they seem."

"Well, why didn't you just say so in the first place?" Dania stood up and stalked several paces away, gazing into the woods.

"So just what do you propose to do when we encounter them again?" Maurin turned his palms up. "I'm guessing they won't just give Aric up willingly."

"Whatever we do," Valasand said, "we should try to act during the day. A nighttime intrusion would give them too much of an advantage."

"Oh, great," Maurin said, indicating the bright autumn sky with one hand. "We'll sneak up on them under the cover of all this pitch-black sunlight."

"Not a problem," Masalla put in. "At least, not in the sense that you're thinking. These Reamar give every indication of being creatures of the night."

"They're nocturnal?"

"No more so than you, Maurin," Valasand said. Maurin's ability to endure late hours had made him a likely candidate for first shift watch while they slept. "But they do seem to do their main work at night. They obviously know the territory around here, and we don't. Attacking when they're strongest is not my idea of a lark. No, I think a daylight approach is what we need."

"Just walk in on them?" Dania turned back around. "Their territory will still be guarded."

"In theory, we should be catching them when they're sluggish and resting from the night's raids. The fact that these cities are generally emptied and not littered with corpses tells me that they are taking captives. We might be able to get some of them to help us."

Captives, Maurin thought. *Aric, please be all right.*

Masalla took another bite of fruit. "There is another possibility," he said.

"What's that?" Valasand asked.

"This path runs by the ruined city with the Well. We could go through the world-gate and try to get some help."

"How long would that take?" Maurin asked.

"A while," Masalla admitted with a shrug. "Unfortunately, the Wells don't just take you where you want to go. You have to map out routes to your destination, and we would have to go through"—he stared off into the distance for a moment—"four Wells before we got to the Temple. Including travel time between the Wells, it could be several weeks."

Dania whipped her head around, eyes flashing.

"Too long." Valasand shook her head. "We don't know how much time Aric has, and Argoneis isn't going to wait for our convenience."

"Well, it's something to consider, anyway." The Warden shrugged. "On another subject, Maurin, I neglected to congratulate you on another culinary delight."

Despite Maurin's self-deprecation, he had been elected the official cook after everyone had taken a turn. He didn't mind; he managed to come up with some creative ways to serve their food.

"It's only rations," Dania growled, and stalked off into the woods.

"She's a real heart-warmer, that one," Masalla said.

"Yes, well, she has her moments." Taking comments from Dania personally was a waste of time. Maurin got up and wiped his hands on his pants.

"I think it's your turn to wash the pots, Dania," Masalla called out.

There was no response.

"That's all right; I'll do them," Maurin said, before she could come back snarling. He started to gather up the utensils, and Talauna followed suit.

"It wouldn't hurt her to do some of the work, too." Masalla leaned forward, chewing on a bit of grass.

"I don't mind; I'm not doing anything else. And I'd rather have her scouting the perimeter." Besides, it wouldn't hurt to get on Dania's good side, assuming she had one. And it gave him a chance to do something with Talauna. He grabbed Masalla's bowl with the fish in it and headed into the woods after her.

———◆———

Maurin and Talauna disappeared into the trees, and Valasand started packing up her gear for the next day's trek. Masalla sat close, leaning back on a rock and watching the activity. His knees jutted up into the air, and he toyed with a bit of ration. A cool night breeze carried the gentle scent of rain and humus, tugging slightly at Valasand's cloak. It also caused Masalla's hair to ruffle with picturesque grace. Had he chosen that spot intentionally? Her mouth crooked at the thought.

"Quite a coterie you have here, Vals." He took a bite of his dried-meat strip. "Interesting assortment."

"They all came to me, Penelo." She inspected the ground around her bedroll for any unwanted visitors. "I hardly had to look. The Source brought us together, and now I have to decide what to do with them, and how best to prepare them for the coming storm."

"Any show promise?"

Valasand sighed. "Maurin, I think, shows the most potential. He's the only one who really has any inkling about what I'm doing with them. Aric was—is—the strongest, and quite the visionary, but Maurin has more control over himself, and a more sophisticated concept of values. He's compassionate and loves justice. He'll be a warrior one day; he just doesn't know it yet. He still claims to have some allegiance to his old god, but he has been Called. I've seen it in his eyes."

"You think he could be a Warden."

Valasand nodded. It was nice, for once, not to have to explain her every thought in detail. Maurin was no dullard, but as a fellow Warden, Masalla was keyed in to her way of thinking. "Yes. Once he has bowed to the Source."

Masalla smirked. "We'll see, won't we?"

"At this point, I haven't spoken with them about the possibility of anything beyond preventing the circus and putting a halt to Argoneis."

"What about the fuzzy little mute waif with the big ears? What's with her?"

"Don't make me regret thinking you could be a good influence on Aric." Valasand pulled the cord tight on her bundle. "Talauna is an inno-cent, Penelo, and very fragile. She hasn't spoken a word since I found her in the slave market, and I don't think it's because she was born that way.

I would appreciate it if you left her alone."

"You have my word of honor," Masalla said, slightly offended. "You know I wouldn't do anything to hurt her."

"I know you would never intentionally wound anyone. But your manner is assertive and overbearing, and she is easily crushed. I'm warning you for your sake as much as for hers to stay away." Valasand regarded Masalla soberly. "She has an empathetic soul. Dealing with her own feelings is difficult enough without the added burden of picking up on the emotions of everyone else around her. Talauna can't take love as a game, as you do. She is just beginning to recover from her wounds, and I don't want to see her hurt again. Maurin is good for her, and, if he will let her, she could be good for him."

Masalla rubbed his palms over his thighs. "There's something special about her, isn't there?"

Valasand nodded. "Above all the others, I was led to her. She has been set aside by the Source."

"I won't touch her, Vals," Masalla said, his voice serious. "Promise." Then he flashed a devious grin, and said, "Of course, when we get Aric back, I may give him a run for his money with that lovely barbarian princess."

Observant man. Not that Dania was exactly subtle. "She'll have you running for something," Valasand said with a shrug, "but perhaps experience is the best teacher."

Masalla ignored her, twiddling a weed between his fingers. "I've had some interesting conversations with Maurin recently."

"That doesn't surprise me."

"He has some fascinating defense mechanisms." Masalla examined her through the fronds. "Have you ever noticed how he pretends to be more out of it than he really is in order to double-check your answers, see if you're being consistent?"

Valasand chuckled. "Maurin has a fine analytical mind, but hasn't yet admitted it. He doesn't like being left in the dark about anything, but he's afraid to let his own light shine too brightly, lest he draw attention to himself."

"Do you know much about his past?"

"Other than the fact that he and Aric are cousins and were stolen from their home world by Argoneis' slavers, I know very little about them. They have not seen fit to divulge much, and I haven't pried."

"Always the polite one."

"Practical," she corrected. "They would be less likely to cooperate with someone they felt they couldn't trust." Valasand shrugged. "Besides which, it's none of my business."

"Don't you think knowing about their backgrounds would help you in their training?"

"Perhaps. I suppose that it could, but for now I am content to have them tell me in their own way, in their own time." Valasand pursed her lips. "I was so surprised to find them all; I didn't want to lose them by pressing too hard."

"Have you seen Jashara lately?"

Valasand smiled, grateful Masalla had the grace to change the subject. "Not as often as I would like, especially since coming to this cursed world. Have you?"

"Once. He mentioned you to me. You were his prize pupil, you know."

Valasand blushed and glanced down. "It never felt that way."

"Oh, he loves you, and you know it," he teased.

"If by that you mean he was twice as hard on me as he was on anyone else."

"I've gotten my share of reprimands."

"Speaking of which..." Valasand said. "Why are you really here?"

Masalla snorted. "I haven't left the Temple in disgrace, Vals."

"Maybe not, but I know you too well. Some of the other women in the Temple used to say you were a good man, but a bad boy."

"Really? Which ones?"

Valasand eyed him sternly.

Masalla sighed. "All right. I'm on a sort of probation. I try, Vals, really I do, but..."

"Trying sometimes isn't enough, Masalla. And you're one of the most trying people I know."

Chuckling, he said, "I think they're afraid I'm going to give the order a bad name."

"I'd say that's a very real possibility."

"Seriously, I'm not very good at this. You know me; I don't steal, I don't lie, I don't cheat, but put a pretty girl in front of me, and..."

"Self-control isn't difficult if it's applied only to areas in which we are already strong." Valasand cocked her head at him. Slowly, he nodded.

"Training Aric might help keep you accountable. In the meantime, we should go back to this Heth Erlire on our way to the Gray Lands. An innkeeper in Mor Tespir told us about an old man living in the woods around those ruins who might be able to tell us more about the Reamar."

"So what are we going to do about them, Vals?" Masalla looked her directly in the eye. "I can tell the others it's no big deal, but you and I both know we're out of our depths here."

"We're out of our depths, yes," she said. "But we are protected by the Vigilant wherever we go, and the Breath will guide us as we move forward."

Masalla tossed away the weed. "May Yasul be with us, then."

———————◆———————

The stream spread out in the evening light, forming a small pool before it narrowed again over a stone lip and fell in a miniature cascade. The sounds of insects and amphibians, making their subdued calls, blended with the quiet splashing of the water.

Maurin squatted and dipped the dishes into the flowing current. For a few minutes they washed in comfortable silence, but then the slippery handle of one of the pans dropped from his hand. He managed to catch it before it could rush downstream and sink, but not before it had splashed Talauna.

"Sorry about that."

A mischievous look came over her face, and she scooped up some water, and deliberately splashed him back.

"Oh." Maurin nodded soberly, trying to stifle the smile playing at his own lips. "All right, if that's the way you want it."

He grinned and set aside the pots, scooping up a double handful of water and dousing her. She gasped and reciprocated with gusto. Within moments, they had forgotten the dishes, and were in a full-fledged water fight.

Talauna caught him full in the face with one particularly good splash, and something solid hit him in the mouth. Stunned, he saw a wriggling form plop back into the water.

He sputtered and made a face. "You hit me with a fish!"

Talauna laughed.

Astonished, Maurin stopped and gaped at her for a moment. Then, with a squeak, his boots slipped on the rock, and he lost his balance and fell into the pool. Everything went black for a moment, then he pushed himself up off the slippery stones in the bottom of the creek. He stood uncertainly, blowing the water out of his mouth and nose and shaking the limp strands of hair out of his eyes.

Talauna threw her head back, pealing with genuine mirth.

Too flabbergasted to be indignant, all Maurin could do was stare open-mouthed as she splashed through the shallow water pouring between the stones and made her way to the bank to help him out.

"You can make noise!" he exclaimed, dripping all over, the water running in rivulets down his face.

She chortled again.

"Aric thought you could, but I really was beginning to doubt..."

Talauna tried valiantly to stop, but the sound was sweet and unaffected, and Maurin didn't really want her to.

"I guess laughter is better than no sound at all," he conceded, then winced. Was that condescending? Why couldn't he get the words to come out right? And now, of all times.

Her giggling fit finally abated, she started to smooth the water out of Maurin's hair, shaking her head slightly. He peeled off his tunic, wringing it out in great spatters on the bank. Talauna removed her traveling cloak and toweled him off with it. She dried his chest and arms, then stopped, cocking her head and giving him a funny look.

"What?"

She glanced down at his pants, then back up at him expectantly.

"You want me to keep going?" he asked, incredulous. "I don't think so."

Impatient hands went to hips.

Sheepishly, Maurin stripped down to his minimal breechcloth, struggling not to be embarrassed.

It's not as if she hasn't seen me like this before, he thought as she toweled off his legs. *She probably doesn't think anything of it; don't be so prudish.* Even so, it was a little difficult to concentrate. A breeze picked up, and he shivered.

Talauna tapped her finger against her mouth, then turned and dashed off toward the camp. She returned shortly with a blanket. He accepted it with a grateful smile and wrapped it around himself. He slid his sopping breechcloth off and added it to the clothes she was wringing out and spreading on the stones.

"So, you can laugh," he said, avoiding the inevitable uncomfortable silence.

At his comment, Talauna looked up and gave him a wry smirk.

"Aric says he thinks you can talk. I didn't really know whether to believe it or not... but you can talk, can't you?" He paused for a moment, searching those fathomless eyes. "Which brings up the question of why you don't talk to me."

He regretted his words as immediately as her expression fell. "It's okay, it's okay," he hastened to add, as she turned her back and continued to fuss with the garments. "It's not a problem."

The Maolori girl finished spreading his clothes out, but now she was avoiding his gaze.

Fool. He shook his head and grimaced. *Are you* trying *to hurt her?* He came up behind her and put his hand on her shoulder. "I'm sorry. Because you don't talk, sometimes I don't watch what I say."

Talauna straightened up and turned around, her eyelashes damp.

"It's so hard, without words. There are so many questions I want to ask you. I could ask, but how would you answer? You do so many things that puzzle me." Maurin hesitated before going on. "I never can tell where I stand with you."

At that point, he came to realize exactly where he was standing: rather close.

A tingle like the wave of energy that surrounded an active flying chariot started at his forearms and raced over his neck and back. He thought he'd done rather well with boundaries up to this point. But he stifled the warning in his mind. Things had been going wrong long enough. If he couldn't count on things going right, at least maybe they might be allowed to go his way. All his life he had put consequences before action.

Consequences be damned. He wanted to kiss her.

How did one go about such things? Did one ask? Did one just act, and hope it would be welcomed, let alone reciprocated? Was he assuming too much? Perhaps it wasn't such a good idea after all. His mind spun. While he was still contemplating, Talauna reached up tentatively, pulled his head gently forward, and kissed him.

So much for that.

Her lips were a trace of satin, and a rush of heat spread from the crown of his head to the soles of his feet. He found himself kissing her in return, intoxicated by the softness and warmth of her touch and the unfamiliar taste of another. Breathless when they broke apart, immersed in the liquid beauty of her eyes, he struggled for words.

"Well," he finally managed, "I would say that was a very effective use of nonverbal communication."

Talauna giggled.

Heart thudding against his ribs, he reached up and trailed the backs of trembling fingers along the peach-fuzz line of her cheek and jaw. She closed her eyes and leaned into his touch. He pressed close to her ear, nearly choking as he whispered, "Talauna, what are you asking for? Because I don't know how much I can give."

She took his hand and clasped it between both of hers, pressing it between flat palms.

His mind raced over all the ways he could interpret that, and he had just settled on the likeliest and most innocuous possibility when he heard the crunching of leaves.

Maurin jerked away, face instantly hot.

Dania approached, scowling and looking him up and down. "They told me to see if you had fallen in."

"Funny thing about that." Maurin cleared his throat. "Tell them we're all right. We'll be there as soon as my clothes are dry."

Unamused, Dania considered the clothes lying damp and wrinkled on the rocks. "They will not dry here this late in the day," she said. "Bring them to the campfire."

"But..."

"Valasand said to fetch you. I am fetching you."

Maurin sighed. How much more humiliation could he take in one day? Grabbing his clothes, he stalked out of the glade, leaving Talauna and Dania to follow him.

"What happened to you?" Masalla called out laughing as Maurin approached the camp. "Decide to go for a swim?"

"I don't want to talk about it," Maurin said, hoping he didn't sound as peeved as he felt. Frustration and relief wrestled his heart for dominance. Valasand's eyes were wide, but whether out of shock or amusement, it was impossible to tell. Maurin looked around for a suitable stick to roast his clothing on, then sat down in disgust. Now they were going to smell like smoke. And wouldn't Aric just have all sorts of things to say right now?

For once, Maurin was almost glad of his absence.

———————— ◆ ————————

Aric found himself escalated to a position of some authority in the cave. Even Matson stopped eyeing him suspiciously after a while. As the days went by, the men stopped to talk to him about his plans to take over the slave ship. How would he do it? What kinds of weapons could they get? He had to admit he didn't know, but there had to be people who did. He asked among the slaves and found out all he could about their experiences aboard the ships. He interrogated the local men and women to see if anyone knew anything about Caileen, and the best ways into the city.

Most of the others were willing to do what he asked of them when he sent them out on errands to find supplies for the trip. At the end of each day, the stockpile of goods got larger, and while the weapons cache was still small, it was growing. Every so often, he would venture out of the cave, but he had to do it when no one was looking. He had become too important to the others to endanger himself in the "outside" world, especially after one of the men reported seeing some soldiers bearing Argoneis's insignia searching through the woods.

The day they all agreed that they were as ready as they could be for the trek, a scout returned with news of the great hunting wolves of the Reamar. "There was a pack of thirty Oarar, maybe forty of them, and they were all in formation."

"What are we going to do?" one of the women asked Aric.

He scowled in annoyance. "What can we do? Give every man a weapon, guard the entrance to the cave, and hope those things don't come within leagues of here."

But they would. Of course they would.

That night was a sleepless one, interspersed with the ghastly cries of the bear-wolves howling off in the distance. Yet even though the sound came no closer, no one wanted to venture anywhere near the mouth of the cave. If only there were some way to shut it off. He had the men spend the better part of a day cutting down trees and shaping them into logs, but left it to to those more inclined to such things to devise a structure that would hold a door. He was no engineer, and for the moment, the cave stood as nakedly vulnerable as a suckling babe.

"I'm scared," Poppi said.

Aric heard the words, but did not listen. Tension was high, and the stillness almost as disconcerting as the voices of the Oarar, because it simply meant waiting to see if the next howl would be closer. He kept to himself as much as he could. If only he could see Maurin. Where was his cousin? Was he searching for him, or had he given up hope? The people who went back into Mor Tespir said the city was dead, but that didn't mean anything. Maurin was stronger than he let on, and besides, Valasand was with them. She wouldn't let anything happen to any of them. Somehow he would find his cousin again, and then they would be off this world even if he had to tie Maurin up and drag him to a ship himself. Though he wondered briefly what Dania felt in his absence, he found he didn't really care. It was hard to care about anything right now. There were more important things to worry about.

The fog came the next day, and he knew they were doomed. There was nothing to say, nothing to advise. They gathered the soft-needled branches of some strong-smelling evergreen, using them first to erase all tracks they could find, and then to line the entrance of the cave; hopefully that would help mask the scent of human residence.

He told the men to stay in and be ready for anything, and the women to gather the children as far back into the cave as they could get. There were some small hiding places where a few might be able to squeeze, if they had to. Cooking fires were extinguished, and only torches far enough into the cave that they could not be seen from the outside were left lit. It was darker now than it had ever been. The fear gripped harder as the hours went by. No one spoke; they knew silence was their only hope.

Aric started pacing, trying to ignore the faces gazing up at him, waiting for some word of encouragement. Nothing came to mind. Gratitude, fear, concern—what could one really feel surrounded by living corpses? He had buried this one deep, but at last there was no denying the reality of this vision of perdition.

Holis's husband stood lookout at the entrance of the cave again. He was a good man, with sharp instincts. He would know if anything was wrong. Then Gade's terrified voice broke out into the silence of the cave. "Here they come! They—"

Aric winced at the sudden horrible sound of Gade dying, his last word choked off by the bite of enormous jaws. The cave erupted into screams. Chaos struck.

"Get the children to the back!" Aric shouted, running. "Get the children to the—" He broke off as he saw Poppi's mother go down. The Oarar had her by the throat. He had a brief glimpse of the horror in the girl's eyes, and he knew what happened next. He turned so he wouldn't have to see it.

It was only a dream, you said, Maurin's voice chastised him. *Only a dream.*

He thought he saw the crumpled form of Holis on the floor, and was glad. She would not have to live with the loss of Gade. The Oarar swept through the cave, snarling and snapping, and turning life into death with every twist of their heads. A few energy weapons went off, but the creatures were so quick that if one fell, another took its place before a follow-up shot could be made. A green mist oozed around the bodies. Spears were nearly useless against the pack.

Cold sweat ran down Aric's brow. It would be over all too soon. He made his way toward the mouth of the cave, hoping against hope he might escape the doom he had brought on them all.

He could just make out the mouth, twilit in the fog, and free of the menacing forms of the Oarar. His feet dragged like lead. He ran, but seemed to make no progress. Yet somehow he got closer. He was almost out.

Then he heard the growl behind him. Somewhere in the dim, icy distance he felt his bladder let go. He froze in the presence of the beast. His limbs would not obey his commands.

"Don't touch this one," said a voice from the gloom.

Ahead, the mist-enshrouded forms of men emerged from the trees, mounted on large serpentine steeds like the ones Aric had seen in the swamps.

"He is mine." The man who had spoken beckoned to the Oarar behind Aric. It came to stand at his side, glowering at Aric with baleful green eyes. The men were all helmeted, and the man in the middle had the oddest one of all, a gray helm that swept up and forward like a pair of blunt-tipped horns, or handless arms. He dismounted his steed and reached up to remove his helmet. Straight blond hair fell over his shoulders as he revealed his smiling face.

It was the Reamar, Guilan Vail.

"We have been searching for you, Dreaded One."

CHAPTER 33
GODS OF THE GRAY LANDS

"Oh, this is a friendly-looking place." Maurin stared at a veritable fortress of wood on a pronounced hill. The stockade covered about five acres, its walls made entirely of rough-hewn logs over thirty feet high, all sharpened to lethal points at the top. Arrow-slits were arranged strategically around the bastioned palisades, and armed men guarded the open gate. Outside, people worked in cultivated fields. Livestock bleated over the wind.

"Woodsmen's village," Masalla explained, his face dour. "We're as likely to find food and help here as we are anywhere within a hundred leagues."

Maurin sniffed at the air and coughed. Yes, his clothes still smelled of smoke. "We've stocked up on enough food for an army."

"That's for the wilderness. Always eat local if you can."

"If the locals don't eat you first," Dania muttered.

"What do you want here?" called one of the guards in an abrasive voice. The other, a large man with a thick beard and a mane of red hair flowing past his shoulders, lowered his spear as he spoke; not so much as to be a threat, but enough that anyone watching would be aware he had not forgotten he was holding it. Side to side, the two guards' bulk took up most of the gate.

Valasand strode forward. "We are in need of refreshment and a guide."

"Guide to where?"

"The Gray Lands."

Red Beard choked. "Why?"

"We have some unfinished business with the Reamar."

"Well, I suppose you'll do all right with the food and all. The guide..." He shrugged and stood aside, gesturing for them to pass. "You can see if anybody'd be willing to do it. I guess there'd be no harm in allowing you to ask."

"Thank you," Maurin said as they walked by.

The guard dismissed him with a snort.

Inside the walls, the village consisted of dozens of rough wooden houses, crudely put together and held up with the occasional incongruous beam. The villagers themselves tended to be big-boned, and as tall as Masalla—some even taller. Even the women were sturdy, their somber, weathered countenances a testimony to life in the outdoors. They dressed in old clothes, but not so old as to be considered rags. Most of their garments draped nearly to the ground, concealing all, and many wore cloths over their heads as protection from the sun. Hands were gnarled and muscular, accustomed to labor. Most of the woodsmen carried spears and long-bladed knives. The few hand cannons Maurin saw holstered in cloth strips and leather were ancient, much-repaired things.

"I wonder why they don't have bolt-throwers?"

"They don't have anywhere to charge them." Dania shook her head. "Never trusted those things. Rich man's folly. Stick with blades; they don't lose their charge when you need them."

The woodsmen regarded the group with some apprehension as they passed through. One by one, the villagers stopped what they were doing to watch the newcomers. A little girl caught sight of Dania, shrieked, pointed, and ran to hide behind her mother's skirt. Talauna trotted along in tow, gazing about with bright-eyed interest.

"All right," Valasand said, acting as if every eye in town was not on them; "I think we'll be safe enough here." They headed for an area that might have been a market—if one could call five stalls and two modest-sized stores a market.

Maurin ground his teeth. Though he knew setting off by himself to try to find Aric was folly, every delay felt like abandonment.

"What'll you be needing, dear?" An old woman appraised the War-den with a sharp eye.

"Just some food," Valasand said, inspecting a lumpy purple fruit. "We have a long trip ahead of us."

"Oh? What brings you out this way?"

"The Reamar," she hazarded, watching for a reaction.

"Really," the the fruit vendor said flatly. "And what would you be having to do with the godlings?"

"They've been raiding villages like yours, and even larger cities," Maurin volunteered. "My cousin was taken in Mor Tespir, and we're try-ing to find him."

Valasand winced and murmured, "I hadn't intended to give them quite that much information."

"If it helps them talk..."

The old woman interrupted. "Seems you don't know too much about the Graylanders. Once they have you, they don't let you go. Not too many people end up going after them. It's the other way 'round."

"We fought them, and they fled," Dania put in curtly, stepping for-ward and glaring in challenge at the woman. She remained impassive, but several swarthy men nearby burst out laughing.

"Did they now?" The vendor shrugged, unimpressed, and spat off to the side. "The Reamar don't run from no one. If they left when you got there, it's because they didn't want nothing from you. If you've come chasing them, you'd best turn your tails and head off back where you come from. The Reamar don't like to be followed, and if you think you've got the drop on them, you'd better think again. They're toying with you, blue-girl, and you'd better run while you still have your soul."

"Thank you for your advice," Valasand said, then paused at a com-motion from around the corner. Cries of outrage grew steadily in intensity.

Maurin followed on her heels, pressing through the gathering crowd of villagers to see what was going on. "Now what?"

Roped and staked to the ground was a gigantic anthropoid. It was an elegantly fashioned mammal, covered in short white hair, with light blue eyes. Dried blood made parallel tracks on one of its sinewy forelimbs. The animal brayed in fear and struggled against its bonds. A few feet away stood a man with a large axe.

Talauna pushed forward and knelt beside the creature and wrapped her arms around its thick neck. She glared fiercely at anyone who happened too close, baring her small teeth at the angry throng.

"What is that?" Masalla said, clearly impressed.

"I think it's a Talormine," Maurin said. "I'm not sure; I've never seen a white one before. They seem to be the wild men of this world."

"Wild woman, apparently," Masalla remarked.

"You would notice that." Maurin snorted in disgust; that wasn't the sort of thing that was readily evident. Even after having it brought to his attention, he wasn't quite sure how the Warden had arrived at his conclusion.

"All right," Masalla said, clearly struggling not to smile at the incongruity of the picture. "Put away your weapons. We're not going to let anyone get hurt here." He looked at Dania pointedly. "Are we?"

She didn't respond, seemingly torn between her readiness to fight the villagers and her amazement at Talauna's intercession.

Maurin answered for her. "No, we're not." They really didn't need this complication right now.

"What is going on here?" Valasand asked the man with the axe.

"This horsehead's a man-killer," he drawled, "and going to be put down."

"Whom did she kill?"

"One of our flockherds and his dog. She was raiding the flocks, and they found her out."

"Did they attack her?"

"She killed a man. What more do you need to know?"

"Does anyone speak this creature's language?" Masalla's crisp baritone rose above the sounds of the crowd. For a moment, he got nothing but incredulous stares and snide remarks as he regarded each of the faces in turn. "Does anyone know how to communicate with this Talormine?"

"Elder Wanulf does," a girl of about ten said.

Masalla crouched down. "Thank you, young lady. Can you fetch him for me?"

"Yes, sir." She ran barefoot across the dusty ground, elbowing her way through the crowd and back through the gates.

"Who do you think you are," the axe man said, brandishing his weapon, "coming into our village and disrupting..."

"We have no wish to cause you trouble, sir," Masalla said. "But neither do we wish to see blood shed this day. Give us a moment to hear the Talormine's story."

With the crowd settled down, the horsehead also quieted, and watched with keen interest.

"Here he is, here he is!"

The crowd parted to make way for a scrawny old man with wisps of white hair blowing about his face. The little girl had him by the sleeve, gesturing at him excitedly. "This is Elder Wanulf. He knows how to talk to the horseheads!"

"Is this true, sir?" Valasand asked.

"I know some of their language, yes," the man said, his voice thin and frail in the wind. "When I was a boy, I was taken by a band of them, and lived with them for a few years before I escaped."

"Can you tell us what this creature wants?"

The old man did not reply; instead, he simply walked up close to Talauna, and addressed the Talormine with a series of harsh syllables. Clearly shocked, the creature barked a reply lasting nearly a full minute.

"Her name is Shallar," he said. "It means *snow*. She is far from home and searching for her cubs. They were taken alive long ago by a hunting party."

"Does she know where to find the Gray Lands?" Masalla asked.

Wanulf grimaced. "Why would you want to know that?"

"Just ask her."

The old man wheezed out the question.

"She does."

"Why did she kill that man?"

The elder translated again. The strain of speaking in the fashion of the Talormine was clearly taking a toll on his voice. The crowd was mesmerized.

"She said she was hungry, and was in the barley fields, and he set his dog on her."

"It weren't his, it were mine!" objected a sickly man with a drooping black mustache. "That beast killed my dog!"

"It bit her," Maurin said. "Look at her arm."

"I will pay for the loss of your animal," Valasand assured the man.

"Ain't no replacement for a good dog," he grumbled.

"You think your gold is going to make up for this, eh?" another woman sneered as Valasand doled out much more than the dog's worth in coins into the reluctantly accepting palm of the herder. "It's all well and good to pay for a dead animal, but a man's been killed."

"That is true, and that is a serious matter." Valasand turned her attention to Elder Wanulf. "Tell her I will purchase her life in exchange for her services as a guide."

"To the Gray Lands?"

"Yes."

He shook his head. "You city folk are insane."

"Probably. Be that as it may, that is our destination."

"You can't trust these horseheads. She'll kill you the moment your back is turned. And if she doesn't do that, she'll lead you off into the wilderness, then run away and leave you there."

"I take full responsibility."

He shrugged, then turned to translate again.

"Ah, Vals," Masalla murmured. "It's so nice to have you here to represent the inimitable virtue of the Wardens. How many slaves do you own, now?"

Valasand's jaw clenched, and Masalla chuckled.

Wanulf listened to the Talormine's response, closing his eyes for a moment. "She has agreed."

"Excellent. Tell her we will be stopping at the ruined city on our way."

"Heth Erlire? What is wrong with you people? First the Gray Lands, now the city of the dead. It's haunted, too... the Ghost still roams those woods, posing as an old man, they say."

"Tell her, please." Masalla frowned, and he addressed the crowd again. "I don't suppose anyone else speaks this creature's language?"

He got a chorus of negative replies.

"I'd take you, father, but I'm afraid the trip would be too much for you."

"The trip? Ha!" Elder Wanulf held his fleshless chin high. "I could walk to the end of the world and back. But not with a horsehead. No, sir. Once was enough for me." He smiled at Masalla, then turned back toward his home.

"Not bad," Maurin muttered.

Masalla nodded. "Elevate him in the eyes of his people and let him bow out with dignity. Always pays to show respect to your elders."

Valasand made arrangements with the would-be executioner for the ransom payment. "Dania, will you be so good as to cut our new companion free?"

Dania unsheathed her dagger, and the Talormine's eyes grew wide. She strained against the ropes, a high-pitched whine coming from her throat. Dania severed the restraints with a practiced efficiency.

The Talormine stood in an instant, unfolding her massive frame and towering above all of them. She snorted, and turned her head from side to side, as if deciding which one of them to kill first. Maurin tried to get close to Talauna, but she stood between the Wardens and the creature.

"Aren't you the big one?" Masalla considered Shallar with approval.

She lowered her head and stared him in the eye, nostrils flaring. Then she turned to Valasand. If the Warden was intimidated at all, she gave no sign of it. Before anyone could respond, the Talormine whirled on Talauna.

Maurin gasped and clenched the hilt of his sword. Not that there was anything he could do. The creature could snap Talauna's neck in a heartbeat.

She looked up, unafraid, and Shallar nosed her cheek, then rubbed the underside of her jaw against both sides of Talauna's neck. Talauna, in turn, reached up to stroke her behind the ears.

Maurin exhaled and took his hand off the weapon, and Dania visibly relaxed.

"Let's get out of here," Masalla said.

Valasand nodded. Without a word, she headed toward the gate. Maurin picked up on the cue, and fell into step, Dania and Masalla close behind. Talauna gestured at the Talormine. The creature loped forward and joined her, uncertainty in its eyes.

The crowd followed them, uncomfortably close, but none threatened to touch the Warden or her entourage. As they neared the edge of the forest, the villagers dropped back. Maurin half-expected a barrage of fruit—or worse, spears—to follow them on their way out, but these people were too practical for that. They merely shut the gate soundly behind them.

When they were well out of range of the village, Maurin started laughing.

"What's so funny?" Dania asked.

"That was wonderful!" Maurin grabbed Talauna and spun her around in a little jig. Then he pulled her tight and kissed her on the cheek.

The Talormine gave a bark of astonishment. Talauna looked taken aback but pleased. Dania stood with her mouth agape, and Masalla's eyes were wide and filled with mirth.

Blushing, Maurin stammered, "Well, she saved the Talormine's life. And now we have someone to lead us to Aric."

The others just stared.

"All right, all right," he confessed. "I got carried away. I'm sorry."

"I think she liked it," Masalla said. "Something tells me you should get carried away more often."

Valasand gave the other Warden a dismissive wave. "And now you can see why I said the Source would provide."

Maurin had to admit that was a pretty big coincidence, but he wasn't quite ready to ascribe it to divine actions.

Neither could he deny the possibility.

Talauna formed a fast friendship with Shallar, much to Maurin's surprise. He had halfway expected the creature's size to intimidate her—she barely came up to the Talormine's chest—but he probably should have known better. Still, it was strange watching the unlikely duo. Talauna picked flowers for Shallar, which the creature promptly ate. The Talormine brought Talauna a small dead animal, which she sadly gave over to be added to the evening meal.

Shallar slept curled up at the roots of a tree on the edge of camp. Contrary to the elder's warning, she gave no indication of running off, though Maurin kept an eye on her. Before he roused Masalla for his watch, he added a couple of logs to the dying embers of the fire, then poked at the ashes until it roared and crackled again. Maurin's bedroll was beside Talauna's, and as he knelt, she scooted closer and opened her blankets for him.

He looked at her in desperation. "I can't..."

She pressed the tips of her fingers to his lips and smiled as if to say, *I know.*

"Just a hold?" he said around her hand.

She nodded.

Maurin lay down beside her, draping his arm over the taut curve of Talauna's middle, but she moved it quickly, situating it a few inches higher, above her belly. With a sigh, she snuggled back against him, and placed her arms over his, hugging them to her as if afraid to let him go.

Talauna's hair spilled over his chest as she settled in, comfortable and content. His unshaven chin nestled in the dark, springy curls, and soon he closed his eyes.

Insects chirped. Small animals chattered, and the night-birds made their lonely calls. The sounds of the dark continued as they had from the beginning of time. Their lullaby soothed Maurin to sleep as he cradled Talauna to him and drifted at last into unconsciousness.

———— ◆ ————

Once more, Aric awoke and wished he hadn't. Dreaming and waking were equally awful now. They traveled by day and by night. Aric's wrists were tied to the saddle horn of a Reamar steed, and Guilan Vail rode just ahead of him. Though only mist fell at the moment, lightning still cracked overhead, causing his ears to ring. His head and neck felt whiplashed from all the riding he had done while unconscious, and his entire body hurt. Soaked to the skin from the recent rain, and chafing in the saddle, he couldn't help trying to undo the knots.

"You might as well stop thrashing around so," Guilan Vail said over his shoulder, a few loose strands of blond hair whipping free in the wind. "You'll only hurt yourself, and I tire of hearing your oaths."

Aric spat out a fresh string of obscenities at his captor.

"Unless you want me to gag you, as well, you would do yourself a favor by staying silent. I will let you get down when you need to, and I will make certain you don't starve, but everything else is entirely up to you. I trust you are intelligent enough to know when you are in danger. It is only a fool who knowingly puts himself in peril, and though you do impress me as being young and rather rash, you do not strike me as being a fool."

"Thanks, I guess," Aric grumbled, subdued. He glared in miserable fury at the back of the man's head.

Guilan made no further comment. That little speech was the most Aric had heard out of him since being taken captive. The Reamar didn't respond when Aric asked him what he meant by saying they had been looking for him, or why he called him "Dreaded One."

After riding in silence for a while that first day, Aric tired of trying to memorize his surroundings. He suspected that if this Guilan Vail didn't want him to see, he would have taken measures to prevent it. No secret route, then, and apparently no concern that he could or would escape. Still, he kept his eyes open.

Few were left after the attack in the cave, and those were put under some sort of command. They obeyed the orders of Guilan Vail without question, without words, without hesitation.

Without souls.

Could they ever be made whole again? Even now, though they had long since dropped out of sight, he knew they were following the Reamar, step by step. A handful of them were positioned on the Reamar steeds like baggage. For what purpose they were brought along, Aric could not guess.

Stopping for rest was rare. The Reamar drove the animals relentlessly, but the strange beasts never seemed to tire. The reptilian steeds carried them swiftly across the plains and into the foothills of the mountains. The animals had no reins; Aric supposed whatever power the Reamar held over their human thralls was just as effective over their creatures of burden. The Oarar bounded in a protective circle about the party, unnaturally silent.

Something seemed off about the landscape surrounding him; it went by in a blur, rippling and twisting as if he were piloting the chariot instead of riding a steed. They were going much faster than they should have been able to, if he was seeing correctly. The sides of the valley rushed up in steep slopes on either side of them. Clouds undulated like waves, radiating outward from some point ahead. The light was odd; it made everything around him appear gray. There were no more trees, as such; only a persistent surreal tangle of thick vines and brambles. Might he be dreaming again? Lightning flashed, illuminating the landscape in hues of stark blacks and shining grays.

Dear gods. The Gray Lands. In all his time here on Argoth, he never supposed the name might be literal. The roots wove through the earth, penetrating it and erupting from it in a never-ending labyrinth of bone-sheen vine. Nowhere could Aric see even the smallest splash of color. He ached from the cold, and the air here was strangely dry, but when they finally reached their destination, he nearly forgot his agony.

In the midst of the valley, like a monolithic spike thrust into the ground, was the most unusual mountain he had ever seen. Leaning at a stark angle, the jagged thorn of stone stood taller than the sides of the gorge, and filled half of the floor. It loomed larger and larger as the caravan dropped lower, and several crooked barbs reached up from its midsection. Then it hit him.

It's not a mountain.

It's a tree.

A tree it was, unlike any he had seen in his life. And yet, he knew this tree.

Buried in this dark valley is the grave marker of the gods.

Oh, how he hated his dreams.

Of monumental proportions, its bare and twisted branches stretched forth to the heavens, and its roots—its roots plunged into the earth to depths unknown.

The Oarar walked ahead in dignified unison, like an honor guard, and the reptilian steeds had been pulled out of their run, and into a quiet, stately march.

"Come, boy," said Guilan Vail, his voice and demeanor almost friendly. "Ride with me."

Aric didn't have much choice. His animal followed Guilan's lead,

and both of them rode to the head of the procession. Lightning crackled behind the tree, burning the stark, jagged silhouette into his brain. Hundreds of Reamar waited for them.

No. They're waiting for me.

Chilled beyond the effects of the rain, Aric realized every single one of the Graylanders' eyes was focused on him. He couldn't imagine what he had done to win the enmity of an entire race, but he was sorry already.

Two Reamar warriors helped Aric down out of the saddle. It had been hours since they had stopped to allow him to relieve himself, and his legs were so sore he could hardly move. Guilan Vail held him by the back of his shirt.

"What's going on?"

"You will see."

A low chorus or chant began somewhere in the distance. The Reamar were no longer looking at Aric, but gazing back toward the base of the tree. A massive procession made its way slowly toward him, wreathed in mist. The elaborate robes of the Reamar stood out like orange and red licks of flame spilling through the slate landscape. The stream extended from some remote point near the base of the mountain-tree, and kept coming. It seemed someone of importance was headed his way.

The voices grew in intensity, and soon the air throbbed with the sound of worship in song:

Réu Samnavé
Vara Bendedwé
Aishèlan sur Vanosla
Duyasula bel Caroma

At length, Aric got a good view of the one who had the throng transfixed. Four muscular servants carried an ornate palanquin. They came to a stop not far from him, and allowed the rider to emerge from under the awning. A solemn, upright individual walked with deliberate steps up to Aric and his captor. The man was ancient-looking, and yet ageless. His head was completely bald, and he had no sign of any facial hair. Red-trimmed orange-and-yellow robes brushed his ankles, and he kept his arms crossed and hands hidden. Dark, unfathomable eyes peered brightly at Aric from under smooth brows. A coterie of dignitaries flanked the man, and an aura of immense calm and power emanated from him.

One is coming who will bring about the downfall of our race, and the end of our world. We are upon the cusp of destruction.

Aric shook his head. This couldn't be happening.

"Lord Réus," Guilan Vail said, releasing Aric and going down on one knee, bowing his head. "I have brought the Dreaded One."

"Greetings, young human," the man said in a quiet, cultured voice. "We have been anticipating your arrival."

Aric gaped in stunned silence. The robed man smiled thinly and pulled his hand out of his sleeve, gesturing to the prodigious tree behind him. "Welcome to Darkhorn Fell."

CHAPTER 34
THE PRESENCE OF ENEMIES

"Where is Talauna?" Maurin woke to find the Wardens drinking some steaming brew in mutual silence by the smoldering remains of the campfire.

"What, she's gone again?" Dania said, squinting from her bedroll. "Doesn't the girl ever stay put?"

We wouldn't even be here if you had stayed put. Though, for that matter, the same could be said of Aric tenfold.

From the looks of it, Masalla was trying to shake off the groggy residue of a mostly restless night. He nodded off into the woods. "She headed in that direction a while before you got up."

Going off into the woods first thing was understandable, but something wasn't right. Maurin cast away his covers and strode off. He followed the trail and found her sitting against a tree, holding her stomach. She had obviously been sick. Watery eyes glanced in Maurin's direction as he approached, but she didn't acknowledge his presence in any other way. He dropped to the ground beside her.

"Hey," he said, "Are you all right?" He put his arm around her shaking shoulders and drew her close, brushing damp tendrils of curly hair away from her forehead. He pressed the backs of his fingers against her flushed cheeks. Talauna repositioned herself, curling up on her side, with her head in Maurin's lap, her left ear folded against his leg.

"Poor Talauna," he murmured, lightly stroking her hair. "You don't feel well at all, do you?"

She shrugged.

She's not a child. Stop treating her like one. "Is there anything I can do?"

Talauna shook her head. He held her like that for a while, then put a hand gently on her shoulder. "They're probably wondering where we are again. Do you think you can make it back?" She gave a nearly inaudible sigh, but got up with his help. Talauna took a few steps and vomited again. Maurin held her until she was finished.

"What's up?" Masalla asked when they returned, seeing Talauna's face.

"She's sick," Maurin said.

Valasand headed over and put her hand to Talauna's forehead. Talauna stared blearily at her, but before the Warden could say anything, the Talormine pushed through, taking Talauna from both of them.

"Hey!" Maurin objected, but Shallar snapped at him. He smoldered, but Talauna waggled her fingers at him and sat by the embers of the fire. The Talormine stroked her hair with thick digits and making soft comforting noises. When Talauna was relaxed, Shallar turned and uttered an emphatic soliloquy of barking syllables at the others.

"I don't know what she just said, but she meant it." Maurin scratched his head.

"Oh, for an interpreter," Masalla said. "I should have dragged the old guy along with us so we could know what was going on in that wild brain of hers."

"You could have carried him," Valasand said wryly.

Masalla shrugged, taking another bite of his sandwich. "Snow could have carried him, and one or two of us, besides."

"So what's wrong with Talauna?" Maurin asked, turning to Valasand.

"I don't think anything is seriously wrong," the Warden said quietly, watching the Talormine. "We'll keep an eye on her and stop if she gets worse or needs to rest."

"Maybe it was something she ate," Dania suggested.

That was always possible, Maurin supposed; Talauna was perpetually picking berries off bushes and trees as she went along or stooping to dig out some hidden mushrooms. She had offered such morsels to the others, and although they generally refused, up until now, she showed a knack for finding and eating only the non-toxic varieties.

Genuine illness was another matter, however. It wasn't uncommon to contract something serious when traveling, and as long as they had spent in the open, they certainly had all the wilderness exposure they needed to be infected by some disease—or worse yet, infested by noxious parasites. Perhaps a relic of their time in the swamp? So far, the worst they had endured were the ubiquitous insect bites.

Eventually the great beast let Talauna get up, and she returned to Maurin's side. Fortunately, she didn't seem to mind him hovering.

The rain began about an hour after they set out, Masalla in the lead. It fell in heavy sheets on the forest, dripping in a steady rhythm from the leaves, and turning the earth under the travelers' feet into mud. The cloaks protected their upper bodies, but their legs were soon soaked to the skin. Talauna plodded along with her head down, paying little attention to their surroundings, occasionally lifting her eyes to glance wistfully at the water running off the leaves. Under other circumstances, Maurin sensed, she would have liked nothing more than to run and play in the rain. He allowed himself a momentary and slightly guilty flight of fantasy. Her hand was still warm on his arm, but other than walking a little more slowly than usual, she seemed to have recuperated from the morning's illness.

Masalla, apparently deciding that walking in silence was boring, launched into a series of tales of his fantastic adventures and misadventures on faraway worlds—most of them true (at least, so he claimed). The

Talormine grazed on leaves and insects as they walked, and what might have been a small rodent.

Maurin saw an irregularity in the distant land through a clearing in the trees and out across the hills. He interrupted the Warden and pointed. "What is that?"

Masalla followed his outstretched finger. "We've almost reached our first destination. Those are the ruins of Heth Erlire, where I first came through that Well. It was once a very beautiful city, they say. It fell, and now the ghosts are all that remain."

For some reason, Maurin didn't think the Warden was joking. His pace quickened as he realized they were within less than a league of a way out of this evil place. If only Aric were here! But, no. Even though his vow to Valasand seemed paltry and trite at the moment, he couldn't just leave. After Aric was found, there was serious work to be done.

The rain drizzled out, and the Talormine shook herself, spraying droplets in all directions. Maurin pulled his hood back, and residual water trickled down the neck of his shirt. The sun was coming out, though, and the humidity started to rise. He inhaled deeply in the fresh breeze, relishing the beauty of the newly cleansed landscape, and desperately wishing for different circumstances.

As they neared, he could see the ancient stone under the moss, the order underlying the chaos. He imagined he saw shrines and market-places rising from the dead ruins. Massive columns stood broken and defeated, and roofs crumbled inward. It was a sad sight, a mysterious testimony to a forgotten past.

"The locals seem to treat the city as sacred ground, and give it a pretty wide berth," Masalla explained. "The people I've talked to say it was the site of a great battle, and somewhere in the dead city lies the entrance to the underworld. The Well, no doubt."

Above, a white bird flapped away out of the branches.

"Are we camping there tonight?" It seemed logical, as opposed to sheltering in the wild, as they were otherwise sure to do.

Shallar pulled to a halt. Talauna reached over and pressed her palm against Maurin's chest. Masalla noticed and gestured for them to come to a halt, a fox on the alert.

"What is it?" Maurin asked.

"Someone's coming," Valasand said somberly. Dania raised her knives.

They stood for a few moments in silence, and Maurin heard the almost imperceptible rustling of feet on dead leaves. Gods, they had good ears.

A man approached them from the path ahead. He had no beard and was older than anyone Maurin had ever seen. He leaned on a staff, yet walked with a surprising nimbleness. A battered hat flopped over his downy white hair. Upon seeing them, he halted.

"Greetings, Father," Valasand said, getting a respectful nod in reply. "What brings you to this neck of the woods?"

"You."

"I see." The Warden did not act in the least surprised by his response. "Have you been waiting long?"

"Not long. You are just in time." The bright-eyed man nodded slightly, then turned to Masalla. "Are you here to return through the Well?"

The Warden's mouth quirked. "Not this time. I wasn't aware that I had been observed coming through."

A wan smile passed over the stranger's face. "Very little happens in these parts of which I am unaware." Turning on his heel, he headed back up the path. "Dinner is prepared, if you will be good enough to follow me."

"Is this the old man in the woods we're supposed to be looking for?" Maurin whispered as soon as he was pretty sure he was out of earshot.

Valasand raised her eyebrows. "You've known him as long as I have."

Masalla grinned. "Offhand, I'd say the signs are pretty good. He's an old man, and we found him in the woods."

Maurin bit back a snappy reply.

"Did not Elder Wanulf say the Ghost of Heth Erlire poses as an old man?" Dania asked.

Valasand smiled. "Yes, that is what he said."

"Well? What if this 'ghost' is luring us to his lair?"

Masalla shook his head. "I don't think we have to worry about having our souls sucked out by this guy."

"Well, it's possible, isn't it?" Maurin asked, frowning.

"For the sake of respecting any intelligence you may have left, Maurin, I'm not even going to dignify that with a response."

"Thanks."

Masalla's expression softened. "Whoever this man is, he is a servant of Yasul. But I shouldn't expect you to know that."

"But how…?"

"I'll explain some other time."

They followed the rest of the way without speaking. The man led them to a cottage built in a wedge between two enormous walls of stone in the steep granite hills. Opening the door, he gestured silently for them to go inside. Strange old artifacts filled the little house. Maurin couldn't figure out what most of them were supposed to be, though he thought he recognized an oil lamp, a mortar and pestle, and a clay water jar. Despite the archaic nature of his quarters, it seemed the man had all he needed to live in relative comfort out here in the woods.

The mysterious stranger hung his hat on a hook by the door and procured small stools and cushions for them. The main room, clearly designed for a single occupant, was a bit crowded, but they managed to seat themselves anyway. He set bowls in front of them while the Talormine curled up in a corner apart from the rest of the group.

Maurin wasn't particularly thrilled to eat things when he didn't know what they were, but the old man presented them with something like venison and fresh vegetables. The round of bread, just out of the oven, tasted wonderful, and Maurin said as much. The old man simply nodded.

"So what brings you to my realm?" the hermit asked, speaking for the first time since they met on the trail.

Valasand dabbed at the corners of her mouth with a cloth. "We are looking for the valley of the Reamar. Not long ago, we crossed paths with their followers, and the city fell to a dark power that stripped it of all life. During that attack, one of our group was taken. We believe these creatures have some evil purpose in mind for him."

Maurin set down his spoon, surprised by her candor.

"They fear him," the hermit said, nodding. "Since the founding of their realm, the Reamar have known their days are numbered, and that one will come who will end their quest for eternal life. Long have they stayed hidden from the eyes of their vanquishers, striving to regain their power and glory." He sniffed. "It has been said of the Reamar that they do not know how to die, and do not care to learn."

"So they are immortal, after all?" Maurin asked. The others were all finishing up their meals. Dusk approached, and the evening calls of the forest creatures grew louder, the drone of insects heavy in the air.

"Immortal?" The hermit leaned back against the wall. "No longer, but they wish to be. And there are ways to cheat death, I assure you." His eyes grew distant. "There are ways," he said again, more softly. He seemed lost in his own thoughts for several moments. Then he smiled, as if shrugging off his momentary lapse. "Many who sought eternal youth thought that if they learned the ancient secrets of the Reamar, they, too, might live forever. Those who traveled in the direction of Eulith Soren— or Darkhorn Fell, as it became known among men—were never heard from again. But I see you do not know the history of this world."

"Just a little." Valasand pushed aside her bowl. "It's only recently this region caught our attention."

"Ah." The old hermit gave her an amused, almost smug look. He adjusted himself in his seat, clearly preparing for a tale. "Then I think it is time you should learn."

"Is this going to take long?" Dania bit out.

The old man seemed taken aback, and Valasand frowned reprovingly.

"Aric is waiting," Dania insisted, refusing to be cowed.

"The more we know about his captors," Valasand said, "the better we can help Aric when we find him. Be patient."

Dania growled and sat back on her muscled haunches, not so much relaxed as in a kind of calculated inactivity.

Valasand waited expectantly. Talauna seemed fascinated as the old man used a thin taper to light a long-stemmed pipe. She regarded him with wide-eyed wonder as he took a deep pull, and exhaled a fragrant smoke.

"What tales I could tell you of the children of the gods, and how men forgot what truly happened all those centuries ago. How oceans boiled, and continents shook, and whole worlds were lost to the wars of the divine rivalry. Yet those days are past, and only the ever-mindful eye of the Source has kept them from returning."

He sounds as if he remembers them firsthand.

"After the wars, the Glorious were scattered, and many fled across the empty seas, attempting to find new homes where they might reign as they once had. But they found the worlds would no longer sustain them, and they became a blight on the very land they touched. Many simply secluded themselves and died, despairing of regaining the glory for which they were named."

Maurin longed to take up a dye stylus and a roll of parchment, but felt Aric's absence keenly as he listened to the old man's tale. This was exactly the sort of thing his cousin would have hated.

Talauna waited for just the right moment, and when the hermit wasn't looking, snatched the tin of tobacco from the hearth and stuck her nose into it inquisitively. She sneezed, and her eyes watered.

"In the years after the great wars, it was rumored that one of the rebel overlords had survived, along with his followers. But they were stranded here, their great temple fallen from the heavens, splintering and forever marring the pristine beauty of this once-innocent world. Many died in the descent, but their souls still sought out life, and living and dead alike among the Reamar began to prey upon the children of Argoth."

The old man stopped for a moment and stared at Talauna. Startled, she blushed, and drew behind Maurin. Feeling her hand on his side, he entwined his fingers with hers. Yet their host maintained his gaze on the girl for several seconds, and she squirmed under his attention.

"When the Reamar first encountered those who came to explore and develop this land, it was... terrible. They found a worthy prey in mankind. They subsisted on the gentle inhabitants of this world, but they relished the notion of feeding upon the favorites of Yasul, for these, too, were messengers of the Source. No longer could the Reamar hurt the Vigilant, who had remained loyal to the One, but they could exact their revenge upon the beloved purveyors of the faith. Yet the Reamar did not engage in wholesale slaughter, but attacked on the sly, invading dreams and luring the children of men to their doom. From that time forward, legends arose, stories from the dark mists of time that told of the cursed gods who walked the face of the planet in search of human souls to devour. Mankind lived in the fear of the night, and learned to hide himself from the terrors of the wild.

"With the rise of civilization and the shelter of city walls came the sense of security. People ceased to look cautiously around before closing their windows for the night. In time, the Reamar were all but forgotten, the memories of their deeds becoming little more than amusing stories with which to frighten young children."

"Why didn't the Reamar kill them all?" Maurin asked.

The hermit's eyes reflected a great pain. "For the same reason you would not kill all the cattle in your fields, or cut down the trees in your orchards. I'm afraid that when the slave trade began, bringing great numbers of people to this world, the Reamar's power began to grow once more. They have been biding time, you see. Waiting for the coming of one who could destroy them—or bring them redemption."

"Do the Reamar not know of the Well?" Valasand's face was drawn with strain, and she wrung her fingers around her staff.

The old man grinned, and Maurin jumped. For a moment, he saw him not as the kindly, wrinkled host, but as a shining being grander than words could tell, with eyes both ancient and wise. Maurin could barely make out features in the swirling patterns of light; it was as if the creature simply didn't fit within this world. He blinked at the painful brilliance of its presence, and the illusion was gone, and once again, the old man sat there. No one else seemed to have seen anything unusual, but Valasand smiled at him.

"No. The secret of the gate has been kept through much suffering and death, and when no man breathed in Heth Erlire, I was assigned as its guardian."

Masalla bowed his head toward their host. "Tell us, then, Father; what should we do now? We have sought help, and found none. I did consider going through the gate, but we would likely lose our chance to help our companion."

"The path of the gate is not for you," the old man said. "Not yet. For even if you had the time, this Well is unpredictable, and does not comport itself as it should. No, it is the will of Yasul that you go alone to Darkhorn Fell, and deal with what you find there."

He sighed, standing and collecting himself. "You may take shelter here for the night. I will be up and about my tasks in the morning, so feel free to make use of whatever provisions you may find. In the meantime, I shall leave you with one word of caution." He pointed at the Warden and her companions. "Your enemy is not your enemy. And when you find your friend, you may not find your friend."

Valasand's chin lifted. "Thank you."

The old man nodded. "I go now to my bed. I have told you all that I can."

"Thank the gods," Dania muttered under her breath.

"May you rest well, Ancient One," Valasand said.

The old man looked back at her, wistfulness contorting his already wrinkled face. "Would that it were so." He nodded again, and went into another room, drawing a curtain behind him. Maurin heard no sounds of him getting ready for bed or shuffling and snorting as most old men do as they settle down for the night. As the curtain closed, sudden and complete silence descended, as if he had simply cut himself off from their world.

Rest did not come easy that night.

———————◆———————

Aric was bathed and powdered by several female attendants, all of whom had lifeless eyes and slack faces. He tried to engage them in conversation, but they seemed unaware of his presence, as dead to the world as the denizens of Mor Tespir. Strange to be in such an intimate situation and yet feel alone in the room. With slow, methodical movements, they dressed him in a dark green robe with black trim and filigreed silver edges.

Afterwards, two large guards escorted him to a cavernous banquet hall. At the head of a long, low table awaited the god-king, Lord Réus. Aric estimated about fifty Reamar, not counting the dozens lining the walls. All eyes focused on him.

"Come, young human," Réus said, gesturing to the spot to his right. "Join us."

Aric paused a bit at the appellation, but sat anyway.

Musicians strummed on odd stringed instruments, while singers wailed in harmony. Cushions took the place of benches or seats. Serving girls poured wine from amphora into beautifully wrought goblets.

Hard to wrap his mind around the fact that he was inside a tree. The entire structure was a labyrinthine honeycomb of tunnels and arteries, and none of it appeared to be carved. Darkhorn Fell was not true wood; it was more like rock or bone, as if the very earth had started to sprout and grow. Like the surrounding lands, it was slate gray. As if to offset their surreal and drab surroundings, the Reamar themselves dressed in bright colors, their accoutrements almost gaudy.

Aric seated himself on a pile of cushions. Beside him, Lord Réus smoked in silence from an ornate hookah, clearly of Caileenian manufacture. How many of the Reamar's possessions had once belonged to their victims?

A tall blonde woman glided up to Aric, preparing a gold bowl of fruit and a small flagon of good wine, in which he indulged with a small thrill. Krige would have loved it here. Then she left. Assuming the servants were humans, and not Reamar—well, if they were any indication of the slaves Argoneis had been sending down here, it was obvious the Reamar were picking the cream of the crop. He had yet to see anyone ugly, or even imperfect, here in Darkhorn Fell.

Aric glanced up in anticipation as she returned with a large tray of aromatic roasted fowl. As she set the dish down in front of him, she said, "I hope you find your meal pleasing, Dreaded One." Her gaze was warm and riveting, and there was no mistaking the nature of the interest in her dark eyes and full lips. He almost forgot about the god-king and the fact that he was hungry. Aric looked down, his cheeks growing hot.

And I thought getting captured by the Reamar was going to be a bad thing. He swallowed his first bite, and asked, "How long have you been preparing for this banquet?"

"Since this morning, Dreaded One."

"But... how long have you known you were going to have it?" he pressed. There was too much here for one day's work. Either he had been expected, or the banquet was being held for some other reason.

"About a month, my lord."

A month! Every hair on Aric's body stood up. A month?

She was still watching him, but there was something odd about her eyes.

It's just like the people in Mor Tespir, he realized. *It's like someone's looking through her.* She was the only servant who had shown any signs of life; the others had performed their duties mechanically. *She's a puppet.* But a puppet for what? Or for whom?

He felt sick, and almost didn't notice when she moved on.

All the while, the bright eyes of the god-king burned into him, studying him, scrutinizing his every move. He exhaled a curling tendril of smoke. "As you can see, young one, we have sought you a long time."

"I doubt it," Aric said, swallowing. "I think you have the wrong guy. What do I have to do with you?"

"You dream truly," Réus said. "You have heard our voices from afar, and you have come."

"I dream, yes. I might even have dreamed about your people. But I dream about everything. I wouldn't take it personally, if I were you." Aric took a swig of wine.

"Your fate, young one, is inextricably entwined with that of the Reamar." Réus looked stern. "It has yet to be determined whether you bring salvation... or doom."

Aric couldn't help laughing. "Are you joking? I'm no threat to you."

"Do you know that for certain? Perhaps you simply do not know your own true power. Or perhaps you do know, and are hiding from it."

"So what do you want from me?"

The god-king smiled as he gestured to Aric. "Primarily to meet you."

"Next time, send an invitation."

"Guilan Vail was acting under orders, but not my own," Réus said. "I trust you will be pleased to learn that none of your original companions have been harmed. Meanwhile, since you are here, I see no reason for your stay to be unpleasant. Consider yourself a guest of the Reamar.

Anything we can provide to make you more comfortable"—he spread his hands magnanimously, indicating the alien splendor of his surroundings and the beautifully furnished meal set before him—"and you have but to ask."

Aric nodded. "In that case, I'd like to get back to my friends."

"I'm afraid that is impossible."

"Thought so."

"You dream of us, young one, but you may not be aware that we dream of you."

A cold prickle lifted the hairs at the nape of Aric's neck.

"Oh, yes, you are in many of my waking dreams, and those of all of the Reamar. Though separated by the oceans of space, we are all subject to the power of the ineffable force that moves worlds. We of the Reamar know it as the Lifestream. It is the power life gives itself, to bind the worlds at large to one another, and weave your consciousness to ours."

"Okay...?"

"The current of the Lifestream moves strongly in your life." Réus gently waved two fingers side to side. "A nudge of fate here, a slight twisting of circumstance there. You have always experienced it, though no doubt you knew not what was happening at the time. Each moment of your existence is at the crux of a myriad of roads, each one of which leads to an infinite number of ends, and each one of which bears equal weight in matters of fate. And it is because your soul shines so brightly in the dimming glimmer of our world that we sought you out. We know our fate is bound to yours. In what way, we have yet to ascertain."

Aric didn't know how to respond. He squirmed under the god-king's gaze.

"Just as life creates the power of the Lifestream," Réus continued, "the Lifestream serves life in an endless cycle of self-preservation. So it is that when a destructive force begins to gain an edge, and those who would destroy life begin to take power, the Lifestream takes countermeasures."

"Not sure I follow you," Aric said around a mouthful of meat, struggling to concentrate on what Réus was saying.

The god-king showed no qualms about his manners. "Life, no

matter what form it takes, is all connected. Perhaps it would make more sense to think of each of us as only a part of the entire fabric of a thriving body. The destructive forces are like a plague. It wants to thrive, but can do so only at the expense of the living. Therefore, the Lifestream sends agents to purge the body of the sickness."

"Okay, I get it," Aric said. "I suppose I'm the destructive force?"

"Why, no, young one." Réus's smile was almost beatific. "We are."

CHAPTER 35
WAKING DREAMS

After the banquet, the same huge pair of Reamar guards escorted Aric to his quarters. There were no doors in Darkhorn Fell, but the men stationed themselves outside the lengthy corridor leading to his room, making it clear they didn't have to go anywhere for a long, long time.

Nothing better to do than to get ready for bed. He didn't appear to be in any immediate danger, so he could at least plan his escape in comfort. He was full, and the wine coursed through his veins. All things considered, he felt warm and relaxed.

The room itself was like something out of an artist's nightmare, a cavern-like alcove of surreal haunts and bogeys. The veins and ripples in the mountain-tree's webbed and tunneled milieu formed strange shadows on the walls. With a little imagination, he could see distorted faces and slender, disembodied arms interweaved in sensual embrace around the entrances and windows; the entire surface of the room was a quasi-organic tapestry, constantly wrestling itself. Columns like those one might see in a cave joined the floor and ceiling. From what he had seen, the entire temple looked like this from the inside.

Royal accommodations, huh?

Oddly, though, as unsettling as the effect was, there was something remotely fascinating, even familiar, about the room. Jets of green flame lit his surroundings, licking the walls at random intervals. He shivered a little at the flickering impressions of lengthened cheeks, closed eyes, solemn expressions—not carved and presented, but implied and felt. He reached out and laid his hand on the dark gray wall. It was cold, like stone, and felt wrong somehow; almost as if he weren't really touching the wall itself, but a representation of the wall.

Satisfied that he was alone, Aric stripped off his robe and tossed it onto the floor. Sighing, he approached what he supposed was a wash basin. He had seen nothing mechanical in Darkhorn Fell; water merely trickled constantly in various intensities from assorted places in the walls, sometimes collecting in a pool, which more often than not was just an odd extrusion on the surface. From there it would run off and along a rivulet in the floor, to disappear into the echoing depths of the caverns. The incessant running water made the cool air in the temple clammy. He put his hand into a stream, and jumped.

What in the hells?

The water wasn't just flowing downhill, but simply away from the source. It ran up the wall and across the ceiling, as well. He fought to control his breathing. This all felt like a dream, but it wasn't. So normal rules didn't apply here. He could deal with that. He hoped.

He had seen no mirrors in the temple, but as he ducked his head to wash, he started at a fleeting reflection over his shoulder in the glassy black surface of the water. He spun around, but saw nothing. The room was empty. He washed his face, eyeing the misbehaving water with suspicion, and toweled off with what he supposed was the appropriate cloth—it was a little difficult to tell what everything was for in this place. For all he knew, he might have been supposed to wear the whatever-it-was.

Oh, well.

When he turned again, his heart nearly stopped. Something was hanging from his ceiling.

No.

Standing on his ceiling, as comfortably as if on the floor.

Disoriented, he made out a cloaked figure against one of the thick stone columns, vaguely bat-like in the gloom. Heart beating cold in his chest, Aric reached for his weapon and cursed. Not only had his weapons been taken from him, but he was currently without protection of any kind. He wrapped the damp cloth around his waist and stared.

"Who are you? Where did you come from?"

"Do not be afraid." The woman's voice had dark velvet overtones. "I am not here to harm you."

Aric felt a little dizzy as the figure walked across the ceiling toward him. She continued down the wall until she stepped out of the shadows and stood before him, stopping only a short distance away. A hooded maroon cloak stretched to her bare feet. From the way the garment draped over the woman's body, he suspected it was all that stood between the stranger and himself.

"What do you want?" he asked, trying to keep his voice steady.

"For a long time, I have watched you from afar, and tried to make myself known to you."

He couldn't see her eyes; he saw only the motion of her lips as she formed words his ears could scarcely comprehend.

"I have loved and desired you since before you were born. My spirit has searched for you through all the known worlds. I have seen you fly the skies and sail the empty seas until the tides of fate washed you to my shore. Emissaries have sought you out since first the slaver's ship brought you to this world, and I sent my own son to protect you from those who would have done you harm. He recognized you in Langfort, and grasped for you in Mor Tespir. How desperate I was when I thought you had slipped from my embrace. Long have you heard my voice—I know, because long have I called for you. And you have answered me, and loved me in your waking dreams."

This can't be happening, this can't be happening, this can't... Aric's heart pounded as he gazed at her. "You!"

She nodded. "Yes, my love. It is I. And I have grown eager for you; you cannot know the ache of centuries of yearning."

The figure reached up, loosening the hood and dropping it. Waves of thick chestnut hair tumbled forward. Her arms were bare, and her skin was flawless. Startling blue-green eyes, highlighted with gold, engulfed him entirely.

The world spun around him.

He knew her face, and the feeling of her gaze. How many times had he seen her, hoped for her? How long had he loved her?

She smiled at his reaction and glided toward him. "And to wait, knowing that you had finally been brought to me, even now, having to watch through the eyes of my handmaiden as you ate and spoke with Lord Réus. It has been a long time since humans have had the honor to sit at the table of the Reamar. Yet the privilege was ours. To Lord Réus and Lady Aishè, you are the Dreaded One. To me, you are beloved."

Steady now. You must be dreaming again.

"No, my dearest Aric," she assured him, "you are not dreaming. I have been waiting for you for longer than you can know. Though my world has been but a dream to you, it will soon be more real than the one in which you were born."

"I don't understand. How...?"

"Cherished one, our love cannot be bound by space or time." Her voice lowered into urgent intensity. "From the foundations of the worlds, it was fated that we should meet. I came forth to you; diligently have I sought your face. And now, I have found you."

She opened the cloak and allowed it to slip to the floor. In startled ecstasy, Aric saw he had been right. She was so beautiful, so perfect, that she was more clothed in her nudity than she had been before. She kissed him, then, pressing her body to his, and holding his head tenderly. Her embrace filled him with a longing such as he had never experienced and had always known. The worlds turned, suns were born and faded to nothingness, and the flow of life surged through his soul as he drank in the sweetness of her being.

"Ulora," Aric said, knowing her name as surely as he knew her face. "I've crossed the empty seas for you."

She smiled and put a finger to his lips. "No more words."

———◆———

The Gray Lands drew near. Their proximity weighed like a smothering blanket on Maurin's soul. But if Valasand was right, each step brought them closer to Aric. Determination quickened his pace, lending strength and speed to his stride.

"You should probably slow down, Maurin, or you won't be good for anything when we arrive," Valasand cautioned. "This is unfamiliar territory, and we don't know how the Gray Lands are guarded. The Reamar may be expecting us to come after Aric."

Dania's eyes flicked over at them, then she stared straight ahead as if she had heard nothing. Masalla watched them, no doubt ready to jump in with his own opinions at the slightest hint of an opening. The old hermit had been gone by the time they awoke that morning, and they had set out after eating a substantial breakfast. Masalla wished to press on as long as they could without a break.

"Bring them on." Maurin took in his surroundings with unusual alacrity. No detail of the green rolling hills passed unnoticed. He might not have Aric's skills at reading the land, but areas in the path ahead indicated where many feet had passed, and recently. His gaze stayed forward, yet his eyes absorbed the entire landscape.

"Something is bothering you."

"You think?" Maurin retorted, matching pace with her, and not particularly caring if the others heard or not. Immediately, he flushed. "I'm sorry. Yes. Yes, something is bothering me."

"Beyond your cousin."

Maurin nodded. "It's been on my mind since the day you told us what your plans were. Us. Argoneis. All of it. But especially..."

Masalla met Valasand's eyes, and then drew Talauna and Dania away with a subtle head gesture, leaving enough space between them that Maurin could speak with a semblance of privacy. Dania raised her eyebrows, but didn't object, and Talauna nodded, though she kept slipping furtive concerned glances back at Maurin.

"Yes?" Valasand prodded.

"Yasul. The Breath. What is it?"

Valasand smiled, as if pleased that he would bring up that particular subject. "The Breath is the voice, the moving spirit of my god. It whispers to me, guiding my thoughts and actions."

"Is that who you were talking to in your rooms that day?" Maurin knew he was giving himself away, but he didn't care.

"You were the one listening?" Valasand asked, her voice almost hopeful.

"No. Aric."

"Oh. Oh..." Valasand dropped back several steps.

Maurin frowned and paused until she started to walk again. "What difference does that make?"

"Aric heard a messenger of Yasul, an instructor of the Wardens of the Gates. He speaks for the Source, but not with Yasul's voice."

"How did he get there? And where did he go? Where is he now?"

"The Vigilant—they're hard to explain. More significant is the fact that Aric could hear it."

"How so?"

"It could, in part, be the reason the Reamar have an interest in him. Not just anyone can hear beings like the Vigilant, or see them. Typically, it takes a spirit attuned to the Breath. But if he can hear these things, even as he has visions..."

Maurin wrestled down his disappointment. "I don't understand. How does it work, then?"

Valasand gave a sharp soprano laugh. "Do you think you could narrow that down any?"

"I'm serious. How does one get 'attuned to the Breath'? I want to know how to find Aric. You say he's not dead. But I don't feel that; I don't feel anything—I'm just scared."

"You feel more than you think. Your concern is a good indicator he lives."

Maurin frowned. "What do you mean?"

"Were he dead," Valasand put in quietly, "what would there be to fear?"

"Oh." He considered that for a moment. "I guess I hadn't thought of it that way."

"You might not have heard the Vigilant, but your spirit's insight is deep and clear. You need to learn to trust it."

"So I can just act on whatever strong impulse happens to come into my head?"

"Don't twist my words." Valasand thumped her staff sharply on the ground. "Listening to your own common sense and listening for the whispers of the Breath are not the same thing. In fact, that is one way you may know when Yasul is speaking to you; what you hear may well be contrary to what you believe to be the wise or sane thing to do."

"Great. So you follow an insane god." Perhaps Aric had been right all along.

"Not at all. I follow *the* God. The Source of all. If Yasul thought like a man, Yasul would not be God. Yasul would not be a god at all." Valasand rested her hand lightly on his forearm, and he stopped to face her. "Do you remember telling me about that day in the woods of your homeworld, when Aric showed you that if you wanted to see animals, you had to wait, and be still?"

"Yes. Are you saying that's how the Breath is? If I chase it, it will run away?"

"No. Those who seek the Source are rewarded. I'm saying that in order to hear the voice of Yasul, you must first silence your own. Your angry desires can drown out even the voice of your Creator."

"My 'angry desires?' What do you mean?"

"Maurin, I am not as blind as that. Don't insult me further by pretending not to know what I'm talking about." Valasand's words were clipped and harsh. "I warned you about your complacency, but even more so against your personal vendettas. You were perfectly content to have nothing to do with Yasul until now, weren't you?"

Maurin stared furiously. He had no answer.

She pressed on: "You want to draw on the power of the Source because you feel helpless about what happened to Aric."

"Valasand..." Maurin started, but could go no further. Disconcerted, he spread his hands out, palms-up. "I'll admit there's some truth to what you say. But what good does it do to follow a god who can't or won't help you?"

"Did I say that? Relying on the Breath for help and trying to control the Source are two different things. No one controls Yasul. The reason I warn you about your anger is that it can control you. Your anger is your greatest strength, and your greatest weakness. You have good cause to fear it. But it is not sufficient to fear it; you must learn to control it."

She smiled compassionately. "Don't worry, Maurin. Yasul will be with us, even if you do not yet feel it. One day, you will realize the truth."

"And that is?"

"That you are Yasul's, and always have been. Your devotion to Baelon was nothing but a prelude to real worship, to a life spent in the service of the Source." She nodded as a white bird flew over them, heading south. Toward the Gray Lands. "One does not hear the Breath for nothing."

Maurin mulled over her words in silence, and hardly anyone spoke the rest of the day. When they finally stopped to make camp for the night, Maurin helped until he was no longer needed, then set off into the woods by himself. His body was shaking so hard that he didn't realize Talauna had walked up behind him until he felt her arms around him. Maurin turned, and she led him further away into the privacy of a hollow between three trees. Sitting down, she pulled him to her. Maurin wept then, cradled against Talauna's breast as she reclined against a fallen tree. She kissed his forehead and stroked his hair, making whispery shushing sounds as he sobbed. When at last he regained his composure, Maurin leaned into her, and just allowed her to hold him.

"Sorry," he said at last, his voice breaking. "I'm just—it's Aric. I've failed him so badly. I guess I've always felt like his father, or something. Aric's parents and siblings—"

What to say?

Aric's mother had died giving birth to his sister, and his father had gone mad with grief. He killed Aric's older brothers, and no doubt would have killed Aric, as well, if the master scout hadn't happened to walk in and stop him. Aric's father had shoved Rale aside and run off. The men of Athure searched for him for weeks before finally finding him in one of the volcanic ravines about two leagues from the city, his neck broken. Aric never knew his little sister; she died shortly after her mother.

Too much. Far too much.

"—they died when he was very young. I'm all he has." Maurin absently caressed the palm of her hand with his thumb. "My own father was always so busy with the affairs of the temple and counsel to the king, but I always watched out for Aric, tried to keep him from getting himself into trouble. I even took a vow to my god in exchange for the preservation of Aric's life when he was ill."

Maurin paused for a moment his throat tight with the recollection. How much did she understand? Hard to tell, but talking felt good.

"We grew up together; I don't remember a time when he wasn't there. I guess I always saw him as my little brother, too. I taught him everything I knew, and took more pride in his accomplishments than my own. I was always fated to preside over the Temple, and possibly even the city, eventually, but Aric... Aric could go anywhere, do anything he wanted. I wanted freedoms for him I would never have." He choked. "I don't know what I would do if he were gone."

Talauna held up his head, moons reflected in her fathomless dark eyes. A simple blink of long lashes, and he was undone. She kissed him and clasped him tight again. Maurin stroked her arm, and settled down, laying his head in her lap to gaze up at Talauna's passive, beautiful features. What did she ever see in him? What he saw in her—well, that was easy. She was a calm spot in his angry, chaotic world. A stable, innocent well of peace and acceptance. She harbored no grudges; she was not bitter. Whatever pain she carried locked within her, she did not let it affect how she treated those around her.

Who are you, Talauna? Why do I feel such peace with you?

Talauna's questing fingers plucked at his hip, and she extricated a length of purple silken ribbon from his pocket. Maurin winced as she fiddled with it curiously. The end must have slipped out somehow. After a moment, she handed it back to Maurin.

"You want to know what this is?" Suddenly overwhelmed with guilt, he scooted into a seated position and held the ribbon out full length.

Talauna nodded.

"It's a wedding band. At the end of the ceremony, part of it is wrapped around the bride's wrist. She has one, too, a green one, and the same is done with it. It symbolizes their union."

Talauna reached up and felt the ribbon, letting it slide between her long fingers. She took the end and wrapped it around her own wrist, then peered up at him, an unspoken question in her eyes.

Maurin winced. "I... I can't. The other half of this already belongs to someone else."

Talauna's direct, unblinking eyes allowed him no room to escape.

"I don't know where she is; I don't know what's happened to her."

Confusion and disappointment—and more than a little hurt—swirled over her face. She gave a deep sigh.

"I'm sorry. Truly I am, from the depths of my heart."

Talauna did not meet his eyes, but neither did she move, so he just sat there, stroking her hair. He could practically hear Aric now: *Nice work, Maurin. Did it again, didn't you? Can't you just love her and be done with it? Why do you have to cling to the past?*

If there were an easy solution to life's dilemmas, he would gladly take it now.

Talauna slept in her own bedroll that night, not too far away, but not too close, either. Maurin lay awake, pondering what to do. His bed, such as it was, felt empty of late; something he had never experienced before. It made sleeping difficult, and concentration almost impossible.

"You confuse her." The voice was pitched low for only Maurin to hear.

He looked up from his bedroll. Valasand had taken first shift, and sat close, regarding Talauna thoughtfully.

"What?"

"I've been watching you. I know you are struggling with your feelings for her and your devotion to your old life. But from her perspective, there is a discrepancy between what you feel and what you do, whereas she always acts on what she feels."

Maurin rolled over, his back to the Warden and the Maolori. "If I acted on what I felt, I wouldn't be true to myself."

"I know. And your principles are part of what make you desirable to her. You may not know how much Talauna restrains herself around you; she does it only because she sees you holding yourself back, and mimics the one she admires the most..."

Maurin ground his teeth. "That doesn't really help."

Valasand continued as if he hadn't spoken. "...but you need to come to a decision about a path. The closer you get, the more you push her away. It's unfair to keep her in limbo."

Valasand moved away to give him some space, but Maurin said nothing, his thoughts a turmoil. The Warden was right. If he wanted to be with Talauna, he should say so, and cast away the past. But if he couldn't, he should leave her alone. Hadn't she been through enough? Was he selfish for wanting her? Was he selfish for not telling her?

Guidance. He needed guidance. When he felt composed enough, he began to murmur in his mother tongue: *"Ar Dia Baelon, kum caratos me li ton'ia, il ste rus matoi varatoia. Ira vas Talauna, un Kirai, un Aric..."*

He stopped short, then waited. As always, his prayer was greeted by silence. But it seemed to him something was wrong; this was more than just the quietude of a god too busy to bother with mortal concerns, or even answering through Maurin's own inner voice. This was the silence of the void.

Have I prayed to nothing all these years? Despair crept in, tainting his soul. *Is Valasand right?*

"Yasul," he said tentatively in Aran. It felt strange, even traitorous to address this foreign god. "I don't know you. I don't even know if you really exist. But if you do, reveal yourself to me. Help me. I love my cousin, and I would do anything to get him back. If this venture requires my death, so be it; I care nothing for myself. But let him live."

Once again, he had appealed to the divine on Aric's behalf.

Once again, he wondered if there was any point.

As before, there was silence. But he felt a strange peace come over him. He didn't sleep much that night, but somehow, it didn't matter. He was on the verge of something, he realized, but what?

———— ◆ ————

She was gone when he awoke.

Typical.

Aric swore. Just once, he would like to have a relationship with a woman who at least stuck around long enough to say good morning. He felt strange—drained and dizzy. Barely able to move, he dragged himself over the edge of the bed and flopped onto the floor.

Ulora. Ulora Vailorscha.

A princess's name. Beautiful, with a touch of mystery.

So Guilan Vail was her son? That didn't seem possible, given that

Guilan was clearly older than she was.

Vailorscha. Mother-of-Vail.

Nothing much made sense around here, but he didn't care. If Dania had seemed familiar to him upon their first meeting, he had known Ulora all his life. And yet, why should that seem so strange? What was he supposed to feel, when meeting face-to-face the woman whose features had haunted his dreams for years? But what was making him feel so odd? He might be in love.

And yet... and yet...

He reached sluggishly for his breeches, his body fighting every command he gave it. Disconnected, he prepared for the day as if wallowing through water. He shook his head to clear the cobwebs.

Interesting. His shoulder no longer hurt when he moved. Gingerly, he tried rotating his arm.

Nothing. Perfectly normal range of motion. Not a twinge of pain.

Completely healed.

Aric grinned.

A serving girl—Ulora's handmaiden, the one who had stared at him so intensely the night before, brought him a plate of fruits and cold meat for breakfast. Still muddled, he did not think to dismiss her, so she simply stayed and watched him eat. Odd, but hardly the oddest thing he'd experienced since his arrival.

When she saw Aric was going to eat no more, the handmaiden cleared her throat, softly suggesting that they go see her mistress, because his presence was desired. Aric tried not to stagger as the girl led him through the alien corridors of Darkhorn Fell to Ulora's quarters. It was all he could do to stay on his feet.

Unlike the austere strangeness of his own, her suite beggared description. Vast maroon draperies hung from the ceiling, and roots had grown into ornate gray chairs. He swayed a bit and saw a root-framed pit filled with water in an antechamber—a bath, perhaps. Golden goblets and jeweled chains festooned the room, and her bed writhed from the center of the floor like a tentacled nest crowned with luxuriant red cushions.

And it was there Aric's lover awaited. Her thick, chestnut hair lifted and moved subtly, as if blown in a gentle wind. Sharp blue-green eyes greeted him, and she opened her arms in a welcoming embrace. Though her kiss left him initially euphoric, fatigue threatened to overwhelm him. His stomach cramped, and the room kept swimming. Was something in the water here making him sick, or was some residual guilt rearing its head? If this was guilt, it was the worst case of it he'd ever had. He felt as though all his energy and vitality were being siphoned off.

"You look unwell, my love," she said. "Lie here on the bed, and let me soothe you."

The handmaiden bowed low and took her leave.

"Ulora, what does Réus want from me?" Aric asked as she stroked his brow. The vertigo grew steadily worse, yet questions still nagged at him. "He said something about the Lifestream, whatever that is, and fate, but I still don't have any idea why I'm here..."

Ulora looked thoughtful. "Well, my love, just as I have been waiting for you, the lord Réus and the lady Aishè have also been waiting for someone. Réus has seen this person in a vision. We all shared in this revelation. The Reamar have searched the furthermost reaches for this special person, in hopes that we will be able to greet him when he arrives."

"So it's a man, then?" Aric blinked, but his vision remained blurry.

"We don't know; it could be a woman. It is definitely a child of man."

"I thought you said he had seen this person in a vision." Aric strained to look at her.

"It was not the face of this Dreaded One Lord Réus saw, but the shining strength of his spirit. Whoever it is will have great power, and the high priestess—the Lady Aishè—believes he will use that power to... to help our people." She frowned, but quickly brightened again. "And so it is very important that we recognize him."

"Réus seems to think it was me," Aric scoffed, though he hardly had the energy to be sarcastic. "Someone is due for a major disappointment."

"We don't know. It could be you. There is no reason it should not be." She smiled down at him, and traced his cold, sweating brow with a single long finger. "Great power flows in your veins, and shines in your soul. Greater, in fact, than I have seen in one so young for a long time. It is obvious for those with eyes to see. I believe you are the... anticipated one."

"Anticipated one, hmm?" Aric said, sitting up. The room started spinning again, and Ulora's image doubled. "That sounds better than Dreaded One. What aren't you telling me? What are they so afraid of?"

Ulora hesitated a moment before answering. "There are those who believe you are here to destroy us. One of these, the young priestess Siaran Thoud, has even fled the Gray Lands, believing there is no sanctuary from you. Others would have killed you if they found you, fearing your power. But I have done all I can to keep you safe from them."

"I don't get it. Why would I want to destroy you? And what do you mean when you say I have some great power?" He should be grateful, he supposed, but it was hard when he just felt more confused than ever.

"Simply that the Lifestream flows strongly in you, Aric, and you may be unaware of your destiny. I believe that in your dreams lies the power to unleash the might of the Reamar." A slight quirk of the mouth. "Or unmake us."

"Now you're sounding like Réus. Or Valasand."

"Is Valasand your lover?"

"No, I don't have another lover." Did Dania count as a lover? Dallying or not, she probably had. Not anymore. She seemed a distant memory. Ulora's features blurred and ran as he struggled to get out, "Valasand is a Warden of the Gates."

"Ah yes. Perhaps it is she that Réus seeks." She laughed. "Though I doubt it. You are stronger than you know. I do not think this Warden you speak of has even an inkling of your power."

"What are you saying?"

"Réus's time is over," Ulora said, her voice soothing and reasonable. "The new era will arise, but it will be the Dreaded One who sits on the throne. The high priestess herself has foreseen this. With the coming of the Dreaded One is the dawning of a new age of power for the gods of the Gray Lands. The followers of the Glorious shall soon worship at the temple of Aric Ulorashain."

Aric pushed away. Him, rule over the Reamar? What was she thinking? He found it impossible to swallow past the lump in his throat, and the room grew dark. "Ulora... what... what's happening to me?"

"I must confess that I have taken something from you, my love,"

Ulora said, perfectly calm. The coils framing her bed seemed to writhe and grasp for him, to drag him down and swallow him. "I have drunk of your spirit and supped of your soul." She held him so he could not look away. "Now, it is your turn. From this moment on, mine will be the last face you see when you go to sleep, and the first thing you see when you awake. You are no longer in the dream, my cherished one, but in the reality of my love. You will draw from my power as I draw from yours, and we will be one in a way you could never imagine."

CHAPTER 36
VIGILANT

"Get up."

Maurin groaned and squinted in annoyance as Masalla's pointed boot toed him in the rear. "That was no full night's sleep."

"Maybe not, but we need to get ready to go." The Warden held up his hands in a helpless gesture. "Valasand's orders."

Maurin grumbled and tossed over in his blanket, trying to catch just a few more moments of rest before facing the day. He felt someone gently but urgently shaking his shoulder.

"I'm up, I'm up!" he growled at his assailant.

Talauna frowned, and her eyes said he needed to get moving.

"All right," he acquiesced, managing a sheepish grin. "I guess the morning air won't kill me." He rolled up his blanket and stuffed it into his pack.

Talauna turned toward the woods, ears pricked up. Shallar's ears flattened, and her mane bristled. Dania's hands went to her knives. "Did you hear that?"

"Hear what?" Maurin asked.

"It sounded like voices."

After a moment, the noise repeated off to the left, in the last stretch of the forest. Maurin listened carefully. "Those aren't voices. It's just some animal."

Talauna grabbed Shallar's huge hand and sprinted off back into the woods, heedless of the others, dragging the Talormine along. Shallar shook herself free, dropped to all fours, and loped off ahead of the girl.

"What are they doing?" Maurin asked, incredulous. "Talauna, where are you going?"

Valasand just shook her head.

Maurin ran after the Talormine and the Maolori, cursing the branches swatting his face. He caught up just in time to see Talauna's feet disappearing over the top of a jumbled pile of rocks.

"Talauna! Snow! I mean, Shallar!" he called in a loud whisper. "Hey!" Reluctantly, he climbed up into a hilly area covered with mossy stones and trees. Brushing himself off, Maurin crept forward through the leaves.

Talauna and Shallar leaned over a large outcropping, transfixed. So earnest and common of purpose were they that Maurin might have thought them deep in conversation. A loud snorting sound interrupted the stillness, followed by a heavy wheeze.

"Oh, gods. Talauna!" he hissed. "What are you doing?"

Before them, in a clearing, a gargantuan pair of wild forest balodonts stood guard over a den. Close cousins of the pachyderm they sold in Langfort, these beasts grazed from the treetops, ambling around, but taking care to avoid a third figure huddled at their feet far below. The large calf held Talauna's attention.

"What? What is it?" Masalla said, suddenly beside him. Dania sidled up moments later, her jaw dropping when she saw the creatures.

"If they catch wind of us, we are in such trouble," Masalla warned. Dania growled low in her throat.

"Are they dangerous?" Maurin asked. "I think they're herbivores. They domesticate smaller ones all the time in the city."

"This is a nest, and that"—Masalla pointed—"is a newborn. The most harmless greens-eating animal in the world is a terror when you get too close to its young. We need to get out of here."

"Talauna," Maurin whispered thinly, "come away from there!"

She threw a peevish glance over her shoulder, stuck her tongue out, and turned her back on him. Resting on her fingertips for a moment, Talauna got up and took several slow, deliberate strides forward.

Maurin gaped after her, making impotent gestures behind her back. Valasand, who had just caught up and joined them, drew in a sharp breath between her teeth, but made no further sound.

It didn't take long for the parents to see her. With a warning bray, they lurched toward Talauna, the ground shaking with each step.

"Oh, no!" Maurin started out after her, but the Talormine stopped him with a vise grip. Shallar locked eyes with him, then turned back to the clearing. Maurin tried to pry the thick fingers away from his arm, but he might as well have tried to cut reinforced steel with a butter knife.

The animals came to a sudden halt. The smaller of the two barked hesitantly, then lowered its head and drew its snout within a few feet of Talauna, who didn't even come up to its knee. With a smile, she stretched out her hand, stroking the bristly skin of the creature's massive forehead.

"Unbelievable," Masalla said.

Valasand smiled. "She has a gift."

Dania stood with her fists on her hips. "We don't have time for this!"

With a bawling moan, the larger animal pushed forward, and Talauna scratched behind its ears.

"Mother or father?" Maurin murmured to Masalla.

"Do I look like a flaming flockherd?"

"Father," Valasand answered. "Definitely."

Now quiet, the two adult beasts enjoyed Talauna's firm petting. After a moment, when the creatures were breathing softly and rhythmically, Talauna reached back, motioning.

"What does she want?" Dania asked.

"She wants Maurin to go in there with her," Valasand said.

"Me?" Maurin's voice broke.

"Yes, you. It was to you she beckoned." Valasand raised an eyebrow at him. "Are you going to hurt her feelings?"

Gritting his teeth, Maurin inwardly cursed the Warden for putting it like that. Hurting Talauna's feelings was one thing. Putting himself in a prime position to get trampled was another. Nevertheless, he walked forward stiffly, afraid his legs might give way any moment as he approached the towering beasts. Animals this large existed back on Sangrine, but his people had been content to let them stay in the wilds. No one was insane enough to try to domesticate them. Or talented enough, he supposed, reluctant to acknowledge what he was seeing.

After an eternity, he was by Talauna's side, staring dumbly at the smelly giant. Talauna favored him with a smile, which made the whole trip worth it. When she realized he wasn't doing anything, she reached over and grabbed his slack arm. Placing her own hand over his, she raised it to the animal's head, making him stroke it with a rough pressure. After a moment, when he was comfortably occupied with one, she took his other hand, and had him petting the heads of both of the creatures.

Then she slipped away.

"Talauna?" he murmured, trying not to panic. *Just keep a grip on yourself and entertain these beasts until she gets back.*

Talauna scampered over to where the calf lay, and caressed it. It licked her hands in pleasure, and she spent several minutes playing and petting. When she was done, she went back to where Maurin was about ready to collapse from anxiety.

Talauna spent a couple of minutes moving her calf-scented hands closer to the parents' nostrils. Maybe she was allowing them to get accustomed to her scent mingled with their calf's. Then she gestured to the others. Shallar dropped heavily from the overhanging rock and landed in a graceful crouch. Valasand walked down, followed by a reluctant Dania, and Masalla brought up the rear.

"Well, girl," Dania groused, "that was just about the stupidest thing I've ever seen. If we don't make too many more of these little side-trips, we might just be able to reach the Gray Lands before winter."

If her gruff demeanor was intended to mask the fact that she was concerned, Maurin thought, it wasn't working. Father had once said anger was often fear in disguise. Maurin knew it—he took several calming breaths himself—but still blurted out, "What is it with women and babies?"

"Maybe she's trying to tell you something, Maurin," Masalla teased.

Talauna just gave them a placid smile. Then she turned her attention back to the animals. The two adults were focused on her, their heads close to the earth. She went to each in turn and pushed downward on their snouts. The animals knelt before her, then settled their great lumbering bulks on the ground in submission. The others were just as confused as Maurin; only the Talormine stood unfazed.

With a quirky grin at Maurin, Talauna scrambled up the leg of the largest beast, grunted, and swung herself over its back and sat astride its neck. She gave its side a few firm slaps and looked meaningfully at the others.

"She must be joking," Dania said. Maurin didn't think he'd ever seen her so pale.

"I don't think so." Valasand seemed to have recovered from her shock. "Penelo, help me up."

Masalla shook his head, but followed her to the other beast, which stayed perfectly still while she maneuvered up its back. He clambered up after her. "Dania, are you with us or with them? I don't think Snow wants to ride."

He was right; the Talormine made no movements in that direction. She waited stoically.

"I don't want to ride," Dania said, her expression grim.

"Suit yourself. You'll have a long walk."

She gave him an exasperated grunt, then shoved Maurin toward Talauna's mount. "Go on. I'll get on behind you."

Sweat broke out on his forehead as he approached the beast's side. The tough skin expanded and contracted with each heaving breath.

Aric, you'll never believe what we're going through to get you. Maurin braced himself, trying to quell the roiling in his stomach. He did his best to ignore the creature's strong scent and the power of the massive limbs, and treated it like a living mountain, climbing up after Talauna. He nearly leapt off when the animal shivered, as it might when bothered by flies, and had to make himself hold still until his heart stopped racing. He struggled to make it the rest of the way, and when he reached Talauna, he held her tightly around the middle. She shifted his arms up, looking back over her shoulder to see if Dania was coming.

The gladiatrix shook her head and vaulted up over the balodont's flank, coming to rest a few feet behind Maurin. Talauna nodded at Shallar, and the Talormine headed off in a southerly direction, this time picking a path with a wider clearing between the trees.

Maurin's stomach lurched as the beast beneath him got to its feet, and he was suddenly and intimately acquainted with several branches. He glanced over to see that the other animal had also risen. The calf was up on its feet and watching its parents. With a snort, the large male took the lead, and followed Shallar's trail out of the woods, the newborn on its heels, the mother bringing up the rear. They made a brief stop at the camp, where Shallar tossed their gear up to them, then set off at a pace no doubt quite leisurely for these enormous animals, but alarmingly fast for Maurin's tastes.

"Valasand is right," Dania said in grudging amazement; "you have a gift, girl."

Talauna just patted the beast and looked straight ahead.

———◆———

"Yasul, hear me. Guide me. Help me. Give me strength."

Valasand sat in a glade far from camp. Her heart hammered and sweat dripped from her brow. She laid her staff across her lap and placed her head in her hands.

Minutes went by, then hours. She prayed, and waited in silence, and prayed again. Nothing. A tear wound its way down her cheek. "I feel so weak. What should I do?"

She heard the rustling of wings, and smiled, squinting into the sudden glow of the apparition. "Jashara!"

"You seem troubled, Little Flame," Huge dark eyes blinked in the midst of the brilliant figure shimmering hazily before her. "Take comfort. Yasul has heard you."

Valasand loved the sound of his voice, heard all too seldom of late. "I am afraid I have failed badly, Master."

"How so?" The glowing visitor gave the impression of raised eyebrows, though of course he had none to raise—as far as Valasand could tell, anyway. The Vigilant were so nebulous, so mercurial. Visits from them outside the Temple were rare, and when they did make an appearance, they swirled in and out of reality like fiery sheets drifting in water.

"We seek one of our companions, the first one to whom the Breath led me. I believe that even if we find him, it may be too late."

"We have seen this. Why do you believe as you do?"

"He is gifted; he has the soul and sight of a prophet. He is the one who heard your voice as we spoke in the mansion. But he is young and inexperienced; I should have nurtured him more, lent him more wisdom. I should have told him his ability to dream is a gift to be used for the glory of Yasul."

"And you think you may have failed because of that." His brilliant gaze penetrated her expectantly.

"Yes," she near-whispered, eyes downcast. Successes were so much better to report. "I truly do not understand what has happened, or what I need to do." Valasand met the kindly but overpowering gaze, and her throat tightened. "This is beyond my abilities, and it frightens me. What if I fail in this challenge?"

"Life goes on." He smiled, but not without compassion. "Probably a little harder than before."

"Thank you," she said dryly.

"Ah, Little Flame," Jashara said, his rich voice resonating with ethereal beauty. He laid a comforting hand on her shoulder; a nearly useless gesture, since she felt no physical sensation other than the peculiar tingle that always accompanied one of his visits. "You have always known, but never been able to accept, that you are not perfect. And that because you are not perfect, you will fail. Failure is part of life. Yasul does not hold failure against you. You must learn from your failures, build upon them. You see so little with your human eyes."

"So you keep reminding me."

"You do not know you have failed," he admonished.

"You never did like to make things easy for me, did you?"

"If life were easy, you would not care to live it."

"I could stand it being a little easier," Valasand griped. "So what am I supposed to do now?"

"You are doing what you must, even as my brother, the Guardian of the Well, told you. Yasul has decreed that you must seek out this young man who has attracted the attention of the Reamar. All else has been hidden from me. Even we do not know everything."

"I wish you could go with me."

"That time will come, Little Flame. But for now, our abilities to intervene are limited by the wisdom and decree of Yasul. We continue to guide and instruct, and act as we are allowed. We are but envoys in this realm. In the meantime, you are not to rely on us, but your strength in him."

Valasand nodded. "I know. But it's so hard, sometimes."

"Whoever told you it was going to be otherwise?" The paternal glow of his smile outshone his natural glory.

"It certainly wasn't you."

"You are a good student to me, and a faithful servant to Yasul. You will be rewarded."

"I don't want a reward."

Jashara laughed. "Nevertheless, a reward is yours—and there is nothing wrong with looking forward to it. But for this life and this moment, know that you are watched over, and never are you out of the sight or care of Yasul, even when all seems silent, and hope has fled." Her instructor and guide folded in on himself, the light winked out, and in a split second, Jashara fluttered away as a white bird. She watched his passing wistfully, too deep in thought to notice the other presence behind her until she heard her voice.

"You commune with the gods?"

Valasand whipped her head around. It was Dania. "You saw?"

Dania nodded, her face pallid in the moonlight.

"Not gods," Valasand said, "though many have called them such. Jashara is one of the Vigilant of whom we have spoken. Servants of Yasul, instructors to the Wardens."

Dania sat beside her. "Tell me."

INTERLUDE
FIRSTWORLD

Show me.

As you wish, my love.

It begins with a word; a word that comes from nowhere, and from everywhere. I cannot understand the speech, but it is power and energy and majesty given voice. All is dark. Then a pinprick of light rotates slowly around a black void. A swirling mass of plasma spins outward from the darkness within the darkness, like water flowing backwards, a whirlpool in reverse. It is a fountain, pouring forth the stuff of worlds. More lights coalesce, appearing on the edges of the expanding eddy, and the voice divides—no, multiplies—becoming a chorus of unimaginable beauty. The fountain continues to whirl, and the universe spreads itself before me like a tablecloth.

What am I seeing?

Firsttime.

Unfolding before me, I see the formation of countless stars, planets, worlds upon worlds upon worlds, time dilating and distorting, edges of the newborn cosmos ancient even as the center is still being conceived. When the fount of creation pours itself out, near the center of the universal tapestry lies an infinitesimal point of blue-green light.

Firstworld?

Yes.

Pristine. Immaculate. I have dreamed of beauty, of death, of everything under a dozen suns, but have never before seen perfection incarnate. Realm of glory, realm of flesh; intertwined, inextricable, balanced. Life blossoming and growing on every plane, fecundity, sheer bliss of existence.

It lasts but the blink of an eye, or so it seems. Somehow, it is spoiled. The rejoicing I had sensed becomes a desperate lament, a mourning of loss I can't even begin to comprehend. The stars become blazing flashes of light, warring with one another. Swords of spirit clash; glorious, shining beings moving whole worlds in their struggle. The sense of grief grows unbearable, and I feel tears running down my cheeks.

At the same time, I see wars on the Firstworld, evil against evil, arrogance, pride, perversion, ever-decreasing good. Discovery of gateways to other worlds. Flight. The children of Firstworld begin anew, whole cultures arising independently of one another on these islands of the empty seas, separated by immeasurable space and time. I turn away as I see a cosmic enforcer aimed directly at Firstworld, set to smite the planet in two. Surely nothing can survive such a blow.

The battles of the higher realms continue and abate. Victory—no, defeat. Dark eyes fill my soul, surrounded by a light so painful I can hardly stand to look. Then the mighty ones are humbled, their visages diminished. Their light gone, they become gray and withered mockeries of their former selves. They crawl off into the dark, crying, pleading, cursing.

Not fair!

How could you!

We hate you!

The shadow figures flee. I watch as a vessel carrying thousands of them spins and twists through the vast emptiness between the stars. Cold and lifeless as its inhabitants, or so it seems. It is like a shard of rock, or a disconnected branch, asymmetrical, ugly. Lethal.

What is this?

The seed of a new beginning.

The shard drifts, tumbling end over end, and it approaches another planet nearly as beautiful as the Firstworld. It is raining, the clouds rent by the sudden intrusion of a massive meteorite, a blade of obsidian stabbing the sky in violent rage. Streamers of steam and mist follow the colossal missile down to the planet's surface, where it impacts, piercing and impaling the world like a javelin thrown by the gods. The land bubbles and warps, and I feel the shock waves as it attempts to reject this intrusion, this blasphemy that stands now at an odd angle, defying the very mountains framing it.

I see them, now—they crawl, broken, miserable, out of the crack the ship created. Dark spirits fill the winds, and howl through the night. The first tribes of Maolori, coming to see what evil star had descended upon their world, are set upon and killed, their lives soaked up like water with a sponge. Animals, too, fall to the wounded rage of the Gray Ones, and almost as soon as the seed is planted, the legacy of death begins.

Cities rise and fall, and gray tendrils spread like a spider web, radiating outward from the base of the fallen monument and cleaving to the land. Roots penetrate deep into the earth, and the former vessel itself begins to grow as the power of the Reamar grows. Thick buds form along its top and side, and leafless branches twist and grow; tenacious fingers of an obscene hand. The transport of the Reamar grasps at the terrain even as it seems to stretch upward to grapple with the moons. The land is transformed and absorbed into the mountain-tree, grafting itself into a new warped reality.

I feel the burning hate of the Reamar, the desire to crack the shell of this world open and rebuild it anew in their likeness. Time means nothing; I know not when I am born, nor how I am tied to the fate of these beings. But as my own awareness grows, so grows the strength of the Reamar. I see the Gray Lands expanding, the potency returning.

I see Ulora.

Oh, how I see her.

I see her beauty, her strength, blossoming like a flower in the midst of a desert. I see myself; I am hunted. Hunted for longer than I could have known. Perhaps longer than I have been alive. Then I see the dark eyes of another woman who wants to kill me, the woman who slaughtered hundreds, if not thousands, in my name. My innards churn as I realize that innocents have died so I might not have the chance to fulfill my destiny.

But I didn't want any of this! Who is this woman?

She is not important right now. I will keep you safe from her.

Among the chaos, I see the golden-haired figure of Guilan Vail, ever watchful.

He hunted me down like an animal.

Your hunter, and your protector. I sent him so you would not end up like these others, my beloved.

Why?

Because I love you. I always have.

Just as the roots of the temple-tree had penetrated and cleaved unto the fabric of this world, so Ulora's essence pierces and weaves into mine. I am aware of giving, of taking, of blending, of living, of dying, the ebb and flow of an unfathomable union. I love her, and make love to her, our bodies and souls intertwined. Dream-world and reality commingle, the power of life surges through my veins and energizes my spirit.

Am I Aric? Or am I Ulora?

We are both. We are—I am—one.

Yes. I am yours.

As I am yours, beloved. We belong to one another; we are one another. And together, we shall be glorious.

CHAPTER 37
OTHERWORLD

Dania hadn't expected to see the Gray Lands so soon. But there they were, nestled in the depths of a broad valley. In the middle of the afternoon, the animals had just topped a hill when they pulled to a stop. Dania's thoughts turned black as she surveyed the scene before her. To her left, the low arm of the Danir mountain range rose like broken teeth. The peaks climbed ever higher into the distance, while the speckled green slopes at their feet turned into steep hills covered with heather and brush. Ahead, several leagues away in the valley, an ashen stain stretched off as far as the eye could see. It was as if a terminal malaise had stricken the land itself.

Dania squinted at the border of the Gray Lands, where the verdant folds of the earth gave way to a snarl of evil monochromatic vines. The vegetation on the edges was sickly and twisted. The plants had taken on an odd hue of green, and leaves and stalks were bent, deformed.

Dying.

The Talormine had led them to the right place, clearly, but had she ever been through the Reamar territory? Did she know the way to this Darkhorn Fell? How could they ever get there in time, or navigate this alien domain? Would they even be able to help Aric if they found him?

The level ground dropped into a broadening valley, both sides rising above them as they traveled. Curved and twisted like the path of an ancient river, the canyon soon became nearly wide enough to be a valley. Though no water flowed through the land, a mist rose in a great cloud, making everything hazy. The fog swirled above and through the Gray Lands. At the widest points of the gorge, she could not see the walls of rock on either side.

But then the veil parted, and Dania gasped despite herself.

Twisted and thrust out of the ground at an unnatural angle, the silhouette of the tree of ages loomed ahead like a massive citadel, an unbreakable testament to its own strength and ancient glory. Wreaths of mist drifted around it, adorning the spire in a death shroud.

"Darkhorn Fell," Valasand whispered.

Hard to miss after all. Dania halfway expected Shallar, having brought them this far, to bolt. She did not. Apparently even the horse-head still felt obligation to the one who had saved her life.

"Cheerful place," Masalla said.

Maurin went pale. "Don't be afraid," Dania said, though she wasn't quite sure why. He tossed a strange look over his shoulder at her.

For the Holy One, there was no beginning. Yasul was, and is, and always will be...

Dania couldn't quite get her mind around what she had seen last night, or understand all the things Valasand had told her. But she knew that for the first time in her life, she felt true freedom. With that knowledge came something she wasn't really quite sure how to handle, but Valasand said it was joy. It seemed incongruous here, in this place of doom, but Dania's spirit remained unfettered.

If the Highest of the High saw value in her, perhaps she could learn to see it in herself.

What kind of sacrifice does your god require?

None, save yourself.

What do you mean?

You must become Yasul's, entirely and irrevocably. Are you willing to give up who you are in order to become the person you are meant to be?

"So what, exactly, are we going to do when we get there?" Maurin's voice intruded into her thoughts.

Valasand cast her gaze upon the forked spike of the eldritch tree. "I honestly don't know, Maurin. Yasul will guide and protect us; more I cannot say."

At one time, this answer would have been most unsatisfactory. Maurin slumped at Valasand's words. Yet Dania felt a certain peace and assurance in them. "We shall find Aric."

The animals grew skittish, and the closer they came to the encroaching Gray Lands, the more reluctant they became. Finally, they stopped altogether, and refused to move any further.

"I guess we're on our own," Masalla said.

Talauna patted the beast on the neck, and it knelt, situating itself on the ground well away from the unsettling edge of the Reamar world. Once the entire group had climbed off the animals' backs, the creatures leapt thunderously to their feet and loped away, just slowly enough that the calf could keep up. Before long, they were out of sight. The group spent a few minutes massaging their buttocks and legs, and Maurin pressed his fists into his lower back. The ride had been anything but gentle.

"Let's be on our way," Valasand said. "This isn't going to get any easier."

With a deep breath, Dania took the first step across the threshold. The air congealed around her with the cold stillness of a cave. The tangled hedge of vines reached above her head. The root-like tendrils of gray did not so much break the ground as merge with the dead and powdery soil. Peering up, she could not see the sun.

They pushed deeper into the Gray Lands. Dania thought she caught a glimpse of shadowy forms flitting through the murk. She had an acute sense of being watched through the uncanny silence. No birds flew overhead, no animals rustled through the leaves. For that matter, the stark gray vines were bare of leaves. She pressed on one, and it refused to yield.

Maurin tried his strength on the same vine. When it didn't move, he braced himself, and put his whole force behind the effort.

"Might as well try to move a mountain," Dania mused.

Maurin stopped, breathing heavily from the exertion. "What is this place?"

"We are heading toward the heart of evil," Valasand said. "Remember what Masalla said; the Reamar do not wholly inhabit our world. We have entered theirs now."

Pity for Maurin stabbed at Dania. She could see the pain in his eyes, and knew he was wrought with fear over the fate of his cousin. She wished someone cared that deeply about her.

Then again, she thought, *maybe someone does.* Valasand's words regarding Yasul's persistent love came back to her. Still, a yearning she had not allowed herself for years tugged at her heart. The man who called himself her father—was he still alive?

They walked for days, it seemed, in a perpetual state of twilight,

ducking under the vines here and crawling over them there, tearing clothing and scratching skin. It got dark much later than Dania expected, and
stayed dark longer. Time crawled in this place. They had no wood to
burn for a fire, and so they simply wrapped up in their blankets and ate
from their dry rations. No one spoke. No one wanted to. The silence of
the Gray Lands was deafening.

Dania began to wonder if they had lost their way, but Masalla
pointed out that the roots were getting larger, so they must be getting
closer. As the massive vines gained in size, so did the spaces between
them, and before she knew it, Dania found herself not at a clearing, exactly, but a gap allowing her to see the base of the mountain. She realized,
in one heart-stopping moment, that the entire Gray Lands radiated outward from Darkhorn Fell, and all the roots and vines met their terminus
at its base. The Gray Lands were the tree of stone, whose roots spread
outward and reshaped the very fabric of the world.

She glanced at the Wardens. No one even commented. Maurin swallowed, and Talauna squeezed his hand. The bristles of Shallar's mane
stood erect, and her long face was pinched and drawn. At last, Valasand
gave a slight nod and moved towards it; Dania followed as if in a dream.
The ground dipped toward the base of the tree as they drew nearer, and
an opening appeared in the rock. Above the larger opening were two
smaller indentations in the surface of Darkhorn Fell. Dania had a strong
impression of a face with elongated features; high, sharp cheekbones, and
a gaping maw dropping open into the earth, waiting to consume those
who passed through. A bizarrely fleshed skull loomed over them, the
brow swept back into a grotesque parody of a pointed headdress. The
ground, as it rose around them, had the appearance of outstretched arms,
drawing them with fingerless malevolence into that horrible mouth.

The illusion faded as they walked forward, and the perspective
changed the hazy light on the tree, but she couldn't help feeling unsettled
anyway.

*Valasand says the Source is always near, even walking with us through
dark valleys. I hope she is right.*

The Talormine sniffed and stopped in her tracks. Talauna held up a
warning palm, and Dania heard a distant muffled sound, like the

simultaneous beating of multiple rugs. As it drew rapidly closer, she recognized the strokes of giant wings.

A chorus of angry shrieks burst out, and the mists boiled with the strangest creatures she had ever seen. Larger than a human, they had the wings of a bat, and the sloped foreheads and powerful jowls of apes. The black forms bore down on the party with a vengeance.

The first one reached for Masalla with its thumbed feet, but his sword was out in a trice. It gave a screeching howl and flew off as the Warden slashed. Dania saw Talauna lifted from the ground by another, and threw her dagger with all her might. There was a horrible scream of fury and pain, and Talauna fell crashing through the vines. Her abductor wheeled in the air and turned back on Dania. It opened its powerful jaws, and dove straight for her.

Dania set her legs and slashed with her remaining knife. The animal fell in a crumpled heap at her feet. It moaned, and attempted to straighten up, but the Talormine strode over and stepped on the back of its neck, snapping it. The creature shivered once and lay still. Then, as with the Reamar in Mor Tespir, a black and green plasma exited the creature's mouth, leaving the body a withered husk. The misty energy took shape, a headless mass of darkness that was all wings. Two malevolent spots glowed near the center, where the shoulders should have been. Dania spasmed with a sudden chill.

Valasand did her best to keep the creatures at bay with her staff. The phantom flew at her, ephemeral claws reaching out to rake at her heart. She swept at the dark form, but the wood passed through it harmlessly. The specter entered her body, and Valasand gasped, staggering backwards, grasping at her chest. The creature was upon her in the blink of an eye. It swept down, and Valasand was lost under a barrage of billowing, insubstantial wings. The formless horror battered her, beating her down. Dania vaulted over and struck at the bodiless beast, but her blows simply passed through the cold void of its spirit.

"Stand back, Dania." Masalla walked up, almost calmly, and addressed the creature: "You! Shadow-spawn! Leave her alone! This one's soul is not yours to claim."

It was all the distraction Valasand needed. When the specter turned its attention upon the other Warden, she rolled to her knees. She muttered what Dania assumed was a prayer to Yasul. With a scream to match the creature's own, Valasand plunged her staff into its center, shattering the phantasm. The shreds of its spirit fluttered away and dissipated into the mists.

At the specter's death-scream, the other flying demons retreated, screeching in rage and fear. The mists swirled around their departing forms, and many of them settled on vines not too far away. One of them spread its wings and uttered a hoarse cry, soon taken up by the others. It was a piercing combination of a shrill squeal and the throaty vocalization of a primate.

Exhausted, Valasand rolled over and lay in the dust. Dania rushed over to the crumpled form beneath the cloak. Masalla was at her side in an instant. "Vals?"

There was no response.

You cannot die... I will not let you...

For a moment, Dania was a young girl again. A bloodthirsty audience applauded as a great woman fell. Dania shook the sounds out of her head, clamped her teeth together, and focused on Valasand.

Dropping to his knees, Masalla helped Dania turn her over. "Come on, now, don't give up here. You're tougher than that."

Valasand moaned, and opened her eyes, drifting in and out of consciousness. "Penelo?"

Dania closed her eyes, determined not to show her relief.

"What happened?" Masalla demanded.

Valasand closed her eyes. "Help me up."

Dania grasped one arm, while Masalla supported his comrade's other. Together they pulled her to a shaky standing position. "How did it get to you?"

"I'm not sure, exactly." She frowned. "Its claws were at my heart, and then..."

"Look sharp," Dania said.

Wolf-shaped creatures with the bulk and mass of summer bears bounded forward out of the dark thicket of roots. They growled fiercely and circled the party, green eyes glowing with malice. Behind them, the mists shimmered, and countless mounted warriors emerged from the shadows.

It seemed one moment as if the Reamar moved so fast the eye couldn't follow, and the next, they appeared to be under water, their long hair floating in unseen currents. The one in the lead focused directly on her, his dark locks swaying about his face. He drew his sword, an evil-looking blade, with a weighted curve and a jagged top edge.

"*Ka vada khadamar!*"

"I don't like the sound of that," Masalla said, shifting the grip on his sword.

"Nor I." Maurin placed himself between Talauna and the wolves. The Talormine's sides heaved, and she poised to leap at any moment. The other warriors had their weapons drawn, as well, and leapt to the attack, rushing the six companions as one.

In a heartbeat, all was chaos.

The leader set upon Masalla, swinging his sword in a blur of motion. But the Warden was prepared. Masalla's blade passed under the sword one instant, and through his attacker the next. Dania barely had time to be impressed at the couple of wolves lying at Masalla's feet, when she had to fend off a few of her own. Valasand, still pale and shaken, but clearly regaining her strength, stared down a Reamar warrior who circled well out of reach of her staff. Maurin's opponent was still alive, but a stream of blood pumped from the side of his neck, and each jet was weaker.

"Not bad," Dania said, clapping Maurin on the back. He looked sick. One of Shallar's victims lay in a contorted heap against a massive root, blood dripping from a spot three feet above the body, evidently where the Reamar's head had hit when she threw him.

Then the screaming started.

An unearthly howling shriek of pain, like that of a wounded animal, resounded through the gray tangles, turning Dania's blood to ice. She whirled around and saw Talauna clutching at her leg. A braided Reamar spear had passed completely through the Maolori girl's upper thigh. Blood flowed steadily from the wound, and Talauna was close to passing out, her eyelids fluttering, and her eyes starting to roll back.

Maurin was at her side, crying out her name in panic. The warriors and their wolves moved in with the steady assurance of vastly superior strength. Dania was good, she knew, but there were too many of them, and the hateful supernatural glow in their eyes told her there would be no victory for her today. There was nothing more she could do. A strange peace settled over her. Pity she would not be able to help Aric get away from these demons.

She had just about made up her mind to charge again, and take as many of the Reamar with her as she could, when a familiar voice called out.

"Stop! Let them go!"

CHAPTER 38
REVELATION

"Aric?" There was no joy in the recognition; Maurin was too stunned.

Sitting astride one of the reptilian steeds, his cousin wore ornate dark pants gathered at the ankle and puffed out at the waist, and an intricately filigreed coat of shimmering green and black. Aric's hair now fell to his shoulders, as if he had been gone for years. And his left ear sported a silver earring with tiny figures scrimshawed into its elegant curve.

He didn't look at all glad to see them. "What are you doing here, Maurin?"

"Coming after you; what do you think?"

"There's no time for this," Dania said. "The girl is injured."

"Call off your dogs, young one," Masalla said, his eyes cold and hard.

Aric seemed as if he would like to retort, but instead he nodded, and the man beside him gave a quiet order in a fluid language. The other warriors bowed—as did their steeds—and turned in unison, walking off into the mists. The great hunting wolves lowered their heads toward Aric, and also left. Only he and his companion, a blond man with shining eyes, remained.

Masalla sheathed his sword, moving with rapid strides over to help Maurin stanch the flow of blood from Talauna's thigh. Valasand stripped away the leg of Talauna's pantaloons with clinical efficiency.

"Thank Yasul this weapon isn't barbed. Hold her still, Maurin." Placing one hand on the Maolori girl's leg, and grabbing the spear with the other, Masalla took a quick breath. Then with a smooth motion, he pulled the weapon out and cast it aside, causing Talauna to cry out again. Sobs of pain racked her body. "Press here."

Maurin gritted his teeth, looking from Talauna to the distant eyes of his cousin and his blond Reamar companion. Valasand used the strips of cloth from Talauna's ruined pants to bind the wound, pressing two knots of fabric against the holes to add pressure. Shallar hovered, and Talauna fainted.

"What are we going to do?" Fortunately it was easy for Maurin to focus on Talauna, because otherwise it would be all too easy to strangle Aric for his seeming indifference.

For the first time, the man riding the beast beside Aric spoke: "Bring your little one into Eulith Soren, and she will live."

The Wardens exchanged a quick glance and somber nods.

At a gesture from Valasand, the Talormine swept the girl into her arms, carrying her as easily as she would a baby. Talauna's head lolled against the creature's broad shoulder. Aric turned his mount back toward the base of the temple, and his companion did the same. They kept a slow pace so the others on foot could keep up. For a while, Maurin could say nothing.

Dania, however, had no such reservations. "We came for you, Aric, thinking you had been taken. But you weren't taken, were you?" she accused, face clouded over. "You left us."

Aric kept his eyes on Darkhorn Fell. "I didn't leave you. I heard somebody calling me when the fog rolled in. I... just followed the voice. I couldn't help myself."

"I'll bet you couldn't," Dania said.

Aric tapped his own temples questioningly. "So what happened to you?"

It took Maurin a moment to realize that he was talking about the new streaks of white in his hair. "One of your friends got a hold of me, and didn't want to let go," he finally managed to say. "We made a trip across this entire country to rescue you, and here you are, being treated like royalty, giving orders to these... these..."

"What made you think I needed to be rescued?" Aric shrugged. "Would you rather find me in a dungeon, being tortured or starved to death?"

"Well, no, of course not," Maurin floundered. "But..."

"I'm in no hurry. In case you haven't noticed, they seem to like having me here."

"That's obvious." Something in Aric's countenance bothered Maurin. The arrogance and smugness in his tone was overbearing, even for Aric. This was not his cousin as he knew him. "But this isn't your place."

"How do you know?" Aric asked, not really defensive, but clearly baiting him anyway. That, at least, was in character.

"Well," Maurin said at last, "I'm glad to see you're all right."

Dania walked in silence on the other side of Shallar. For once, it seemed, she didn't even have the strength to comment further, let alone fight. She bit at her lower lip, and her forehead furrowed. Cold waves of nausea swept over Maurin at the intensity of her emotions.

Talauna's face was pale, and she remained blissfully unaware of the betrayal they all felt. Maurin envied her.

Aric jerked his head over his shoulder at Shallar and Masalla. "Who're they?"

"Penelo Masalla, Warden of the Gates. This is Shallar; she agreed to help us find you. Though I'm beginning to wonder if our efforts are worth anything in your eyes."

Aric shot him a resentful look. "I'm grateful. But you shouldn't have come."

What have they done to you? Maurin walked up closer to Aric's reptilian steed and pitched his voice low. "What's wrong with you? Have you forgotten who these people are?"

"Do you even know who these people are?" Aric cast his gaze down at Maurin.

"I've a pretty good idea, and I can't believe you're in league with them. Have you forgotten Mor Tespir already?"

"Shut up, Maurin. Now isn't the time."

They neared a dark furrow in the base of the tree, between two of the most prominent roots. The group walked into shadow, but Maurin wasn't aware of actually going through a passageway. Rather, the air got colder around them, and they plunged into a darkness defying explanation. Soon a light flickered ahead, and they walked toward it, their footsteps dull and muffled.

Aric and his companion led the group into a cavernous vault, in the midst of which towered a twisting fountain of pale green flame. It swayed gently and licked at the uppermost reaches of the chamber, but put off no smoke or heat. If anything, Maurin realized, the air felt colder as they got nearer to the glow. It illuminated a dismal gray world honeycombed with baffles and channels, all leading off into darkness. The twisting heights of this enormous hollow went far above what he could see, turning, no doubt, with the angled bulk of the tree.

A chill slid down Maurin's spine at the overwhelming sense that the whole temple was aware, and alive with a single purpose.

They were not alone. Shadows moved around them, resolving into hundreds of Reamar falling into step, a procession of the damned. Maurin's heart almost stopped when he saw them walking straight down the dark inner surface of the tree toward them. From the tunnels and arteries woven throughout the entire surface, more Reamar emerged like insects from a nest.

The Reamar's clothing and hair billowed around them, stirred by that same current he could not see or feel. None of them uttered a sound. He couldn't figure out any ethnic pattern; there were people with light skin, people with dark skin, almond eyes, blue eyes, green eyes—all cold and accusing, and filled with hate. He saw a few younger ones, but no children. The very youngest—adolescents—still wore the same stony, knowing scowl of the adults. Maurin shuddered as he recalled the unholy ritual in Mor Tespir.

Then it hit him.

These are slaves!

The Reamar must have been using the bodies of the humans Argoneis sent them, inhabiting them as casually as they might don another set of clothing.

Valasand nodded at him in sorrow, her expression telling him that she, too, had guessed the truth.

"This must end," the Warden said quietly.

Resentment mounted in the air, an almost palpable desire to get rid of the outsiders.

Or devour us.

Maurin thought his skin might just crawl right off his bones.

After Aric and the Reamar dismounted and handed off their steeds to an attendant, the group passed from the large inner chamber into a narrow tunnel seeming no different from the others. The horde had dropped back when they entered the crevice, and they were now alone with Aric and the Reamar man. Throughout the passage, tendrils of greenish flame danced like wisps of swamp-fire.

The uphill passageway terminated in a columned hall. A bald man sat at the end of it on a throne resembling a miniature version of Darkhorn Fell itself. His expressionless eyes shone with an air of languid solemnity as the group approached.

"Lord Réus," the blond Reamar said, "we present to you companions of Master Aric."

"Greetings." The voice was like the whispering roar of a distant waterfall. "I am Réus of the Reamar. I am honored that you would travel so far to visit my home. But what has happened here?"

"Lord Réus." Valasand bowed from the neck. "We sought our companion, and were set upon by your forces. Our young friend was injured in the melee."

Ten Reamar surrounded the throne, five to each side. The male at Réus's left hand had long dark hair and stern blue eyes. The resentment he bore the newcomers frosted his handsome features and cut through his self-important veneer.

The priestess to the right of Réus took Maurin's breath away as surely as if he'd been dealt a physical blow. Incomparably intense dark eyes bored into him. The presence of this one, Maurin thought, would be enough to wither the strongest of men. Her hair, which fell almost to her feet, was so dark as to appear black in the dim light. She had the appearance of one who seldom, if ever, smiled.

Next to her stood a heart-stoppingly lovely woman, with all the grace and poise that only a lifetime of self-refinement could give a person. Her eyes were lucent cobalt snares, the pupils unnaturally small in the dim light. They hid everything, and saw all.

Maurin despised her immediately.

The god-king stood and indicated the spot before his throne. "Set your wounded here."

Maurin tried not to think about how much it looked like a sacrificial altar.

Valasand gestured to Shallar that she should lay Talauna down. Though her expressionless Talormine face remained nearly impossible to read, she complied. Talauna moaned. Blood seeped around the makeshift bandage on her leg and dripped onto the floor.

Réus knelt above her, and laid one hand on her forehead, the other on her leg, just above the wound. He glanced up at Masalla. "You have come for us."

"Yes. I had heard rumors of war, and of gathering power. Entire villages are left deserted, or filled with people with empty eyes. We have seen this for ourselves."

"Interesting occurrences, no doubt," Réus said flatly, "but why would these things concern you?"

"We are Wardens of the Gates." Masalla inclined his head, keeping his eyes riveted on the god-king.

Maurin glanced at Talauna and bit his lip. Couldn't they hurry?

"Do explain."

Masalla stepped forward. "We serve the order of the Breath, the Temple of the Source, whose sphere of influence extends across the stars. We are keepers of the ancient Wells, through which the progenitors of our race passed when they first pioneered the worlds."

Maurin struggled to rein in his temper. He had placed his trust in Valasand. Surely if Talauna were in any immediate danger, this Warden wouldn't bandy words with this ruler of darkness. Then again, they were at the mercy of the Reamar, and no doubt Masalla realized that.

"I know of your order," Réus said, though his tone did not indicate whether he was impressed by it. "Your coming has been foretold. There exists a prophecy about a liberator of the chained, one who would open a gateway to freedom. Is that how you arrived here?"

"I arrived on a ship," Valasand said. Masalla didn't reply. Perhaps he felt they had already said too much.

Talauna moaned again, and Réus stroked her forehead with surprising gentleness. "Be still, little one." She went limp at his touch. He closed his eyes and focused inward.

A cold wind passed through Maurin's body, stirring his soul. Looking at the others, he realized he was not alone in feeling the pull; the Reamar was drawing energy to himself, siphoning it from the rest of them. Maurin attempted in vain to shake off the draining sensation

"What are you doing?" Dania strode forward, clenching her fists at her sides and gritting her teeth.

"Quiet, Dania," Masalla said.

Valasand nodded, and held up a restraining hand, provoking an incredulous stare. Dania no doubt thought she had lost her mind.

The other Reamar watched Réus with indifference. All except the powerful woman with the dark eyes; she appeared angry, for some reason Maurin couldn't fathom.

"Your connection to this one is the strongest," Réus addressed Maurin, keeping his eyes closed. "You will feel the sharpest tug."

And so he did. He sagged to his knees, and with a sickening pull, he had a sudden odd sense of entering, of becoming one with Talauna in an intimate union no one else could possibly imagine. He felt his soul touch hers, and mingle with it. Maurin's own heart beat in unison with hers, lending strength to her fading pulse. Awe gradually replaced the shock of the initial sensation as he merged with her inner being, traveling down the pathways of Talauna's bloodstream, feeling her breathe.

There was a slight deviation in the rhythm, a flutter that Maurin couldn't quite place. The pulse was compounded by a lesser echo, a vibration within a vibration—alternate rhythms in the core of the girl's being. Alarmed, he thought he heard himself call out, as if from a great distance, but no one responded.

He felt the break in the continuity of Talauna's otherwise healthy body, the pain and inflammation surrounding the gap, the interruption in the rhythm, like a stone in the middle of a smoothly flowing stream. He weakened with her as each beat of Talauna's heart brought her closer to permanent darkness.

Everything went black.

Then the others were around him, patting him awake, and Shallar helped him to his feet. Slowly, his vision cleared, and the Talormine let him go when he was steady enough to stand on his own. The sensation of having his life drawn off was gone. In its place was an odd feeling of melancholy, a realization that he had come close to Talauna in a way he could never explain or duplicate.

"She and her offspring will live," the god-king said.

"Thank Yasul," Valasand murmured, closing her eyes.

"She and—what?" Masalla said.

"This little one carries a child within her," Réus explained.

"She's pregnant?" Maurin gasped, shock overriding his pain.

"I knew it!" Aric said. The Reamar woman smiled.

Suddenly, it seemed, all eyes were on Maurin.

"Don't look at me like that!" Maurin snapped at his cousin. "If she is, it's not mine, you idiot!"

"She must have been pregnant when I ransomed her at the slave auction," Valasand mused.

Aric bit his lip, looking strangely disappointed. "Krige, you drunk old buzzard." For a moment, Maurin thought he saw the compassion he knew of old.

Réus stared at Valasand. "A child of great destiny," the god-king continued, as though he had a bad taste in his mouth. "In four months' time, she will give birth to a female who will grow to be a mighty weapon in the hands of your god."

———————— ◆ ————————

Valasand had stayed behind with Réus. Though she must have her reasons, Maurin hated having her out of sight. It felt like abandonment, but was the fear he felt for her, or for the rest of them? Dead-eyed slaves led them down a series of corridors to a large, ovoid room. Sheets of flowing formations partitioned the chamber into three smaller sections. A single low bed lay in the main area past the first separation, and Shallar laid Talauna down gently in its center. Under the sticky sheen of drying blood, the wound was healed.

The slaves exited without a word, leaving them to their own devices.

Blood covered Maurin's hands, so he laved them in a stream flowing sideways along the middle of the wall. The Talormine snorted and followed suit when he indicated her soaked coat.

Several cushions and mats lay on the floor. Maurin sat on a cushion beside Talauna and pulled the sheets up over her. The Talormine circled the floor next to the bed a couple of times, then dropped to all fours, and half-reclined between her and the entryway.

"I don't know what I'd do if you were gone," Maurin whispered, ruffling Talauna's tempest of massed curls. "This may well be the second worst day of my life."

"So... this pregnancy complicates things a bit," Masalla said from across the room. "And you say you didn't know about this?"

"No."

"You two spent all that time together, and you didn't even notice?" Dania asked skeptically.

"How was I supposed to know?" Maurin exploded. "She doesn't look pregnant."

Why was he feeling so jealous of Talauna all of a sudden? He wanted her all to himself, and wished the others would—could—just go away.

Selfish. Stupid.

Gently, he grasped her limp hand. He stroked it for a while, then rested it against his cheek, clasping it there in his own, and curling her little fingers around his.

Talauna's mouth was partly open, her petal-soft lips seemingly inviting a kiss. Seeing no reason to refuse such a polite invitation, he kissed them. Talauna's breath caught for a moment, and Maurin froze, fearful he had wakened her. But she let it out in a coo of contentment and rolled closer to him.

Shallar snorted at him, and kept an eye on Maurin, though she seemed willing to let him stay beside her.

"My silent angel," he whispered, stroking Talauna's ear with his thumb. "I could float away on your sea of calm, and never turn back." How he wished she could—or would—give voice to whatever lay inside her... her happiness, her sorrows. "Don't worry. I won't let anything happen to you. Ever."

"We have a visitor," Dania said, stepping aside with a look of distaste.

A voice made its way through the entryway, reverberating in Maurin's mind even as it fell softly on his ears: "It's just me."

He watched in stunned disbelief as his cousin strode briskly into the room—on the ceiling. Aric seemed to realize what was wrong, reoriented, and walked down the wall to get on their level.

"I see you've picked up a few tricks, youngster," Masalla said.

Aric's pointed silence weighed on Maurin like lead. "I just came to see how you were doing." He glanced at Talauna, then at his cousin, who still held her hand. "Apparently, not too badly. I'm glad. You were starting to worry me."

"Worry you?" Maurin frowned.

"I thought you were never going to do anything about that girl," Aric explained smugly.

"Do anything? I haven't done anything."

"So you say. Maybe you should."

Maurin stiffened. "Aric, I am married, after all..."

Aric held up a hand, and the billowing flames in the room flared and then wavered, as if a strong breeze had blown through. Maurin's heart skipped.

"You aren't married," Aric corrected, oblivious to the incredulous stares focused on him. "You told me yourself that you aren't sure if Kirai finished her part of the vow. And even if she did, what does that matter now? You don't know where she is, and you probably never will. Are you going to stay 'married' to a girl you'll never see again, or get on with your life?"

Maurin fumed. The urge to slug his cousin in the mouth was overwhelming.

"Oh, Aric, darling, there you are." The striking woman from the throne room sidled up beside him in the entryway, followed by the blond man.

"Are you going to introduce us to your companions?" Masalla asked.

"I am Ulora Vailorscha. I am a priestess to the lord Réus, and this is my son, Guilan Vail. Aric is my guest here in Eulith Soren."

Maurin didn't have time to wonder at the strangeness of the introduction of this man as her son, because the Reamar woman leaned close to Aric, and whispered something in his ear that elicited a chuckle. Then, to Maurin's astonishment, she kissed his cousin full on the mouth, and murmured again. Aric blushed and averted his eyes, not meeting Maurin's shocked gaze.

Dania stared in stony, unblinking silence at the couple across from her. Aric studiously avoided her accusing eyes. Maurin actually felt sorry for her; he didn't know what had gone on between Dania and his cousin, but clearly, she had grown attached to him, and Aric's behavior stung her as surely as salt in a wound.

Aric was handsome, true, and had never had any trouble attracting the gazes of women back home. But what did he have to offer this one? Maurin liked to think charitably of his cousin, but he sincerely doubted it was Aric's charming personality. What was it about his spirit that drew the Reamar like iron filings to a magnet?

"Well, young one," Masalla said sternly, "are you joining us?"

Aric squirmed. "Not just yet. I have something I need to do."

Maurin couldn't believe his ears. "Are you joking?"

"No. I'm sorry, Maurin. I'll be by later." He turned his back on them and left with Guilan Vail and Ulora.

Too stunned for words, Maurin gaped after them in disbelief.

"Come on, Maurin," Dania said curtly. She gripped him by the arm, guiding him toward the bed, where he sat by Talauna.

"Found, but lost," Masalla said, with a grim smile. "Are you all right?"

"Not really." Maurin swallowed a lump in his throat, blinking away tears that kept threatening to fall. "I'm not even sure all this is real. I keep thinking I'll wake to find this all just a bad dream."

"It is a bad dream," Dania said softly. "But I don't think there will be any waking."

CHAPTER 39
SHADES OF IMMORTALITY

"The Reamar began their page in this world's history as a scourge of man, but now—little more than the stuff of legend." The god-king's personal guards flanked Valasand and Réus on their journey through the bowels of Darkhorn Fell. "We are all that remain here, although some survivors may be scattered among the stars; perhaps a few of our temples still roam the heavens. If there are others, we have been too long separated by time and circumstance, and so pass the millennia in ignorance of them."

A growing unease settled upon Valasand as they descended past dozens of green flaming vents and natural fountains. With a chill, she saw the stream branch off, flowing up crevices in the walls.

"And what of the slaves? I know your secret. Daman Argoneis supplies you with human slaves from other worlds, and those you do not feed upon, you inhabit."

Réus nodded curtly and indicated the right-hand tunnel with a flick of his finger. "Though our bodies endure for ages, they do wear out with time. Many of us were killed in the initial descent to this planet, our spirits unhoused and set to wander in darkness and agony. The discovery that we had the ability to move into a human shell is ancient by your standards, but relatively new to us. For hundreds of years, we kept ourselves renewed by drinking from the Lifestream at the source, absorbing soul after soul in an effort to regain our eternality.

"Yet I knew that this could not continue, for we would soon drain the world dry, and be stranded here, starved by our gluttony. Though he does not know it, Lord Argoneis saved us from extinction by bringing offworlders to us. With the growing population, we are able to live through them without killing, though to do so limits our abilities somewhat. I am all too aware of those who would have liked to see me dethroned, so they could go back to the days of wanton butchery, of lust for power and hunger for life. But those days are gone; I have kept the Reamar alive by shielding us from the attention of outsiders."

Valasand saw it then, in a vision so powerful it nearly swept her away.

The Reamar, the Gray Lands—one massive organism, cleaving to the world like a parasite, draining it of its vitality, channeling it back to this place, and focusing the raw essence of life into a power the likes of which she could scarcely imagine. As the Reamar grew in strength, the Gray Lands spread, and so the cycle built on itself. Her own words came back to haunt her.

To dream is to walk with one foot in the physical world and the other in the realm of the spirit. Aric's stride takes him on that path in his waking moments and in his sleep... He is the perfect bridge between their world and ours.

The Reamar had been awakened in Aric's dreams. He was a conduit for their power. Valasand saw this world sucked dry of life until it was nothing but an empty husk. And if, in their expansion, the Reamar happened across the Well, or took over one of the ships passing from world to world, they would spread across the stars like a malignant gray plague.

"Do you hate humans so much?" Valasand asked, nearly twisting her ankle on a dip in the floor of the passageway.

Réus pursed his lips. "Our battle in this physical realm, our dungeon, was ever against Yasul's clay-children, what many of my kind believe to be a vile mockery of our once-glorious race. They had already achieved a favored status in the eyes of their Creator. Overnight, we learned to hate mankind. And so it was the ultimate humiliation that in order to destroy him, we must be chained and bound to his form."

"And what do you want with Aric?"

"The Reamar share a vision, a phantom revelation of a Dreaded One whose coming will change our world. Some believe this is something to fear, and others believe we should welcome this One." He cast his eyes down. "Guilan Vail was sent to look for one of our own, a priestess of the utmost importance to us. When he came across your Aric, he sensed the fathomless power in his soul. Guilan suspected he was the Dreaded One that haunts our very being."

"And so villages, entire cities, were wiped out to prevent his ever reaching you?" Valasand asked, sick at the thought. Fatamor. Mor Tespir. Untold others. How many thousands had died to keep Aric from destroying the Reamar? And just now, even if it were somehow in his ability, it seemed that was the furthest thing from his mind. "So now that he is in your possession, why do you let him live?"

"One of my priestesses believes there might be a better path to take, that his strength might be exploited through his weakness."

"What do you believe, Lord Réus?"

The god-king smiled. "I believe that whether Aric is the Dreaded One, or whether by his presence he brings the Dreaded One, he is crucial to the fate of us all. The boy is strong; his spirit shone like a beacon from across the empty seas. Ulora believes he is like a key that unlocks our power, and as he grows in age and wisdom, so will his gift be the foundation of a new age for the Glorious."

"And if you were to discover that he meant harm to you...?"

"I would utterly destroy him," Réus said without malice.

Futility and sadness without measure shone in his eyes. Perhaps it was time to risk everything in one fell swoop. "You're tired of this life, aren't you?"

The god-king gazed at her with somber dignity. "You see much, do you not, young human?"

"I'm not young."

"To me, all humans are young."

"You're evading the question," she pressed. "You're ready for it to end."

He led her deeper in silence, down main paths and meandering passageways, always descending, until Valasand had a distinct impression they had gone below the level of the earth, and were now tunneling into the deep-reaching roots of the tree. Parts of the channel were so steep that she had to use her staff for balance.

At last he responded. "I must confess you are nearer the truth than you know. I have talked with the Lady Aishè about the fact that it may be time to allow our race to diminish, to cease to be. Aishè was my conspirator in the rebellion against Yasul and his Vigilant, and holds fiercely and tenaciously to even this damned existence. She considers herself the mother of the Reamar, and tolerates no threat to her children."

Réus sighed. "It is difficult to bear hate for endless centuries, and I find I no longer wish to take the life of others—even a life so frail and insignificant as that of a human—so that my own meager awareness might be extended by a fraction of an age. Even if we endure until the death of the cosmos, I know that one day, I must face the Source again, and when I do..." His voice trailed off.

Valasand almost felt sorry for him, though she knew he stood before her today only by the sacrifice of thousands of lives throughout the eons. "That is something we all must face. Yasul welcomes all those who welcome Yasul. Even those who have abandoned the path may once again turn in that direction. All must bow before the end, but those who bow willingly belong to the Source."

The god-king regarded her, and she saw the reflection of millennia in his eyes. "It is too late for that, I fear."

"It is not too late." Valasand dared to stop in front of him, forcing him to halt, as well. They had come to a large, high-ceilinged chamber. "Yasul would have you back, if you would have Yasul back. The wars are over, and there is a time of peace ahead. The question is: will you accept it?"

"Perhaps you are the Dreaded One Aishè fears," Réus said, with a slight smile. "Certainly what you propose would bring about the end of our race, and our way of life."

"Better to die once in Yasul than die eternally apart from your Creator."

He glanced at her sharply, then gestured for her to continue walking. The god-king remained silent, and the only sound was that of their footsteps as they walked deep into the ravenous void. Glowing green mists swirled slowly, creating an eerie tableau. Condensation gathered on lumps and projections on the floor of the vault and dripped upward to the ceiling.

"Do you know what it is to live forever, Warden Valasand?"

She shook her head.

Réus nodded toward the darkness. "This is what it is to live forever."

A shadow flickered in the torchlight.

The dark screamed in her face.

Valasand jumped back, colliding with the god-king, then flinched away.

"Do not fear. As long as I am here, they will not harm you."

Hundreds of pallid gray wraiths drew near, stopping only a few feet from them. They all had the same soulless eyes, black ovals abnormally large in the sockets, with no discernible pupil or iris. They did not seem to see so much as reside in the place where eyes should be. Yet, sightless or not, the creatures honed in on Valasand and Réus.

Another one of the skeletal figures screamed, and the others took up the chorus. They didn't even seem to be breathing; their chests didn't move, and the sound went on longer than a good lungful of air should have allowed.

Valasand waited to speak until they had stopped and started to wan-

der off. Even then, she couldn't force the tremor out of her voice. "What are those... ghouls?"

If the god-king was offended by the appellation, he didn't show it. "These are Reamar who desired and sought to regain their immortality, but refused to pollute themselves by sloughing off their cursed bodies and taking on human form. Deathlessness consumed them. At first there was little change. But by degrees, it slowly ate away at them, until there was nothing left but what you see here. Their power and strength are intact, but their minds, their souls, are gone." For a moment, Réus turned introspective. "There is nothing remotely godlike—or even human—left of them. They have sunk below the animals."

Indistinct, translucent phantoms filled the air above them, forms without substance. Valasand tried hard to keep her face from showing any expression: no fear, no revulsion, no pity. But again her voice betrayed her. "And these shades?"

"They are living death," Réus said simply. "Disembodied specters of my fallen race. We call them *Geuslahan*—Harvesters, in your tongue. They reap the souls of men without care or concern for rank or privilege. Their spirits eternally hunger for life, and glean it from everything they can."

"This is not immortality," Valasand murmured. "Surely you know that."

"As long as I live, they must remain here. And on this issue, you must trust me: I alone among the Reamar have the strength to maintain command over these beings."

"What would happen if they were to break free of your grip?"

"They will not."

"But if they did?"

Réus sighed. "The Harvesters are attracted to the lifestreams of the living. Were they to break loose, they would instinctively seek out and absorb the essence of the nearest creature. They would saturate their own being with the power of life."

"Why do you show me this?"

"Because, young Valasand, you have traveled far to tarry in the jaws of the beast, and I believe you need to know against whom you stand."

"It need not be that way, my lord," Valasand said, looking him directly in the eyes. "I did not realize it when I set out to rescue our wayward young man, but Yasul has made clear to me that I have come for yet another purpose."

"And what would that be?"

"To bring the offer of new life to the Reamar."

CHAPTER 40
INITIATE

"In the long ages since the downfall of the Glorious, I have watched entire civilizations ebb and flow, and I have seen the living suffer the torments of the damned. I have looked mortality in the face more times than I can count. Indeed, I have known more agony in my life alone than one should have to suffer, for always, when I saw death before me, I turned away, and chose to live."

Surreptitiously positioned behind a twisted column rising to meet the vaulted ceiling, Aric listened as Aishè spoke. The high priestess sat with her back partially to him. Ulora and Guilan Vail stood before her.

"We stand at the cusp of creating our civilization anew," Aishè continued, "or seeing it crumble into dust—all because of the lusts of one young human male. In your arrogance, you have taken him into your arms, and now the fate of our entire race rests in the thrusts of his loins." Aishè turned to face Ulora, curiously calm. "It is intriguing to me that between a human's legs lies the ability to affect the course of history."

Aric shuddered. How much did she know? How much had she seen? Could she look through Ulora's eyes just as Ulora looked through her handmaiden's?

"I am your servant, as always, my lady." Ulora bowed. "Aric is but an infant, even in the eyes of his people, and who better than a babe to raise as one of my own?"

Aric bristled. She caught his eye over the high priestess's shoulder, and he ducked back around the pillar. Apart from that one flicker of recognition, she did not indicate in any way that she was aware of his presence. Had she known all along he would follow her?

"Lord Réus may have his visions of the Dreaded One," Ulora said, "but since before my own son was born, I have had visions of Aric. I thought to bring him into the world myself, but eventually realized that was not to be. I have called to his spirit from the time he was conceived. He is my beloved, my intended. I cannot let him be destroyed. His power can be wielded to our benefit."

"Would you let our people be destroyed for his sake?" Aishè did not give her time to answer. "The enemy is come, Ulora Vailorscha. We harbor them under our roof, and meanwhile, I watch as my beloved Lord Réus gives us over to this Warden."

Aric dared to peek out again.

"My lady?" Ulora's face turned questioning.

"One of his servants has come to me in secret. The god-king has consulted with this Warden, and she attempted to sway him to return to Yasul, to have us become hated minions of the Source once more."

"Does he not care if we die?" Guilan seemed genuinely surprised. "We are all a part of him, from the least of us to the greatest. Why should he wish his own death?"

"Yes," Ulora said with a quiet savagery. "Why should he wish it?"

"We cannot allow this," Guilan whispered.

"No," Aishè agreed, "we cannot. We must not return to those days."

"But the Reamar do as Lord Réus commands," Ulora said. Something in her voice told Aric that she was baiting the high priestess, testing her.

"Of that, I am aware. I have known Réus since the beginning of beginnings; I am not surprised by this. He has grown weary. I must persuade him of the folly of this path."

"And if he cannot be persuaded?"

Guilan and his mother drew nearer to the high priestess, conversing in tones Aric could not hear. Might as well return to Ulora's quarters and wait for her. He didn't know what to make of what he had just heard, and he wasn't sure he wanted to.

He nodded to the handmaiden as he passed, then collapsed onto the bed. Lying there, he stared at the frost left on the wall by the writhing curls of flame. What had he just been privy to?

It wasn't long before he felt her slide between the sheets.

"You are not so silent that I cannot hear you, my love," she said as she began to massage his shoulders.

"So I'm a baby now?"

Ulora chuckled. "Words, beloved. The high priestess must not think you pose a threat to her."

"Tell me," he said as he relaxed under her ministrations, "what's going on here."

Ulora's hands paused in the middle of his back. "What do you mean?"

"Well, for starters, why does the high priestess hate me so much? She is the one who was hunting me, wasn't she?"

Ulora hesitated. "Yes."

"Why?"

"She thought you might be a threat to us. As I told you, we have awaited the arrival of the Dreaded One with some trepidation. He could mean a new life for us, or our death. Is it any wonder that she does not trust you? Or me either, for that matter, since I have taken you under my wings?"

"I suppose not."

"I knew she would have Marèse Shavad kill you as soon as you were discovered. So I sent Guilan along with her hunting party to make certain you were spared. After all, he had already seen you once before in Langfort; he knew whom to protect."

"What's the deal with him?" Aric flipped over to face her. "How is it that your son looks older than you do?"

Ulora gave Aric a surprisingly soft and maternal smile. She played absently with his hair, running her fingers through the curls. "Guilan is one of a new generation of Reamar. There were no births among the Glorious; we were all that were, all that would ever be. But when we learned to take on human form, our new bodies afforded us a whole new spectrum of sensations and possibilities—including procreation."

"How old is he?"

"I gave birth to my son seventy-eight years ago," she answered, her voice once again warm and comfortable. Her finger traced across his chest. "The Lifestream has kept him young."

Aric's stomach churned. He couldn't wrap his mind around the fact that this beautiful woman before him was, well... ancient, for lack of a better word.

"When we were in Mor Tespir I dreamed... it was a dream, wasn't it?" He frowned, unsettled. "A girl gave herself to the Reamar. She was...

someone else when she woke up."

"She had taken on the power and person of the Reamar."

"So what happens to them?"

"Their bodies live on in our glory, and their memories live through us."

"But they—their souls—they die, don't they?"

Ulora glanced away. "There is no death in the Reamar."

Aric couldn't help feeling she was evading him. "So you've been offered new bodies? Personally?"

"Several times," Ulora said easily. She frowned at his expression. "What's wrong?"

"What were you like, you know, before?"

She widened her eyes, raised her hands like claws, and made a face at him. "An old hag," she said in a rough, pinched voice.

"Seriously," Aric chided.

She sighed. "I was dying. My body was injured in a battle with the humans, and there was no hope of recovery. Some followers of the Reamar came across it when I was nearly gone. A young girl, Renna, was with them, and offered herself as a sanctuary for me."

"So this is her body?" Aric said, looking down appreciatively, yet still with a sense of unease.

"No. This was a long time ago; well before Guilan was born. Many have offered themselves to me since."

"So what happened to her?" He wasn't going to just let her go on this one.

Ulora frowned. "What do you mean?"

"Where is she now? If you... moved into her body, what happened to the girl?"

"Aric, I am she. Renna—and all since—became me." Her gaze was earnest. "All that they were now lives in me. I have knowledge of every life lived, both in my body, and in those of my followers."

Aric still couldn't help thinking that she wasn't telling him the whole truth. It sounded as if the immorality the Reamar offered was strictly for themselves. Their worshipers just followed them blindly, giving up their bodies for a false hope of eternity.

Yet, why would she lie to him? Their souls were spliced, one unit. He could feel her presence as surely as he felt his own. She had already told him that she was his destined bride. And hadn't she kept him from certain death at the hands of the fearful high priestess?

"I don't know about this," he said at last. "What am I going to tell Maurin?"

"You must tell him you have found your destiny."

"For some reason, I can't see that going over well. They'll want me to go with them."

"I know." Ulora nuzzled his neck lightly, giving him her most sultry smile. "But I don't want you to leave."

"I don't want to, either," Aric said. "But I may have to."

"Stay with me, beloved," she pleaded, hurt. "You know you are one of us now."

"But... my cousin," Aric countered. "He's my only family. He needs me."

"*I* need you."

"You could come with us," he suggested.

"My place is here," Ulora said stiffly. "As is yours. You do not understand, cherished one, what it is to wait for an eternity for the other half of your soul. Your spirit was strong enough to call to me from across the empty seas. You have the sight to touch not only your own future, but the destinies of those around you. You have such power, Aric, the depths of which you have only begun to plumb. Let me teach you how to control this gift of yours. With my tutelage, you could aid those you love by guiding their fates, and kill your enemies with a thought."

"I don't want to kill anyone."

"You need not ever kill; not if you don't want to. But you can have the power to right worlds of wrongs. The key to the universe sits in your hand, love." Ulora's voice took on grand and glorious tones. "When you stand at the door, will you be brave enough to open it, or will you cower on the threshold?"

"I've got to get out of here," Aric said. He leapt from the bed and started pacing back and forth. "I need to think."

Ulora rose, grasped him by the shoulders, and looked squarely into his face. When she spoke, her voice was husky with passion and desire. "Stay with me, Aric, and I can help you control your own destiny. You can go wherever you want. You need not be bound by this world or any other. Your Valasand knew this, but did not want to tell you. You can be a god."

"I don't want to be a god."

"Stay," she repeated, undaunted, "and you will have the opportunity to see what we truly are, and what we can offer you."

"Oh?" Aric raised his eyebrows, but still affected disinterest. "What's that?"

"The chance to live forever." She smiled at his reaction. "For starters, you might say."

Aric rubbed his chin. "I want to be able to know what my dreams mean, and to keep them out of my head if I don't want them there."

Ulora nodded. "To control one's dreams is much more desirable than to be controlled by them."

Aric lapsed into a thoughtful silence. The power welling in his body and soul beckoned to him to explore its depths. The freedom he had sought for so many years called with a siren's song. He looked back at Ulora. Gradually, his frown surrendered to a smile.

"Teach me."

Ulora flashed a predatory grin. "To begin with, you must understand that the body is not the womb of the soul; it is merely the puppet of the spirit."

He frowned. "I don't understand."

"Think of a pair of lovers coming to one another. Their bodies respond, slaves to what their spirits desire."

Aric arched his eyebrows. "I always sort of thought it was the other way around."

Ulora snorted softly. "When you come to me, you act not on some crude flaming of the body. No, your physical shell but faintly reflects the true burning of your spirit. Focus, and you can see into my soul. Do you feel the pulsing of life in my heart? Do you hear the cry of my life's blood as it flows through my veins? *Drink deep, it says, drink, and be filled of me.*"

Aric's breathing quickened with Ulora's. She gripped him more tightly.

"Put me out of your mind, my love." Her voice came softly, hypnotically, accentuating the rhythm of his heartbeat. "Close your eyes, and hear my words. Your lover is no victim of mortal frailty. By choice, she is vulnerable for you, Aric. She is ready and willing to give the essence of her being for you. She loves you, Aric. Only you matter to her; she gives herself freely."

"Ulora..."

"Do not think. Just listen. Your lover stands before you. Take her into your arms," Ulora coached him from a misty distance; "draw her into you. Feel the energy of her life wrap itself around you, embrace you. She wishes to become one with you. Not just her body, but her entire being. Her vitality will flow into yours. Reach in, take it. Accept it. She must consent; you take nothing from her that she does not give willingly. Free your body and soul of their confines. Stretch forth your hand, and grasp the heavens."

Somehow, as he reached out, Aric was aware that they were not alone. He opened his eyes. Before him stood not Ulora, but her handmaiden. Arisnè breathed in ragged gasps; her eyes glazed. The girl's body was limp, relaxed in his hands.

"She gives herself," Ulora repeated, smiling. "Now take her."

CHAPTER 41
OLD HURTS, NEW HURTS

Maurin jolted awake, finding his hand still in Talauna's. She was conscious and staring at him apprehensively. Taking his hand, she pulled it over and pressed it firmly to her stomach. He watched her, curious, feeling the warmth of her belly through the sheets. Then something fluttered under his palm; the baby, kicking. Barely there, but unmistakable. A reassurance of life and health.

And hope.

"You smile any bigger, Maurin, and your face is going to split in two," Masalla said.

Maurin ignored him; he saw happiness and relief mirrored in the Maolori's face.

"Oh, Talauna. Did you think I would care?"

She flashed him a smile, showing rows of small, even teeth.

"I'm so glad you're all right." He squeezed her hand, then started at a touch on his shoulder.

"Shhhh," Valasand said, sitting beside him. "It's all right. I'm back. But it's time for you to go to bed."

"But Talauna..." Maurin began, in tired protest.

"Will be fine," Valasand finished. "You've been keeping watch long enough."

"I'd rather stay." Maurin rubbed his neck.

"Maurin." Her tone brooked no argument. "Go... to... bed." She softened a bit at his hurt look of resignation. "You'll do her more good by getting some rest. We're going to need our strength and wits about us."

He nodded, getting stiffly to his feet. "Can I ask you something first?"

Valasand's eyes betrayed her weariness, but after a moment's hesitation, she nodded. "Come outside with me."

They stepped into the outer corridor and moved some distance away from their room.

"What is it, Maurin?"

"Why do you think Talauna doesn't speak? Do you think she was raped?"

"Does it really matter?"

"Does it matter?" Maurin repeated, his body tensing. "Does it *matter*?"

Valasand regarded him evenly. "Perhaps I should rephrase the question: What difference does it make? Something she experienced has locked her firmly inside herself, and that is the reality with which you have to deal."

He started to retort, and found he had nothing to say.

Valasand continued. "You need to ask yourself whether you accept her as she is, or want her to be someone she might have been."

Maurin pondered that for a moment. "I see your point," he conceded, his sudden burst of temper waning. "But it still angers me that anyone could treat her so badly."

"As well it should. But don't let your anger stand in the way of your concern for her well-being. She likes being with you; if she feels that you constantly pity her, or if you become incensed every time you think about her and her past, that could change."

"So am I supposed to pretend that it didn't happen?"

"No," she said bluntly. "There is no way you can ignore her past, especially when it affects the present as much as this does. But if you can't accept her, past and all, you may need to think about just why you're wallowing in self-indulgent fury."

"Wallowing in...?" Maurin stared at her, incredulous.

"That's right. What has happened, has happened, and cannot be changed, no matter how much you may want it to be otherwise. Not only is it a waste of time to dwell on those things we cannot change, but in the end, it will consume us."

Talauna's pleasure whenever he entered a room. Her relief when she saw he was not angry at her for being pregnant. The way she always sensed what he needed, and when. Seeking her core, learning what brought her joy, the wonder of sharing a new life with her—that was one of the easiest decisions he would ever make.

"These past several days," Maurin pressed on, "it seems as though maybe she wants to say something, or something is on her mind, but—of course, it's Talauna—she's always holding back. She never quite starts. Do you know what I mean?"

"So the question in your mind is not really 'Why doesn't Talauna talk,' but rather, 'Why doesn't Talauna talk to me?' Is that correct?"

"Ah, I guess so."

"Why won't she talk to you?" she said softly. "Well, that's a very difficult question to answer directly, Maurin. Why do you think this is?"

"She doesn't trust me yet?"

"I believe she does, to a great degree. But Talauna has grown comfortable in her own silent world. She may feel it is safer to let others do the talking for her. Wounds of this sort do not heal quickly, and even when they have healed, the scars will be sensitive for a long while. You'll simply have to be patient."

Maurin's throat hurt, and he didn't trust himself to speak.

Valasand gave him a searching look. "Maurin, you did not cause her pain, and you cannot take it from her."

He nodded in response.

"But you can help her bear it."

Maurin looked up, feeling a sense of new purpose. "Thank you."

Valasand smiled. "One day, when you are least expecting it, Talauna will call you by name and speak her heart to you. On that day, you will know you have won her."

———— ◆ ————

How dare this demon harlot steal Aric away from them—from her? How much resistance, if any, had he even put up to the Reamar witch? He had so readily given himself to Dania that first night. Her eyes burned inexplicably, and she cursed him for his weakness. Then she cursed herself for hers. What had they all risked so much for anyway? If he wanted to be a demon's plaything, that was his business, but he had made it theirs. He'd crushed his cousin's spirit. He'd put Valasand and Talauna in danger. He'd wasted precious time and sidetracked them all from doing what truly needed to be done. Argoneis still sat on his throne, the circus still loomed. And Aric, the little scat, stood there with that smug grin on his face—so proud of himself for bedding a goddess. Too young, too stupid to see that he was a pawn in whatever game she was playing.

Having made her excuses to Masalla and Valasand, Dania crept through the shimmering corridors of Darkhorn Fell. She waited patiently in the shadows for guards to pass, then sought her target with a lethal surety of motion.

A hard, cold knot had settled in her stomach ever since the Reamar woman had kissed Aric. Afterward, Dania had brooded in complete silence, rigid, avoiding everyone's eyes. Words would not suffice in a situation like this. Her ire turned to cold fury, and she drew her knives. One swift, simple cut, and the problem would be gone. Aric would have no reason to stay here.

She passed through a small antechamber and into a large, round room. Small gouts of cold flame writhed on the walls. She pulled up short at the sight of a young man and woman sleeping side by side. The maroon covers were pushed down to their waists, and their skin shone a whitish green in the pale, unnatural light. His left arm hung slackly by his side, and the woman's dark hair spilled over his shoulder in a cascade of thick, wavy tresses. Her flawless complexion and figure befitted a deity—a testament to her power; even in sleep, she resonated an ageless beauty that beggared description.

She regarded the couple for a few moments, then approached the bed.

"For you," Dania whispered.

She centered the dagger over the demon's heart, pulled back her arm, and prepared to plunge the blade home. She drew a soft breath, the knife flashed...

Aric's hand swept up, intercepting the killing blow.

With a gasp, he opened his eyes, but did not let go of the blade grasped in his palm. Aric raised his head off the pillow, holding her dagger in a death grip. Several dark splatters of blood dripped between Ulora's breasts, and her eyes shot open.

"Sleep." The Reamar woman said it like a curse. "Human bodies are so frail."

Ulora's expression did not change; she made a sudden sweep of the hand, and a green flash nearly blinded Dania. She flew backwards through the air, landing hard against the far wall, her knife flying out of her hand. Stunned, her body tingled as it fluoresced and coruscated with green fire.

"I would never have been caught off-guard thus in the old days," Ulora said in disgust, rising gracefully from the bed. "You saw her in your dreams?"

Aric nodded, wrapping a corner of the sheet around his hand and making a fist. He winced.

"You're dead, witch!" Dania rumbled low in the back of her throat.

She forced herself to leap up, and flew upon the Reamar with a scream.

Ulora whirled around, her arms out to her sides. A bright sphere of energy encased her body. Dania rebounded without ever having touched the woman. Misty green tendrils swirled off her, and her joints ground with arthritic pain.

Dania spat, and somehow managed to rise to her feet. "I will rip your heart out with my teeth!"

Ulora gripped at the air in front of Dania, making a fist. The gladiatrix gasped as her chest and arms were squeezed by an invisible force. She could hardly breathe. Ulora tossed her hand downward, as if throwing a scrap of garbage to the floor. Dania felt her body crushed by an unseen weight, and she fell flat. The wreaths of green energy were blown away as if by a strong wind.

"Wild one," Ulora said, kneeling, "why do you attack me?"

"You stole him!" Dania hissed.

"What is he to you?"

Dania simply glared. Aric avoided her eyes.

"Ah. You were lovers. Are you pledged to one another?" When neither responded, Ulora nodded. "I thought not. Let me tell you something. Whatever may have once been, he is mine, now—he always has been. I will share his body with you if it pleases him, but his soul is mine, and I would advise you not to challenge me for him. To compete with me would mean your death."

"Your death!" Dania shrieked. She struggled to raise herself, but her body collapsed beneath her, unwilling to hold her weight. She sagged to her knees. "I have killed over three hundred foes. None has faced me and lived!"

"You are vicious, aren't you?" Ulora shook her head in mock concern. Then she leaned in close, almost intimately, speaking softly into Dania's ear. "Know, then, fearsome one, that I have devoured entire nations, and the hunger within me never dies. I have drunk up the souls of nobles and peasants, and my thirst grows ever stronger. I am a mouthpiece of Eulith Soren, a priestess of the sacred order of the Reamar. I have consumed your like at the rising of the sun, and a hundred more by its setting."

Without another word, Ulora grasped Dania by the throat. Dania's arms went up reflexively, but her eyes locked on the Reamar woman's. Ulora seized her soul with an inescapable gaze, and Dania felt her vitality draining from her with each passing second. She shivered and twitched, but the Reamar woman would not release her hold. Her heart hammered as it had not since her first time in the pit; a green glow passed from Dania's neck and into Ulora's hand. The veins in the Reamar witch's slender arms throbbed and glowed with each ebbing of Dania's spirit.

She had seen her death a hundred times over and expected to embrace it. But never this... this blasphemy. Weakly, she pried at the immovable fingers.

"Let her go," Aric said sharply. "She won't attack us again."

Ulora hesitated, then unclenched her grip. Dania fell to the ground in a gasping, crumpled heap. The twisted ceiling spun, and darkness threatened to eclipse her vision. She forced herself onto her stomach, Aric's words of rescue mocking her as she crawled away like a wounded dog.

"Very well," the witch said, her fading voice radiating disdain. "If she means something to you, I will let her live, for your sake. But she can no longer stay here."

CHAPTER 42
WEB OF DESTINY

"Wake up."

Masalla's voice jarred Maurin from slumber, and he opened his eyes to several Reamar guards filing into the room, hostile and ready for a fight.

"We have been summoned," Masalla said ominously, "by the high priestess herself. And she doesn't seem to be in any mood to wait."

Maurin looked around. "Where's Dania?"

The Warden shook his head. "She left wanting a privy hours ago, and never returned."

Talauna slid out of bed, testing her leg gingerly. She seemed dizzy as she hobbled forward, so the Talormine slung her over her shoulder. Talauna grasped her neck to hang on, wrapping her legs around Shallar's middle.

Maurin composed himself as best he could and stepped out into the hall with the others. The Reamar escorted them through the labyrinthine corridors of Darkhorn Fell. Maurin glanced over at Talauna from time to time, but said nothing. He had no strength or wit for words of comfort.

At the end of a long vessel lit by the ubiquitous cold flame vents, he saw a low entrance leading to a larger chamber. He expected the guards to announce them. Instead, they stood aside, each with his back to a wall, and waited for Maurin and the others. It took him a moment to realize that they intended for them to go on in alone. He took step after heavy step toward the arch.

Maurin forced himself to pick his feet up as he went into the vaulted room. Talauna slid off Shallar's back and stood next to him. It was almost too dark to make out any details of his surroundings. A low brazier burned with a flickering green flame, and beyond that, he saw a triangular flash of white skin above a dark robe. He stepped forward cautiously. The woman had her head bowed, and sat cross-legged, arms out to her sides, palms up. They must have caught her in the middle of meditation.

"Stop."

Maurin pulled up short at the sonorous voice, his legs obeying her command instinctively. Without moving any other part of her body, she slowly raised her head and opened her eyes. Maurin gulped with apprehension at the intense woman he had seen upon their first entering the temple. He nodded uncertainly in greeting, the rhythm of his heart growing steadily faster.

Slowly she unfolded her limbs, arms first. She raised them to her sides, her shoulders rippling with the muscular grace of a dancer. She rose, then; rather than standing, she seemed to be lifted to her feet. The high priestess regarded him with those inscrutable eyes. "You are the one known as Maurin. Is that correct?"

"Yes, it is. I mean, I am." He cleared his throat nervously. "Who are you?

"I am known by many names," the high priestess said, her voice high and eerily musical. "You may call me Aishè."

An enormous pressure squeezed Maurin's brain, and everything started to go fuzzy. So hard to think...

Aishè suddenly turned her eyes back upon Maurin, her heavy veil of hair swinging behind her. "I sense your hatred of us, young human. You wish us harm, do you not?"

Maurin's heart hammered in his throat. His tongue suddenly felt too big for his mouth. He started to panic; every nerve in his body was singing, alive with a high-pitched vibration.

"I want nothing to do with your people," he finally managed. "I never have. I came only to get my cousin back."

"No. You have come to destroy our way of life."

Valasand stepped forward, seemingly unfazed by the potency of the woman's presence. Maurin silently thanked her, relieved to be free, for the moment, from the Reamar's spell.

"I have offered the chance to change it; not necessarily to destroy it."

"To alter us is to destroy us. In the long ages since we were cast from our rightful place, we have endured, have held death at bay. What you ask of my lord would be the end of our race."

"The end," Valasand replied, "and a new beginning."

"What if I cannot change?" the Reamar challenged.

Valasand locked eyes with Aishè. "You will change, one way or another. Neither you nor I can stop this from happening."

The high priestess remained silent for a long time. "You are of course correct. The time for change has come. I must think about what this... change... means to me."

Valasand was totally unmoved. "As Maurin has said, we've come to rescue Aric from one of your priestesses who has established a powerful influence over him. She exploits a fledgling in an attempt to draw him away from those he loves, and that which he knows to be right. Moreover, I do not believe he is the Dreaded One you seek."

The high priestess turned her attention on Valasand, her eyes cinders burning into the Warden. "You savagely hunt my children. When you harm them, you do as much to me." Raising her voice, she called, "Bring forth the prisoner."

A half dozen Reamar guards walked into the room, surrounding a miserable Dania. Though none touched her, she stood uncharacteristically silent, eyes downcast. After her followed Aric with his new lover and Guilan Vail.

"You claim to bear us no ill will," Aishè said, inclining her head toward Dania, "yet this one has attempted to murder one of our priestesses in our very sanctuary."

Slack with defeat, Dania didn't respond.

Maurin could hardly believe his ears. Aric quietly held up a palm marked with a fresh pink scar.

"Ordinarily, this action would be met with immediate retribution," Aishè said. "However, I understand that your companion acted out of ignorance and jealousy"—Dania bristled—"and so her life will be spared. But you must leave at once. We can no longer harbor you in Darkhorn Fell."

"We will leave. All of us." Masalla waited for Aric. "This is your last chance, young one. Come with us."

Aric shook his head. "I can't."

"What?" Maurin strode forward. "Yes, you can! You must!"

"I'm not leaving, Maurin." There was pain in Aric's eyes, but he wouldn't look directly at him.

His chest seized. "Aric, you're not one of them. You're my cousin. What's wrong with you?"

"Maurin, all my life I've been looking for someone to tell me what my dreams mean. I've found her here."

"A Reamar is the woman of your dreams?" Maurin shouted. Aric flinched. Talauna gazed at him in sorrow. "Do you even hear yourself?"

For the first time, Aric had the grace to stammer. "They've been searching for me even longer than I've been searching for them. There's so much I have to learn. Can't you understand?"

"No! No, I can't understand! Aric, you're not yourself; you're under a spell. You have to leave this tomb! We can go wherever you want, just don't give in to this!"

"I'm sorry, Maurin. I've made my decision. My place is here."

With that, Aric turned on his heel and left. The guards parted, and Dania growled in Aric's direction as she moved to join the others. Maurin couldn't move.

Ulora regarded him with an unmistakable air of satisfaction. "You love him, don't you?"

"More than life itself." Maurin whispered. *As only a relative, a true friend, and perhaps even a brother, can love.*

Ulora walked over, her eyes glittering ice. After a moment's quiet reflection, she asked, "And what makes you think that I do not?"

Because there aren't all that many people who are even able to put up with him, he thought, but said: "Because one does not use the person one loves." Maurin steeled himself for her response. "I know of your kind, and I know what you do. Do you want to love him, or consume him?"

"Is there a difference?"

Maurin shuddered at her sweet smile and reptilian gaze.

"Aric represents your hopes for the future," Ulora continued. With languid, gliding steps, she paced around him. "You have been bound all your life by the customs of your people, by circumstances beyond your control, and by your own code of honor. In Aric you see the chance to live vicariously, to see him avoid pitfalls you could not, and to take action where you may not. You have hope for him that you dare not hope for yourself."

Too shocked to be stung by her words, Maurin stood agape.

"I understand better than you think, young Maurin. You see, I, too, have great hopes for Aric." She smiled. "You should know that we have sought your cousin for some time. His soul called from across the void, but we knew not where he was. We are worshipped on other worlds than this, and it was among our followers on your home planet, Sangrine, that we found an adherent willing to tell us where to find him."

For a moment, the full impact of her words didn't sink in. Then his knees buckled. "You sent the slavers?"

"Of course."

Maurin blanched. All that had happened to them was because of Aric. Everyone they knew whose lives were affected or lost, all those from

Athure now in bondage on an alien world, were there because his cousin was a dreamer?

Ulora trailed a finger across Maurin's chest, a line of cold in its wake. "We occasionally give Argoneis suggestions regarding possible worlds to visit. Of course, we could not tell him of the importance of yours, or he would have gotten suspicious, and started culling the slaves himself. Usually he gives us first pick, but for some reason or another, in regard to the ship you two were on, he did not. Thus it took us a while to find Aric even once he was here on *Ha'argota*—Argoth."

Maurin's stomach kept tying itself in knots. "Who worships you on Sangrine?"

Ulora tossed chestnut locks. "There we are known by a different name, but I remember quite well the young man who directed us to your world. His sister, or some relation, was about to be married, and he wanted her throne for his own. Y'atan, I believe his name was?"

Aric was right. The gods be damned. Aric was right all along. Maurin clenched his teeth in fury.

Kirai's cousin.

"Jathan," he whispered.

"Farewell, Maurin." Ulora's smile was the quintessence of feminine beauty, and her eyes the bottomless hunger of black eternity. "Depart Darkhorn Fell in the knowledge that Aric has chosen me... over you."

CHAPTER 43
BORDERS

Krige sat bolt upright, startled out of another drink-induced slumber. His eyes took a moment to focus, and he realized he had fallen asleep waiting for Phoecius to arrive. The governor had sent word that he must speak with Krige immediately, and in person.

The candles had waned to mere wax puddles, and the fire died to embers. He recoiled in startled shock when he saw Sedrick standing before him in the glimmering twilight of the great hall, silent and unmoving.

The steward hardly appeared to be breathing, and he stared without blinking at Krige. How long had he been there?

"Gods, Sedrick," Krige said crossly. "You gave me a start, slinking around like that."

Sedrick made no reply, or any kind of indication he had even heard his master.

Krige frowned. "What is it?"

His servant's jaw trembled for a moment, and then his mouth flopped open, slack. A string of drool made its way down his chin and onto the lace lapel of his dark maroon coat.

"Sedrick?" Krige's voice quavered, and he edged back in his seat.

The servant's arm raised, an outstretched finger pointing accusingly at him.

"Aster Krige." The voice coming out of Sedrick's mouth was not his own. Krige had most recently heard it from the young boy who came to threaten him into silence regarding the dealings near Langfort. He went cold. *"It is I, Aishè of the Reamar."*

"My lady?" He forced himself to stay calm this time. The Reamar were unsettling enough in person, but to have them visit this way was beyond unnerving; it bordered on haunting. "What do you want from me?"

The arm lowered, but still Sedrick did not blink. *"Some human interlopers will soon leave the borders of our domain."*

"Human interlopers? I don't understand."

"You will intercept them," Aishè said. *"While the Warden and her consorts have failed to wrest the Dreaded One from our grasp, his heart is still weakened by love for his cousin. We must remove this temptation from his life."*

Suspicion began to grow in Krige's heart, and he felt his palms starting to sweat in anticipation. "Who are these interlopers?"

"Two Wardens of the Gates, who count three slaves among their number, as well as an animal from the wildlands."

"Why didn't you take care of them while they were in your territory?"

The expression being wrangled on Sedrick's face suggested that the forthcoming answer was not a pleasant one to the speaker. *"The blood of those loved by the Dreaded One must not be on Reamar hands."*

So even you have things you're afraid of. Krige snorted softly. His mind started to race. "Just out of curiosity, is one of the slaves a *M'luri* female?"

"Yes."

He exhaled slowly, trying not to let his emotions show. *Talauna's alive!* "Very well. I will dispose of them for you."

Sedrick's mouth worked soundlessly for a moment, and the reply seemed to come from the bottom of a well. *"Be sure they are dead. Particularly the male slave. Stand not in the path of the Reamar. This weak vessel will serve as a reminder to you of what has passed between us."*

"Pardon?"

Sedrick's body went rigid, and Krige watched in horror as a spasm racked him from head to toe. He heard a sound akin to an outrushing of breath, and Sedrick's hair lifted on end. From the roots to the crown, the remaining color fled, replaced with purest white. His eyes grew wider as the flesh around them wrinkled and shrank, and his fingers contorted into agonized claws. His feet lifted momentarily from the floor as if by some unseen force, and then he fell, crumpled in an awkward heap on the hearth.

"Sedrick?" Krige rose warily from his chair, edging closer to the motionless form. "What have you done to my servant? Sedrick!"

The eyes, devoid of life, stared at the ceiling. Cautiously, Krige reached out and grasped the man's wrist, then drew back, appalled at the cold.

The guest-announcement bell, though not particularly loud, sounded like an alarm in the crypt-like silence of the room and nearly sent him into arrest. The bell rang again a minute later, and then realization set in.

"Oh, right, I guess I'll get it." Krige wiped his hands and scurried off through the halls and down the stairs into the main foyer.

"Krige? Krige, are you there?"

Governor Phoecius. Tremendous.

"I'm here." He fumbled with the door, opening it with a groan.

The governor of Langfort stood on his doorstep with several of his servants, all thoroughly surprised to see Krige himself. "Where is your steward?"

"I gave him a holiday," Krige said, puffing a little. "Won't you come in? We can go to the—no. Let's go to the conservatory."

"Thank you."

Within minutes, the two men sat in the tree-lined garden. The birds seemed despondent and quiet since Talauna had gone. Krige collapsed into his painted metal chair and held a hand to his temple.

"Is something wrong?" Phoecius asked.

"No, just a persistent headache." About the size of the Gray Lands. "It will pass in time."

"You shouldn't drink so much—"

"What did you wish to discuss with me at this late hour?" Krige interrupted.

The governor's face melted into a disgusted lump. "The Reamar have broken their treaty with me. They said they were only interested in finding this missing priestess, but they know she's not in Langfort, and people are disappearing anyway."

Did you expect anything less? Krige sighed. "I think it's safe to say the Reamar are not trustworthy."

"If this keeps up, I won't have a city anymore! They're ruining me! Do you know we have to tow our chariots well outside the city walls before they'll even work? Those Reamar spoil everything they touch!"

Krige struggled to listen, his mind on Talauna, and how he would get her back. He could fly out there himself; his new pilot was pretty good, though not up to Aric's caliber. But Krige really didn't have the ability to take the Wardens by force; their fighting skills were legendary, and his small chariot wouldn't seat that many people. He knew he would have to rely on Argoneis's men. They were already searching the countryside; all he would have to do would be to give them a nudge in the right direction. But somehow, he would have to get to them first.

"Governor," he said suddenly, "Are there still passages of airspace safe to fly through?

"Of course! There are huge pockets of dead space between the cities and the Gray Lands. But what difference does that make? Just because I can safely fly roundabout ways doesn't mean it's not a considerable incon—"

"How would you like to get in Argoneis's good graces?"

"That would be a miracle," Phoecius said, "considering he practically thinks it's my fault the Wardens are here."

"I know where they are," Krige said.

"What? How?"

"Never mind that now. Argoneis's men are already looking, but you can get to them first. Just do me one favor."

"Anything!" Phoecius's eyes glittered.

"One of the slaves is mine. A Maolori girl. Bring her to me, and say nothing of her to Argoneis. The rest, you can deliver to him, and receive whatever reward he may bestow."

———— ◆ ————

Valasand craned her head over her shoulder. The moons spilled mercury oceans of light over the stark landscape of the Gray Lands. What secrets lay buried, deep as the millennia, in the root-tunnels of the gargantuan tree?

"It's not your fault, Vals," Masalla said quietly.

"Really? Whose fault is it, then?" Valasand gestured back in the direction of the Reamar kingdom. "If ever there was a monument to failure, it's that. I've failed with the Reamar. I've failed Aric. And should I need reminding, all I have to do is look at Maurin's face. His heart is shattered, and can you blame him?"

"You gathered this group for a purpose, Vals. The Breath guided our paths together; you know this does not change that fact."

Maurin and Talauna walked together, several yards away. The Maolori girl limped slightly, and Valasand saw a painful echo of herself as Talauna leaned into him. Maurin's head hung nearly to his chest, and his feet dragged as if weighted with lead. He hadn't spoken a word since leaving Darkhorn Fell. Valasand suspected he was in shock. Talauna had tried to comfort him, but while he never pushed her away, he simply stared straight ahead with his eyes unfocused, and didn't respond to her caresses. She shed the tears that he could not.

Valasand gestured tightly as she spoke in a low tone. "Talauna is pregnant. Maurin is going to be useless in any kind of combat. Dania is so conflicted that I can't get through to her. Shallar—who knows what's going on in her head, or where her loyalties lie, besides with her missing cubs? I believed—with all my heart, I believed—that we could rally the slaves, halt the circus, and overthrow Argoneis. But I can't see my way through this. It's hopeless."

Masalla regarded her sternly. "Vals, I think you know better. When have things ever gone smoothly for the servants of Yasul? How many things have you personally sacrificed over the years? Your plans have been spoiled, but they may have been too small. There is still a long road ahead back to Caileen."

"And believe me, I plan to spend every step telling Yasul exactly what I think of this mess."

Masalla raised an eyebrow and smiled. "You do that."

Dania drew near, her brow furrowed in thought. Black stubble covered her scalp; apparently she had stopped shaving her head.

"What is it, Dania?"

"This is all my fault. I tried to murder the Reamar witch."

"Yes, you did," Valasand said. "I won't pretend what you did was right. But I understand why you did it. These are confusing times."

"I will never be good enough for your god." Dania ground her teeth. "I am an animal."

"No one is 'good enough,' Dania," Masalla said. "If perfection were required, I suspect I would be far from Yasul's heart indeed."

She frowned. "What are you saying?"

"Simply that you cannot earn your way into a family." He smiled. "You have to be adopted."

Dania mulled that over for several moments in silence.

Valasand searched everything she had been taught, weighed it against the turmoil of her emotions, and finally cast it all aside. Hopefully it would make sense to Dania; it scarcely made sense to Valasand. "We are constantly learning, Dania, and each day strive to do that which pleases the Creator. But it doesn't mean we will always succeed. And some-times—oftentimes—the Source demonstrates power through our weak-nesses."

"I don't understand."

"I think what Valasand is saying," Masalla interjected, "is that Yasul makes sure we know we are not the shapers of fate. We play the parts we are called to play, but ultimately, we are not big enough to thwart Yasul's plans."

Valasand caught his glance and forced herself to smile.

Dania frowned. "What's wrong with Talauna?"

"What?" Masalla asked.

Valasand followed her gaze. The Maolori girl had stopped in her tracks, and the Talormine had dropped into a tense crouch. Maurin looked around, as if waking from a dream, and Valasand put all her senses on alert.

Oh, Yasul, not more trouble. Not now.

Then she heard it: the familiar humming sound of air-chariots. An-other second, and she saw them. Four sleek assault-style shuttles, rising above the valley's edge, and bearing down on them fast.

"Back! Back to the Gray Lands!" If what Masalla had said was true, the chariots might not be able to operate in Reamar territory. Right now, it was their only chance; they were out in the open. She turned on her heel and ran, glancing over her shoulder to see if the others had heard. The Talormine slung Talauna over her back again and loped on all fours, gaining speed every second.

Apparently, the pilots of the four craft had also heard of this anom-aly. Two of them sped ahead, cutting the group off from the border of the Gray Lands.

"The Reamar set us up," Masalla spat.

The craft came to a swift landing, and almost as soon as they had touched down, bay doors opened, spilling forth dozens of uniformed men. Valasand pulled to a stop, as did the others. There was no point now; they were surrounded, and the men all armed with bolt-throwers and shock cudgels. She took them all in with a calculating glance, and looked over at Dania. The gladiatrix had come to the same assessment:

they were outnumbered and overpowered.

Governor Phoecius of Langfort stepped out. "So we meet again. Come. Lord Argoneis wishes for you all to star in his circus."

"Where is your Yasul now?" Dania asked bitterly.

Valasand had no response.

CHAPTER 44
SECOND THOUGHTS

"Aric, my love?"

"Yes?"

"Have you seen my handmaiden lately?"

Well, that didn't take long. Aric took a deep breath. "I let her go."

"You what?" Ulora's expression was a mixture of irritated disbelief and amusement.

"I set her free. I put her on one of those weird horse-lizards and told her not to stop riding until she couldn't see the Gray Lands anymore." He decided not to tell her about Arisnè's grateful parting kiss. Bad enough to risk Ulora's anger; there was no point rousing her jealousy.

It wasn't often she was struck speechless. Had Ulora been anyone else, Aric might have enjoyed the moment. As it was, he just felt uncomfortable and hoped she wouldn't be too upset with him.

She pursed her lips and raised her eyebrows. "May I ask why?"

He shrugged. "I felt guilty, I guess."

"Guilty for what? You did her no harm."

Aric shot her a scowl. "Did her no harm? I nearly killed her!"

"Nonsense. She woke with perhaps a slight headache, a little nausea, and no memory of your love." Ulora's tone softened as she added, "Her loss."

"She's not my lover; you are. And I don't care what you say, there's nothing loving about practically sucking the life out of someone just because they happen to be there."

"If you put it in such provincial terms, dearest, of course it's going to sound—"

"I just wanted her to go live a normal life. Is that wrong?"

Ulora snorted. "She's just a human, love."

Aric whipped his head around. "I'm just a human."

If she felt at all chagrined, it didn't show. "We both know well that you are more than a mere human."

He didn't reply for some time. The memory of Arisnè's body prone and limp on the floor only seconds after he touched her horrified him. He still couldn't quite figure out what had happened; one moment the handmaiden was standing in front of him, the next, she was comatose, and he was floating in midair.

"My love," Ulora said, placing her hands on his shoulders and affecting a patient tone, "it is you who does not understand. If you feel you are preying on the innocent by practicing your skills on such as Arisnè, allow me to find you a criminal to reduce to his proper state. You cannot deny your gifts, not when you are so close to fully realizing your potential."

He sighed. "Perhaps."

Aric didn't like it, though. Not one bit. True, he had felt euphoric and powerful at the initial influx of vitality. But with it came a strange sensation of becoming someone else, of absorbing into himself something never meant to be his. And that it had come at the girl's expense went against the very grain of his being.

Maurin always used to say that innocence, once lost, was never regained. Aric bit his lip. He had always hated it when his cousin played adult and tried to be the teacher. But it felt like only yesterday that he and Maurin were exploring the forests outside Athure, laughing and playing, gossiping over futures that would never come to pass.

The healed scar on his palm was the only relic of Dania's attack. But what about the scars on his soul? They were not so easily healed. He had come so far, and felt so empty.

He understood what Ulora was saying. Arisnè wasn't dead; she wasn't even damaged. She had fully recovered.

The question was, would he?

———— ◆ ————

Krige spent the next couple of days in agony waiting for Talauna. Toward the end of the second day, she was delivered to him along with a grateful note, vague and unsigned. He could tell she had been crying, and something was different about her. Once Phoecius's men had gone, he pulled her into a tight hug. *Every man knows a master cannot truly love his slave,* he recalled himself saying the night he made the decision to sell Talauna. *What did I know?*

Talauna stiffened at his embrace.

"What's wrong, my little beauty?" he asked, still grasping her small shoulders. "Aren't you glad to be back?"

She tilted her chin up at him in anger and defiance.

"Well, never mind," he said, taken aback. "It's been a long journey for you, and I'm sure you must be tired. I'll have some of the maids draw you a bath."

He had sent his wife to visit her sister for a week. He wasn't sure how he would explain Talauna's return to Mirian, but he still had a few days to think it over. Meanwhile, he would prepare such a homecoming as the Maolori girl had never seen. He had the servants make up the bed and sprinkle flower petals over the sheets and the floor. He made sure some aromatic oils were set heating over small braziers, and a large bowl of fresh fruit was set by the bedside. He bathed himself and slipped into a silken robe. Then he reclined on the bed, waiting for her, sipping a mild wine. He didn't want to lose himself to the drink; not tonight.

Aric had not been amongst the Warden's party. Mulling over the words of the Reamar's high priestess, he realized his former pilot must be the so-called Dreaded One. How interesting. No wonder that Vail character had taken such an interest in him. What could possibly have been so special about the lad? It certainly wasn't his piloting abilities; they were useless where he was now. Right now, he couldn't care less. He had Talauna back, with Argoneis none the wiser.

The doors opened as the maids brought her in clean and dry and smelling of roses. She wore a short bathrobe, and her curly mane spilled fetchingly over the collar.

Krige smiled at her. "Come here," he said, and patted the bed beside him. "How I've missed you!"

She sat on the edge of the bed, eyes downcast. He scooted up behind her and caressed her shoulder. She remained unmoving as a block of wood. Krige leaned over and kissed her on the cheek, and tasted salt. Surprised, he pulled her around to look at her. Tears were streaming down her face.

"Talauna, dear, you're home," he said, trying not to sound angry. "Come to bed." Smiling, he slid his hand down her shoulder, taking the robe with it. "You won't need this."

To his stunned surprise, she grabbed the cloth and pulled it back up over herself, glaring at him. She clenched it tightly in front, then walked around to the other side of the bed, where she crawled under the covers, facing away from him.

Krige wished he'd chosen a stronger drink.

CHAPTER 45
DELIVERER

For the fourth time, the man went down. For the fourth time, he got up. Maurin heard the laughter from above, laughter at the futile attempts of the struggling duo to overcome each other. The combatants doubtless knew their lives were forfeit, but still they fought as if it mattered.

Almost a week since their capture, and the circus would begin tomorrow. Maurin went through the motions as the trainers gave him an intensive course in gladiatorial combat, but remained hollow inside.

He'd felt the pricking pain of life again when Talauna was taken from them in Langfort. Twice he had promised her he wouldn't let anything happen to her, and twice he had failed to keep that promise. Part of his brain realized there was no way he could have kept her safe from all the dangers of all the worlds—least of all this one—but it still ate away at him. There was, however, one promise he could make and not break, and he vowed to himself that should he ever be reunited with her, he would make it.

Slim chance of that, though. The most he could hope for now was that his end would be as quick and painless as possible.

He hadn't seen any of the others since their arrival in Caileen. They'd been split up, not allowed to know each other's fate. The Talormine had run off before they were surrounded outside the Gray Lands, and he couldn't really blame her. None of this was her problem, after all. Hopefully wherever Shallar was, she would be able to find her cubs.

"The eve of death." A tallish woman stood in the corner, keeping her distance from everyone around her. Her lustrous blonde hair was shorn unevenly and hung in ragged tatters about her face. She could not have been that much older than Maurin, but her gaunt, haunted look said she had seen all too much in her years.

"One can only hope," he muttered, too low for her to hear.

She tried to keep her voice steady and unemotional. "In one of the games, there are several men and one woman. They like us helpless and beautiful." Her tone turned acid. "The woman isn't given any weapons, and she's set out into the middle of the arena, and that's when they release the wild animals."

Maurin cleared his throat. He didn't really want to hear more, but she continued anyway.

"The woman is the flag; they have to get her to some point of safety, and if she dies, the whole team is executed. Either way, Argoneis wins his blood."

"What happens if the team makes it?"

"Supposedly, a certain amount of prize money is afforded for each win. A slave could buy her way to freedom, if she got through the entire gauntlet."

"You don't think that's likely?"

The woman shrugged, and a tear wound its way down her cheek. "No. There are rules; you're not supposed to kill your slaves with no reason. But we're talking about Argoneis here, the man who impales a slave on a sharp pole, and times his dinner on how long it takes for the slave to die. He would think it funny if every one of us ends up dead."

Maurin shuddered and looked out away from the troubled eyes of the blonde woman. He didn't see the two men fighting anymore. "What does he hope to gain from all this? Power? It seems he has that aplenty."

"Pleasure," the woman said, disgusted.

He turned back and regarded her silently. "How did you get here?"

She shook her head, her hair hanging in limp strands over her eyes. "I dared to stand up to Argoneis. He mutilated my father, tortured my mother to death, and kept me in a dungeon, tormenting me until he decided he would rather put me in the games than kill me outright or sell me anonymously."

"Were you one of his slaves?"

The woman laughed a bitter laugh. "Hardly. I am... I was the countess of Sal Dalinde." She turned away, her shoulders slumped. "Now, I'm just a statistic, one of hundreds of Argoneis's disposable playthings."

"I'm sorry." There didn't seem to be anything more to say.

"I never thought much about my slaves," she said, her eyes distant. Maurin wasn't really sure if she even realized he was still there; she appeared to be talking to herself. "I always avoided the games as much as possible; I have no love of bloodshed. Daman would have accused me of being weak, no doubt, but he's the weak one. How well I know that now. Weak, and cowardly, and... cruel. Cruel above all else."

Maurin pictured Argoneis as a spoiled and arrogant child, pulling the wings off insects and torturing small animals. Had there ever been a decent or loveable bone in his body? Somehow, Maurin doubted it.

"Don't fear." A burly and incongruously optimistic wispy-haired old man spoke up. "We have only to wait for the deliverer."

"The deliverer?" Maurin raised an eyebrow.

"Ledes," another slave said, rolling his eyes, "you keep saying someone is going to come to deliver us. When?"

The elder leaned back and sighed. "Soon," he said. "Very soon."

"The deliverer," the countess repeated dully. She did not sound comforted.

"I'm not sure I understand," Maurin said.

"It is a prophecy," Ledes said. "Many have read it in the stars."

"Would that be the stars as seen from this world, or your homeworld?

Because the night sky here is nothing like the one I know." Had he asked to bait the man, or out of genuine desire for knowledge? Maurin shook his head.

Ledes chuckled. "Young man, many have seen this for years before coming to this world as slaves. When the Breath sends a message to Yasul's beloved, it doesn't matter where they are."

"Oh... you're one of those. There is no escape, old man," the woman said with a sharp laugh. "The only way out of here is death."

INTERLUDE
SHADOW OF DEATH

The day is so sunny as to be almost painful. The crowd squints at the combatants in the arena. I fight for all I am worth; none yet lie dead in my wake, but I have managed to stay alive so far. Sweat glistens off my body as I swing my sword with all my might. The chaos of battle surrounds me. The cool mountain air is thick with the scent of blood and fear.

A shadow spreads over participants and onlookers alike as a huge black cloud billows and rolls over the mountains.

Dania clenches a trident in one hand and a knife in the other.

"What are you doing?" I see no pity, no remorse. Just the cold calculation of a lifelong killer.

"Defend yourself, Maurin."

I hesitate, but she does not. She lunges forward, and I dodge, but she is too quick for me. With a practiced sweep of the leg, she swings around and connects with the backs of my knees. Then I am on my back, and she has her foot on my chest.

She raises her trident for the killing blow...

CHAPTER 46
PLEDGE

"Aric?" Ulora's voice called him from the arena. "Aric, wake up, dearest."

Aric stirred, fighting the urge to lash out. He didn't want to leave; he had to help Maurin. This was wrong, it was all wrong...

"Beloved, it's all right. Please come back to me."

Aric gasped, and rolled off onto the cool floor of the room, dragging the sheets with him. He didn't answer for several minutes, but lay there panting, soaking with sweat. She came to sit beside him and cradled his head until he calmed down enough to speak.

"What have you seen?"

Aric forced the words out of his mouth, speaking around a throat so tight he could hardly breathe: "Maurin is going to die."

Ulora's eyes filled with concern. "Oh, no, beloved. How can this be?"

"Dania—the one who attacked you—is going to kill him in the arena." Aric shook his head. "Something's happened; they must not have made it back all right." A sudden suspicion filled him, and he tore away from Ulora's embrace, glaring at her. "Do you know anything about this?"

She looked wounded. "No, love; why would I?"

Aric searched her soul for signs of deception. He could sense none, but then, there was so much he didn't know about the Reamar, even now.

"I have to help him." He got up, and was dressed and in the corridor. It took him a moment to realize that he didn't recall having put on his clothes or leaving the room. Ulora stood smiling beside him.

"You are Reamar," she said. "You are coming by instinct to understand our realm."

"I'm not sure I do," he said, looking himself over, and back at the room he somehow just left. The gray tunnels of the tree were now grand corridors of a vast palace, brilliantly festooned with colorful banners and lavish decorations. He no longer strode on the stony floor, but on a rich green carpet toward a grand staircase.

"Aric," she said, walking now beside him, "the world in which we dwell is but a shadowy dream to most. But to you, it is as real as the one you left. And you are a living conduit of the planes. Before long, you will be able to walk the world of the flesh as if it were but a dream."

Aric considered the transformed halls in awe. "And all this?"

"The reality you choose to inhabit."

And then he understood. He closed his eyes, and when he looked down again, he was clad in green armor, a blazing sword clenched in his fist. He filled his vision with the arena in which he saw Maurin, and he was there. But it was empty.

Ulora gazed out across the landscape of dream with him. "You have created this place, Aric, but we are still in the Gray Lands. In order for us to travel to other places by the power of will, the Gray Lands must grow."

"And how does that happen?"

"By our direction, and our existence. We are one, the Gray Lands and the Reamar. But there must be a connection, and I believe none of us has ventured into Caileen long enough to establish a presence."

Aric knelt for a moment and ran his fingers through the dust of the empty arena. It turned to ash in his hands, and when he stood again, all was as it had been; he stood in the corridor of Darkhorn Fell, with Ulora at his side. But something nagged at his memory: gray vines in an alley-way, on the night he escaped Lord Krige's mansion.

"One has."

"What?"

"Your missing priestess, Siaran Thoud. I know where she is. She's hiding in Caileen."

And with the knowledge came the certainty that she had come for his sake, that she had wanted to warn him against the Reamar. He hoped he hadn't betrayed her to punishment. But none of that mattered now. There was a connection, a seed of the Gray Lands planted in the heart of Caileen. And perhaps that would be enough.

"I can't do this alone, and Maurin will die if I don't go to him."

Ulora wore a satisfied smile, like when they made love. "Cherished one, Lord Réus will be able to help you in this task. But I need a pledge that you will return to the Gray Lands."

"A pledge? What kind of pledge?"

In an instant, she was transfigured. A dazzling light overwhelmed her natural radiance and beauty, and he saw her as a vision of glory, a spark of creation. Her face and hands shone, and her voice took on a heart-rending beauty. Surely this was how the Reamar appeared when they were first wrought from the will of Yasul. "Bind yourself to me. For time, and for eternity. Vow that you will be mine forever."

Then the image faltered. As though obscuring lenses were removed from his eyes, Aric saw past the exquisite veil of light, past the physically perfect body she had chosen, and into her soul. What he saw nearly made him gag.

Ulora crouched before him, a shriveled, gray thing of skin and bone. Black, tangled strings of hair hung limply from a shiny pate, and her wiry arms were like claws. Hateful black-upon-black eyes stared at him with an endless hunger, and he realized he was seeing Ulora not as she had been, but as she truly was; a wretched, pitiful creature of anger, spite, and fear.

He blinked, and the hallucination was gone. Ulora stood before him as he knew her; human, beautiful and flawless. She was smiling, and he sensed she didn't know what he had just seen. Aric's heart constricted, but he could not rid his mind of Maurin facing his death. He looked Ulora in the eye, took her in his arms, and words spilled forth from his mouth as if he had been rehearsing them for years.

"Grant me this boon," he vowed, "and I am yours, from this day forward. Your destiny and mine are one. I am of the Reamar, and the Reamar are of me. Your will is my own."

He felt his soul buffeted by a wind, and the light in the corridor dimmed. A chill settled into the core of his being, and the dread of the ages pressed upon him. He sensed a great sorrow somewhere, though he couldn't place it.

"I accept your pledge," Ulora said, smiling with such radiance that he nearly forgot the starved, moribund creature of only seconds ago. "Now let us visit Lord Réus."

Shackled and alone. Was this to be her fate? To taste freedom, only to lose it time and time again? To live in pain and solitude, to have every hope of joy and love stolen for the promise of blood?

Dania counted her fiftieth press-up and slowly exhaled. A ray of light pierced the darkness of her cell, and she rose to greet her visitor.

A broad shape filled the doorway, accompanied by the familiar scent of cigar.

Farel.

"Come to gloat?" she asked, hands aching for her daggers.

"Dania, Dania," he murmured. "I never wanted this for you."

"Then you should never have betrayed me."

Farel leaned against the jamb and exhaled a plume of smoke. "I told you you were too valuable to lose."

"*Valuable* can also mean *costly*," she reminded him. "I hope you got a fair price."

Farel said nothing for a moment. Dania stared him down, unblinking. Finally, he shrugged. "We all do what we have to do. You of all people should know that."

"I know that I was never worth any more to you than the price of a ticket. I know that you lied to me. And I know that I shall never forget it."

Farel nodded, started to speak, and then seemingly thought better of it. He stepped outside and closed the door. "I'm looking forward to seeing you in action again."

Dania stared at the door until the spots in her vision faded and the narrow confines of her cell became clear.

"Don't worry," she promised quietly. "I'll give you a show you won't forget."

That night, on the hard stone bench running the length of the gladiators' quarters, Maurin drifted between dreams and despair. Then he heard it.

MAURIN.

And this time, he knew who it was.

"Here I am." He sat up, wide awake, heart pounding. The tiniest ember of hope flickered in his soul.

HEAR ME NOW, MAURIN, FOR I HAVE CALLED YOU FROM YOUR LIFELONG SLUMBER, AND IT IS TIME FOR YOU TO AWAKEN.

"How can this be? I'm nothing but the son of a priest, and the priest of a lesser god, at that. I'm not worthy of being..."

The voice was quiet, yet Maurin felt an intense pressure on his soul.

I AM THAT WHICH WAS, IS, AND SHALL BE. I AM YASUL.

"What do you want from me?"

EVERYTHING.

"I have nothing to give."

TARRY NO LONGER. THE TIME HAS COME.

"For what?"

BECOME WHAT I HAVE CREATED YOU TO BE. YOU ARE MY SWORD OF RECKONING.

A lifelong devotee of Baelon. Indebted by oaths to the divine. The decision should have been difficult. Yet to be sought out, to actually be spoken to—there was really nothing else he could do.

"I am your servant. Use me as you will."

But the voice did not respond, and the presence had left. A few slaves shifted position, snoring softly. No one appeared to have been awakened by his strange visitation.

But how can I do anything stuck here? He hadn't spoken aloud, and didn't expect a response, so almost jumped when the voice whispered again.

FEAR NOT. I AM EVER WITH YOU.

Sleep overtook him with an incomprehensible sense of peace, and the morning light brought a dawning of a new purpose.

A heady anticipation grew within him, a heartsong of liberation and retribution.

This was what he had dreamed of since the day of his wedding and abduction.

Valasand had once asked him, Are you worthy of your dreams?

He smiled. The time had come to find out.

CHAPTER 47
DAY OF WRATH

First day of the circus, and already Krige wished he were somewhere else. He tried to look away from the carnage below as often as he could without Daman noticing.

Argoneis gripped his armrests in ecstasy, eyes glazed and body tense as he watched the proceedings. He grinned like a carrion bird awaiting its next meal. Yet he seemed unusually agitated, talking and laughing more loudly than his wont. Could it have anything to do with the Warden languishing in her prison cell? She had told Daman with a mysterious smile that his doom was coming, and he would be powerless to stop it. She was hardly the first person to threaten Argoneis, but he seemed strangely unnerved by her mutterings.

Talauna sat by Krige's side in the shade of a large awning. He hated to bring her to places like this, but he took the Maolori girl with him everywhere he went now. His wife had been less than thrilled to discover she'd returned, and had threatened to have her beaten within an inch of her life if she were ever left alone with her. Talauna watched the games with a greater intensity than he would have thought. It was almost as if she were looking for something—or someone. The master of ceremonies announced the reenactment of some centuries-old battle or another, and a new round of gladiators entered the stadium.

Talauna's ears lifted.

———————— ◆ ————————

Maurin stepped out into the bright sunlight of the arena. He should be afraid; he could very well die this day. But he felt a sense of calm he didn't expect in the knowledge that whatever happened, he would be an instrument of the Source.

Help me. Show me what I need to do.

Stationed around the entire circumference of the arena were guards carrying bolt-throwers. No gladiators were allowed to use energy weapons or projectile launchers, but the servants of Argoneis carried them in case of just such rebellious thoughts.

Many of the cadre of gladiators were heavily armed, and even more heart-stopping, armored. For the sake of this particular drama, Maurin was dressed only in a broad vest, tunic, leather sandals, and linen pants. The sword he carried and the shield on his forearm did little to dispel the feeling that compared to others, he was practically naked. And while some of the games were highly structured, this one was a free-for-all. Last one standing won.

He took a deep breath. *I don't want to kill anyone. Most of these people are just scared slaves, like me. Why do I have to go through this?*

The trumpet call heralded the beginning of the melee, and within minutes, he was fighting for his life. Suddenly it didn't matter where these warriors had come from, or if they had wives, husbands, children. One after another came at him, and he fought to disable, but soon it would be kill-or-die, and he couldn't do anything for Talauna or Aric— much less Yasul—dead.

As he fought, the sky started to cloud over, and a shadow fell across the arena. The people in the stands didn't seem to notice. All around him, Maurin heard the shouts of the massive crowd, the clash of steel, and the screams of the dying.

Then he saw her. Dania, outfitted once more in the scant costume armor of the arena, flinging off attackers left and right, her tattooed body standing out like a flower in a field of wheat. Her muscles worked in perfect harmony as she dispatched one after another of the gladiators. His confidence waned and his heart sank as she sprinted in his direction, eyes flashing.

"Dania...!"

She drew back and slashed at him with her blade.

His jaw dropped. He deflected the blow with his shield. "What are you doing?"

"Defend yourself, Maurin."

She swung at him again, then made a jab with her trident. They might as well have been alone in the arena; no one was within yards of them. A chill wind blew across Maurin's sweaty body, and he shivered. Betrayed. Why was she doing this?

Dania lunged again. He spun out of her reach. Didn't want to fight her. Dead if he didn't.

Probably dead if he did.

Maurin shuffled back—*please just let this be over soon*. Dania twisted around, swinging her leg. An impact, and he found himself staring at the sky, gasping for breath. Overhead, the clouds roiled in angry power. A sandaled foot planted on his chest, and Dania's face twisted into a grin as she raised her trident and brought it down...

Next to his head.

"Maurin, it's time to stop playing around. Let's get out of here." She nodded off to her left. For the first time he saw Masalla—the Warden was engaged not more than a few yards away, watching them out of the corner of his eye.

"Be who you were born to be," Dania said, her smile and stance radiating a peace and understanding he would never have expected from her.

From one end of the arena to the other, the ground was littered with the bodies of the slain. Dozens of gladiators still engaged in skirmishes of their own. Maurin stood, drew in his breath, and shouted:

"In the name of Yasul, *STOP!*"

And to his amazement, they did.

His voice echoed, a chorus of "stops" following the first, calling out from one side of the arena to the other. The gladiators turned in surprise, and thousands of eyes—slave and spectator alike—were now on him.

His courage faltered; nonetheless he continued, pitching his voice to reach every ear: "You who are willing to fight for your lives, will you not instead join me in a fight for freedom? Freedom for yourselves and for those you love. Freedom for those shackled to this cursed world and those who have yet to know the pain of slavery! It is time for a cleansing. Let it begin here!"

The guards with energy weapons didn't hesitate to use them. Within seconds, a flurry of lightning bolts turned sand to glass, pelting at his feet as he ran. Dania ran with him, and Masalla joined them.

"Well done, young one," the Warden said, diving into a pile of broken stone pillars and slabs used as props for the previous battle.

"For all the good it seems to have done."

Dania pointed. "More than you think, Maurin."

Dozens of slaves ran toward the gated archways leading to the arena. Many were shot down, but a few managed to get close enough to attack the guards. Masalla cheered softly as the gladiators took the bolt-throwers from their bodies. Others crowded in close to the trio in the rubble, gazing at Maurin and offering him silent nods and promises of support.

"It's beginning," Masalla said.

The far-better armed security forces of the arena used their bolt-throwers and crossbows to make short work of anyone who ventured too close, but the instigators of this riot—Maurin chief among them—were clustered in the middle of the stadium, unreachable except by crossing the vast expanse of sand, and getting close enough to kill. And few seemed willing, at this point, to risk getting ambushed. Pretty soon, Maurin expected, this would reach a standoff, and there would be no bargaining. They would all die.

Then the world turned inside out.

A shockwave, silent, but deafening as a thunderclap, threw Maurin and the others near him to the ground. A collective gasp went up from the crowd. Then the earth beneath them shook and rumbled. The sky overhead blackened to night.

The ground in the center of the arena erupted like a volcano, and a vast gray spike thrust upward, growing taller and broader with each passing second. It spread horizontally, radiating creepers and tendrils outward almost faster than Maurin's eye could follow. Shouts and screams rose over the wind as an interwoven mesh of gray rapidly blanketed the arena.

The spike bulged at the end, then split open from the tip to the base like a seed pod. At first, there was nothing but the sound of the gale. Then, slowly at first, but with a gathering power, a noise made itself heard over the storm: a deep, mournful cry. With a sudden rush, an ink-black jet erupted from the bloom of the gray vine, a smoky cloud of impenetrable gloom. It spiraled into the air in a streaming column. A prickling, invasive chill settled around them like a curtain and began to swirl through their midst. While most of the gladiators stood frozen to the ground, a few took to their heels.

"Stand firm!" Masalla shouted.

The horror threatened to claim Maurin's spirit, but he stood his ground. The clammy caress of the shadow ran over their bodies, as if it wanted to squeeze the last drops of life out of every one of them. But after a moment, the sensation passed. Maurin could only stand there, mouth agape, as baleful shadows—not quite formed, but not quite formless—oozed through the air past them and flew out into the stands.

The screams began in earnest as a sinister wind blew through the arena. Black phantoms raced upwards, striking hundreds of the spectators in turn. A wave of motion in the stadium—people running, then toppling to the ground in succession.

Motes like pollen or dust sped by at the edges of Maurin's vision, then took shape, blurring into reality like some trick of perspective, moving like demons.

Reamar warriors.

Broad horns swept over shoulders armored with gray bone. Ribbed breastplates and shadowed face-paint made the invaders resemble a legion of skeletons. All carried braided spears and bore the countenance of death.

Hundreds—thousands—of them poured forth through the opening in the ground, riding their hissing reptilian mounts. The wolf-like Oarar bounded out and into the pandemonium. Emaciated ghouls scrambled up out of the gap between the worlds, and scattered outwards, latching their long, thin arms onto guards and spectators. The humanoid creatures screamed as they leaned in, flashes of green light and mist rising from their victims. Ledes, the old slave, emerged from the catacombs. He didn't seem at all surprised by what he saw. Masalla grabbed him by the arm and whisked him back, standing between him and the horrors, sword at the ready.

Then a figure soared upwards and out of the ground, his clothing rippling around him. He held his arms out to the sides and flew over the heads of human and Reamar alike until he landed at Maurin's feet.

Dania spat. "Aric."

"I told you the deliverer would come," Ledes said brightly. "You just have to have faith."

CHAPTER 48
A NEW ERA

"This is her doing," Daman muttered, his eyes bulging out of his head. His fingers gripped the arms of his chair so hard his knuckles had turned white.

"Aishè?" The name was out before Krige could stop himself. The encounters with the Lady of Darkhorn Fell were too fresh and vivid in his own memory.

Fortunately, Daman was too out-of-sorts to notice. "That Yasulite witch. I should have killed her when I had the chance."

It was hard to imagine what the Warden would have to do with the Reamar and the sudden screaming chaos in the arena, but that wasn't important right now. "If she's responsible for starting this, can she stop it?"

"Let's go, Aster." Argoneis leapt from his seat, almost colliding with Krige in his haste to leave. He turned to Anice. "Ready my chariot. We need to get back to the palace."

Krige couldn't agree more. Swallowing his panic, he reached for Talauna. The Maolori was gone.

———◆———

"Good. I'm not too late."

"Too late?" Maurin looked as if he might be going into shock.

Aric glowered at Dania. "Haven't had a chance to kill him yet, have you?"

"Several times over," Dania said, with a caustic sneer. "What makes you think I would take it?"

"I saw you," he accused. "I saw you about to kill Maurin."

"Dania was just trying to get close enough to talk to me!" Maurin said. "She wasn't going to hurt me!"

"Humph." Aric regarded the chaos around them. Off to his left, a Reamar warrior had pinned a man to the ground with his spear. To his right, a group of the feral Ancients scavenged another. Several of the Harvesters had apparently chosen to take up residence; all around, corpses scrabbled to their feet in jerky succession, emitting horrible-sounding screeches. "I don't know what to say."

"You came back because you thought I was going to die?" Maurin's tone softened.

Aric shrugged, embarrassed. "You're my cousin."

Maurin's face twisted up, and he smiled through his tears. "I thought we'd lost you."

Aric chose to ignore that for now. It seemed simpler.

"What is going on here, young one?" the Warden asked.

"I went to Réus," he said. "Told him that you needed help." He swung his sword around at the corpses littering the arena. "It meant bringing them here, but it's all right; you're protected."

Masalla drew closer. "What do you mean, protected?"

"I had him leave everyone with a slave-brand alone." He gestured to the scattering Reamar warriors and the gray specters in the distance. "The Reamar can share their thoughts; Réus imprinted it on all of them."

"Not all slaves are branded," Maurin growled, "and some of them wear their marks covered."

"And I don't have one," Masalla put in. "Nor does Valasand."

Aric nodded. "I know, but it's a risk I had to take. Look, it's all right. Réus is controlling the Harvesters."

"And this is supposed to make us feel better?" Maurin flipped his hand in a broad gesture encompassing the entire stadium.

"He's changed, Maurin. He wants the Reamar to change."

The Warden cocked his head. "Vals," he murmured, "you're incredible."

"Come," Dania said. "There are still slaves beneath. Let us free them."

Aric nodded and rushed forward. Maurin and the others ran beside him down the dark entry to the catacombs, and into the cells. A cohort of Reamar warriors led by Marèse Shavad flanked them, spears at the ready.

"What's going on?" a young woman asked, rubbing at her upper arms.

"The time has come," Aric said. He shook his head at the odd sound of his voice, and the words that came out of him unbidden. Where had that come from? He cleared his throat. "It's time to go, I mean."

A leg stuck out from around the corner, and he rushed forward. It was one of the guards. Aric reached toward the body, a wisp of green energy swirling about his fingers, and the man's keys were suddenly in his hand. He tossed them to Maurin, who regarded him with a strange expression. "What?"

"We're definitely going to have to have a talk when this is all over." Maurin started undoing shackles.

"Let's see if there's another set," Masalla said.

"You thought I was going to kill Maurin," Dania said as she released the woman from her bonds.

"You tried to kill Ulora."

"That was different." She raised an eyebrow. "Give me another chance, and I will."

Masalla took charge. "You two can argue later. Right now, we need to make sure some things are taken care of. I'm going to try to take control of the mountain port."

"The ships aren't due for some months now," Aric said. "There's no risk of anyone getting off-planet."

"Most of the fighting vehicles and heavy energy weapons will be there," Masalla explained. "No one must get in the air."

He didn't add *least of all, the Reamar.* Aric heard it anyway. He nodded, turning to Marèse Shavad. "Will you send fifty of your warriors with him?"

The Marèse inclined his head. "It shall be as you say, Dreaded One."

"Great," he said. "And don't call me that."

The Warden scowled at him.

"Don't worry," Aric murmured to Masalla. "The same thing that keeps the airships from sailing over the Gray Lands keeps the Reamar from getting on them. It'll be all right."

Suddenly Dania jolted, and her eyes widened. She sprinted out of the catacombs faster than he had ever seen her move.

"What was that about?" Maurin asked.

Masalla shrugged. "Whatever it was, we don't have time to chase after her. Are you ready?"

Marèse Shavad nodded. Aric watched as the Warden left, escorted by the Reamar. Then Aric slipped around a pillar and into a dark corner. *Something's wrong.* He closed his eyes and took a deep breath.

Then the vision took him again.

* * *

The time has come.

The surging pulse of the growing Gray Lands under my feet feeds me a current of strength, fear... and emotions too powerful to name. Roots and vines crawl up the walls of the city, merge with the stone, graft themselves into the fabric of this world. Towers and streets are overgrown and interwoven with the indomitable Reamar tree.

Justice rides in on the wind with the shrieking vengeance of an unleashed titan. Harvesters sweep across the length and breadth of the city, passing over every slaves' quarters and howling through the house, killing or incapacitating anyone they encounter on the way, but leaving the slaves untouched.

Trouble at the heart of the realm. Lord Réus stands with hands raised, addressing the Reamar in some sort of formal ceremony.

"My dear children, for millennia we have cheated death, have held our glorious estate ahead as a goal to be reached, but I have come to tell you that things can no longer be as they have been."

Ulora scowls, exchanging a meaningful glance with the high priestess.

"The time has come for our great race to accept our loss and return to the Source. We have lived a long and powerful existence, but it is in vain. No matter how long we delay the inevitable, our paths lead back to Yasul. And our choice is to bow the knee willingly, or upon pain of damnation."

"Never," Ulora whispers. *"Never in ten thousand years."*

A rising murmur of dissent fades in a rush. I am once more with Ulora and Aishè outside the god-king's private chamber.

"It is time," the high priestess says with sorrow. *"The die is cast, the strong will survive. Extinction is not an option."*

Ulora nods with a secretive smile, handing Aishè a braided spear. The high priestess walks with purpose into Réus's chamber, her bare feet making no sound on the curved stonewood floor.

He sits with his back to her, head bent forward in deep meditation. Réus's concentration remains centered on the battle hundreds of leagues away, on keeping the Harvesters in check, guiding them down the tributaries of the Lifestream.

"My love, my love," Aishè says gently, raising the spear, *"I hoped this day would never come, but you are going to destroy us all."* A tear rolls down her cheek. *"Goodbye, my lord Réus. An eternity was not enough."*

I try to warn him, but no sound comes from my mouth.

With a movement like a striking snake, Aishè drives the spear through his back. The tip protrudes from his chest, and an unearthly scream emits from his soul. I can feel the incredible surge of power as the god-king's lifestream flows into her, his cry becoming her own. Aishè falls to her knees, then rolls onto her side, contorted in uncontrollable spasms beside Réus.

"What have I done to us?" she screeches, her voice a symphony of terror and confusion.

"You have done what I could not." Ulora smiles. *"You have eliminated the only obstacle to the throne. Now, with Aric at my side, I shall usher in the new era of the Glorious."*

My throat tightens.

This is my fault.

Not Maurin's, not my father's.

Mine.

Ulora turns to leave as Réus stops his anguished writhing. The body slumps over, followed by a blast of green energy that blows Aishè against the wall.

And the Harvesters go berserk.

Suddenly free of the controlling influence of Réus's will, the Harvesters shriek and begin killing everything in sight. I watch helplessly as they descend on livestock, leaving whole herds twitching and expiring. They sweep through city streets with the rushing torrent of a storm, darting and pouncing at the humans. But the brand is still burned into what consciousness they have as surely as it is burned into the flesh of the slaves. Though they try, the Harvesters cannot touch them. Those whose tattoos are not visible, or who never received the brand in the first place...

They're not so fortunate.

My breathing quickens, and I struggle to stay in the grip of the vision. I know what must be done. I summon every bit of strength and concentration, and send my mind racing along over the city and through the alleyways until I can focus on one of the black spirits.

Then I seize it.

No longer constrained by the god-king and angry at having its indulgence interrupted, the Harvester tries to throw me off. Distantly, I feel sweat beading on my brow as I grapple with the creature, wrestling its will into submission. My spirit echoes the fatigue my body must be feeling—I can't hold the creature for long.

Straining, I guide the Harvester over the city walls and out into the open country.

Go.

I release it, then start chasing another, and another. As I grow familiar with the distinctive feeling of each one's presence, my resolve strengthens. One by one they succumb, reluctantly leaving their feast for the dark, empty spaces of the wilderness.

Why am I chasing you?

I picture myself flying above Caileen, hovering with arms outstretched. My ethereal body glows like a beacon, and my spirit calls out:

Your master is not dead! I am your master now! Come to me!

Like an upside-down funnel of dirty water, the black spirits spiral upwards toward me. I grit my teeth against their fury and throw my arms out in front of me.

Go! Go into the wastes, and do not return!

The specters wing their way over the city walls, hundreds of them, so massed as to be one dark river of evil flowing out of Caileen. Don't know if they're all gone, but that was definitely most of them.

I can't help but feel a little bit satisfied with myself.

Then, in a soaring rush over land, I'm back at Darkhorn Fell. The entire Gray Lands blaze with a sickly light. Rivers of green fire flow toward the central hub of the tree, billowing and swirling about the outstretched fingers of its branches. The shimmering luminosity reflects off the vaulted ceiling of clouds above, an unholy pyre of countless souls going to feed the eternal hunger of the Reamar.

The very land shivers and quakes with greed, the roots of Darkhorn Fell penetrating deep, growing with each passing moment. They spread not only toward Caileen, but toward other cities, stretching toward the concentration of life as a tree's roots seek out water. Above the fields, streamers of green mist are the only indication of the imminent terror below. Animals in the field bleat or moo in alarm seconds before they collapse, spent. People in far-off cities look askance at the strange phenomenon, then scream as their own lives are drawn away.

Above it all is Ulora, standing now at the apex of the flaming temple with her arms upraised and eyes closed in ecstasy. Wave after wave of rising green energy wreath her, the passing souls stirring her hair and clothing like a strong wind. She soaks in the raw current of sheer power.

Ulora has never looked so beautiful.

Or so terrible.

———————◆———————

The vision dropped away with a jolt of pain. Aric fell, trying to focus through the tingling numbness. A Talormine stood over him with a shock cudgel, and a man wearing the insignia of Daman's personal forces smiled down on him. "They call you the 'dreaded one,' don't they? You're the one who brought these demons to us. What say you and I go to visit Lord Argoneis, and see what all this is about?"

The city's alarms echoed from the towers, spreading their hoarse cry across Caileen and through the mountains.

Out of nowhere, Talauna appeared and leapt on the man, scratching and wailing on him with tiny fists. The man howled and shook her off.

"Bring her, too," said another guard. "She's evidently a part of this."

Aric mustered his strength and lunged.

CHAPTER 49
AT THE GATES

Revenge. Sweet and bitter, raw and visceral. The day of reckoning had come, and at last Dania would taste justice. Farel lay beneath her, radiating fear. She tightened the grip on his throat, her other hand poised to plunge the dagger into him the moment he flinched.

To his credit, he scarcely breathed. Of all people, he knew it would be futile to try to escape.

Dania's mouth twisted. "You..." Words failed her, and her throat tightened. "Do you know what you have done to me?"

"I can't undo it," Farel said, as close to remorse as she had ever heard him. "I would if I could."

"Maybe you can't make it right," Dania said. "But I can."

She tightened her grip on the dagger.

He closed his eyes.

And she hesitated. A drop of moisture fell on Farel's chest, and then another. Her vision blurred, and her arm quaked.

Farel opened his eyes. "Dania...?"

"Don't you move." She ground her teeth. "Don't you dare move..."

And then a shadow hit her with the strength of a gale, and she tumbled away. A writhing black mass glowed green, enveloping her, and then turned on Farel.

His eyes bugged, and he tried to get to his feet, but it lifted him from the ground. Dania watched helplessly as he floated and twitched in the embrace of the shade. His howl of fear turned into a dry rasp, and his rimed and withered corpse landed with a thump as the Harvester flitted off to seek out new prey.

"NO!" Dania screamed after it. "You can't take this from me!"

———— ◆ ————

The attack came just as Maurin was freeing the last of the prisoners, but the Reamar were prepared. Even now, the invaders' spears skewered one after another of Argoneis's men. Green light flashed all around the catacombs. Several of the dark warriors absorbed the lives of the dying, then turned around, revitalized, and attacked with renewed force, their bodies saturated with energy, wisps of green mist swirling about them as they moved.

Maurin recognized one Reamar warrior as Guilan Vail. Unarmed and surrounded by Argoneis's men, Vail raised his arm from his waist to shoulder level, as if summoning something. An odd glow took shape in the air around him. The Reamar snapped around in a sudden motion, and a ring of green energy went out from him like a shock wave, hitting all his attackers at once. They fell, convulsing. Vail kneeled over one of the spasming men on the ground, leaning in for the kill.

If one did not know better, one might have thought the warrior and his victim locked in passionate embrace. But the green, hazy energy passed from the man on the ground into the Reamar's mouth. With each breath, Vail seemed to relax, and when he stood, his eyes were closed in a kind of meditative bliss. He placed his arms down to his sides and floated above the ground, hands crackling with energy.

One of the surviving security officers panicked and fired one lightning bolt after another at the Reamar. Maurin could only watch as Vail walked with casual confidence towards the man, feet never touching the ground. The Reamar dodged the electric blasts, his movements so graceful that they seemed slow and languid, yet not one bolt hit him. He shifted from side to side in a blur, and the air appeared to warp around him. When he was upon the man, he thrust his spear into his attacker's abdomen. The weapon glowed, and Argoneis's man clutched at his chest and gut with hands turning into claws even as he sank to his knees. The light faded from his eyes and gleamed anew in the eyes of the Reamar. A slight smile was all the victory the warrior exhibited for having taken a life and kept it. As one, the Reamar swept in again like a flock of carrion birds and finished off the rest.

It was all over in a matter of minutes.

Maurin couldn't feel his extremities. These creatures—so steeped in darkness.

And Aric was becoming one of them.

Suddenly Guilan Vail stood before Maurin. "Where is the Dreaded One?"

"What, Aric? Isn't he here?" Maurin forced his jaw to close and strained his eyes scanning the blasted arena.

"No." Urgency edged the Reamar's voice. "He must be found."

"Are you talking about that young man who came in with you?" asked one of the recently freed slaves.

"Yes, my cousin," Maurin said. "Did you see where he went?"

"He was captured, milord," the slave said. "The lord regent's men took him."

Maurin and Guilan glanced at one another. "Took him?"

"Yes, milord."

They could have just killed him. The fact that they didn't...

"We have to get to Argoneis's palace," Maurin said abruptly. "Can I ride with you?"

Manifestly displeased, the Reamar nodded and instructed one of the warriors near him to dismount. He gestured Maurin toward the steed.

"I'm going, too." Dania stepped up to Maurin's side, face drawn tight.

"Where were you?" Maurin asked as another Reamar relinquished his animal.

She swung herself into the saddle, deliberately avoiding his eyes. "Never mind."

Guilan Vail clucked his tongue, and with a stomach-churning lurch, they were off. The city distorted and blurred as they rode, whipping past buildings and alleys. Gray tendrils and vines reached up through the stone of the streets everywhere. Time warped around them, the Reamar beside him shifting and re-focusing with each galloping step. Dania's tattoos formed a trailing smear of blue and white.

Guilan Vail gestured, and reality warped into shape around them as the reptilian steeds slowed to a stop.

And there it was. The beautiful spire of Daman Argoneis's palace lay straight ahead. Maurin could make out the guards patrolling the walls, growing steadily more anxious. One of them, a young man with a round face, was inspecting the gray veins climbing the battlements.

Guilan Vail casually dismounted, then cocked his head.

"Watch out!" screamed one of the guards.

But it was too late. With the swiftness of a raptor, an indistinct shadow swooped over the wall of the palace and smothered the young man, covering him with an inky black veil. Maurin swallowed in a dry throat as the other terrified guard fired several shots into it with his energy weapon. With a barely audible swish, an impression of wings, and a baleful glare, the shadow lifted. Below, the body of the young guard was riddled with bolt-thrower scorches. His hair had turned white, and his round cheeks had sunken into hollow flesh on his skull.

A horrifying scream rent the air as the Harvester turned on the other guard. Within seconds, a second specter joined it, and they dove into the compound. Maurin heard shouts and wails from inside the walls, but soon, all was silent.

Even Dania looked a little sick.

Maurin struggled to find his voice. "Now, to open the gates."

Guilan Vail let his arms drop slack to his sides, then raised his hand and made a fist, his eyelids slowly opening as he focused on the palace before him.

"*Rai'nak shalunar!*" He brought his arm down with a sharp motion, splaying open his fingers as if throwing rubbish to the ground.

There was a dreadful pause, and then a sudden crack. A split appeared in the mortar in the tower. Another crack, and a series of webbed fractures spread across the stone of the gateway.

Gravel and dust poured out of the walls as the weight shifted, and the massive gates fell, drawing the supporting walls into a pile of loose rubble. Only a framing latticework of giant gray roots remained.

Powerful allies, these. And powerful enemies.

———————◆———————

"What do you mean, they aren't coming?" Argoneis screamed, nearly apoplectic. "We're under attack! Of course they're coming!"

Krige had never seen Daman in this state. The Lord Regent paced, his hair matted with sweat and dark circles forming under his eyes. His breath was foul, and he was biting his nails ragged.

Talauna shied away further, disheveled and on edge. Krige had tried to convince the guards who brought in the Maolori that she belonged to him, but they insisted on confirmation from Argoneis before releasing her. He had no choice but to accompany them back to the Lord Regent's palace, along with the shackled and unconscious Aric. Glad to have retrieved her, yes, but this was the last place he wanted to be right now.

Oh, to be home, away from Daman and the Reamar, curled up beside Talauna, and sipping at a gentle wine.

The patience of the Captain of the Guard wore thin. "I've contacted the governors of Daupin Tarine, Birn Aloi, and Langfort. The baron of the Shiloan Landing sends his cordial apologies, but says he's not to be bothered with these things."

"What?"

Sabatha answered through gritted teeth. "Governor Phoecius of Langfort said he would love to help, but he's afraid of the repercussions if he sends his men to give us aid in this matter."

Krige bit back a smile. This was the Reamar's doing, no doubt. They must have gotten to the governors, somehow. He imagined Phoecius getting a warning like the one he himself had received from the Lady of the Reamar, and suppressed a chuckle when he thought of how he must have taken it. Caileen was going to the seven hells outside, and yet, Krige couldn't help feeling a detached sense of amusement; there was something refreshing about seeing Argoneis like this.

"Repercussions?" Daman ranted. "Repercussions? What does he think is going to happen when I get my hands on him? That filthy, spineless weasel! I'll cut out his heart with a pair of nail scissors, starting at his toes—"

"No one has responded to our call for assistance, Daman." There was, for once, an accusing note in Sabatha's tone. "Whatever we do, we do on our own."

Daman swore. "Release the castocs!"

Sabatha nodded curtly and motioned to Anice. "Contact the keeper; tell him to let the animals out. Then double the guard around the palace. Make certain no entrance is left with fewer than ten men."

"In the meantime," Argoneis said, "let us see what this young man is made of."

Krige felt Talauna tense beside him, but he ignored her. She hadn't let him touch her since he rescued her, and he wasn't feeling particularly sensitive right now.

Aric, bound to a rack, closed his eyes.

Subduing the boy had apparently not been easy. Distracted by Talauna, one of Argoneis's men had let him get too close after the initial stunning, and suffered for it. Aric had gone for his throat. The other guards rushed in with their shock cudgels, but the man was already in a coma.

Apparently, Aric had become quite dangerous during his time with the Reamar.

"Be careful, Daman." Sabatha laid a hand on his shoulder. "You don't want to do anything permanent. He might be useful as leverage."

"Are you questioning me?" Spittle flew from Daman's lips in his furor. "You *dare* to question me?"

"No," Sabatha said calmly. Though, of course, he did dare. Daman was no match for Sabatha physically. Krige suspected that if there was one man in the world in whom Argoneis could not inspire fear, it would be Sabatha. "I'm simply suggesting that at this point, we may wish to have some negotiating power with the Reamar."

Daman looked ready to fly into another rage, but as quickly as his fit of temper had begun, it was gone. He took a deep breath, ran a sweaty hand through his blond locks, and exhaled. "Very well, then, Captain of the Guard," he conceded lightly. "You're right, of course. But this boy will talk."

"As you say, my lord."

Daman tightened a lever, and Aric cried out.

With the Lord Regent preoccupied, this would be the perfect opportunity to slip away with Talauna. Krige turned, motioning for her to follow, but once again she was no longer beside him.

Krige could barely contain his frustration. Did she not realize that only with him would she be safe? Where could she have gone now?

———————◆———————

"Is this a trap?" Maurin scanned the courtyard for any sign of activity. No bolt-thrower fire greeted their arrival, and apart from the alarm sounding over the city, the place was strangely still.

"They must be inside." Dania shifted her grip on her daggers. "Nothing here but corpses."

"Well, that's encouraging," Maurin said. "At least they won't fight back."

"Wait." Dania stiffened. "Something's moving."

Maurin's gut went cold, and he readied himself to engage. Guilan Vail's expression remained placid.

Dozens of uniformed figures shuffled toward them out of the shadows. Not slaves. Dania hissed. But they drew nearer, sharing the same blank expression Maurin had seen on the faces at Mor Tespir.

He shuddered. Thralls. Little more than walking corpses, people whose souls had been supplanted by the will of the Reamar.

A few whispered words from Guilan Vail, and the thralls preceded them across the open courtyard and into the main building. Past the foyer, great columns stretched up to a ceiling several stories above them. Each of the first two was a marbled pillar with a gilded staircase coiled around it in the image of a gigantic serpent wrapped around a tree. Maurin started to cross the palace floor, but Dania blocked him with her arm.

"Don't."

A small contingent of Argoneis's men waited ahead in the shadows. A familiar pair of dark-skinned humans and several massive Talormines stood in the lead, holding energy weapons, spears, and crossbows. Sabatha, Anice, and their guards had apparently been waiting until the others were all inside, but with their ambush spoiled, they began firing anyway. Maurin hit the floor. One after another of the Reamar thralls fell, throats and abdomens erupting in sharp points of blood, others burned by the jagged bolts of electricity. The remaining thralls pressed forward, oblivious to the danger. Some of them got through, and set upon their attackers, growling and screeching like animals.

Still, Argoneis's forces spread out and moved forward with determination. Dania planted her feet on the ground, set widely apart. She took a deep breath and clenched her teeth.

"I will take them," she said decisively. The guards ran toward her, firing as they came.

Without warning, a large white form lunged forward and grabbed the straps of Dania's breastplate, sweeping her up with one powerful motion and pulling her back. Startled, Dania yowled, and Shallar loped off toward a promenade with the gladiatrix dangling from one fist, squirming and kicking.

"What are you doing?" Dania's cries echoed off the stone walls. "Put me down! Let me go!" Maurin was hard pressed to keep up with the Talormine. "You great fool! I can take care of myself!"

Shallar set Dania down behind the stone barrier. She staggered a bit, took a deep breath, and promptly used it to start hurling furious imprecations at the Talormine, who watched her wild gestures impassively.

"Where did you come from?" Maurin exclaimed, grinning. This seemed to be the day for surprising reunions. "Where have you been?"

The Talormine jerked her head to the side, indicating an unguarded hallway.

"Go," Dania said. "We'll hold them off!"

Shallar leapt forward, grabbed Sabatha by the throat, and hurled him across the room. He hit the wall and slid unmoving to the floor. Without missing a beat, the Talormine seized another of the soldiers and snapped his back. She smashed yet another's head against a pillar.

Ducking, Maurin raced down the corridor as crossbow bolts and energy streaks flew over his head. He turned one corner after another, descended a series of stairs into the lower levels of Daman's palace, and around another corner. He heard no sound of pursuit, so he slowed down and walked briskly through the damp stone labyrinth.

From the end of the corridor, a Talormine guard drew a massive khopesh from its belt.

Maurin halted. *Oh, great.*

The Talormine lurched forward, swinging to decapitate him. Maurin met the blow, but the sheer force and weight behind it drove him back. He staggered, and his tunic caught on one of the torches.

Let his size work against him.

Maurin pulled away from the wall, jerking the cloth free, and tearing it halfway down his back. The guard swung again. Maurin dropped, and the crescent blade carved a chunk of the wall above his head. A plume of powdered stone and gravel rained down. Maurin scooted himself along on his back with his heel and elbows, the advancing Talormine looming over him. Its massive khopesh whistled through the air with each stroke, dropping ever closer like a pendulum. Maurin's shoulder found the cold stone of a stair, and he scrabbled up a few steps.

Come on, just a little bit closer...

The Talormine raised the blade over his head and brought it down with all his weight. Maurin rolled to the right, but kept his left arm out, bracing the pommel of the sword against the steps.

At the same time the Talormine swung down, Maurin kicked out with his right foot, knocking one of the Talormine's narrow-footed legs out from under it. With a bawling cry, the enormous beast fell forward, impaling itself up to the hilt on Maurin's sword. He felt a wrenching jolt of pain. His arm was pinned, and his wrist sprained, but the beast was dead.

An energy bolt hit the step next to him. How many more? Maurin swept down with his right arm and unclipped a bolt-thrower from the belt of the dead Talormine. He struggled to free his hand from the dead weight of the creature's body, crying out in pretence of mortal anguish. One of Argoneis's men poked his head around the corner, and Maurin shot it. *Don't you come any smarter than that?*

Terrific. Now the others wouldn't come out where they could be hit.

They were there, though. He could hear them whispering and breathing.

And suddenly screaming.

A ghastly moan sounded in the narrow confines of the hallway, and bolt-thrower fire erupted in wild, crazy spurts. None of it was directed at Maurin, though. Cautiously, he stuck his head up over the dead Talormine, straining to see around the corner. He could not, but the light had suddenly gone dim, and a phantom gloom ate away at the tunnel. The sound of struggles decreased, and the last of the shots echoed through the corridor.

With a metallic-edged moan, a Harvester rounded the corner, its billowing blackness sparkling with traces of green. Maurin fought to unpin his arm. *Got to think fast, got to move, got to get out of here, got to... PLAY DEAD!*

Maurin flopped down, locked in a strange embrace with the corpse of the horsehead, and shut his eyes. A howling wind rushed over him, tossing his body and threatening to pick him up, but after what seemed like an eternity in the caresses of a demon, it passed.

Cautiously, he opened his eyes. The Harvester was gone. No sign of anyone else. He braced himself against the stairs and rolled the Talormine off. He let the weight of the sagging body do the work of withdrawing the sword. Realization hit just as he was about to tie back the torn corners of his tunic. Maurin craned his neck to see the exposed flesh of his shoulder.

His slave brand was visible. Cold fingers gripped his heart. That was too close. How stupid could he be? If anything could tell the dead from the living, it would be one of those things. But Aric had said they were protected, hadn't he?

Maurin tore his vest off and cast it aside. He removed the remainder of his tunic and used it to wipe his sword, then considered the Talormine's bolt-thrower. If that last blast was any indication, the weapon was nearly drained, and he couldn't risk his life on a weak shot. Would the presence of the Reamar affect those, too? No wonder Dania didn't trust energy-based weapons. He tossed it aside and staggered on down the hallway, not looking at the pile of dead men.

He came to a corridor of barred wooden doors. A large key ring hung on a hook. Argoneis's dungeon? He grabbed the ring and dashed forward, stopping at each door as he called for Aric.

Several cells down, he heard a feeble female voice. "Maurin."

"Valasand!"

Her cloak hung on a peg outside a cell with her Temple medallion. He fumbled with the keys, trying several until he found one that fit. The door swung open to reveal a squalid cell. Valasand lay on the floor, bloodied and bruised.

Maurin rushed forward and covered her with the cloak. "What has he done to you?"

"Never mind," Valasand rasped, gazing at him through swollen lids. "Something has... changed in you, Maurin."

He nodded. "I heard the Breath call, and this time I answered."

"Good," she said, with a hint of a smile. "It took you long enough. Now go... do what you need to do."

"I can't leave you here."

"Yes, you can," Valasand said. "I can't keep up with you, and there's... an evil man on the loose. Go take care of it, Maurin."

"I think Aric is here, too," Maurin said, hesitant.

"Aric is going to have to wait." Valasand's voice took on new strength. "The Source has raised you from the ashes of slavery for a purpose, Maurin. Go be Yasul's sword."

Maurin nodded. He left her and ran further down the corridor. A faint stench in the air grew in intensity the further he went, but he couldn't quite place it. It was freezing down here. He passed a hallway lined with stalls, each one equipped with benches, and some strange hoses and troughs. Maurin frowned.

The next room was a chamber of horrors, the likes of which he suspected had not been seen in centuries. The stifling impression of agony lingered in the air; an overwhelming, nauseous aura of unspeakable suffering that was all too real, and all too recent. A solid chair sat off to Maurin's left; spiked, with a bracket across the front filled with holes and stained with something dark. There were racks, and mottled tables, and hooks, and blades, and instruments of torture such as could have been conceived only in the mind of a psychopath.

Something caught his boot as he stepped forward. Sick to his stomach, Maurin saw that the stone floor had drains spaced periodically throughout, their grates stained with blood.

He turned away quickly, then cried out.

On one of the racks lay Aric.

His cousin motioned to the adjacent room and mouthed one word: *Argoneis*. Maurin nodded in understanding. Choking on a ghastly smell, he rounded the corner and walked into a nightmare.

CHAPTER 50
GALLERY

Dania whirled as an enraged scream resounded through the hall. From behind one of the piles of bodies, a lean form leapt, all sinew and dark grace. A spearhead flashed, just missing Dania's shoulder. She ducked close and returned a sweeping stroke, drawing a line of blood across the other's abdomen.

Anice, sister to Daman's captain of the guard. The cut was not deep, and served only to anger her. The woman snarled ferociously and flew at Dania with renewed vigor, jabbing with the spear and swinging the long-bladed head alternately.

Dania swiped out with her dagger, and only a jerk of the head kept Anice from being blinded. Anice drew back and jabbed the spear at Dania's abdomen. Dodge, parry, thrust, block—*damn*, a nick—swipe—*Ha!* Got the bitch's ribs. The woman fought well. But good as she was, she had not been raised in the pits. Anice threw her entire body weight behind a thrust, and overstepped her balance, her blade whistling past Dania.

Dania thrust one knife into Anice's wrist, pinning her arm to the pillar. With the other hand, she drew her blade across the woman's throat, cutting short a scream. Dania paid little heed to the ensuing spatter of blood.

Dan-ia! Dan-ia! DANIA!

She raised her daggers above her head in victory.

Shallar, her white coat now red with blood, growled and pointed down a dark passageway, where two pairs of yellow eyes shone out of the shadows. Enormous furred avians emerged into the light. Dania knew these animals well: Shiloan castocs, often used in the arena. They drew nearer, hissing. With a great leap, the creature bounded out of the corridor and set upon the Talormine. It drew its talons across her chest, leaving parallel grooves in the flesh. Shallar snarled and rolled over, wrestling with the creature.

The Talormine managed to get around to the back of the animal and seized its neck in a death grip. It thrashed and struggled, scoring her with its talons as she squeezed the breath out of it.

One of the Reamar thralls lifted a sword and slashed at the animal, drawing a gout of blood and a shriek of pain. The creature lunged, knocking him aside, and tore into him with beak and claws. Dania bared her teeth in frustration. She had only her knives, and while she had killed larger animals than this, this one was tricky. She would likely die, too, if she attacked with just her daggers. Her eyes flitted among the bodies until she saw what she needed. She dashed across the floor toward Anice's corpse. Grasping her spear tightly with both hands, she rushed at the castoc occupied with the thrall. With a mighty shove, she plunged the spear into the animal's side, up under its rib cage, and through its heart.

And then she was alone with the Talormine. Shallar lay panting and shaking, barely conscious. Nothing to be done for the creature at the moment. But maybe she could lend Maurin a hand. Dania ran down a flight of stone stairs, and narrowly missed being hit by a flash of energy from a small bolt-thrower.

Not all dead, apparently. She rolled and came up, casting about for the source of the shot. A door squealed. Heaving herself forward, she reached it just before it closed. With a kick, she rocked the door back on its hinges. Echoes of feet running into the distance, a shadow flinging itself around a corner. Dania took off after it, and the footsteps stopped abruptly.

What kind of a fool did this one think her?

She reached the corner and threw herself into a forward roll. Bolt-thrower shots sailed overhead. Those split seconds of confusion were all she needed. She hurled one knife, which lodged in the man's chest. Gasping, he dropped his bolt-thrower and clutched at the handle. She ran forward and made a tight, controlled slash. Blood splattered on the wall.

A sound like the caw of a bird mixed with the hoarse baying of a hound reached Dania's ear, growing closer by the moment. With a ferocious screech, another castoc bounded full tilt at her, foaming and snapping its beak. The claws gleamed evilly in the torchlight. If only she had kept the spear, even grabbed a bolt-thrower off a corpse.

She braced herself for death.

A shrill whistle burst out at her side, and the attack ceased as suddenly as it began. The castoc pulled up short, startled, and the arid shrieking died. Talauna stood there, hands on her hips. Making a slight "hmmmph" noise in the back of her throat, the girl gave the animal a disapproving stare. The creature cowed at her feet, its tail between its legs, and its head low to the ground in repentance. It whined pitifully. Talauna made a quick gesture, and the castoc ran off into the recesses of the palace. Then, smiling, she turned to face Dania.

"I don't know where you came from, girl," Dania said. "But I'm glad to see you."

Talauna reached out and embraced her, squeezing as hard as she could. Dania stiffened, then tentatively patted the girl's back. Her vision blurred for some reason, and she coughed before speaking.

"Do you know where Aric is?"

— ◆ —

Mounted on poles and nailed to the walls, chained to posts and hung from hooks—everywhere were hacked and mutilated bodies. Male and female. Some in advanced stages of decomposition, some relatively fresh. Most barely recognizable as human. All had died in states of extreme torment.

The room was the grisly showcase of a demented hobbyist, seared into Maurin's eyes and memory. He staggered back against the wall next to the door, his head spinning, his stomach clenched.

"What do you think of my gallery?"

Maurin stopped short. Argoneis stood smirking next to an ornately dissected cadaver, kindling Maurin's anger anew.

"You murdering bastard."

Argoneis shrugged. "A true artist always has his detractors, and, admittedly, my tastes don't always please everybody. But since the art is mine, I don't suppose it matters, does it?"

"It mattered to them." He stepped closer, keeping his sword out, with the tip leveled at chest height. A strange calm overtook Maurin as he gazed at the man, the heat of his anger cooling into a hardened heart. He had to kill him. There was nothing to save. No mercy, no redemption.

"So." Argoneis's amused smile curled into a demonic façade as he glanced at Maurin's slave brand. Untouchable to the last. "The mighty warrior faces his adversary, hmmm?"

"Call it what you want." Maurin refused to be baited. His grip on the sword tightened until it was almost painful to hold. His knuckles turned white. "You're going to be called into account for your actions."

"You really think you can bring me to trial, slave?" Argoneis scoffed. "You came in here seeking some foolish notion of justice, looking for a way to make me pay, didn't you? Go ahead and try." He held out his wrists in a mocking offer to bind him. "I'll go with you. But no court in the dynasty would convict me."

"You know, you're absolutely right." Maurin raised his sword in both hands. "Justice—"

And then his arm exploded in pain, and his sword flew across the room. He tried to move, but his hand was frozen in place above his head. A quarrel protruded from his wrist, pinning his arm to the stone wall of the chamber.

Snorting, a Talormine giant moved into sight from behind a row of bodies, accompanied by a couple of human enforcers. One had a hook nose, the other had spiky hair.

Maurin cursed himself and tried not to panic. He had let his guard down. Of course Argoneis wouldn't go anywhere without his lackeys.

"You were saying?"

"I was saying you're a dead man." He tugged, but couldn't move.

Fiery rivers of agony flowed up and down his arm.

"I think you have us confused somehow." Argoneis ambled forward. "I can't seem to find Anice or Sabatha anywhere. You wouldn't happen to know where they are, would you, slave?"

"Your bodyguards? Last I saw, Sabatha had just learned that stone walls are tougher than heads."

Argoneis froze, his smile disappearing.

Foolish to bait him? Perhaps. Argoneis clearly had the advantage, but nothing Maurin could do would change that, and perhaps getting him angry would cause him to make a mistake.

Just what would that be, anyway? No idea.

But it was better than cowering.

"His sister... didn't see what happened to her, but between us and the Reamar, your little surprise party got crashed. I imagine you'll find her once you start sorting through the bodies."

The Talormine moved forward and punched Maurin in the gut, driving out all his wind and causing his knees to buckle. He would have collapsed but for the tearing sheet of pain that caused him to jolt upright again when his weight dragged on the bolt in his wrist.

Maurin strained against the quarrel. The shaft had gone between the bones, but he didn't think they were broken.

Yasul, help me. He tugged again, and nearly passed out.

"Do with me what you want..." Maurin gasped.

"Thank you for your permission," Argoneis said dryly. "I plan to."

At a nod from Argoneis, Hook Nose moved forward with a halberd. Before Maurin realized what he intended, the guard thrust the weapon through his left foot and into the wood of the floor.

Maurin screamed.

Pain assailed him from both extremities of his body. Maurin's heart quailed. Death had never felt so real, and his arm and leg formed a diagonal line of anguish through his core. Was this just the beginning?

He forced himself to speak through clenched teeth. "I don't know if you've noticed, but the gods of the Gray Lands have come to Caileen. Why don't you take a look outside? You're not in charge here anymore."

"To the contrary, I have their beloved Dreaded One in my

recreational room. Did you see it?" Argoneis's eyes blazed wild and intense. "There are some wonderful toys in there. Had I known you were going to come visiting, I would have brought you there to greet you in a proper manner."

"Don't take any pains on my account." Maurin pushed again. Spots floated before his eyes.

"Believe me, I won't." Argoneis grasped Maurin's shoulder amiably. "You'll find on that subject, I'm very giving." He looked thoughtfully in the direction of Maurin's abdomen. "I think I'm going to get a blade and spool from the other room."

After Argoneis left, the guard who had stabbed Maurin leered, his breath fetid in Maurin's face. "We're gonna tear you to pieces."

Maurin didn't reply. He kept pressing against his bonds, sending pulses of misery up and down his limbs.

Hook Nose pressed closer. "No one messes with Lord Argoneis and gets away with it."

"Actually, it's Argoneis who should beware," Maurin said.

The guard gripped Maurin's shirt in his fist. "Not really in a prime position to make threats, are you?"

Maurin shrugged against the pain. "It's not a threat. Just a statement. He's offended the Creator, and he's going to be unmade."

"Really." Hook Nose laughed. "And who's going to see that happens? You?"

Maurin nodded. "That's why I'm here."

With one last effort, he pulled.

The quarrel came free of the wall.

Argoneis's eyes widened in disbelief as he walked through the door. He dropped whatever vile apparatus he was carrying and dove aside with a squawk. Hook Nose reached for his weapon. Maurin swung his arm and drove the imbedded bolt through the side of the man's neck. Then, with a cry of agony, he yanked it out. The guard gurgled and pressed his hands to his neck, stumbling back and trying to stop the streams of blood jetting from between his fingers.

Maurin reached for the haft of the pike holding his foot to the floor, but the Talormine was quick; he had his crossbow up in an instant, and shot at Maurin's face.

Spiky Hair was quicker, however, and leapt for Maurin in fury. He caught the quarrel in the back of his head, spraying Maurin with gore.

In the moment of horrified confusion that followed, as the Talormine realized what he had done, Maurin pulled the halberd up and out of his foot. The creature threw aside his empty weapon and rushed at him.

The halberd came up, and the Talormine went down, its thick skull cracked.

Maurin slumped to the floor. Grimacing, he grasped the shaft of the quarrel, and pulled. A gush of blood followed, and he forced himself to stay conscious.

It all happened so fast that Argoneis hadn't had time to react. He stared in disbelief as Maurin picked his sword up off the floor and advanced. Every step felt like a knife in his foot.

"I think we have some unfinished business."

Argoneis backed away in a panic, pushing a desiccated corpse over in front of Maurin, its display rack clattering. He scrambled toward the door, but Maurin blocked his exit. Argoneis grabbed a surgical blade and waved it wildly.

Maurin batted it out of his hand, sending it skittering across the floor. Argoneis tripped over himself in an effort to escape.

Backed into a corner and gasping for breath, he ogled Maurin's bloody sword. "What are you going to do?"

"End your reign of terror."

Argoneis held up his hands. "Wait, wait... doesn't your Warden's law have something against killing in cold blood?"

"I'm not a Warden."

"But I'm unarmed! That would be murder!"

"How many of those you tortured and killed were able to defend themselves?" Maurin snorted in disbelief and tracked Argoneis with his blade. "This isn't murder. This is an execution."

With a quick intake of breath, Maurin brought his sword up in a powerful arc, swung his body around, and carried the blow through.

Argoneis's head sailed across the room, landed on the marble floor, and spun to a halt by a long, purple drapery. The body stood spurting blood for a brief moment, then slumped into a grotesque heap on the floor. A crimson pool spread around the corpse.

"As I was trying to tell you earlier..." Maurin lowered his sword and walked over to the head, kicking it so that it faced up, staring at him with a surprised expression. He leaned close, on the chance any dim perception lingered. Looking into Argoneis's rapidly glazing eyes, he whispered, "...justice doesn't always come from courts."

CHAPTER 51
DAYLIGHT

Dania burst into the room, then halted in surprise. "I hope the others look worse than you."

Maurin lowered his sword, forcing himself to sound light. "Argoneis is as handsome as ever, just a little shorter than he was."

Dania skeptically appraised the severed head. "Over too quickly."

"I didn't have the strength for what he deserved. Besides, I had to make sure he didn't get away."

She nodded her approval. "We should collect that for the slaves' celebration parade."

Maurin shuddered.

Dania pressed his wound with her thumb and fingers. The flow was steady, but didn't seem to pulse with his heartbeat. She cast about for something with which to fashion a bandage, settling on a strip of cloth from the tunic of one of the dead Talormines.

"How does it feel, priest's son, to be the great bane of Argoneis?"

He grunted as she tightened the knot. "My father once told me that having a man's death on my soul would haunt me for the rest of my days, but somehow, I don't think that's going to be the case. I wouldn't have wanted that man's *life* on my conscience."

She stalked over to Argoneis's corpse and extracted a set of keys. "For Aric."

Maurin leaned on her and hobbled back into the chamber of horrors. "Talauna!"

With a squeal of delight, the Maolori girl jumped into his arms, wrapping her legs around him and nearly bowling him over in the process.

It took all his strength to remain upright; his knees threatened to buckle, and his foot throbbed with glassy anguish. Using the momentum of her leap and pivoting on his good leg, he spun her around and leaned against a pillar. He stroked her hair and struggled to breathe, let alone get in a single kiss between every five of hers.

"Don't mind me," Aric said from the rack. Talauna and Maurin broke apart, and she slid down onto her own feet again.

"Oh, shut up." Dania started fitting keys to his manacles.

Aric let his head drop back, gazing at the ceiling with a kind of agonized resignation. "You came for me."

She pursed her lips and nodded. "Someone else did the same for me once. I don't like owing anybody."

"You didn't owe me anything," he said.

"I know."

Aric moved to grasp her hand tightly. "Dania—I can't..."

"I know."

"And you're all right with that?"

Dania arched a brow. "Get over yourself."

"I'm sorry."

She looked him in the eye, and her expression softened. "I'm sorry, too."

Maurin sagged against the wall. His foot was so swollen that the laces of his boot were strained. He winced and shifted his weight again onto his other leg. "So what happened?"

Aric sat up with some assistance from Dania, then coughed. "Argoneis's men got the drop on me."

"I'm surprised you didn't see it coming."

His cousin's face turned somber. "So am I."

Somehow, Maurin didn't think Aric was talking about his capture.

———◆◆———

A procession of the living carrying the dead was not that unusual, but a procession of the dead carrying the living was quite another matter. Maurin had to look twice to make sure he was seeing what he thought he was.

A number of what had to have been the Reamar's victims bore Valasand on a bier draped with red cloth. A wounded Shallar swayed next to her. Guilan Vail walked behind them, his eyes never leaving Aric. Maurin and his cousin leaned into each other, doing their best to stand.

"Réus is dead," Aric blurted when they reached her.

Valasand looked stricken, going a shade paler. "This is fell news indeed," she said weakly. "How did it happen?"

Guilan Vail remained stoic. Surely the Reamar cared something for the loss of his sovereign lord? Whereas the Warden was acting as if an old friend had died.

"The high priestess killed him," Aric said. "And it's driven her mad."

Maurin leaned in close so only Valasand could hear. "Maybe I'm just being a little more obtuse than usual, but am I missing something? The god-king of the Reamar is dead, and this is a bad thing?"

"Réus was all that held the Reamar in check," Valasand whispered back. "He kept a semblance of order in a dominion founded in chaos. With Réus out of the way, and the high priestess incapacitated, there may be a grab for power, and a revival of the old ways."

"It's too late," Aric said quietly. "Ulora has claimed the throne."

Guilan Vail's lips twitched. Was that a smile?

"Talauna!"

Maurin squinted into the ill-lit corridor for the source of the voice. A shadow moved toward them, and Dania held her knife ahead of her. Talauna shook her head and gently pushed down Dania's hand.

"I can't believe it." A man in dark robes staggered forward into the light of the foyer. He stepped over a body, arms outstretched. "Talauna! You're all right!"

Maurin recognized him immediately. So, apparently, did Dania.

"Let me kill this snake," she hissed; "this so-called man who likes to use you."

Talauna placed herself in front of the tattooed warrior, who strained like an animal on a leash. What was left of Maurin's blood boiled. But Talauna had made it clear: this was her battle.

"Come back with me," Krige pleaded. "I swear it will be different for you this time."

"Girl, as he has taken your voice, let me take his." Dania brandished her knives again, fury choking her words. "If you don't want me to kill him, I will make him remember and rue the day he stole from you that which cannot be returned."

Sweat popped out on Krige's forehead, and he turned pale. Yet he stood his ground, addressing only Talauna. He held out his hands to show Dania he was unarmed.

A bit impressive that he wasn't panicking; most men would have run for their lives at the slightest hint of a threat from the gladiatrix. Then again, he probably knew flight was futile.

Maurin's hands were starting to shake, and he was so tired. The pain was coming back in waves, but he forced himself to stand, even if bearing witness was all that was required of him.

"It can be a new beginning for both of us." Krige's voice quavered. "Sedrick is dead. Everyone is dead. But I can take care of you. I love you!"

Dania was primed to snarl out a reply, but Talauna forestalled her with a quick gesture. With a slight limp, she stepped forward and took one of Krige's wrists in her hand. She slid his palm over her belly, and his eyes widened in realization as he felt the bulge in her abdomen. Talauna gazed at him evenly, then dropped his hand and took several steps back. He looked confused as she turned her back on him. Dania followed Talauna's cue, and also walked away, staying with Shallar at Valasand's side as she was carried out of the building.

"Where are you going?" Krige called out. "Talauna?"

They left Aster Krige alone in the great hall of death. When the doors had shut behind them, and the man's plaintive cries could no longer be heard, Maurin smiled at Talauna and took her hand. Together, they walked forward into the light of a new day.

CHAPTER 52
STARTING OVER

Sunlight shone through the windows of the mansion. Dania tossed out the weeds—all right, flowers—someone had put in her room to freshen things up. Maurin? Probably. Seemed like the soft sort of peace gesture he would make.

"Something is troubling you." The Warden smiled slightly from the open door.

"Nothing." Dania shrugged. "Nothing important."

"Dania." The Warden continued to gaze at her until she couldn't stand it any longer.

"This." Dania gestured. Lying atop her bed was a new outfit made of a durable but soft white cloth. She hadn't tried it on, but she could tell it was designed for total freedom of movement, and what was more, specifically tailored to her body. Atop it sat a new woven leather cuirass. She picked it up and frowned. It was perfect for her, and that bothered Dania most of all. "The girl gave me this."

"Yes," Valasand said. "I think Talauna wished to show you she values your friendship. Your old cuirass was the false protection of the arena, with the reek of death still in it, yet you still clung to its safety."

Dania snorted. "The armor I have now I found here. I had to leave my things when I escaped."

"Even so, as a token of your new life, I thought this would make a fitting gift for you."

"I figured you must have had a hand in it somewhere. But now..." Dania grimaced, searching for words. "Now I owe her, and I don't like that."

"And you would like to do something in return, so you are no longer obligated to her."

Dania looked at Valasand, grateful she understood.

"You know, not every gift is given with the expectation of something in return."

"What do you mean?"

"You've been given a much greater gift than this, and there is no way to repay except with your life. Every day we breathe is a chance to start anew. Some never make that choice."

Dania nodded slowly. "It is difficult to think of these things. I'm not sure I understand."

"I'm not sure anyone fully understands. All we can do is to be grateful and live accordingly. That's all Yasul expects of us."

Dania thought for a moment, and said, "All the same, whether she expects it or not, I still want to give the girl something."

Valasand smiled. "There's nothing wrong with that."

"Perhaps a set of knives," she said at last.

Valasand blinked. "Do you really think a set of knives would be an appropriate gift for Talauna?"

"No," Dania admitted. "She wouldn't know how to use them." She pounded her thigh in frustration. "What, then?"

"Though a weapon would not be my first choice as a gift for Talauna, you are probably right. She needs to learn how to defend herself; we won't always be around to protect her, and she is not a fighter."

Dania laughed. "You could say that."

"Perhaps you could give her something a little more suited to her abilities."

"Such as...?"

"I think a staff might be fitting." Bemused, Valasand glanced at her own, then at Dania.

Staff. The word carried her back home, to the wagons and tents of her nomadic youth. The chieftain of their caravan used to explain, as he carved his staff, that just as the tattoos covering him from head to toe reflected who he was inside, so each new ring of symbols on the wood was a reminder of his exploits, and the major events of his life. When Dania asked him why there were so few rings on it when he was so old, he had chuckled and answered that he had a dozen more staffs like it at his home; he was just starting a new one.

Dania pictured herself telling Talauna about him and explaining how to carve out a life-staff for herself.

The notion appealed more than it should.

Valasand's voice jarred her from her thoughts. "My master told me once that the new wood was symbolic of new growth, and that just as the branch was cut away from the tree, so it would find new life in my hands."

"Your master?" Dania asked in surprise. "You were a slave?"

"Teacher, I should say. Jashara, whom you saw briefly before we entered the Gray Lands." The Warden looked somber. "My entire life has been spent in willing servitude to Yasul; I suppose you could say that I am a slave. But I would have it no other way. You see, Dania, there can be a certain freedom in service, too."

She nodded. "That would not have made sense to me before."

"And does it now?"

"I think so."

A soft smile crossed Valasand's face. "I'm glad." She paused. "There's something else, isn't there? What is really bothering you?"

Dania chewed her lip. "He was there. Farel."

The Warden's voice dropped low. "I see."

"I had him in my grasp. I wanted to kill him. But... I couldn't. And before I could make myself do it, one of the Harvesters got him."

Valasand reached out as if to caress Dania's arm, then dropped her hand. "You were faced with the choice of whether or not to kill him. That choice was taken from you, and you feel robbed." She rose to leave. "Though it may not seem so now, perhaps that, too, was a gift."

A gift. It certainly didn't feel that way. All these years. Her childhood stripped away, her adulthood bathed in blood and hopelessness. Was there no reckoning for such? Or did reckoning have to come by one's own hands?

"Valasand?"

"Yes, Dania?"

"What will you do next? You came to this world to bring down Argoneis, and he has been brought down."

"Well," the Warden said, considering, "it may be a while before we can arrange for ways to return the former slaves to their homeworlds, but Masalla is working on that. He'll be taking over temporarily as the official Temple representative, at least until someone can come in from off-world to assess the situation here."

"Can you not tell the Vigilant? I thought they traveled between the worlds without gates or ships."

"They are not at our beck and call. And they have much to do when they are not relaying messages or instruction to us. One never knows when they will show up, or where they go when they leave, so we can't rely upon them to do our work for us."

"What about the Harvesters? They've been scattered across the countryside."

The Warden nodded. "Aric was trying to help, but they will eventually have to be dealt with. And soon I will have to return to the Temple to report on all that has transpired."

"I want to go with you."

Valasand's eyebrows arched in surprise, and then she smiled. "Are you sure?"

"Where you go, I go." Dania looked down for a moment before glancing back up again. "If you'll have me."

———— ◆ ————

The snare was broken and the captives set free. Maurin had played a major part in the overthrow of Argoneis, and while it all seemed monumental, he also suspected this was only the beginning. Yasul had called him out, and nothing would ever be the same.

After all the passageways and crannies of Argoneis's palace had been checked for slaves in hiding, Valasand had given Maurin permission to go back in and cleanse the place with fire, to rid the dungeons and torture chambers of the sense of death and agony. He had gone into the former temple with dozens of former slaves. It was remarkably liberating, wrenching apart Daman's instruments of torture with prybars and axes, then burning them in the public square. He would have liked to bring the entire building to the ground, to keep it from standing as a monument to the rewards of evil and decadence, but Valasand wouldn't allow it. She wanted it to serve as a monument to the way evil could overtake even the holiest of stations, and possibly eventually do a formal rededication of the building to Yasul.

One thing was clear, and that was that nothing was ever clear.

The damage done by Aric's rescue attempt was irreparable, the Gray Lands grown beyond all prior boundaries. For all that, Maurin had no doubt Valasand was right: the Reamar had been used as an instrument in Yasul's own will. Without them, there could have been no victory over Argoneis. They would have to be dealt with, of course, but that would come later. For now, it was enough that his loved ones were safe.

At least, as safe as could be, given the circumstances. Aric had returned with them to the mansion, ostensibly to make sure everyone was all right before he returned to Darkhorn Fell. With every attempt Maurin made to persuade him to stay, Aric's eyes turned haunted, and he would just shake his head. His cousin was becoming more distant and alien each day. Once a brother in spirit, now nearly a stranger. One day, Maurin feared, he would wake up, and Aric would be gone for good.

Maurin shook his head. No more. He had promises to keep, and he would not allow his own fears to get in the way again. For now, Aric was here, and who knew what the future would bring?

He paused at the entry to the library, where Valasand and Masalla discussed the countess of Sal Dalinde, who had taken over as regent of Caileen. Shallar interjected her own grunts and mutters from time to time. Would she soon resume the search for her cubs? He smiled and shook his head as he walked past and headed upstairs.

He found Talauna in her room, giving Dania a hug, and was surprised to see the smile on the tattooed warrior's face. A newly-cut staff lay against the wall. Dania wore an outfit he hadn't seen before; it still hearkened to her warrior nature, but seemed to soften her somehow. There was a mature light in her eyes now, not tempered by anger or hatred. She nodded at the Maolori girl, then exited, punching Maurin lightly in the arm. At least, he assumed the hit was meant to be light, since she was still smiling happily when she did it. He winced and rubbed his bicep as she left, then turned and closed the door.

"Talauna," he said, "I have something for you. Come, sit with me."

She favored him with an impish smile, tugging playfully at his white locks. He kissed her, and they made their way over to the window seat.

For a few moments, they gazed together out over the sunlit woods of the mountainside. A brisk breeze flowed through the window.

The last few months had made a difference in Talauna. Her face was round and radiant, and her belly swollen. How could he not have seen it before? But then, he had been blind in so many ways.

Maurin made sure he had her undivided attention. Reaching into his pocket, he pulled out a long silken purple ribbon, fumbling a bit as his fingers refused to grip as they once did. "This is the last piece of my old life." He wadded it up and tossed it into the fireplace, where the embers of last night's blaze still glowed. For a moment, nothing happened, then it started to blacken, and quickly shriveled into ash.

He drew another ribbon, a new yellow one, from his other pocket. Silently he returned Talauna's gaze, then reached out, and grasped her arm. He gently wrapped the ribbon in a spiral around her wrist. He continued past her hand and onto his own scarred arm. In short order their hands were bound together by the cloth.

She looked up at him with an unspoken question.

"Yes." Maurin nodded. "I'm sure. More than anything."

She broke out into the widest and happiest smile he had ever seen, and he was lost in a barrage of kisses. When they finally separated, her eyes brimmed with tears of joy. In a soft voice, she said:

"I love you, Maurin."

POSTLUDE
PROMISES TO KEEP

"Aric?" The voice comes to me like the first breath of air after an eternity underwater. My eyelids flutter open, and Ulora stands before me. *You must come back to me. I long for you.*

"I can't," I reply. "Not yet."

Ulora crosses her arms over her chest, a bit of human body language she picked up who-knows-how-many centuries ago. I can feel the cold unquiet in her soul.

"Not yet." Her voice carries an implicit demand for an explanation, and her eyes betray the wrath she will unleash should I attempt to go back on my word. *"You promised me, beloved. You are well; your friends are on the mend. It is time to take your place among the Reamar. Your destiny lies ahead; soon you will be what you were born to be."*

"I have to be sure of something first."

She drops her arms. *"I cannot imagine it is all that important. You must leave your human concerns behind, my love. It is not befitting a god to be anxious over these transitory things."*

"Love is forever; isn't that what you're always telling me?" I hate arguing with Ulora; she has thousands of years on me in experience, and

there is no way I can compete with her intellectually. Wiliness compounded over the centuries mellowed into a sort of crafty genius. "I still love my cousin. I want to make sure he's going to be all right. His wounds are severe."

The expression on her face goes beyond skepticism. *"Very well, but do not forget your vow."*

"I won't."

I hate to admit it, but I wish I'd listened to Maurin. The wretched vision of Ulora's true nature will haunt me to the end of my days. What have I gotten myself into?

She smiles, and for a moment, I almost forget.

For a moment.

"I understand. You must be assured that the ones you care for are in good health. But soon, when you have had a chance to say your farewells, you must join me at Darkhorn Fell. I am waiting for you."

"Of course, my love." I nod, trying not to let my trepidation show, and force myself to smile. "I'm looking forward to it."

AFTERWORD

A little over thirty years ago, while I was in college, my cousin Jeff and I had an idea for a novel. Originally intended to be a single book written more or less for our own enjoyment, it was an amalgam of a number of stories we ourselves had always liked. As we brainstormed and wrote back and forth, the tale grew, and we discovered that it was likely going to be longer than one book could hold. More significantly, we realized that it could be a "real" book; not just a story we told for ourselves, but one that others might benefit from, as well. We were aware that a number of the influences that went into the "cauldron of story" (as Tolkien put it) were not particularly good in and of themselves, but just interesting notions whose concepts far outshone their execution. That was something we wanted to change as we laid out the initial framework for the worldbuilding. A bit ambitious, perhaps, for a boy in his teens and a young man barely into his twenties, but we wanted to tell a vast, interconnected story whose execution would (hopefully) be worthy of its concept. Whereas Tolkien delved into Greek, Norse, Finnish, Latin, and other cultural mythologies to create his world, I decided that we would use the alternative science/ancient alien/UFO culture as an interesting starting point for our own mythopoeia. While full of strange and sometimes crazy ideas, it had the advantage of appealing both to futuristic and quasi-historical frameworks, and might even be used to explore deeper spiritual concepts in abstract ways.

I have had many people ask me, upon reading *Bid the Gods Arise* in its manuscript form, whether the characters of Aric and Maurin are meant to be reminiscent of my cousin Jeff and myself. The answer to that is a resounding yes... and an emphatic no. When we first conceived the story, we tried to imagine what young men of similar temperaments, who shared a familiar relationship, might do in a completely different world.

Every author uses a form of shorthand, particularly those dealing with speculative world-building. So much was strange and alien in our world that we wanted people to have something tangible to grasp onto as they read—in this case, realistic human relationships. And as any sitcom writer can tell you, family feuds are instantly identifiable across the board. The notion of closer siblings (such as brothers) set at odds is a trope in the genre, and while I did strive for mythopoeia, I put my foot down when it came to outright plagiarism. So the choice to make Maurin and Aric cousins was a natural one, as it was a relationship about which I could easily write.

Yet when we sat down and started drawing out the story and characters, our first thoughts were not what would we do in a given situation, but what would Maurin or Aric do? The idea was not to create doppelgängers of ourselves, but rather to cast familiar templates into unfamiliar roles, so the reflection is only an homage as seen through a glass darkly. While it is impossible for those who know me or knew Jeff not to see certain similarities, there are times that I have more in common with the other characters than Maurin, and Jeff was a much kinder and more giving person than Aric ever was (though his tendency to be a smart-alec definitely inspired some of the earlier drafts of the character).

When Jeff died, and the shared storytelling experience was suddenly thrust into my lap, I determined that I would try to make decisions regarding the characters and the story based as much as possible on the early discussions we had, remaining true to our initial concepts. When I came to a crossroads, I frequently had to ask myself what Jeff might have suggested, thus keeping the story as much in the vein of what we had always intended from the outset.

That having been said, there are many ways in which the story is necessarily different. I have grown, both as a person and as a writer, and the story reflects that (though I confess that I had to resist the temptation in this latest edition to use my older perspective to "fix" some issues that would have altered the canon too greatly). While there are some elements to the novels that we might not have considered back in 1994 when the story was first conceived, I like to think that had Jeff lived, he would have approved of the choices I made in expanding our original vision.

ACKNOWLEDGMENTS

I can't take full credit for this one.

I've heard it said many times that no book—particularly no first novel—is ever written by one person alone. There may be exceptions to this nearly universal rule, but this is certainly not one of them. A story in its purest form is an ever-growing entity, a living, breathing thing reacting to those whom it touches. It "grows in the telling," as Tolkien would put it, not solely because of the accomplishment of the author, but in part because of the imagination and input of the audience. With each new interaction, the tale becomes that much richer, adding spice and flavor to what the master called the "cauldron of story." Therefore, I must humbly thank several people without whom this book might not have been written.

The first, and most obvious, would be my cousin Jeff. From the outset, I loved telling stories with and to him, and when we first conceived this novel, we had no idea how far it would go, nor in what directions. He did all the initial brainstorming with me, as well as aiding in the creation of several of the characters, names, and situations. Many of the formative ideas were his, infusing the plot with a richness and spirit it would never have had, had I been the sole creator. The book has taken a long time to finish, and I regret that he will never read it. Jeff was and is always my truest inspiration, my muse.

The second person who aided in the gestation of this book is my very good friend and co-storyteller par excellence Mark McDonald. He helped shape the narrative in great depth and detail, adding major plot elements, structure, realistic characterization, psychological insights, and scenes, giving the story more emotional power and validity. When Jeff was too busy—and later, no longer able—to help in the creative process, Mark guided me through some pertinent parts of the story, provided a framework for many disparate elements, generated a wealth of ideas and material, and argued faithfully with me over the technical issues. In many ways, he could really be billed as the coauthor; Mark's input cannot be measured in terms of quantity or quality. After a necessary re-write, I decided to return to a story closer to the original concept Jeff and I had in mind. But much remains of Mark's input, and the story is infinitely better for it.

The third person who supported this work creatively was my late friend Matt Marcy, whose art I first spied when visiting Oregon to make preparations for my second trip to Africa. Matt's painting captured the essence of the story. He had agreed to do the cover art for the entire series, and died before he could see the final cover for the first novel. Though the dictates of consistency necessitated the replacement of his art, I will be forever indebted to him for his enthusiastic love for the project, and his spirit, like Jeff's, will continue to imbue the future novels.

My wife, Jai, who is the Scully to my Mulder, has studied plot much more than I, and did a traumatic edit of my book before my final draft. While it had me reeling (and frantically searching for missing parts), I—somewhat grudgingly—had to admit that it came out stronger and more streamlined in the end, and thank her unequivocally for it. Her suggestions proved invaluable.

Vickie Smith and Michael O'Donnell, my college English teacher and mentor, respectively, were the first to encourage me to write. Without them, this book would never have come to be. Michael has always done everything within his power to help me in all aspects of my life, beyond my literary ambitions. Many thanks are due my father, for his unparalleled knowledge of the English language, and my mother, for teaching me to love reading at an early age.

My "first readers" were absolutely indispensable, letting me know what worked and didn't work in their eyes. Very special thanks to my friend Chad Pape, who read over my manuscript in its early stages, offering encouragement and immensely helpful insights on how the story could be improved. Chad has been wonderful at getting me to accept nothing but the best from myself as a writer and as a person. He put a great deal of effort into writing out detailed editorial notes and giving me tremendous suggestions. He was also a friend and supporter through the toughest times of my life.

My original writers' group, The Red Inklings (Gwen, Vicky, Ilona, and Brenda) all gave me valuable suggestions. I would be remiss if I neglected to mention my nickname squad: Adam "Toto" Marley, Brian

"Mouse" Johnson, and David "Poet" Warren, the "crazy Canuck."

Angela Preston generously read through an early draft, as well as some of the sequel, and was kind enough to let me know in no uncertain terms that I had left her hanging. Years later, I still use her memorable phone call as an impetus to get a move-on in my writing. Craig Flanary, whose generosity is without compare (as are his steaks), was a hard and ruthless editor—the best kind. The seeds of several of his ideas took root in this story and grew.

Eternal gratitude to Ken McIntosh and Victor Vieira of my Flagstaff writers' group. They have been like the finest doctors delivering a late-term baby; I couldn't have polished and shaped what was then the final draft without their help. They went through the manuscript with me word by word, and kept my feet to the fire in terms of presenting the best possible book. In Denver, Ira Davis and Jena DePooter gave me some great insights. Thanks also to Amy McDonald for some last-minute suggestions. A very special thanks to Jim Cline for the phenomenal cover for the first edition, and to Kent Powderly for introducing me to him.

For the fourth edition, I decided to re-brand the series with some minor tweaks and a stronger sense of genre. Caleb Havertape came through in spades with cover art that captured the epic scale and ominous mood of Darkhorn Fell as it had never been represented before. I'm forever endebted to him for his contribution, and my only regret is that I can't present a full-size poster with each book.

My beta readers for the revised edition were Amy MacDonald and Catherine Hinkle. Amy caught typos and editing relics that had somehow managed to survive six years in print, and Catherine's eagle eye caught innumerable instances of twenty-year-old (weak) writing. The volume you now hold would not be what it is without their input.

Apologies are due to any who offered good advice that I ignored for whatever reason. Any errors, omissions, or otherwise bad choices are the sole responsibility of the author.

Original novel soundtrack by Dennis S. Mowers
available on dsmowersmusic.com, Amazon, Spotify, Bandcamp,
Soundcloud, and iTunes

What is a novel soundtrack?

It's a reasonable question. After all, if you're familiar with soundtracks at all, you are going to be accustomed to their being the scores to films or possibly even video games. But a novel soundtrack? What is that, anyway? Perhaps not surprisingly, it's essentially the same thing: music inspired by the characters and events of the book itself. The precedence of music written for literature goes back centuries. *Romeo and Juliet*, *Sleeping Beauty*, *The Divine Comedy*, *A Midsummer Night's Dream*, *Moby Dick*... the list goes on. And that's just classical music. The worlds of Tolkien, Verne, and others have been the foundation for rock operas and heavy metal. *The Lord of the Rings*, *The Wheel of Time*, *The Kingslayer Chronicle*, *The Way of Kings*, and certain *Star Wars* novels—all of these have official and unofficial music written by talented composers inspired by the novels themselves.

Is the soundtrack meant to be listened to while one reads the book? Probably not, though of course nothing would be stopping you. Not everyone reads at the same speed, and the music is not designed to capture the exact reading pace of a scene anyway. Rather, the soundtrack plays out a few key scenes and features cues that represent certain characters. Like a tone poem, the music tells a narrative based upon the novel of the same title, and allows the reader and listener to revisit and be immersed in the world in a whole new way. In a sense, the "movie without a movie" concept is very much in play here, with music that you would probably assume accompanied a feature film.

When I first approached Dennis to ask if he would be interested in scoring the music for Bid the Gods Arise, I knew it was an unusual request, but I had already heard his fan music for certain entries to a franchise I knew we both enjoyed, and had a taste of his talent. When he sent me the cues as he was recording them, I was stunned. I had expected something vaguely evocative of the mood of the novel, but he went far above and beyond my wildest dreams. He continually surprised me with content that delved creatively into the heart and soul of the world and the people inhabiting it.

From the ominous themes for Argoneis and the Reamar to the tender, contemplative music for Maurin and Valasand, the eerie, almost golden age siren call of Ulora, and the heroic and hopeful theme now associated with Aric—Dennis never failed to deliver, and always managed to nail the exact "sense" of a scene or character. And the powerful, desperate music he composed for Dania is revisited in a poignant variation for his suite for Blood Song (and as an unexpected bonus, he utilized lyrics of my own in what might be considered the "end credits" of that piece, giving what might have been a mere snippet of in-universe poetry a heartbreaking depth). Even more than Dennis's ability to evoke the mood of a powerful scene, I admire his insight into characters, and the ability to reach straight into their hearts. His powerful portrayal of The Wells of the Worlds is as canon as the words themselves.

I highly recommend that those who enjoyed the books check out the soundtracks. It is my hope that they will open up a whole new avenue of enjoyment, and help boost a talented young composer on an already promising career. Should I be fortunate enough to have my books made into movies (as they were first envisioned), I sincerely hope that Dennis will still be available to take my calls, because I cannot now imagine my story world without his music.

Liner Notes by Dennis S. Mowers

UNQUIET DREAMS/EVE OF DESCENT: The beginning of this book was so mysterious and unsettling that I immediately felt inspired to write music for "Unquiet Dreams." Before reading even a hundred pages, I had a demo for this ready to go. The theme (which is very inspired by the style of Howard Shore's Lord of the Rings scores) eventually became a motif for dread and peril throughout the rest of the soundtrack. Since this isn't a film score, I thought it appropriate to create motifs for certain moods and expressions as well as other ones for specific characters.

Based partially on the style of John Powell, the "Eve of Descent" part of this piece was never originally meant to be a part of this soundtrack. I wrote a demo of this track for a game soundtrack I was working on with Smashing Graphics Game Studios, but it never felt right. It didn't match the rest of the game's soundtrack very well. I ended up reading the beginning of BTGA again, and as I was reading "Eve of Descent," I felt this sense of peace as Aric and Maurin felt freedom for the first time, even though it was very brief. In my head, this theme started playing, and I knew it absolutely had to be a part of the BTGA soundtrack. I edited "Unquiet Dreams" and made this track a two-parter. I couldn't imagine the soundtrack opening any other way.

MAURIN: Maurin's theme, although placed very early in the track list, was one of the later additions to this soundtrack. This piece represents the innocence that Maurin holds onto throughout this book. I actually wrote "Broken Vows" before this, and I thought it would be a good idea to take the music that represented Maurin's life as he knew it crumbling and falling apart before his eyes, and turn it into something sweet and innocent. In the middle of this track, it becomes minor for a bit, and then somewhat dissonant. This is because Maurin occasionally is pulled away from his old life, and I wanted to show through music the internal struggle that he faces constantly throughout the story.

BROKEN VOWS: For "Broken Vows," the first huge turning point in the story, I wanted to show just how quickly life fell apart for Maurin and everyone else. It starts off with a wedding march that shows off the regality and traditions of the ceremony. Things quickly go south, and Maurin and Aric lose everything from their old lives. I wanted to capture the apocalyptic sense of this chapter, as well as the chaos and destruction. One of the themes found in this would eventually become Maurin's theme, but I intentionally never used any of the other music in "Broken Vows" again. This was because I wanted this part of the story to feel very separate from what happened after. As much as Maurin felt a constant tug back to his old ways of life, I wanted to make it perfectly clear that there was no going back.

VALASAND, WAYFARER/THE REAMAR: Valasand is such an interesting character. She is definitely the wisest of the bunch, and I wanted to show just how put together she is, in almost a legendary way. As for the Reamar section of the piece, I wanted to show just how scary this group of beings could really be. Although their intentions are nowhere near as malicious as they seem, they still seem like a very dark force, even to the end. I chose to put "Valasand's Theme" and "The Reamar" together because they at first seem like two opposing forces. We very quickly learn, however, that Valasand has the ability to help the Reamar, and that made they're not so much on opposite sides as we thought.

BLOOD GODDESS: Dania intrigued me from her first appearance in the book. We learn early on that she's a fighter and a warrior, and doesn't take garbage from anybody. But her escape is what really inspired me to write music for her. Throughout this chapter, Dania doesn't say much. It's her actions that count, and the thoughts in her head as she commits violent murders as retribution for the torment she has gone through. In such a short amount of time, we learn so much about her character. I wanted to show through the music that she is a machine of destruction, but that she also has her own problems and inner turmoil.

LEAVING CAILEEN: The group's departure from the city of Caileen reminded me of a car chase. The group tries to find a way out of the city as they are being pursued by Argoneis' forces. It was such a fun read and it seriously kept my intention. I wanted to show the feeling of freedom as they find a ship to steal, only to have the music come crashing back into chaos as they are forced down moments later. There's a certain theme in here that first appears in this track, and ends up being the central theme of another. There's something very special about it, but I'll discuss that in the other track's notes.

DAMAN ARGONEIS: Say what you will about the Reamar, but the most frightening thing about this story is Argoneis. That's why I chose to begin this piece with the same "dreadful" music that I introduced in "Unquiet Dreams." This character is brutally unpredictable, extremely dangerous, cruel, and sadistic. In this piece, I didn't want even a shred of hope to shine through. This is why at the beginning and end there's dissonance in the strings that surround the rest of the music. There's no way out, and the whole time you're utterly trapped in darkness.

ULORA (OF DREAMS AND NIGHTMARES): Ulora's character motives can be shady, but somehow one can see reason in them if they look deep enough. She's an extremely ambiguous character. When we are first introduced to her, we know nothing about her or who she is. However, even after we know her and her backstory, she is still somewhat of a mystery. You're never really sure where her loyalties lie or who she really cares about. This piece was meant to bring out that ambiguity, and highlight the serenely mysterious air that she has around her.

THE DREADED ONE: This name might be a bit misleading if you don't know the story (or to whom it refers). Aric, whether he likes it or not, is pretty much the reason this story happens. It is his existence that sets everything in motion. There is something legendary about him, even if he is only human.

    This theme, which was also used in "Leaving Caileen," has a special place in my heart. Years ago, there was a website called Notessimo. This was my first real introduction to composing music. My first original composition was done on Notessimo, and it was this theme. It sounded different, and the instruments didn't sound anywhere near as pretty or realistic as this does, but that theme has always been important to me. Ever since then, I have tried to find places to use it, whether it was in a chamber music piece, or for a trombone group, etc. But it was made with fantasy and fiction in mind, and I've finally found its home in this soundtrack.

Note to the Reader

If you have gotten this far, you've already purchased and read this book. Thank you! In doing so, you have done your part in supporting indie authors. If you enjoyed it and would like to read further volumes, I would ask you to consider taking a few moments to go one step further. Reviews increase an author's visibility and rankings, and especially in the case of indie publications, make it more likely that there will be more in the future. Amazon, Goodreads, and Barnes & Noble are all good places to start, and it doesn't have to be long. A simple sentence or two is all it takes, and could make all the difference.

About the Author

Robert Mullin is a cryptozoologist who has traveled to Africa three times in search of a possible living dinosaur. He was featured on an episode of the History Channel's television show Monster Quest. He is also the creator of *The Star Wars Chronological Companion*, one of the premier fan timelines.